THE Art OF THE CHASE

NEW YORK TIMES BESTSELLING AUTHOR

LAUREN DANE

Published by
Mills & Boon
An imprint of Harlequin Enterprises (Australia) Pty Limited
(ABN 47 001 180 918), a subsidiary of HarperCollins
Publishers Australia Pty Limited (ABN 36 009 913 517)
Level 19, 201 Elizabeth Street
SYDNEY NSW 2000
AUSTRALIA

MIX
Paper | Supporting
responsible forestry
FSC
www.fsc.org   FSC® C001695

CONTENTS

Also available from Lauren Dane

Second Chances
Believe

Goddess with a Blade

Goddess with a Blade
Blade to the Keep
Blade on the Hunt
At Blade's Edge

Diablo Lake

Diablo Lake: Moonstruck
Diablo Lake: Protected

Cascadia Wolves

Reluctant Mate
Pack Enforcer
Wolves' Triad
Wolf Unbound
Alpha's Challenge
Bonded Pair
Twice Bitten

de La Vega Cats

Trinity
Revelation
Beneath the Skin

Cherchez Wolf Pack

Wolf's Ascension
Sworn to the Wolf

Chase Brothers

Giving Chase
Taking Chase
Chased
Making Chase

From Lauren Dane

The Best Kind of Trouble
Broken Open
Back to You

Whiskey Sharp: Unraveled
Whiskey Sharp: Jagged
Whiskey Sharp: Torn

Chased

Author Note

Hey there, all you lovely reader friends!

Way back in 2006 I got an idea that I knew I couldn't sell to the publisher I was with at the time, so I took a chance on a new publisher and a new editor with my small-town contemporary romance.

Twelve years later, the Chase Brothers series has been reissued, but with the same beloved editor, Angela James, who continues to kick my butt and make me a better writer.

I've done very little to change these books. Some grammatical stuff here and there, but though I like to think my writing has come a long way in those intervening dozen years, I wanted to keep these the way they were. The heart of the stories is unchanged. The heart of this group of friends and family is unchanged.

The Chases remain a personal favorite of all the books I've written and it's always a pleasure to see them reach new readers even now. If you're a new reader to the series, welcome to Petal! I hope you enjoy your stay. If you're returning, welcome back!

Either way, I'm glad you're here.

Lauren

Chapter One

At the sound of the doorbell, Liv dabbed her eyes and cursed to herself, seeing they were still red and puffy. She'd have ignored it on any other day but Cassie and Maggie were picking her up to take her to drive over to Polly and Edward's fortieth wedding anniversary party.

Letting out a resigned sigh, Liv answered her door to her friends, both dressed to the nines.

"You've been crying." With a concerned look on her face, Maggie pushed her way into the house and Cassie followed.

"I'm fine. Really. I'm nearly done, I just need to fix my eyes. I don't want you two to be late."

"I've spent all afternoon with Polly, and Cassie took care of the setup. Edward's out with Polly, he's taking her for a drive. I think they're going to make out at the lake. And that means you're going to tell us what's going on." The look on Maggie's face told Liv she wouldn't back down.

"Brody." Liv sighed, turning to the mirror so she could repair her makeup.

"Brody what? What did he do?"

"Not what. Who. That rat bastard cheated on me with Lyndsay Cole. I walked in on them yesterday afternoon at his apartment. Got off work early and brought him some dinner. I got a lot more than the thank-you I was expecting."

"He did not! She did not! That bitch," Maggie hissed. "That man-stealing bitch. I'm going to make a Lyndsay doll and stick her full of pins."

Liv snorted a laugh. "You always make me feel better. And someone was already sticking her full of something. But don't blame her. She wasn't in a relationship, Brody was. Pig."

"I hope his pecker falls off," Cassie said through clenched teeth.

"Or maybe it should get like a thousand paper cuts and then have lemon juice poured on it. And I hope Lyndsay gets a cold sore. A big one and a wart on her chin." Maggie nodded.

"With a big, black wiry hair that grows out of it and no one tells her," Cassie added.

"You two are the best." Liv grinned and turned around, finger-combing her hair and smoothing down the front of the sweater dress she'd chosen for the party. "I feel better than I have since yesterday when I found out. I wish I could say he sucked in bed, but I'd be lying. What is it about me? Why can't I find someone? Something real?"

Maggie sighed. "You found out yesterday and you're only telling us now?"

Liv shrugged. "I couldn't face anyone. I caught them and I couldn't get it out of my head. You and Kyle had a date, Shane and Cassie had only just returned from their honeymoon and Dee and Arthur just finished the move to Atlanta. She's already got high blood pressure and I don't want to make her pregnancy worse. I came home, ate too much ice cream, watched *Thelma and Louise* and went to bed.

"I know Brody and I weren't engaged or anything. I didn't think he was the one, but I thought perhaps someday... Oh I don't know what I thought but I do know we were supposed to be exclusive. It could have been right someday to move to the next step. You know, he could have broken up with me. He didn't have to fuck someone behind my back."

Cassie hugged her tight and Maggie followed. "He's a pig. He's a pig, a jerk and a dick."

"And an ass. And his nose is big," Cassie added.

"Marc asked if I wanted him to kick Brody's ass." Liv grinned.

"You told Marc? You told Marc Chase before your best friend?" Maggie's eyebrows flew up.

"It just happened. He came by this afternoon looking for Shane. Something about the party. Anyway, he came by to look at my legs and flirt a bit and he asked if I was coming tonight with Brody and it just came out. He was very sweet about it."

Maggie harrumphed but looked mollified. "Well, I suppose if you have to unburden such a shitty story to someone, it may as well be someone who looks as good as Marc does."

Liv laughed. "He does, doesn't he? Lawd, you should see the damned place every time he walks through, women coming out of the woodwork to be seen."

They all walked to the car and admittedly, Liv felt better.

"I just want someone I can trust. Someone I can come home to at the end of the day and share my life with. I want to be in love and get married and have kids. Not tomorrow or anything but I feel like I'm very far off schedule." Liv chewed her bottom lip as she pulled her seat belt on.

"Love doesn't have a schedule, Liv," Maggie said from the back seat. "And you *will* find love. You will, I promise you. This thing with Brody isn't about you at all. He didn't cheat because you were bad. He cheated because he's a jerk."

"And Matt?" Liv's heart still ached a bit when she said his name.

"Matt is a good person, don't get me wrong. But he was not right for you. He's not right for anyone just yet. She'll come along though. But you aren't her and I'm sorry because I know you wish it was different. He's not ready."

"I want what you have with Kyle. What Cassie has. What Dee has. I look at Polly and Edward and think about how they've had forty years together and I wonder why I can't have that."

"You *can* have that. It'll come."

"It's only because you're pregnant that I don't smack you for saying that. People who are so happily married it makes my teeth hurt can say that stuff awfully easily. You have Kyle who looks at you like there's not another woman on Earth. Cassie has Shane who can't take his eyes off her for three minutes."

Maggie laughed. "No one but you two and Kyle knows about the pregnancy so watch it. Polly will kill me if she hears it before Kyle and I can tell her. As for you? Lotsa frogs in this world, Liv. Your prince is out there."

Liv groaned. "Maybe I need to sign up with a dating service or something."

Cassie shrugged. "I don't know, Liv. I mean, do those things work? Maybe you just need to get out there and meet people. Or give people a second chance. You're very picky. There are some great men in this town."

"Who are all married, cheaters or quite happily single like those damned Chase boys."

"Well, there's always Marc. He's damned good-looking. Sweet too."

"Maggie Chase, Marc is way too young for me. Not to mention the fact that he goes through women like potato chips. I'm done being a potato chip."

"He is not too young for you. It's not like he's twenty or anything. But you're right about the potato chip part. Let's just look for someone appropriate then. In the meantime, you need to stop riding yourself so hard about this."

Easier said than done. Liv knew it wasn't a problem with her looks. Without vanity, she accepted that she was beautiful. The kind of woman who got second glances everywhere she went. She had a good job, a good life, she was intelligent and most people thought she was funny. She did have a bit of a smart mouth, but it wasn't like at nearly thirty-five she could change that part of herself. And she had self-respect, damn it. She would not start lying and biting her tongue just to appeal to men!

"You could always ask for Polly's help." Cassie winked as Liv groaned. "She's got her finger on the pulse of this town. She can find you an eligible man in minutes, I'd wager."

"You know, I may take her up on that if this goes on too much longer."

They pulled up out front and Liv sighed at the exterior of the house. Matt had strung white fairy lights in the trees out front and the lights inside burned out a warm, inviting glow. Truth be told, Liv missed being a regular part of the Chase family more than she missed Matt. Missed the house and Sunday dinners. Belonging to the Chase family had felt really wonderful.

"Ugh, I'm such a fucking whiner," she mumbled before joining Cassie and Maggie to go inside.

"By the way, nice tan." Liv put her arm around Cassie as they entered the foyer. "All that vacation sex really relaxed you."

Cassie laughed. "Shane, the sun, fruity drinks and lots of hot monkey love. I've never enjoyed myself more. Come on through, the present table is in the sitting room but we've set up the food in the back so that's where everyone will be."

"They're here!" Kyle yelled as Polly and Edward approached the door.

As Polly and Edward came into the house, everyone gathered shouted "Happy Anniversary!" Polly clapped her hands and started smooching up on everyone she could grab as Edward just took it all in with a calm smile.

They'd tried to plan a surprise party but Polly was too nosy and she'd found out early on. Instead, her sons and daughters-in-law had made Polly and Edward agree to let them plan the event and to stay out of the way until it was time to start.

Getting out of the way, Liv went to hang up her coat and bag before going back to the living room. She saw Polly Chase's hair first and then the rest of her as the crowd parted to let her through.

"Why, hello there, Olivia. It's good to see you, honey. I'm glad you could make it." Polly click-clacked on over in her stiletto heels, that giant, lacquered wall of hair not budging an inch as she moved.

Liv bent and hugged Polly, wishing her a happy anniversary. "I wouldn't miss it for the world. You and Edward are a fine example to the rest of us. I hope I can find what you two have someday."

"Aw, well, it's all Edward. The man is quiet, lets me have my way, doesn't say much. A good father and a good man. I'm fortunate." Polly turned and Liv followed her gaze to where Edward Chase stood with Matt.

It was hard to see him, even after a few years. There'd been a time when she'd believed Matt Chase was the one for her. He was attentive and fun, they had sexual chemistry that was off the charts and Liv kept thinking that soon he'd fall for her too. But it never happened. Sure, he had affection for her, but as they'd reached the year mark he hadn't moved even an inch toward marriage or living together. She'd tried to deny it, tried to pretend he'd change but in the end, she knew he didn't love her and never would.

Pride intact but heart broken, she'd left their relationship because it was time to go. She wanted something permanent and it wasn't fair to just spin her wheels with a man who'd never want more than a Saturday date.

Matt saw her and smiled. She waved in return.

"That boy is a fool." Polly shook her head and Liv warmed. "Tells me you're his best female friend. I said he doesn't need any more friends, he needs to settle down and if not with a beautiful, successful woman like you, who? I swear. Kyle was always the sweetest one so of course it wasn't a surprise when he ended up with Maggie. Shane, well, he's been a trial since the moment he was born but Cassie can handle him just fine. Marc doesn't think he needs forever but I think he needs it more than any of the others do. Matt though? I'm afraid he's going to be in for a rude awakening when he finally realizes just how much he let go when you left."

Fighting back tears, Liv squeezed Polly's hand. "Thank you for that, Mrs. Chase. That means a lot to me. He and I weren't meant to be. I wish that weren't so, but it is. And he is my best guy friend, even if he can be a total butthead. You raised four good boys. The last two will do fine when the right woman comes along."

"I'll have you know I have my eye out for a good man for you. I heard about that punk Brody Willitson from my Marc earlier today. Never liked him and he wasn't good enough for a girl like you, honey. Don't you worry though, I've got my ear to the ground." Polly winked. "Now get yourself a plate and have a drink, the night is young."

Liv watched, amused, as Polly ambled off to greet the next person who'd arrived when she saw Maggie with Marc.

"Hey, you two." Liv picked up a plate and began to fill it.

"Hey, Liv. I keep meaning to compliment you on that dress. Is that the one you bought online? That dark purple color is gorgeous on you." Maggie touched her arm.

"I have to agree with Maggie on that one, Liv. Now, as much as I like you in short skirts, this one is very nice. The appeal of a curve-hugging sweater that's a dress is not lost on me at all. The boots are sexy too. A little bit dominatrix. You got any secrets to share, Livvy?"

Liv laughed to cover the warm surge in her belly that always came when Marc flirted. She knew he was full of it and flirted with every woman he met, but still, it made her feel tingly all over.

"Have you seen the bench we got them?" Marc held his

arm out and Liv took it, letting him lead her out of the room, through the kitchen and out into the large backyard.

"Kyle landscaped this little alcove for it. He says the roses will bloom over the arbor in the summer and night-blooming jasmine is planted on both sides."

The bench sat in an isolated corner of the yard with a pretty white arbor over it and a fountain nearby.

"Momma saw the bench last year during the insanity after Christmas when they were planning the wedding and Cassie told Shane and it went from there. You see the plaque?"

On the back of the bench, there was an inscribed plaque with Polly and Edward's name and anniversary date.

"It's impossible to shop for them but this and the album of all the pictures we had made from the slides my daddy had have been the biggest hit yet." Marc sat down and Liv joined him.

Liv warmed at the affection in his voice. "It's really beautiful out here. Kyle did a great job at making this little place. Like an oasis for the two of them to come and sit together."

"He'll read and pretend to listen to her and she'll talk and cross-stitch and pretend he's listening when she's really just planning on getting me and Matt married off."

Liv laughed out loud at the truth of that statement. "They work."

"They do. One day, if I can have what they do, even a shadow of what they have, I'll be lucky."

Liv nodded as she picked at the food on her plate and Marc helped himself to it as well. The noise from the party wafted out on the air but their corner of the yard was an isolated haven. They didn't talk, instead just looked at the stars and picked at Liv's food.

"We should probably go back inside," Liv said, standing. She needed to get back inside before she gave in and leaned her head on his shoulder.

"Yeah, it'll be cake time soon. I love cake." He pressed

a quick kiss to her cheek. "Don't forget that you owe me a dance later."

"We'll see."

"No seeing about it, Olivia Davis. You owe me a dance and I mean to collect." Popping a stolen olive into his mouth, he drew her back into the house, letting her go ahead once they reached the porch.

Man oh man did he love to look at her. Tall, long legs, big brown eyes that always looked like she had a very naughty secret and hair as black as a raven's wing. Straight and glossy and usually in some short, stylish 'do. Her clothes were just shy of outright sexy but it was clear she was a woman who knew what looked good on her body and she dressed accordingly. Not too tight but certainly clingy enough to highlight the high, round ass and the legs. She wore heels high enough to show off hard calves and tilt her ass and breasts out just right. The blouses and sweaters lovingly showcased her perky B cups.

He adored her smile. One of those smiles women had when they knew something delicious. Her accent was nice and thick—sexy, soft Southern sin—and she always sounded on the verge of laughing.

Liv Davis was just an all-around package. Funny, intelligent, independent, very feminine but capable too. She never ceased to make him smile when he thought about her. And she was the only woman he knew who flirted as well as he did. He had to admire that.

Once they got back inside, Liv got pulled into a cutthroat game of canasta with Marc, Cassie and Shane.

"Sheesh, I was hoping your mind would still be addled with all that honeymoon nookie but you're a shark with the cards," Liv joked with Cassie.

"I don't play to lose, Liv." Cassie sniffed and tossed down some cards, reaching to draw more.

"I love it when you're vicious, beautiful," Shane said and Marc rolled his eyes.

"Stop before it starts. No cow eyes over the cards. Chase family rule."

Liv laughed. "I like that rule."

"I hear the music starting up in the other room, Olivia. You promised me a dance don't you forget." Marc winked.

"Let me just do this." Liv tossed down her last suit and stood with a smile. "I don't play to lose either."

Cassie laughed and Marc stood. "Okay then, darlin', let's dance."

Liv took his hand and let him lead her through the house to the formal living room where the music was playing.

With an artful flourish, he pulled her into his arms and against his body. They both froze a moment and moved a bit apart. Swaying slowly, they chatted about town gossip as Reba sang over the stereo speakers.

That night when she finally got home, sore feet and all, the small of her back still tingled where his hand had lain when they'd shared a dance. "I must be ten kinds of fool for even entertaining the thought," she mumbled to herself as she tossed and turned.

But her dreams had other ideas.

Chapter Two

Marc happened to find himself standing in the front window of The Sands looking through the glass at Liv Davis as she reached out and touched the cheek of another man. The affection in her eyes startled him. He would have felt jealous but the man was clearly thirty years older than she was and the touch wasn't sexual at all. There was something else there he hadn't seen with Liv before, a sort of yearning.

When she looked up and saw him, surprise won over her face followed by a smile. There was nothing else he could do but go inside after she looked at him that way.

"Hi there, sugar." He strolled up to her table.

"Hi, Marc. Listen, I want you to meet my dad. He's visiting my sister in Atlanta for a week or so and came out to see me as well. Dad, this is Marc Chase. Marc, this is my father Bill Davis."

Marc shook the other man's hand. "It's a pleasure to meet you, Mr. Davis. Liv has spoken of you often. How's life in Florida treating you?"

"Sit down, boy." Bill Davis gestured to the place next to Liv, and Marc liked the man even more as he sat. "Florida is good, my lungs are much happier now, although I miss my baby girls. I was just trying to convince Livvy here to move down to be near me."

Marc didn't like the feeling in his stomach at the thought of that desk in the mayor's office being filled by someone else.

"But what would we do without her, Mr. Davis? Maggie might expect me to listen to all that girl talk if Liv wasn't around."

Liv snorted. "If I moved down there all his little girlfriends would be put out. He's the king of his senior community. He thinks he wants me and my sister there but he's got a harem to take care of him and they'll put up with a lot more than we will."

Marc stayed for pie and had to get moving. He had a meeting at the bank about a small business loan. But as he sat waiting to speak to the loan manager, his mind kept returning to the night of the anniversary party. It'd felt good with his body against hers, his hand at the curve of her back, holding her there, warm and soft, the scent of her in his nose. The itch to taste her rode him hard, he'd wanted to kiss her pretty bad but his father had cut in, stopping him before he did it.

It wasn't like he hadn't thought of asking Liv out before. At first she was freshly broken up with Matt and it was too soon. But the year mark had long passed and he'd brought it up to her and she'd deflected it. She didn't seem to take him or his advances seriously and he'd never really tried to make it more clear.

They called him into the meeting and he cleared his mind and got it back on business. In the end, the papers were relatively simple and Marc signed on the bottom line, in triplicate, and took out a loan he tried not to think about the size of. Some minutes later a few blocks away, he signed the lease on a space that would hold his gym and where he'd also run his personal training business from.

"When do you need me to help paint?" Kyle asked from the doorway.

Marc turned to face his brother. "Don't offer if you don't mean it. I'll put your butt to work."

"Of course I mean it. This is your dream, Marc. I'm your brother. You helped me on weekends how many times when I was getting the landscaping business up and running? That's what family does." Kyle came into the space. "This is a good spot. Central. Good lighting."

"This your place now?"

"Hey, Matt." Marc waved and his heart warmed to see Shane darken the doorway as he followed Matt.

"Well, now. This place is nice." Shane looked around the room.

"The paint is waiting at Pete's to pick up. The mirrors are ready. The floor people delivered the supplies to Pete's as well. I took off all next week." Marc walked around, envisioning just where he'd put everything. It wouldn't be a large gym but focused on the personal needs of not more than ten people working out at once. The space had been a gym some years ago so there were already two dressing rooms in the back with showers and lockers. He didn't plan on a juice bar or water aerobics. His place would be simple. But he would work with others to refer out as needed. He could help his clients with nutritional counseling but he'd been in contact with a woman in town to help with cooking classes or even meal delivery for his clients on an as-needed basis.

"Okay, we'll strip the walls before we get the flooring down. Get the paint up, the mirrors in and then do the floors. Where's the equipment?" Shane, ever the organizer, made Marc smile.

"Murph is letting me store it there until I'm ready."

"When's your last day at Murphy's?"

Murphy's was the gym in Riverton that he'd worked at for the last five years as a personal trainer.

"The end of the month."

"Well, tomorrow is Saturday, let's get in here first thing and get these walls cleaned up. You're coming to Momma and Daddy's before The Pumphouse tonight, right?" Kyle asked.

"I wouldn't miss this announcement for the world. Should I act surprised when Maggie tells us all she's knocked up?" Marc grinned.

"How'd you know?"

"Kyle." Matt rolled his eyes. "What other sort of big announcement is there? And she's been pretty green on and off over the last two months. She hasn't had a beer that I've seen since before Christmas and she's got a tiny little bump in her belly."

"And her boobs are bigger," Marc added.

"Thank you for that, Marc. So much tact." Shane chuckled. "Congratulations, Kyle. We figured you'd tell us when you were ready. After the miscarriage, we knew you'd want to wait to tell people this time. Although I'm absolutely sure Cassie knows but hasn't said."

Kyle laughed. "Count on it. I wasn't allowed to tell anyone but I know darned well Maggie told Cassie and Liv. Those three are thick as thieves. I was sorry to see Dee and Arthur move to Atlanta, I know Maggie misses her sorely."

"Yeah. Things are changing. You're gonna be a daddy. Shane is married and not grumpy all the time. Matt, well, Matt is still Matt but you know what I mean."

"I know I saw you looking at Liv last night like she was a steak and you were a starving man," Matt said to Marc, eyeing him closely.

"That so? And if I did?" Marc wasn't sure if he felt defensive or not. He didn't feel embarrassed though.

Matt sighed. "What's your game? I may have messed things up with her, but she's one of my best friends and I don't want her hurt. After this mess with Brody, she doesn't need some guy who only wants a one-night stand."

"Look, Matt, you're my brother so I'm gonna let that insult

slide. I like Olivia. She's gorgeous on the outside but I like her insides too. I want to be her friend. I *am* her friend. I'm not an asshole."

"I'm not insulting you. But she's not a notch on your bedpost."

"And that's not an insult?" Marc's voice rose and Kyle stepped in between them both.

"Whoa. That's enough. Matt, you're being insulting. Marc isn't some slutty user. Have you ever seen one single woman in this town hate him? I've never seen him less than respectful to a woman. And Marc, Matt is just trying to say that if you're not looking for something long-term to not start anything with Liv." Kyle put a hand on each of their shoulders. "You two are brothers. Stop it now."

Shane grinned. "You're good at that, Kyle. If you ever get tired of landscaping, you should be a counselor. And, Marc, for the record, I think a woman like Liv is exactly what you need. I'm not trying to convert you to the ways of a married man but I do think it's time you started thinking about being with a woman for longer than a few weeks at a time."

"I'm sorry if I offended you, Marc." Matt patted Marc's shoulder.

"Me too. Let's go to Momma and Daddy's and listen to the squeals of delight before we go play some pool."

Marc played pool and thought about the whole night. From the elation of finally carving out something for himself to the joy of Kyle and Maggie's announcement.

He'd been the baby of the family, living in the shadow of the other men in his life. His father, an upstanding pillar of the community. His oldest brother who'd always been the kind of guy you could trust to get your back. Upstanding, intense, loyal to his family. Kyle, good-hearted, hardworking small business owner, a wonder with the ladies until Maggie came along and now a devoted husband and soon-to-be parent. Matt, who liked to pretend he was just an affable, lazy guy but who excelled at everything he'd ever done. Perfect grades in school, highest scores when he went to the academy and well liked and respected at the firehouse.

It was hard to find your identity when your brothers were all such fine men. And he'd been content enough working at Murphy's, but over the last two years, he'd realized just how much he liked being a personal trainer. He wanted something of his own and closer to home. He wanted to help people live healthier lives in his community.

Maybe it was time for some more changes in his life.

He watched Liv and thought some more. Wondered if the longevity of her appeal to him was a matter of her unavailability or whether she was someone he could actually have a relationship with.

There was really only one way to find out.

"So uh, when did you and Marc start looking at each other like you were imagining each other naked?" Cassie asked as she drank her beer.

Liv started. "What?"

Maggie just raised an eyebrow and Liv sighed. "Okay. Okay. I don't know. I've always thought he was handsome. It's just flirting. Don't go picking out china patterns for me. He's way too young and as I said before, he's not looking for anything serious or long-term and I'm done with men who aren't. I may look and he may look but that's all it is. Looking."

"And I said he's not too young. He's what? Six years younger? That's not a thing. Men go out with women ten, fifteen years younger all the time. And I share a bedroom with the former wiliest bachelor in all the county. Apparently when these Chase boys decide to settle down, they do it for real." Cassie shrugged.

"You've seen Marc right? He's really hot. He works in a gym, his body is off the chain. He's got the most beautiful green eyes and I love that his hair is the darkest of all the boys. Nice, sort of just-rolled-out-of-bed features too. Of course I'm gonna look. Sheesh. A woman would have to be dead not to look. But that's all there is to it. Now, moving along to another topic. How did the announcement go?"

"As predicted. Polly is probably out buying furniture for the nursery right now. She insisted that they have a room for the baby at their house for when they babysit and so she or he will have a comfortable place to sleep when we're having dinner there or whatnot."

Cassie burst out laughing. "Yeah, like that baby will be put down in a crib with Polly around. I'm glad you're doing it first. Between Polly, Edward and those boys, you're never going to be able to hold your own baby."

"I'm happy for you. You and Kyle are going to be such great parents." Liv smiled.

"And you two will be the best aunties a baby could ever wish for."

"Free babysitting for life. What girl could ask for more?" Liv winked. "So when do we start the childbirth classes?"

Maggie laughed. "We've got a few months. I'm gonna need you to take a heavy hand to keep the delivery room clear."

"You got it, ace, I'll be your hired muscle." Her best friend and the person she loved most in the world was having a baby. Wow. They were all growing up and life was changing.

A pang sliced through Liv as she wondered when and if she'd be having a baby with a man who adored her as much as Kyle did Maggie. No one had ever looked at her that way, with such love and adoration, she had no real frame of reference for being cherished.

Marc looked down from his place on the ladder to see Olivia walk in.

"Hey there. What brings such a beautiful lady into my gym on such a nice day?"

She looked up and they locked gazes a moment. "You're just a jack-of-all-trades, aren't you? You're an electrician too?"

"Oh this is pretty simple stuff. The lights look better when they're set into the ceiling instead of hanging, I think." Finishing up, he came back down and put his toolbox aside. "What can I do for you?"

"Do you have room for another client? I've been feeling winded and out of shape doing simple stuff and it's harder for me to maintain my weight than it used to be. So I figure I could use your help."

And she was helping keep his business afloat too. He warmed, thinking about her wanting to help him out.

"I don't see an ounce of fat on you. And I think I've looked closely enough." He winked and she laughed. "Well, let's sit down and talk about your goals and what you're looking to do with yourself."

He interviewed her and got a better idea of the kind of services she'd need from him.

"I'm not going to let you slack, you know. I'm a tough taskmaster."

"And I'm not some weak little girl either. I can take it and my ass and upper arms need it."

Craning his neck, Marc checked out the area in question. "Honey, your ass is just perfect. Do you want to work out here or at your place?"

"I don't have the equipment at home so I guess here."

"Well, let's get some measurements then." He stood and indicated the scales.

"Do I have to?" She blanched.

"I don't know why women are always so freaked by the scale. It's just one indicator and it doesn't mean anything at this stage. You have nothing to worry about. Now come on."

"Should I take my shoes off?"

"Do you want to? It's not going to make much of a difference you know. If it makes you feel better, you go on. I bet you have pretty toes anyway."

Marc was very matter-of-fact when he worked with clients. He didn't coddle or pump up egos for no reason. He gave praise when it was due, and criticism in a constructive manner.

She sighed and stepped on the scale. With her shoes on. He liked her grit.

"You're well within normal weight range for your height." He took a body fat measurement and then brought out a tape measure to get her arms, legs, waist, hips and chest. Taking all the numbers down.

He discussed targets with her and they set up a schedule.

"I'll give you the family discount," he said, reaching for her credit card. "If you're not satisfied at the end of one month, I'll give you a fifty percent refund. But you have to work at it."

"You are not giving me a discount. You just started your own business. Later, when you're a mogul here in Petal, you can give me a discount. And I told you, I'm not afraid of hard work."

"I like the set of your mouth when you get uppity." He gave her the family discount anyway and watched her as she walked out the door and to her car. He jogged to the door.

"Hey!"

She turned and waited.

"Walk tomorrow. You have enough time to get home from work and change out of your clothes. Walk and it'll be a nice warm-up."

He couldn't help but love the way her eyes narrowed at him and her hand cocked on her hip. But she only nodded and got in her car, and he laughed as she pulled away.

"Feisty."

As promised, she showed up the next night—on foot. The walk wasn't that far and she found that the time enabled her to get rid of her day and begin to focus on working out for herself.

"Good evenin', Olivia." Marc handed her a key. "This is for the locker in the dressing room. You can stow your stuff in there. Come on out and we'll get started."

There were two other people working on the machines when she emerged from the dressing room. He'd said that there would be other people working out when she was there but he'd be available to her one-on-one when she needed it. Apparently, there were just simple gym members and those who needed less than a one-on-one trainer. She liked seeing his business getting off to a good start. Wanted things to work for him.

He went through the weights with her. Showed her the proper way to lift the weights and to extend her muscles. Instructed her on each machine and made notes in her personal log about her stamina. Which embarrassed her. She was used to being good at things, but she was out of shape and pretty darned sweaty and tired by the time she was done.

But she'd be damned if she let that get to her. No, she'd work her ass off to get it in shape because she said she would. And anyway, it would keep her from obsessing about her lack of a love life.

Of course, it did help that he looked so darned good. It was easy to mentally wander off to her happy place while her muscles screamed for mercy. For his part, he hadn't flirted at all, had kept his behavior professionally genial. Still though, he smelled good and when he leaned over her to adjust the weights on what she thought of as the thigh buster, she wanted to take a bite out of him.

"You're done for tonight. This will be your workout on Mondays and Fridays. Wednesdays and Saturdays you'll do aerobic exercise. We'll go for a run on Wednesday morning before work as planned and Saturdays I've got a bike ride set up for my clients who are interested. This week I thought the lake trail would be good. I can get an idea of where you're all at staminawise. And then I'll set up individual appointments with you as necessary. Have you ever tried kickboxing or rowing?"

She just stared at him for long moments until he laughed. "What?"

"Nothing. I've just realized I'm paying you to kill me."

"You're paying me to extend your life, Olivia. Now go on. I'll see you Wednesday morning at six. I'll swing by your place to pick you up. You okay to walk home?"

"It's five blocks. People are still out and about and it's Petal." She softened a bit. "But thank you, I appreciate your asking."

"Okay then. Take it slow, don't dawdle but let your muscles cool down."

Liv had the foolish need to kiss him goodbye but a new client came in. A female one who giggled at him. Gnashing her teeth, Liv remembered herself, pokered up and waved quickly before leaving.

As she walked home, she gave herself a stern talking-to about this new infatuation with Marc Chase. She needed to keep in mind who Marc was. No, *what* Marc was. A very nice, very flirty guy. She wasn't anything more than another woman to wink at. A woman six years older than he was. She wasn't Mrs. Robinson and he wasn't what she was looking for, even if he was interested in her romantically, which he wasn't.

It was a fun, flirty friendship. Period. End of sentence. She'd be a fool to entertain anything other than that. And Liv Davis may have been staring spinsterhood in the face but she was not a fool.

Chapter Three

Liv sat eating her lunch at The Sands, looking out onto Main Street. It was a Wednesday, she'd had a good run that morning with Marc. Even though it had been a month and he didn't need to run with her every week anymore, he still did, said it kept him healthy too.

Wasn't like she was going to complain. She liked hanging out with him. When she'd been going out with Matt, Marc was the saucy little brother. She knew him but only as someone to say hello to on the street and to talk to about shallow topics at Sunday dinner.

She never got to actually know the Marc Chase who cared deeply about physical fitness and nutrition. The Marc who was a lot deeper than she'd given him credit for.

"Are those potato chips on your plate?"

Speak of the devil. Liv looked up into those gorgeous green eyes and blushed. "Yes. Baked, not fried. I swear. And I asked for half an order. No mayo on the sandwich and you can see it's nine-grain bread."

Laughing, he slid into the booth across from her. "Good job. Trans fats are the worst. And anyway, if you use all your calories up on crap, you can't have smothered pork chops for Sunday dinner."

That was another thing. He cared about eating right and living healthy but not in a fanatical sense. He enjoyed life and wanted his clients to as well.

"I save my weekly splurge for Friday nights at The Pump-house."

He laughed. "I have to do extra time on the rowing machine for chili cheese fries."

She only barely managed to bite back a comment about how good his stomach looked as he used the rowing machine. Flex and release, flex and release, the muscles in his abdomen were hard and toned and she squirmed a little in her seat as she thought about it.

"Can I join you? I haven't had lunch yet."

She nodded and he ordered. There was something about him that made her feel relaxed. Well, stuff about him that made her feel nervous and edgy too but that was the lack of sex. It had been six weeks since she'd had sex and she felt like she was going insane with the stress. And the marvelous hunk of man cake in front of her just ached to be licked from head to toe.

A giggle bubbled up before she could stop it. The lack of sex really was driving her mad.

"What's so funny?" Marc's smile was infectious and she laughed again.

"Nothing. Just a silly thought I had that I'm *not* going to share."

"Ah. A sex thought. About me I bet. I know I have plenty about you. I can say that since we're not working now," he added.

"You're incorrigible. I'm old enough to be your, um, baby-sitter."

"Trust me, Olivia. Momma left us with a few babysitters here and there, not very often, you know, because they never came back after the first time. But none of them looked like you. We might have behaved if they did."

"Oh you guys. Did you torture a bunch of teenaged girls? Setting fires and egging cars?"

"We never set fires."

Liv began laughing anew at the thought of the four Chase boys terrorizing their babysitters.

"It was all Shane. I just followed along. I'm totally innocent." He put his hands up, struggling against a laugh.

"Oh no more. I'm going to choke on something," she gasped out through the laughter. "You, innocent?"

Marc realized as they laughed together that something really essential had passed between them. Had changed. She wasn't Matt's ex-girlfriend anymore. She was his friend. Totally separate from her former relationship with his brother. Free from that. What they had was unique to the two of them and it all sort of clicked into place.

"Okay, so innocent probably isn't the best word choice. But Shane is an instigator. He may be the sheriff now but it's only because he was such a lawbreaker when we were kids. Oh, Daddy used to get so mad. And my dad rarely gets riled up. Momma, well, she'd grab for whatever son she could grab a hank of and hold on to, screeching the whole time. Once she had your ear, you were done with, and you may as well just submit or she'd never let you go. But Daddy? He'd bide his time until we all thought the coast was clear and then he'd corner us in his study or the kitchen and man we'd get it." He smiled at the memory.

"Your mother is something else. I love her to death but she scares the hell out of me."

"I'd say she was all bark and no bite but that'd be such a lie. She's fierce for such a tiny scrap of woman. Taught me a lot about courage. My father taught me about justice and honor but Momma taught me courage and tenacity." Marc wondered what she'd think about him and Liv and realized the moment he thought it that his mother would be all for it. Liv had already passed inspection and been approved. It was Matt who fucked up.

"I love the way she terrorizes John. The mayor, that is. This whole Founder's Day event has been fun to plan but every time she enters the building he tries to jump out his office window. He tries to charm his way around her but she sees right through him and he just gives in with a heavy sigh."

Marc didn't like the first-name thing. Wondered if she had a thing with the mayor and then discarded the idea. John Woodward was not the kind of man who could hold a woman like Olivia Davis for longer than three minutes. He certainly couldn't match her in bed. John was too timid and gentlemanly. Marc knew what Liv needed between the sheets. Passion. Energy. Creativity and if he wasn't wrong, a bit of a dominant hand.

"You going then? To the picnic and parade?" Marc asked, he hoped not too eagerly.

"Wouldn't miss it. Should be a big shindig and your mother has worked really hard with the Historical Society. And I love a good party." She crumpled her napkin and grabbed her bag. "I need to get back to work. It was nice to hang out with you today." She put a hand on his shoulder to stay him. "Don't get up. I'll see you later, Marc. Have a nice afternoon."

"I'll see you Friday," he called out, relieved his voice hadn't cracked at the weight of awareness of her as a woman. Holy moly, he wanted her bad. Seeing her laugh like that, her head tipped back slightly so her neck was exposed, all creamy and supple, made him want to lick all the way from shoulder to earlobe. Wondered if she would give a little shiver of delight. Wondered what she'd taste like.

Groaning, he put his forehead in his palm. This couldn't be happening to him. He was not going down like his older brothers had. No way. But he would taste Olivia Davis. To get her out of his system, of course. Once they'd had each other a few dozen times the desperate need he felt would wear off. Yeah. That was it.

Torture. That's what it was and she had to end it. Liv looked at Marc Chase as he sat on a blanket with Becky Sue Radin. The teeny little blonde stared at him like he was a cupcake. And Liv loved cupcakes too, but since Marc hired on as her personal trainer she hadn't had one. That was clearly her problem. A lack of cupcakes. It was all Marc's fault. Cupcake deprivation had led her into sexualizing everything.

Huffing out a breath in frustration, she turned her attention back to Bill Prentiss, who'd been telling her all about his prize-winning steer. *Fascinating.* Okay, she was being unfair. Bill was a perfectly nice man. Owned a ranch outside town. Made a good living. Worked hard and was quite a handsome specimen. Marriage material even.

He held her hand gently, respectfully and paid attention to no other woman but her. These were *good things* and if she wanted forever, she'd have to stop this ridiculous attraction to men like Marc and Matt Chase, who didn't think ten minutes ahead of their little misters.

No, Liv Davis was done with the sweet-talking ladies' men of the world. They might be fun as all get-out between the sheets but there was more to life than between the sheets.

So she smiled at Bill and flattered him because he deserved it. It was all *her* issue that she had some kind of messed-up gene that found unworthy men attractive. She had to stamp it out. Retrain herself. Yes. That's exactly what she needed to do. Retrain herself.

"Bill, I'll be back in a few minutes. I just need to check in on the ladies around the corner to be sure they've got enough ice and everything they need."

He stood when she did and she cocked her head, smiling.

He really was a nice man and she'd be a fool not to go out with him again if he asked.

"I'll be right here, Liv. Unless there's something I can do to help?"

"That's very kind of you but, no thank you. I just promised the mayor that I'd be on the lookout in case the Historical Society ladies needed anything. Back in a bit."

Of course, as she'd figured, Polly Chase didn't need a thing. She had the entire evening planned to perfection, including the pie booth. Polly thanked Liv, pressed a peach popover on her and Liv headed into the building to get a sweater out of her office as the evening had gotten a bit chilly.

"Hey there. Whatcha doing in here?"

She nearly jumped out of her skin when Marc spoke behind her as she left the building on the side away from the crowds. "Jeez, give a girl a heart attack!"

"Sorry. I ran to my truck to grab a blanket. It's getting a bit cold. Should have known. It is mid-April."

He made no move to leave though. Standing there, staring at her mouth in the moonlight.

"Do I have sugar on my lips?" She felt slightly guilty for eating the popover and made a promise to herself to go and grab Bill a piece of something sweet.

He stepped forward and she had no place to go, the wall was at her back. "I don't know. Do you?" he murmured, his body just shy of touching hers.

"I...uh." Before she could say anything else so spectacularly witty, he closed the last inch between them, his hand moving to cup her cheek.

"You're one of the most beautiful women I've ever seen. I've always thought so. Soft. You smell good too."

"Marc..."

His lips brushed hers, just the barest hint of pressure but within a breath, that soft touch exploded and need so dire it scared her welled up and swallowed her whole.

It must have been the same for him because he angled his mouth and went in for a real kiss this time. A skillful combination of teeth, tongue and lips all working to devastate her defenses. Her fingers gripped his shoulders, digging into the muscles, registering the softness of the sweater he was wearing.

His taste bloomed through her, spicy, delicious. It made something deep within her ache for a moment, seize and then warm all over. A soft moan escaped her and he swallowed it eagerly.

His hands, large and capable, held her hips, the tips of his thumbs stroking over the naked skin just beneath the hem of her sweater, just two inches shy of the bottom slope of her breasts.

That's what snapped her out of it, the longing, the yearning to reach down and move his hands up over her breasts and arch into his touch. She let go of his shoulders, sliding her palms down to push him back gently.

"Holy moly," Marc breathed out.

She nodded.

"When can you leave? We can go get a late drink somewhere or you could come to my place." Marc brushed a thumb over her bottom lip and she shivered.

"I'm here on a date, Marc. God, I shouldn't have done that." Especially because it awakened something deep inside her, a recognition that freaked her out. It was something she couldn't afford to feel. He wasn't capable of giving it back.

"Of course you should have. Olivia, this thing, that kiss has been brewing between the two of us for a long time now and you know it. We can go to dinner another night. I'm sorry for suggesting you dump your date. I know you're too kind to do that."

"I can't have dinner with you, Marc. Not tonight, not tomorrow night."

"Okay, well then come to my apartment. I'll make you dinner after I've had you three or four times." He grinned and she groaned, pushing him back so she could move away from the wall. She felt cornered in more ways than one. She vowed to eat a cupcake that very night. Two even. This addiction to dangerously handsome men without an ounce of desire to commit would be the death of her.

"There'll be no having!"

"Oh now, Olivia, don't be offended. I didn't mean it to sound crass."

She shoved a hand through her hair. "No, not that. I'm not offended. I'm flattered. Confused." Panicked, scared, freaked, aroused and a dozen other things it would not pay to feel. "But it can't happen, Marc. Not ever."

He narrowed his eyes at her. "You're joking. Olivia Davis, that was the single most hottest kiss I've ever shared with a woman and you were on fire in my arms. I felt your nipples through your sweater. You wanted me, you can't deny that."

Oy. "I'm not denying that. Yes, yes there's chemistry but there are too many reasons to not give in."

He put his hands on his hips. "Like what? You're single, I'm single. We're attracted to each other and you know we're going to be hot in bed together."

"Marc, you're too young for me. I'm six years older than you are. And," she held up her hand to silence him, "I've just recently decided that I'm done with casual relationships. I am not going out with another man who thinks of women as a box of chocolates and he has to sample every one. I want something real, something lasting and that's not what you want. I'm not judging you, Marc, but I want a relationship. I want to end up married."

He paled so much she could see it in the moonlight. She laughed tightly. She'd known it but it hurt to see his reaction anyway.

"See? Even the word freaks you out. You and I are friends. We really are and I like that. I like *you*. But this can't be more than a friendship, spectacular kiss or not. Now, I have a date who'll be wondering where I am and you do too if I'm not mistaken. I'll see you on Monday when I come to work out."

She hurried off before she changed her mind.

Watching her walk away, Marc slammed his fist into his thigh in frustration. *Friends?* After that kiss? His lips tingled with her taste, his cock throbbed, pressing against the fly of his jeans.

"Too young my ass," he mumbled, heading back to where Becky Sue waited for him. It wasn't like Liv was old. She was gorgeous and totally in shape. He knew that for sure. He'd seen her body enough as he worked with her over the last month.

Images of her stretching and sweating assailed him until he pushed them firmly out of his mind or he'd go find her and fuck her against the trunk of the nearest tree. God, he wanted her bad and he knew she wanted him too. That was the kicker. This artificial barrier she'd created over their age difference was just dumb and she was using it to keep him away.

As he turned the corner he saw her with Bill, head tipped up, body leaning into his as they watched the sky. As if Marc had called her name, she turned toward him. Her gaze caught his for long moments until she let go and returned her attention to the fireworks.

Frustrated, he glanced back toward the blankets where Becky Sue waited with Cassie, Shane, Maggie and Kyle. He smiled when he caught Kyle placing his palms over Maggie's growing baby bump. They were good together.

He froze a moment. Marriage? Liv said she wanted long term. Said she wanted to get married. Okay, so he wasn't too young to have a nice fling with her but he was definitely not interested in marriage. *Yikes.* No, he'd go back to being her friend, sport a few furtive fantasies about bedding her and continue on with his happily unencumbered life. Marriage was for suckers and he was most certainly not a sucker. Yeah, sure.

* * *

Friends my ass, Marc thought as he watched her take another lap in the community pool one Saturday morning a month after that kiss. She was made for the water, swam like a freaking seal and, even in a nondescript one-piece swimsuit, she looked hot.

He shouldn't even be there. He didn't need to be. Her Saturday workouts weren't even in his schedule. But he found himself unable to resist being near her when he could be.

"Hey there!" she called out as she pulled herself out of the water and grabbed a nearby towel. "Whatcha doing here?"

He stared at her a moment, watching the water beaded like diamonds on her thick lashes, her dark hair slicked back against her head.

"I played racquetball with Kyle earlier. We just finished and I saw you and thought I'd come say hello." He looked at her upper body and nodded. "You're really coming along, Liv. Your shoulders look fantastic."

She blushed and he cursed his ridiculously friendly cock for bounding to attention.

"Thank you. Two months of working out will do that, I suppose. At first I thought it'd be hard to work it into my schedule, but really, it's not that bad and I'm used to it now. Plus, I like the way I feel."

He liked *her*. Damn it. This friends stuff wasn't cutting it. He'd gone out with every woman he could but none of them could get his mind off Liv.

"What are you up to just now? I haven't had any lunch. You hungry?" He sent her his best "just friends" smile as he lied through his teeth.

"I'm actually meeting Cassie and Maggie for lunch in about forty-five minutes. Sorry. I'd invite you but we're going to be talking about babies and then sex and stuff you aren't privileged to hear." She grinned and his gut tightened.

"Fine, fine. Keep me out of all the fun. See if I care." He

heaved a theatrical sigh. "Looks like I'll try and catch up to Kyle and Shane as they'll be free. I'll see you Monday then. Have a good weekend."

She waved as she headed toward the locker area and he watched the sway of that delectable ass before making up his mind and heading out to catch up to Kyle.

"Kyle!" Marc shouted as he jogged toward his brother.

Kyle tossed his bag into the back seat and turned. "What's up?"

"I need your help." He briefly filled his brother in.

"Meet me at my house in an hour. I'll call Shane and have him bring some takeout."

Relieved, Marc nodded and headed home to change.

Liv looked at herself in her rearview mirror when she pulled up to the restaurant. At least the strain didn't show. Every time she saw Marc she wanted to kiss him. But he was off the menu. And he hadn't shown anything but a friendly regard for her since that night anyway. And why not? She was hot, damn it!

Oh she cracked herself up. Yeah, right. It wasn't funny that she could not shake this insane jones for Marc Chase.

The marriage comment freaked him out. And good. It wouldn't be right for her to engage in a dalliance with him when she knew it wouldn't go anywhere. *No*, she was done with that. It was time to look past tomorrow morning. It was time she did something for herself and chose a man who wanted to share his tomorrows with her, not just his night and a few condoms.

Man, self-respect blew sometimes.

Chapter Four

Marc let himself into Kyle and Maggie's place and followed the sound of his brothers to the kitchen where they were busily opening up boxes of food.

"Hey there. Grab a beer, we'll get to work in a minute," Kyle called out. Marc cracked a cold one open and sat down at the table in the breakfast nook.

"Didn't expect it to be a full house."

Matt rolled his eyes. "We're brothers. Between the four of us, we've handled a whole lot of women. Kyle tells me this is a woman issue. Let's hear it. Between all of us, we can solve just about anything."

Shane chuckled and bit into a spring roll. "Spill."

Kyle nodded.

"It's Olivia." He looked to Matt nervously, now understanding why Kyle invited him. It would be best to do this all openly so Matt wouldn't be upset.

"What about her?" Matt watched him suspiciously.

"I have a thing for her something fierce. It's not just lust, although I have that in spades. Oh man do I have that." Marc shook his head. "It's more. I kissed her at the Founder's Day picnic. It was," he licked his lips, "specfuckingtacular. I've never, ever, felt that way kissing a woman. And I haven't been able to forget it. I want to be with her but she doesn't take me seriously."

"What did she say?" Shane asked.

"First she said she was too old for me. Dumbest thing I ever heard. Has the woman never looked in a mirror? She's amazing. I told her it was only six years. And then she said she wasn't looking for one night or one week." He heaved a sigh. "I know. She's right to distrust me on that score. She says she's not going out with men who only want something temporary anymore. She says we can only be friends." He rolled his eyes at that.

"And clearly you don't want that. But what do you want because, Marc, she's telling you what she does. She doesn't want to be temporary. You're a temporary kind of guy." Kyle watched his brother carefully.

Marc scrubbed his hands over his face. "I know. I know what I am. What I *was*. And she's right to turn me down based on what she's seen. It's not like I've made a secret of it. But you all know." He looked at Matt and laughed before turning back to Kyle. "Well, you and Shane know what it is when you want to cast that aside for something lasting."

"You saying you're in love with Liv?" Matt asked, incredulous. "You, Mister Different-woman-on-his-arm-every-night?"

"I'm not in love with Olivia, no. I don't know her well enough. Not like that. But I do know I want more than a week or two with her. I want to explore something long-term. For real. I've gotten to know her as a person, not as my brother's girlfriend and then ex. I'd like to get to know her as a woman now. But I don't know how to get her to trust me enough to let me in."

"And that's where we come in," Kyle said, clinking his beer against Shane's. "Liv needs a good old-fashioned wooing."

Shane chuckled. "You ready to woo? It's like training for a marathon, Marc. She doesn't trust you and that's based on what she's seen for years. You're going to have to forgo other women. Can you do that?"

"Yes. I've tried to date Liv out of my head but it hasn't worked. I'm not interested in anyone else. She takes up my mind every minute of the damned day."

"Olivia is a good woman. Beautiful, giving. Can you take care of that? Work to not hurt her?" Matt asked.

"I can. I swear to you all that I would not be pursuing this if I thought it was just some temporary thing. I don't want to hurt her. I know she deserves more than that. I want to give her more than that."

Matt sighed and held up his beer. "Well then, let's work on the woo, shall we? Four Chase boys all united? She doesn't stand a chance."

Monday evening, Liv walked into Marc's Body By Design and smiled when she saw him there. He sat on his haunches next to one of the machines, talking to Shane.

Boy did they both look fine. Shane was huge. Muscled, hard and now sweaty. She did like that Shane's workout coincided with hers. She loved Cassie to pieces and would never dream of taking on a pain-in-the-ass man like Shane Chase. But he sure was nice to look at.

Then again Marc—with his muscled thighs straining against his shorts and the hard muscles of his back and shoulders visible through the neck of the T-shirt he wore—was a hundred times hotter. He carried his strength easily, gracefully.

She had to gulp and hurry past them to drop her stuff off in a locker before she leapt on him and licked his neck. Why oh why did the sight of a bead of sweat rolling down to the hollow of his throat make her itchy to lick him? Wasn't that sick? That was it. She was sick and perverted. Sweat making her hot, good gracious she needed sex.

When she came out, Shane was leaving. He waved to her,

said he was on his way home to shower with Cassie and, leaving her blushing, walked out the door.

Chuckling, Marc accompanied her to the mat where she sat and began to stretch.

"How are you tonight?"

"Good. Stressful day. Budget time. The mayor is cranky and taking it out on everyone. I wanted to bop him on the head with my stapler today."

He took her arms and pulled, letting her stretch her thighs and back. Standing, he reached down, giving her a hand up.

They headed to the free weights where she began her first rep of thirty. "You need me to kick his ass? John always has been kinda punky."

Liv laughed. "Thank you for that very chivalrous offer, Marc, but I think I scared him back in line. He's not a bad guy, he's just a control freak and you can't control everything at this time of year."

He reached out to correct her arm. "This way. You're going to hurt yourself if you do it like that. You sure look pretty tonight."

She looked at him askance. "Uh, yeah. Straining muscles and T-shirts with exercise shorts always make a girl look pretty. You need a loan or something?"

He barked a surprised laugh. "I'm good. Business is doing well as it happens and you do look pretty. I like the new thing you're doing with your hair. It was sort of sleek and straight last month but I like this tousled, curly thing you're doing."

Liv stilled mentally. It wasn't so much that he was flirting. She could handle flirting. He was…earnest. Sincere. It was off-putting because while she could blow off flirting, sincere compliments and a keen interest in her and her perspective from him felt intimate and had the added effect of making her all tingly. Lawd. She was such a loser.

"Uh, thanks." *Uh, thanks?* Could she be any less coherent? "So, how's your mom?"

"She's good. Says you should come to dinner soon. She and I were talking about you yesterday and we both agreed you don't come around near enough."

Liv put the barbells back and moved to the next station to work her legs. "What's your game, Marc?" She grunted as she pushed the weights the first time. Lovely. Grunting.

"No game. Why do you ask? That's a very half-assed rep, Olivia. Work it, don't puss out."

"Puss out? I most certainly do not *puss out*. I'm tired."

"You're pussing out. Now work it. Your ass will thank you. And I will thank you because you have a very nice ass. You should come with me to open mic night at Lindy's tomorrow. You like live music, don't you?"

She stopped outright. How did he expect her to concentrate when he stood there all hard and yummy, acting sincere and then asking her on a date?

"We went through this already, Marc Chase." Gawd, even she didn't believe the conviction in her voice.

"Stop slacking, Livvy. Move those legs or I'm gonna make you run an extra mile on Wednesday morning."

She snorted. He was gonna make her? "I'll have you know I now run Monday, Wednesday and Friday. I run lots of extra miles." She gritted her teeth and pushed out the last four reps, sweat beading on her temples.

"Good for you."

She heard him arranging the weights as she settled in, grabbed the bar above her head and pulled, working her biceps and shoulders.

He leaned over, his mouth just a whisper from her ear as he adjusted her hands on the bar. "You smell good, too. No chemicals, all woman. I like that."

"I can't concentrate when you do that." Her voice came out breathy and she felt faint.

"What?" He straightened and indicated with a nod that she

continue. "Talking about how good you smell messes with your concentration?"

"You know damned well it does. What are you up to, Marc?"

"Finish up." The bastard sauntered away and made some notes, so she ignored him and completed that set. He left her alone for the next two machines but came back into her space when she did her lunges.

"Good. I like the way you're holding your back. Nice work."

She was suspicious, yes, but his praise warmed her despite that.

When she was done, she hurried into the back to change and get going. She'd shower at home and she wanted to get out of there before the giggly client came in. One of the Scott girls if she wasn't mistaken. Couldn't be over twenty-three and the mere sight of her made Liv want to scream and snatch her bald for fawning all over Marc.

When she came out he was waiting. Alone. The lights were turned off but for the very front spots and he had a messenger bag slung across his shoulders.

"Ready?"

"For what? Where's the bottle blonde who giggles incessantly?"

Marc reddened and choked back a smile. "Sarah? She has evening classes this quarter at the community college so she comes in during the afternoons now. Shall I tell her you were asking after her?"

"Yeah sure, smartass. Well, I'll see you Wednesday then."

"Wait. I'm all done for the evening. Let me walk with you. It's a nice night."

Liv narrowed her eyes. "You live in the opposite direction."

"I know. I want to walk with you. Is that a crime?"

"I'm not kissing you or inviting you in." God knew if she invited him in, she'd be naked with him inside her within three minutes.

"Well, we can work up to that. It's a fine evening and I like your company. Come on. I'll be a total gentleman."

She sighed. "Fine. On the way you can tell me your game, Marc."

He locked up behind himself and chuckled as he joined her. "Sugar, I am not playing a game. This is serious. I mean to woo you, so shut up and let me do it."

A burst of pleasure broke over her at his statement even when she knew she should be stern. "You're going to woo me?"

"With every ounce of effort I possess. You don't stand a chance, Liv. You could just give in now and save me the work but I doubt you will. Enjoy it. I know I am."

"What do you think you're going to get out of this? I've said I'm looking for something long-term. You're not a long-term guy."

He took her hand and looked deep into her eyes. "I didn't used to be, no. But I find myself thinking in terms of what it would be like to take you camping over the summer. Do you ski? I know of some excellent places to get in good winter skiing. I love to take trips and travel around." He paused when they reached the walk in front of her little house. "Look, Liv, I know you don't have any reason to believe me right now. We both know my history. I can't wish it away or pretend it didn't happen. So I'm going to show you I've turned over a new leaf. Prepare to have the hell wooed out of you."

Bringing the hand he'd been holding to his mouth, he brushed his lips over her knuckles and her nipples hardened. She only barely held back a whimper.

"Marc, you're wasting your time," she whispered. "Don't do this to me. Please. You and I both know you don't do women for longer than what, a week or two? You're only interested in me because it's a novelty for you to be turned down."

"I'm genuine here, Liv. I thought so at first too. The novelty thing I mean. But I know different and so will you." He took a step backwards. "I'll see you Wednesday morning then. Have a good night."

She tried to speak but he shook his head and she sighed, moving up the walk to her front door. "See you Wednesday. Thanks for walking me home," she called out.

"My pleasure." He waved and sauntered back the way they'd come.

Man, if he wasn't kidding she was in big trouble. Fear crouched low for a moment and was gone.

He wasn't kidding. Damned Marc Chase! She frowned as she looked at the pretty bouquet of French lavender sitting on her desk. His note said that he hoped the scent would help bring her calm in a stressful time at work. Two days before it had been a raisin muffin from The Honey Bear. A healthy treat. Thoughtful and she loved raisins too.

He'd jogged up to her house with it fresh, still warm from the oven.

Heaving a sigh, she sat down and tried to do her work but the scent of lavender wafted around her as she did.

"Pretty flowers. New admirer?" Maggie grinned at her. "Aren't you done yet? You can tell me who sent these on the way to get Cassie."

"I...uh." She sighed. Liv hadn't told Maggie, or anyone else for that matter, about Marc's declaration of wooage just yet. She didn't know what to think much less how to describe it. She shook her head as she shut her computer down and turned to get out of her chair.

"I'm going to run home first, take these there. I don't want them here over the weekend where they'll just die." Liv grabbed the flowers. "I'll meet you at The Pumphouse."

They walked out together and Maggie headed one way while Liv headed home. Once there, she put the lavender on her kitchen table and headed to her room to change her clothes and touch up her makeup.

She looked in the mirror as she freshened her lipstick. Not bad for a woman who'd be thirty-five in six weeks. She probably should have stayed out of the sun more. Worn sunscreen. God, how was she supposed to know it was bad to cook herself every summer until she got a good base tan? Everyone knew you had to get a few good burns before your skin got nice and dark. She sighed. And now it caused cancer.

"Stop it now before you turn into one of those crazy cat ladies, Olivia Jean," she admonished herself in the mirror.

At The Pumphouse, Cassie and Maggie were already waiting. It was a bit lonelier without Dee there but Dee would be spending less and less time in Petal now that she and Arthur had moved to Atlanta and their house had just sold.

"Scooch over, hot stuff," Liv said to Cassie. She tried not to look toward the back where the pool tables were. If Marc was there she'd end up staring at him all night.

"So, flowers huh? Who?" Cassie poured Liv a beer and pushed the glass toward her.

"Did y'all order the chili cheese fries yet? I ran an extra mile this morning and I'm starving." Liv busied herself looking through her purse.

"Hoo boy! This is good. You won't even look me in the eye. It's Roger Petrie isn't it? You've decided you can overcome his, erm, intense love of his animals." Maggie laughed.

Roger Petrie was one of the oddest citizens in town. Well known for his predilection for keeping his animals in bed with him.

Liv stopped rustling around and looked up at her friends. Cassie snickered and Liv just shook her head. "You're totally insane. No. That's not it. You're *jealous*. Ha! Roger is all mine, baby. Between me and his goat, there's no room left in his bed."

Maggie tossed her head back and laughed until her eyes teared up.

"If you must know, it's Marc."

Maggie stopped laughing and looked over at Liv, mouth open in shock. "Marc Chase sent you flowers? Why?"

"He tells me he's wooing me."

"Oh the woo." Cassie blew out a breath. "They're awfully good at the woo, those boys."

"No shit. Kyle wooed my panties right off. Wooed ice cream in my belly button at three in the morning." Maggie sighed. "Damn good woo. I'm betting they got it from Edward. It's always the quiet ones. But why is he wooing you?"

"What? You don't think I'm worthy of woo?"

"Say that five times fast." Cassie laughed. "No, cupcake. I think Maggie is asking why a man with a revolving door in his bedroom is wooing a woman who's declared she's looking for more than a few nights' entertainment. Has something happened?"

"Yeah. What she said. Of course you're worthy of woo. Dumbass."

"You're very cranky now that you're knocked up." Liv couldn't help but turn, and damn if her eyes didn't move straight to Marc's ass. "Boy howdy the man has an ass on him."

The other two women craned their necks to look. "Oh yeah. The nicest of the bunch asswise, I'd wager. Back to you telling us what's going on," Cassie said.

Reluctantly, Liv turned back to her friends and told them the whole story. Including the night of the Founder's Day picnic up until the flowers he'd had delivered that morning.

"Wow. Well, if I may direct you to a statement you made to me in this very booth nearly two years ago now. You said, *when a man like that falls, he falls hard and all the way. There's no middle ground for a guy like Shane.* Now, I think you can turn that around and say the same of Marc. If he says he wants more, I believe him. He may be a randy little dude, but he's a good-hearted, honest man. And he wouldn't pursue you if he didn't think he could give you what you want." Cassie grabbed a fry and popped it in her mouth.

"He's not offering marriage. He's wooing me. God help me, that's enough."

Maggie waved that away. "None of these men are going to offer you marriage from date one. Well, maybe Roger if you buy him some goat chow. But what if? What if this could develop into something real?"

"Goat chow, you're a laugh riot. And I don't know. I've had my heart trampled on and I don't want to go back there again. I'm afraid."

Cassie put her arm around Liv's shoulders. "Ah cupcake, I know that feeling. But you say you want to find something real. Someone real. You'll never know if you don't let it happen. He won't cheat on you. He's too honorable for that. And he's, well, I've seen him in his swim trunks out on my dock swimming in the lake and when I say little dude, I'm just being affectionate. I don't think it's an accurate way to describe his body at all."

"Don't I know it? Good gracious, when we're running and he takes off his shirt to wipe his face? Oh, I want to lick him. But he's so young. I feel like a cradle robber."

"Will you quit it with that already? Not quite six years' difference. You're hot, he's hot for you. What's the issue? He's certainly old enough to knowingly consent. And here's the thing, go out with him and see. If it's not a love match, keep with your plan but you have to date to find Mister Right anyway, don't you?" Maggie sipped her soda and smiled.

Marc saw her come in and nearly ripped the felt with his cue. She was all leggy grace and energy and he loved the shiny lipstick she had on. Reminded him of raspberries.

"Holy moly she looks good enough to eat," he murmured.

Matt chuckled and took his turn. "How goes the woo?"

"She got all stuttery when I brought her the muffin on Wednesday morning and I had lavender sent to her office today. She said it was stressful because it was budget time.

Lavender is good for calming and relaxing. I thought it might help."

"Oh that's good. Damn, you're diabolical, little brother." Kyle looked over at the three women gathered in their usual booth. "She sure is pretty."

"She's beautiful. I love her laugh. And she's cocky, I like that. Called Sarah Scott a giggly bottle blonde."

Matt laughed. "Well, she's spot-on there. Sarah still trying to get you in her bed, Marc?"

"She's too damned young. She might be twenty-two but mentally she's about sixteen. I don't need that kind of trouble. Never have. No, I prefer trouble with inky black hair and brown cat's eyes."

"You know, if you really want to increase your chances of making this work, you should enlist Momma's help." Shane's gaze drifted to his wife's and Marc felt that tug between them.

"That's true. Neither of these two knuckleheads could have landed such fabulous women without Momma's interference," Matt said.

"Well, certainly not Shane but I landed Maggie myself," Kyle mumbled but Marc ignored him.

"Two steps ahead of you. I just happened to mention to Momma that it had been some time since Liv had been to Sunday dinner. Course Momma gave me grief for bringing it up on a Friday afternoon but agreed with me and said she'd invite her for this Sunday. Do not, however, tell Momma I'm interested in Liv. I want to do this my own way and Momma will get up in my business."

"I don't know how you could talk about her that way, Marc. Momma just likes to help." Matt snickered.

"You wait, Matt Chase. It'll be your turn one of these days. And I'm gonna laugh and laugh." Marc grunted once he'd made his shot.

After a few games, it was time to get going. Kyle and Shane

wanted to get home with their wives and Matt had a date to meet across town.

"Liv, can I drop you home?" Marc asked as he caught up with her outside The Pumphouse.

Liv turned and smiled at him and he felt it to his toes. Damn.

"Marc, thank you for the lavender. It was very thoughtful. I walked here. Hope that'll get me some extra credit with my personal trainer. He's such a hard-ass." She winked. "Anyway, I was just going to walk home. It's not far and the night is pretty warm. Thanks anyway."

"I'll walk with you then." He caught up to her and easily kept pace as they strolled down Main.

"Your mother called me a few minutes ago. I can't believe she has my cell phone number." Liv laughed.

"Momma's got everyone's number. You'd do well to just accept it. So what'd she want?"

"She invited me to dinner Sunday. Well, no. Invited means I had the option to refuse, I suppose. This was an order, only said in that pretty, pushy way she's got. Butter wouldn't melt in her mouth but it was still an order. Plus she added a twist of guilt. You know, *it's been so long since you've had dinner here. I'm beginning to think you don't like us anymore.*"

Marc burst out laughing. "I see Polly Chase isn't the only one who's got everyone's number. But you said you'd go didn't you?"

"You know I did. Is she in on your plan to woo?"

He put a hand over his chest in mock dismay. "Olivia Davis! I do not need my mother to help me woo a woman. I'm walking you home on a Friday evening. I've been watching you all night long. I don't need her help, thank you very much. My family likes you, Liv. Including my mother. But I'm not going to complain that you're coming to dinner on Sunday. I like looking at you."

They stopped at her front walkway. "Marc, I don't know what to say when you're like this."

"What do you mean? And you should invite me in. Be polite."

She sighed. "If I invite you in, I'll let you kiss me again and then… Well, anyway. It's a bad idea. I mean, when you're genuine I don't know how to respond. You should just flirt with me and go out with giggle girl. I'm not for you."

Marc took her hand and kissed it briefly. "Olivia, that's pretty hurtful. I'm always genuine. Even when I flirt. I'm not shallow and it's not fair of you to say that."

She shook her head. "No, that's not what I meant. I'm sorry. I'm not saying you're shallow. It's just that when you're flirtatious, you're being lighthearted, silly. I can deal with that. Fling it back your way. But when you're…" She pulled her hand away and shoved a curl behind her ear. "I don't know how to say it. I just know how it makes me feel."

Stepping closer to her, he took her hand again. "And how is that?"

"Off balance. Confused." Her voice was no more than a whisper.

"And you don't like not being in control, do you, sugar?" He cocked his head. He should feel bad for her but he had her on the ropes. She was going down and he wasn't going to stop until she had no defenses left. "As for you not being for me? You know that's a lie. Both of us do. You're for me, Olivia Davis. All long legs and big brown cat eyes. Sex and sin and all sorts of mischief on your face. I like that."

"Oh man. Stop it. This isn't fair."

"Nope. Not fair at all." Quickly, before she could realize his intention, he leaned down and brushed his lips over hers. Just a featherlight touch. His body zinged with her taste.

Blinking quickly, those sexy cat eyes looked up into his, surprise and a hint of arousal in them. "I have to go in."

"Go on then. I'll watch you until you're safely inside. I take it you're not inviting me so I'll wait. Bide my time."

He took in the way she had to swallow hard and then

watched as she gathered her wits about her and took a step back, away from the heat they'd generated. Damn, when they made love the first time it was going to scorch the paint off the walls.

She quickly headed up her walk and rummaged through her bag for her keys. As she unlocked her door she looked back over her shoulder, not speaking for long moments. Finally she said, "Night, Marc. I'll see you Sunday."

He waved and loped back down the sidewalk, grin on his face.

Chapter Five

Liv knew what a mistake accepting the dinner invitation was when she stepped into the foyer of the Chases' home. Marc greeted her, kissing her cheek. But not really her cheek, more like the outermost edge of her mouth.

He smelled good. Different than when they worked out. Marc smelled like warm, sexy man with a bit of cologne. Not too much, but just enough to tickle her senses. And she still wanted to lick him.

"Come on through. Everyone's just hanging out in the living room."

As they'd done when she was with Matt. But for the first time since they'd broken up, she didn't feel that loss when she entered the room where the family had gathered. When she saw Matt sitting there, feet up on the coffee table, she didn't flash to the times they were together. Because Marc took up her thoughts. The way his body was wide at the shoulders but tapered at his waist. The curve of those buns. Yum.

"Hiya, Livvy. Glad you could make it." Edward smiled at her from his recliner.

She smiled back. It was hard not to. Edward Chase was just that kind of man. He smiled and you wanted to smile back as you basked in the warmth of his attention.

Polly moved to give her a quick hug and kiss and Liv settled on one of the couches next to Maggie.

"How's it goin', momma?" Liv touched her friend's belly.

"So much movement now. He or she is dancing around in there. Going to the doctor next week for another ultrasound. Since they couldn't see the gender last time they're giving me another look. I'm really excited. You're still coming, right?"

"Dude, like I'd miss it? Has Kyle changed his mind yet about wanting to know?"

Maggie shook her head. "No. He'll leave the room when they tell me. And you're sworn to silence around him."

"I want it to be a surprise. It'll be cool, don't you think?" Kyle leaned over Maggie.

"I'm not getting into this one. Uh-uh." Liv put her hands up.

"Smart girl. Let's all go in to eat," Polly called out from the doorway.

The Kyle–Maggie baby gender discussion continued at one end of the table while Liv tried not to stare at Marc.

"It sure is nice to have you back at our table, Olivia." Polly passed a platter of her famous smothered pork chops her way.

"It's nice to be here." Liv concentrated on only taking one chop. They smelled so good her mouth watered. "Especially on pork chop night."

Marc laughed. "She is a mighty fine cook."

Marc liked seeing her back at their table too. She fit there with them. As Maggie's best friend and one of Cassie's closest friends, the connections were there. And his mother clearly adored her, which was half the battle. Woe be to any woman one of them wanted if Polly didn't approve.

There was an element of comfort there, but also of *knowing*. She belonged at that table. At his side. Man, he had it bad and he wanted her to have it bad too.

At the end of the evening, Liv helped clear the table while the guys did the cleanup. Marc watched her, so animated and vivacious. Sharp-witted, clever and bright.

"Son, you're besotted," Edward murmured as he approached Marc. "Don't think I've noticed you look at Olivia that way before. She know?"

Marc sighed. "She does. Well, she knows I'm interested but she doesn't think I'm serious. She thinks I'm just out for a one-night stand."

Edward looked him up and down. "Ah, it's uncomfortable when your past comes to bite you on the butt, isn't it, son? One of these days I may just tell you a story about me and your momma. Suffice it to say, Chase men like to run and hunt but once we find our woman, that's it. There's no one else for us. You saying Olivia is the one?"

"Dad, I don't know. All I know is that I've never felt this way about anyone before. I want more than a few weeks. I like seeing her here. Like feeling she's one of us."

"How does your brother feel? I expect you'd have discussed this with him?"

Marc nodded as he looked to Matt, who was joking and flirting with Cassie. "I did. He was worried I'd hurt her but he says he's behind me and this woo plan one hundred percent. I wouldn't want him to feel bad. He knows she wasn't the one for him. And it's been two years now that they've been broken up."

"Okay then. Well, boy, you let me know if I can help in any way. I do like Olivia quite a bit. She's a good woman. The kind of woman who'll be a true partner and won't run when things get rough. But you'll have to catch her first because she's gonna run from you 'til you catch her.'"

Marc laughed and the woman in question turned to face him, a question in those eyes of hers. He winked and she shook her head, turning back to his mother.

Later, he insisted on walking her to her car. "Good night, Olivia. I'll see you tomorrow." His fingers itched to touch her, mouth watered to taste her.

"Night, Marc."

"Don't suppose you'd let me kiss you just now?" He took a step closer so their bodies were just an inch apart.

"I..." She gulped and nodded. Triumph roared through him and he leaned toward her.

"Liv! You forgot your leftovers!" Polly called as she came out the front door.

Liv jumped and opened her door quickly, tossing her purse inside. "Oh, thank you, Mrs. Chase. You didn't need to do that."

Marc wanted to scream in frustration as he found himself jogging up to grab the bag from his mother. "I've got it, Momma."

"Of course I didn't need to. I wanted to. Now go on, drive safe, honey, and I'll see you soon. You need to come back to dinner again. Don't make me hunt you down." Polly waved and stayed put on the porch as Marc handed the leftovers to Liv, wanting to groan as she bent to load them into her passenger seat. Her ass swayed a bit with the movement.

"Okay then. Good night." Liv waved at Polly and sent Marc a rueful smile. "See you tomorrow."

"Yeah. I'm collecting on that kiss. Very soon." He closed the door and rapped the top of her tiny little sports car as she drove off.

Liv didn't know whether to be frustrated or relieved that Polly had interrupted the two of them the evening before.

She smiled as she thought about the slim book of poetry she'd found on her desk when she returned from lunch. Maya Angelou's *Phenomenal Woman* and the little card said, *takes one to know one*. Lawd. Poetry.

But right then her thighs burned through the hell on earth that was StairMaster time. While she tried to ignore the presence of other people, two of them female who flirted outrageously with Marc. And he returned that attention.

It was his nature, she knew. But it still made her sad. She

wanted to believe she was different and truth be told, he'd
made her feel different too. But the other women. Man, she
didn't know if she could deal with it. Maggie had to, Liv knew
that firsthand. The women in town responded to all the Chase
brothers. It was impossible not to, they were lovable rascals
and damned good-looking. Kyle had taken Maggie's feelings
to heart and made a concerted effort to never be more than ge-
nerically friendly to other women. Women fell all over themselves for Shane but he didn't spare a second glance at anyone
other than his wife.

But Marc wasn't hers. No. They hadn't even dated so her
being jealous over flirting was just dumb. And anyway, if she
really wanted Marc Chase, she could have him and these little
gym bunnies didn't stand a chance. Liv might be older than
they were but she had a lot more experience under her belt,
not to mention more intelligence and personality too.

Sniffing with her own self-righteous superiority, she re-
joiced when her time was up and she was free of the wretched
torture device from hell.

"Good job, Liv. Your stamina has really increased." Marc
came over and noted her progress.

"Yes, well. I'm through for the night. I'll see you Wednesday. Oh and thank you for the book. I love that poem."

He insisted she cool down and stretch before going to
change. "I'm glad. I heard her read it on *Oprah* or something
a few years ago. I always thought it was a great poem and I'm
fortunate to have many wonderful women in my life. But it
seemed perfect for you."

The hand he'd been using to make sure she extended her
back properly continued to rest there as she finished up.

"I'm sorry we got interrupted last night," he murmured. "I
have two more clients to see tonight or I'd walk you home."

She smiled. "Do your work. I'll see you Wednesday."

"What? No comment on being interrupted?" He pouted and
it was pretty devastating.

"My goodness. I bet that face got you out of a lot of trouble over your life."

He chuckled. "Some. Come on, Liv. I'm fishing here. Give a guy a break."

She softened. He was very bad for her self-control. "Okay. I'm sorry we got interrupted too. But it's probably for the best."

"It's not for the best, Olivia. In any case, it was only a temporary reprieve. I'm coming for you." He grinned.

"Oh man. Go on, your little booster club is waiting. I'll see you Wednesday." She turned and put a little extra sway in her walk. She knew she was teasing but she wanted him to think of her instead of those two bimbettes.

All the way home she thought of how his eyes darkened just a bit every time he made a move. They didn't change when he flirted. But when he was down to serious business, they darkened from a blue-green to a deep mossy color.

She could not allow this silly flirtation to derail her plans. She needed to find Mister Right and keep her eyes on the prize. It was libido versus brain, she had to keep her brain in charge.

"So, now that we know you're having a boy, I can tell you I went on a date last night." Liv sipped her tea and looked at Cassie and Maggie. They'd had the ultrasound appointment and it had been pretty clear right away that the bundle of Chase in Maggie's belly came with a crank handle.

"Kyle will be begging to know in a week." Cassie laughed and then turned to Liv. "Date with who?"

"Rancher Bill. I also signed up with one of those computer dating places. Of course I got like six hundred emails this morning. Man. You should see some of the stuff they sent me. I wanted to hose off with Lysol afterward."

"Well, that's what? Date number three with Bill? How'd it go? Any action yet?" Maggie stole a fry from Cassie's plate. "It totally sucks that you're healthy girl all the sudden, Liv. Less fries to steal. You do, however, look even better than you did before and that was pretty smokin' hot to start with. Thank goodness I'm spoken for or I'd be jealous."

Liv fluttered her lashes. "Why, thank you. Marc has really worked me hard. Heh, okay that sounds dirty. Some action with Bill. He's a very good kisser. There was, erm, third-base-type stuff going on."

"Third base, huh? And how are his hands?" Cassie asked without a blush.

"Lawd you women are deviants. Sheesh." Liv winked. "He's fine. I mean, he's got nice-sized equipment. He seemed kind of shy about it." Liv shrugged. "I'm sure when we do sleep together it'll be nice."

"Nice? Since when did you settle for nice? And what about Marc working you hard? What's going on with that?" Maggie demanded.

"What about it? Look, I want to be married, damn it. I want forever. A house. Kids. Pancakes every Sunday. You have that, Maggie, and your whole life changed. You're having a child with the man you love. I want that too. I've wasted nearly thirty-five years on men who don't fucking care about me enough to make a baby with me. It's easy for you to sit there and judge, damn it. You have forever." She looked to Cassie. "And you too. Yes, Marc is still wooing and all that but I have a plan. And yes, it's sexy and flattering and he and I have major chemistry. I can't deny it any more than I can stop looking because Marc Chase may be interested in fucking me. Letting myself be distracted by the shiny of hot men like Marc instead of focusing on men who are ready to offer me forever like Bill."

The rigidity in Maggie's spine eased and she sighed. "It's more than that. Liv, I've seen the way he watches you. If all he wanted was to fuck, he'd have moved on by now because you haven't given him any. He hasn't dated in months. I asked Kyle. Don't settle for heaven's sake. You don't have to choose Marc if that's not what you want but if Rancher Bill doesn't rev your motor, there are other men out there. Marriage is forever. If the sex is mundane, it's forever mundane. You're an awfully sexual woman to just accept mediocre." Maggie stared at her, exasperated.

"I've gone that route. Chosen the hot guy with the great chemistry in bed. And it got me nothing but heartache. Maybe I need someone calm. Something calm."

"Fuck that. You don't need something calm. You're lively and you need a man who appreciates that. A laid-back man? Sure, given your level of activity and your personality, that might be a good idea. But Liv, you can have great sex and love. Maggie and I do. Dee and Penny do. Not with each other, *that* sounded dirty." Cassie winked at Maggie, who laughed. "You don't have to settle on forever. I understand you want to be married. I support your plan and I love you. But don't just roll over and give up."

"And has it ever occurred to you, Liv, that you wimp out when it comes to the men you choose? I mean, you choose the Rancher Bills of the world over the guys who could be the real thing for some reason? Protecting yourself or something?" Maggie sighed.

"And has it ever occurred to you that not everyone has a wham-pow connection like you and Kyle? Bill is a nice man. I said his hands were nice. He's a good kisser. He hasn't proposed, it's just been three dates. Yes there are other men out there. I'm not settling. I'm simply asking myself if I've been looking for the wrong thing. And what, choosing a marriage-minded man over a man like Marc is me protecting myself? That's just dumb. I'm choosing better than I have before. People live without grand passion and have spouses they admire and respect and live quite happily."

"I see your chin getting all stubborn, Olivia Davis. Stop it. We're your friends. If we don't tell you like it is, who will? All I'm saying is that you can have great sex, great chemistry and forever," Maggie said, one eyebrow rising.

Liv waved it away. "I'm not stubborn. I have to get back to work. I'll see you all Friday if not before."

"Not stubborn my ass," Cassie murmured. "I only know one person more stubborn than you and I'm married to him."

Liv drank the last of her tea and stood. "I am not even in Shane's league, stubbornwise. You however, are right up there, missy." She kissed the top of Maggie's head and blew one to Cassie. "I'll see you all later. I appreciate the honesty. I do."

And she did. They were right, she knew. But it was just three dates with Bill, she'd see him again if he called. It wouldn't kill her to give the man another chance.

The Pumphouse was packed to the gills, which only agitated Marc more than he already was. He kept looking toward the front and seeing Liv there, laughing with his sisters-in-law.

He also kept seeing various men stop by the table to flirt with her. Oh how he hated that. Everywhere she went she turned heads with that smile. And the bright red, very small top and the white pants she wore that night only highlighted the pale beauty of her skin and the darkness of her hair, which she'd changed again; this time it stood up in a sort of spiky disarray. A bit rock-and-roll. One of her shoes, a high-heeled slide, dangled from her toes as she slowly kicked her foot back and forth under the table.

"You look like a lovesick puppy. I'd be snickering that a woman finally turned the tables on you but I feel too sorry for you. What's the next step in Plan Woo?" Matt clapped him on the shoulder.

"Picnic. I've got the stuff out in my truck. I want to take her out to the lake under the stars. Good heavens, look at Frank Gillchrist. He's making a damned fool out of himself with her. Practically taking up residence in the front of her shirt."

"Go on. Get out of here. You're miserable and you're going to start a fight with someone if you don't just make your move already." Shane took his shot and bumped Marc hip to hip.

"If it brings you any comfort, she's been sneaking looks back here for the last hour." Matt smirked.

"Some. Okay, I'm gone. Wish me luck." Marc put his cue back on the wall and headed toward her booth, single-mindedly ignoring the women who put themselves in his path.

She looked up at him with a tentative smile. "Hey there, Marc Chase."

"You and me, picnic under the stars. What do you say?" He held out a hand.

A moment passed and he wanted to kick himself for putting it that way until she grabbed her purse and took his hand. "All right then."

Well, that was pleasant. If only she let him have his way in everything. Maggie looked up at him through her lashes, a smile playing on her lips. Retribution lay just beyond the encouragement. If he damaged Liv, Maggie would kick his ass. And then Cassie would have a go.

Marc smiled at Maggie and blew her a kiss and, as he didn't play favorites with his gorgeous sisters-in-law, he sent one Cassie's way as well. "See y'all later." Placing Liv's hand in the crook of his arm, he escorted her out and to his truck.

"What is it with you boys and these trucks? I mean, if I didn't know better, I'd think you all were overcompensating for other things that weren't so big."

Surprised, Marc snorted a laugh. "How do you know better, Miz Liv? You been peeking into the men's locker room?"

Opening the passenger door for her, he watched appreciatively as she scrambled up into the seat.

"Wouldn't you like to know?" Liv replied with a smug smirk, making him laugh again. Damn he liked her attitude.

He jogged around to the driver's side and got in. As they drove away from the center of town, he snuck a look at her. He'd like to know, hell yes. But he'd show her himself and he hoped like hell it would be soon or his cock would fall off from disuse.

Liv sat in the giant truck, watching the skies darken into evening. She should not be there with this man. A picnic under the stars alone was a very bad idea. Alone with him was a bad idea but when he'd stalked over and got all bossy, it made her weaken inside. Something about it when he took charge made her all gooey.

He'd looked commanding in those snug jeans and the cowboy boots. His brothers didn't wear boots very often but he did and she thought it was sexy. His shirt flowed over the muscles of his upper body like a caress. Not tight, that would have been tacky, but the material definitely showcased his strength.

She didn't like to be bossed around and she hadn't met a man who could ably take charge of her in the bedroom. She managed her life quite well and was happy being an independent woman. That didn't mean a very in-charge, dominant man wasn't the most delicious fantasy she had. And an unfulfilled one too.

He pulled down a long road toward the lake and parked. "Those are some pretty shoes so I won't make you walk too far. It's just down the path. I saw this little spot when I came out to row the other day. Shane and Cassie's place is just across the way."

Rowing must be why his upper body looked so damned good. "Well, it's working for you. Maybe I'll give it a try sometime. I've only used the machine but it seems like it'd be fun."

"It is. The water is nice and if you come out early enough, it's quiet and beautiful and the water is smooth as glass. Hang on a sec."

He got out and grabbed the ice chest from the bed of the truck and met her around on her side where, he was pleased to see, she'd waited for him.

Instead of waiting for her to get out, he banded her waist with his arm and pulled her down, sliding her body against his until her toes touched the ground.

"Mmm, you feel good," he murmured, nuzzling the hollow

of her throat instead of kissing those lips. He'd wanted to but he'd save it. Savor it. "Come on."

She took his hand and they walked down a path to a grassy slope that led to the shoreline. He spread a blanket down and she kicked off her shoes before sitting.

He joined her, sitting next to her instead of across from her. With a small smile, he unloaded the cooler, placing the food out in front of them.

"Wow. Impressive. Did you make all this?" Liv swept her hand, indicating the array of goodies.

"Hell no. I wish. This is from that new deli that opened up on Elm and Fourth. Roasted vegetables, fresh feta cheese, fruit of all kinds, I got the bread from the bakery, it's some sort of flatbread the guy said. Turkey, olives and oh…" he pulled out a white bakery box, "…cupcakes. Two of them. Buttercream frosting. Because if you can't splurge, life isn't worth living."

"Cupcakes?" Liv sighed dreamily. "I love cupcakes. My goodness, you're perfect. And you got to me just before the food came so I'm starving."

Insanely pleased she'd liked such a small gesture, he grinned as he pulled out some bottled water. "I have wine too if you'd prefer. But when I kiss you, and I will, I want you to be clear-headed."

"Awfully sure of yourself."

He nodded, making himself a sandwich. "I am. Because I want you so much it makes my skin itch. And because I know you want me too."

Her only reply was an intake of breath. He let her hide from answering. For now.

They ate in companionable silence as the night deepened. It was clear and warm and the stars and three-quarter moon gave off plenty of light.

She took a sip of water, nervous. What an effect he had on her! No man had ever made her speechless, not even Matt and she had loved him. But this man pushed every button and she wasn't sure why or how. Six months ago he'd been a pretty face she liked to see every few weeks here and there around town and all of a sudden she thought of him all the time. Imagined his hands on her, his mouth, wondered about how the heat of his naked skin would feel against hers.

In truth, she should be running back to that truck of his. But her body and libido had firmly refused to comply with her brain and she decided to ride it out, see where things went.

He shifted beside her and her heart kicked in her chest.

"Liv," he said softly and it was as if another woman's hands screwed the top of the water on and placed the bottle aside. She turned to face him and couldn't stop a gasp when she found him so very close.

"There you are." He smiled lazily. "You're damned sexy I don't quite know where to start. But I figure the lips are the best first step."

Surely, he moved, closing the last few inches between them. Warm, lush lips covered hers. His hand slid up her back, fingertips teasing her spine and then to her neck and into her hair. He cradled her head, holding her just how he wanted as he deepened the kiss from slow exploration to hungry plunder.

His tongue feathered the seam of her lips and flowed inside when she opened to him. Warm and sinuous, his tongue slid along hers. He wasn't aggressive, but Marc Chase knew what he was about and he kissed her without hesitation. He took what he wanted and gave back in spades.

Liv wasn't shy sexually, she believed very strongly that women had to be in charge of themselves and their pleasure and to demand it if necessary from a partner. But Marc needed no guidance on that score. No wonder the women on his arm always looked happy.

He guided her back to the blanket, his upper body settling against hers. His teeth nipped her bottom lip in short succession, once, twice and then again, his tongue laved the sting away.

She slid her hands under his shirt, exploring the miles of hot, hard muscle there, loving the flex and bunch as she touched him. This was dangerous. Marc wasn't some jovial hunk like Brody had been. This was happening at his pace although he wasn't forcing anything, he was firmly in charge. She normally held the sexual upper hand in the relationship. Damn, perhaps that was why Brody cheated and Matt walked away. Okay, that wasn't something to think on at that moment.

Marc broke the kiss, looking into her face. "You okay? You with me?"

Breathless, she nodded and grabbed his hair, pulling his mouth back to her own.

Marc had to hold his lower body away from hers. If he touched her with his cock she might run away. No, gauging by the way she kissed back, she wouldn't run. But he wanted to fuck her right then, press himself deep into her body and ride her until she begged him to let her come.

And it wasn't time for that just yet. They'd make love, he had no doubt of that. But not out there. He wanted to explore her first. Take his time and make it good. He couldn't do that where they were even if the idea of being caught didn't turn him right on.

Her lips were sweet. Made for him. She was incredibly responsive to his touch, returning his kiss with abandon. And she knew her way around a kiss. This was not some young woman waiting for him to make all the moves. Olivia was not just sexy, she was a woman who enjoyed sex, that much was obvious in her response.

He'd never actually been with a woman he could truly loose all his sexual energies with. The thought that he might be able to with Liv was alluring.

Her hands moved to the waist of his jeans and then to his fly. *Sweet baby Jesus.* He groaned when she grasped his cock, sliding her thumb through the slickness at the head.

"Holy shit. Liv, wait." He didn't want her to stop but they couldn't go at it out there.

"Why?" She looked up at him, her face colored by moon-light, a smile tipping one corner of that luscious, kiss-swol-len mouth.

"Because when I fuck you, I want you spread out on my bed so I can lick and touch every damned inch of your body. Once you stroke me, I lose all sense of proportion and I don't want the first time you make me come to be out here. I want to come in your mouth, Olivia," he murmured and she shiv-ered and moaned softly.

Gently, he pushed her hands away and sat up, putting the food and trash away. "Come on back to my place."

It wasn't so much a request as an enticing order. Liv's en-tire body was on fire for him. She needed him inside her so badly her thighs trembled. The truth was, he'd been a surprise. Who'd known he was capable of such control and deep sexu-ality? He came off as playfully sexual but the comment about coming in her mouth wasn't a line, it was a truth, delivered in a desire-roughened voice, and it set her aflame.

So it wouldn't lead to picket fences but she'd lay good odds it would lead to multiple orgasms and she liked Marc. A lot. What harm could it do at that point to take a little enjoyment in each other until the attraction wore off?

She looked up at him where he stood, cooler in hand. Mak-ing up her mind, she grasped his outstretched hand and let him pull her to stand. But he didn't stop there, he grabbed her around her waist and pulled her flush against him.

Lips just a hair's breadth away from hers, he whispered, "I'm going to make you come so many times you're going to pass out by the time I'm finished."

Her heart raced as shivers worked through her body. "Okay."

Chuckling, he let go to grab the blanket and they headed back to his truck where she settled in, looking out over the water while he tucked the cooler into the back and came around to his side.

The quick drive back to town, back to where his apartment

sat over a shoe store, was quiet but not uncomfortably so. He pulled into the alley at the rear and parked.

Before she knew it she was in his lap, her body straddling his. She didn't even know why she'd done it but there was certainly no reason to waste her situation.

"That'll do nicely, Liv," Marc said with a wicked grin as his wide palms slid up her legs, stopping at the back of her thighs just below the swell of her ass.

Her lips found his with almost desperate joy. His taste roared through her system, enticing, seductive, making her tremble with need. She swallowed his groan, the sound sliding down her throat as she suckled his tongue. It was probably the lack of sex, but she was pretty sure she'd never wanted a man that desperately before.

She wanted to grind herself over his erection but his hands held her up out of reach. When she whimpered, trying to move down, he chuckled and she found herself on her back on the bench seat.

"That's more like it." Quick hands pulled her pants and the tiny wispy panties off. "So beautiful." His fingertips traced the line of her labia, slick and swollen, and she unashamedly widened her thighs to get more of him.

She gasped when he brought those fingertips to his lips, closing his eyes at her taste. "Better than I'd imagined. And I've imagined a lot. Olivia, I'm going to taste you out here where anyone could catch us. You're going to scream when I make you come and then I'm going to fuck you. After that we'll go inside and start again."

Licking her lips at his words, Liv could only manage a nod. Cripes, the man was sex on legs. No one else she'd ever been with could have gotten away with what he'd just said to her. But he more than got away with it, her body, her mind, yearned for more.

"Hands above your head. Hold on to the door." Marc insinuated himself between her thighs, pushing them yet wider and spreading her pussy open before taking a long lick.

Her breath rushed out and pleasure, bright and hot, made her see stars. Her fingers got numb as they dug into the padded door handle. His mouth—tongue, teeth and lips—set about devastating her, driving her toward climax hard and fast.

"Don't rob me of your voice, Olivia," he murmured, stopping for a moment. "I want to hear you. I want to know how I'm making you feel. Stop biting your lip and give me what I want."

All she could do was gasp and then moan when he got back to work. She should be appalled by his behavior but it would be stupid to pretend. And Olivia Davis wasn't stupid.

Instead she complied and let it come as her body primed itself for orgasm. Letting him hear her soft cries and moans as her hips undulated against his mouth.

Satisfaction roared through him as he eagerly took in each sound she made. He'd been surprised when she hopped into his lap and laid some sugar on him after he'd parked but he wasn't one to look away when fate dropped a hot woman in his lap.

He'd push her, see how far she'd let him go, see how much of himself he could be. Embrace the ability to let the full face of his sexuality show and see how hot he could make this beautiful woman spread out on his front seat.

She tasted good, salty-sweet, nearly as good as the moans. Many women hesitated with oral sex, didn't want him to do it, feeling uncomfortable or self-conscious. But not this woman. She let herself be held wide open and devoured. He loved that about her.

Loved the way her pussy fluttered around his fingers when he slid them into her, hooking them to stroke over that sweet spot that brought a gasping sob from her lips.

A deep, gut-wrenching groan came from her as she began to come, her back arched, body clenching around his fingers.

Gently, he backed away, grabbing a condom from his wallet, freeing his cock, sheathing it and moving to her again.

"Up. I think you need to get back on my lap."

She looked up at him and then down to his cock with a smile. "My, I love a man who's prepared." Scrambling quickly, she held herself above him, reaching around and holding his cock before sliding down, inch by inch until he'd embedded himself fully within the heat of her pussy.

Eye to eye with her, he knew right then. Everything shifted. The noise and chaos in his head, the aching need he felt for her, the confusion that his carefully ordered, commitment-free bachelorhood had been discarded and he didn't seem to be bothered—it all fell away. With a sense of clarity he'd never felt before, he saw it. Absolutely without a doubt. He loved Olivia Davis. It should have scared him, freaked him right the fuck out, but it didn't. Instead, a sense of calm settled over him and it was all right. He knew then what Kyle and Shane felt and understood the enormity of the gift he'd been given. Now he had to make sure Liv understood it too but with an inward sigh, he had the feeling it wouldn't be as easy for her.

"Ride me, Liv."

Taking his lips in a kiss, she lifted herself off his cock and slid back down. The pleasure of that heated embrace gathered at the base of his spine as she moved on him, her mouth over his, their tongues sliding together.

He let himself slide toward climax relatively quickly, to take the edge off. Without vanity, he could admit he had a very fast recovery time and he wanted to get her inside where he could stretch out and give every inch of her body the attention it deserved.

Liv bit his bottom lip, slid her tongue through the dimple on his chin, cruised over the line of his jaw as she took him into her body over and over.

She couldn't quite believe she'd let a man go down on her in the front seat of a truck in an alley and now rode him like a pony. All in relative public. And she liked it. Man, she was a deviant because she loved every minute.

Loved it when his fingers found her clit and worked her into another climax and pressed his cock up into her pussy hard and deep as he came. Loved it when he gently sat her beside him and handed her her pants.

"Now that I've taken the edge off, I can dedicate more time to you in the manner you deserve." He tucked her panties into his pocket and his cock back into his pants while she got dressed.

Afterwards, he helped her out of the car and she liked that he kept hold of her hand as they took the stairs up to his place. She'd only been there once before a few years back when Matt had to drop something off.

The first thing she noticed was that it smelled good. She hadn't expected it to. Couldn't say she remembered anything from that last visit but she figured it would smell like most bachelor pads, messy, of unwashed laundry and wet towels.

Marc's place smelled like his cologne and fresh fruit. She saw a set of hanging baskets filled with apples and peaches and knew that's where the scent had come from. His living room windows were large and looked out over the street. It was nicely furnished with bookshelves on the walls and pictures of his family all around.

He kept surprising her and that made her uncomfortable. In the box marked *unavailable bachelor for life*, he was non-threatening because it wouldn't pay to develop feelings for him. But in the box labeled *guy way deeper than she'd thought who loved his family*? That guy was dangerous to her well-being.

"Now." He flipped the lights off before lighting candles set all around the living room. "I'll be right back." He disappeared down the hall, returning after a few moments. "You look gorgeous with candlelight on your skin. I figured you would. Then again, I've yet to see you in a situation where you didn't look gorgeous."

His hands went to the tie at the right shoulder of her shirt and undid it, letting it fall forward. Her nipples, already hard at his presence, hardened even more at the cool air and the look on his face.

"Okay, let's go down the hall before I take you here on the floor of my living room. I've already had you in a truck, I need to mind my manners now."

She laughed and let him drag her down his hallway to his bedroom. A king-sized bed dominated the space.

"I've been dreaming of this," he murmured, pulling his shirt up and over his head. Her heart raced at the sight of him, tawny in the candlelight.

"God you're beautiful."

He stopped and cocked his head, smiling. "Thank you, sugar. I've got nothing on you."

Her blouse lay around her waist and she removed it, laying it on the arm of a chair.

"Nothing on me." She snorted. "Puhleeze. Look at yourself in that mirror there. You're gorgeous. Hard and fit and muscular. I know you know you're handsome, women fall over you all the time and you catch quite a few too."

Chuckling, he unzipped her pants and shoved them down, letting her lean on him as she stepped out of them and her shoes.

"Good gracious." He stalked around her, taking in every inch of her body. A body he'd helped her shape and strengthen. She'd never been ashamed of her nudity but she certainly felt a lot better about her overall tone and shape now that he'd kicked her ass for two and a half months.

"Now you. I want to see all of you."

He stopped in front of her and slowly undid the buttons at the front of his jeans. Each *pop* of the seven buttons drew her nerves, and her nipples, tighter.

He shoved his jeans down and off his body, taking his socks off with them and then stood gloriously naked in front of her.

"Wow." Her mouth dried up. Flat, hard stomach with an enchanting line of hair leading to his very healthy equipment. Listing to the left. She liked that, liked how it'd felt inside her. Right then it was very hard. "I do so love a man with such a good recovery time."

He laughed but made no move to stop her as she took her time looking him over, taking in every inch of his body. Unable to stop herself, she skimmed her palms down his back and over his muscled ass. "This is even nicer unclothed."

When she reached his front again, his eyes were a deep, dark green and a very naughty grin had taken residence on his lips. A thrill worked through her at the sight of that face. Shit, she totally should have started doing younger men years ago. Even as she thought it, she knew it was a lie. It wasn't about his relative youth, it was about *him*.

"By the way? You're not overcompensating. Not at all."

Surprise overtook his features for a moment and he threw his head back to laugh. The floor swept out beneath her and she landed with a laugh on the bed, Marc looming over her.

"Did you like what you saw?"

"I like what I see very much. I'd like it even more if you got busy with all those arms and legs, your mouth and hands and that verra fine cock you've got there."

"On your hands and knees then. Face the other way. I want to fuck you from behind but this way I can see your face in the mirror. See you come with those beautiful cat eyes looking up at me so you don't forget who's bringing you such pleasure."

Holy shit, the man was lethal with the talking. Who knew? Ugh, again with the surprises. He was like the ultimate Pandora's box of naughty.

She moved quickly and he settled himself behind her. They were well matched heightwise, his groin pressed against her ass and the back of her pussy.

But he didn't plunge in. Instead he bent and licked the length of her spine until a soft squeal of surprised pleasure came from her.

"I don't have any neighbors and the shoe store is closed. Feel free to make as much noise as you like." The edge of his teeth found her hip, biting her gently. "I just want to eat you up." He paused and met her eyes in the mirror. "Again."

She moaned as shivers of delight broke over her. She looked back, under the line of her body, watching as he sheathed himself.

"Now then." He pressed the head of his cock just inside her body and waited. One of his hands gripped her hip, keeping her from ramming herself back against him to take him inside. The other stole around her body and palmed a breast, moving to slowly tug and roll the nipple until she writhed as much as she could.

"Please!"

"Please what? Tell me what you want, Liv."

"Fuck me. Please. Stop teasing me and fuck me."

"My pleasure." He slid deeply into her in one strong push before pulling out nearly all the way.

If Marc hadn't already loved her, watching her as he fucked her would have sealed the deal. It took a lot of trust for a woman to let herself be taken from behind like that. More trust to tell a man what she wanted and then to receive it with utter erotic abandon.

Her breasts swayed as she moved back to meet his thrusts, soft sounds broke from her as he played with her incredibly sensitive nipples. She was wet and creamy and he'd never felt anything as good as being deep inside her. His fingertips found her clit again, coaxing her into another orgasm.

And when she came? Holy moly she looked absolutely luscious. Her face flushed, eyes glassy, lips wet from her tongue. He'd seen a lot of women orgasm, but this one was beyond compare.

He loved how easy it was to make her climax as well. Once when he'd gone down on her, another as he made love to her in the truck, a third time with his hands just moments before and now he'd have her do it herself.

"Liv?"

"Mmmmmm?" she responded, lazily, sexily, making him smile.

"I want you to make yourself come."

"I don't know if I can."

"Do it for me, Liv. I know you've got another in you, give it to me."

She hesitated a moment but keeping her eyes locked with his, slid her hand over her belly and her fingertips met the place where their bodies were joined.

Her eyelids slid halfway closed as she began to touch her clit and he watched, fascinated, as the muscles in her arm and wrist corded and he felt the telltale flutters of the walls of her pussy around him.

Sweat broke out on his temples as he struggled not to come yet. He wanted her to go first but the carnality of what she was doing, the way she felt around him, the scent of their sex on the air beat at his control.

"Come, Liv. Come," he urged through clenched teeth as he quickened his pace, fucking into her harder and deeper. Climax gathered in his balls, in the soles of his feet and the top of his head.

Her head shot back and her eyes widened, catching his in the mirror. That luscious mouth opened in a silent howl and, as her orgasm exploded around his cock, his unleashed into her body in wave after wave of quicksilver pleasure until he had to collapse to the mattress, bringing her down with him.

"Be right back," he mumbled. When he walked back into the room she'd sat up and was reaching for her blouse. He jumped onto the bed, tackling her down with him.

"Where do you think you're going?"

"Well. Uh, home I guess."

"Oh I don't think so. I like you right here. It's late and I'm going to make you breakfast before I have you again in the morning."

"You don't seem the type to have women sleeping over. I don't want to ruin your reputation."

He moved to rest on one elbow, unable to resist leaning down for a kiss. "I didn't used to be the type, no. But I seem to be now. I want to wake up with your warm, sexy body ready for me."

"And do I have a say in the matter?" she asked acerbically and he stifled a grin.

"Always, darlin'. If you don't want to sleep over, I'll run you home right now. I'd never force you to do anything you didn't want to. But I would make it worth your while when you woke up."

Seconds ticked by as she lay there thinking and he only barely kept himself from flicking his tongue over those delicious nipples daring his control as they poked up toward the ceiling.

"Will you put cheese in the omelet you're going to make me? And real milk in my coffee?"

Ah, triumph! "Yes. I've got some ham too. Although the milk is skim, the beans are gourmet."

"Good because I don't skimp on breakfast and I don't go in for soy cheese or any of that crap. I want real cheese and real eggs, not that fake egg stuff and I don't want egg whites either."

"Now you're just being greedy." He kissed the tip of her nose and she laughed.

"I am greedy. I like to eat and eat well. I work out and watch what I eat but that doesn't mean I'm giving up the joys of eating pizza or omelets with egg yolks. And don't bother trying to tell me a pizza on whole wheat crust with no cheese is just as good because that's a bald-faced lie."

"You're a difficult woman. It's a good thing I want to sink into your body for weeks. Egg white omelets are just as good."

She made a face and he wanted to laugh. "That is such a lie. I gave up mayonnaise. Okay. I don't eat omelets every day but when I have one, I'm having one. No halfway fake omelet. I want it all or what's the point of eating oatmeal five days a week?"

"You drive a hard bargain, Olivia Davis. You'll have your full egg omelet with cheese and ham."

"Then you'll have my warm and willing body to wake up with."

Sighing contentedly, he pulled her against his body and kissed her temple. "Wanna watch a movie?"

Chapter Six

Before the sun rose, Liv lay in Marc's bed, his arms around her and his heart beating softly against the ear she'd laid against his chest. She should have felt warm and relaxed. Instead she fought back a sweat of terror.

She was in over her head. The sex, oh man the sex had been incredible. Earth-shaking. Hot, hard and deep in more than one way.

Never had she felt connected to a man during and after sex the way she had with Marc the night before. His hands on her body were an anchor, holding her to Earth when she wanted to float away.

She could not feel this way about him. She couldn't afford the emotional capital. The roar of the fear Matt had left in his wake echoed through her, filling every cell.

At the same time, she was frozen, lying there because she wanted him. Wanted him so much it scared her, but now that she'd had a taste she couldn't bear the thought of letting him go. It was monumentally stupid. It was monumentally selfish but she knew she wasn't going to walk away just yet.

Instead, she planned, tried to work out just exactly how she'd manage the situation and her intense attraction to the man at her side.

Until he woke up and decided to greet the day in a very inspired manner.

* * *

"We need to talk about all this."

Marc looked up from his plate, across the table at a very warm, very satisfied Liv. "All this?"

"You and me. Last night."

He smiled. Okay then. It was going to be easier than he'd thought it would be. "All right."

"Clearly we've got some pretty major chemistry. I can't deny that. I can't deny the sex is amazing and that I'm in no major hurry to give it up."

"Good. I don't plan to give it up."

She waved it away. "But it makes sense to talk about our boundaries. Because as I said, I'm looking for something long-term and you're not. So I think that we can continue with this until the attraction burns out and I'll also keep looking. If you find yourself attracted to someone else, just let me know and I'll step out of the way. There's no reason why we can't stay friends. We're both adults. Both sexually liberated. Let's enjoy our time and move on as friends when it's over."

His fork clattered to his plate and he saw red. "What the fuck are you talking about?"

"Language."

"Fuck language, I've heard you curse a blue streak. In fact, I heard it about twenty minutes ago when you ordered me to eat your pussy."

He should have been satisfied by her blush but he was too pissed off. "You think I should just service you while you look around for some man worthy of your forever, Liv? Is that what you're saying? I'm good enough to fuck but not good enough to be with on Christmas?"

"What? Why are you being this way? You're the one who has a flavor of the week on your arm. You're the one who's fucked every damned woman under thirty in this town."

"Thirty-five." The moment he said it he regretted it.

Her eyes narrowed and she put her fork down. "As you say,

thirty-four, thirty-five in a month. In any case, you're the one who has the love-'em-and-leave-'em lifestyle. I've told you up front what I'm looking for. I haven't lied about that."

"Stop being so sensitive about your age. God. It's not a thing. And I told *you* up front that I'm wooing you. I want you, Liv. Not for the next week or two, but for the long haul. But if you don't think I'm good enough, you should go now."

"I never said that and I don't think that. Where do you get this good-enough crap anyway? When did I say any such thing? I'm trying to be sensible. You're the one who nearly passed out when I said I wanted to get married."

"That was months ago and before I told you I wanted to woo you. Before I worked my ass off to show you I was not the same person I used to be. You've changed me, Liv. And I know I've changed you. Don't you fucking lie to yourself or me. The sex between us was spectacular. It wasn't like that with Matt or Brody or any of the other men you've burned through. It didn't work with any of them because you're meant to be with me."

She stood up and he did as well. "Burned through? Are you insinuating I'm a slut? Because pot, meet kettle."

"Oh ho! I never said any such thing. Burned through, as in you dated them and it didn't work out, you moved on to the next guy, same story. And are you saying I'm a slut?"

She closed her eyes and it looked like she was counting to herself. Suddenly his anger drained away and he wanted to laugh. Fear. She was afraid of what they had together and was spitting like a cat in a corner. He could handle that. He would have her in the end. He just needed to wait her out.

"I need to go before I say something I can't take back. I value your friendship more than I value the orgasms you can give me. Yes, it was amazing, but not worth losing you over."

She slid on her shoes and grabbed her bag but he didn't miss the way her voice trembled when she spoke about losing him.

"I'm not finished. Let's talk this out."

"I am. I'll see you Monday."

"For heaven's sake, Liv. You're not going to lose me! This is a dumb fight because neither one of us is being totally honest. I want you. In bed and in my life. You want that too. I know you do."

He saw confusion war with fear in her features.

He softened his voice. "At least let me drive you home so you don't have to do the walk of shame through town. We can talk about this again soon, when you've got your thoughts together."

The rigidity in her spine eased and he knew he'd won at least a small amount.

When he got her home, after they'd both ignored the heady scent of sex in his truck, he'd kissed her before she could scramble out the door. "I'm not going anywhere, Liv. Get it through your thick head. I'll see you tomorrow."

"Tomorrow?"

"Yes. My parents' for dinner. Momma's expecting you."

"I never said I'd go!"

He chuckled. "This is Polly Chase. You never said you wouldn't. When she told you she wanted to see you for dinner more often and you agreed, she took it that you were coming to dinner again tomorrow night." He was *so* lying on his mother and he'd have to go deal with her right then. He knew though, that Polly would be on his side in this battle. Liv would fall and he'd be there to catch her.

Liv sighed. "Fine. I'll see you tomorrow." She got out of the truck and he watched her until she'd gotten safely inside before heading over to his parents' house.

Liv slumped into her house and moved straight to her bathroom. Turning on the taps of her great big old antique tub, she took her clothes off, trying to ignore Marc's scent but it was impossible. Because it was on her skin. Under her skin. In her hair and brain, on her tongue.

With a groan, she went to make herself a cup of coffee, turning off the taps when the bath had filled. Minutes later, she sank into the water and sipped her coffee. She did her best thinking in her bathtub.

He said he wanted her for the long term. But was it just the sex talking? They were friends so did he feel more hindered, less able to give her the truth about how he felt?

And the sex. Oh man, it was way more than just sex. He'd seared her soul-deep. Her body had responded to his in a way that satisfied her but scared the hell out of her at the same time. So dominant and sure of himself sexually, the allure of that was overwhelming.

Giving up control to him had been the most liberating thing she'd ever done. If she'd done that with Brody would they still be together? What about Matt? Did the men in her life leave because she was too much in control?

"I think too much," she mumbled as she put down her empty cup of coffee and slid beneath the surface of the water. The silence surrounded her as the water embraced her body. It was just her and her insecurities and fears.

She sat up and wiped her eyes. Most people saw her as supremely confident and self-assured but beneath that were the doubts. Maybe she wasn't worthy of love. Maybe she wasn't meant to be cherished. It was her, she was the reason they all left. What had she done to chase them away?

The tip of something very powerful had surfaced in her time with Marc and it scared the hell out of her. A man like Bill didn't scare her. He was managed easily enough. Being in charge meant she controlled her feelings and he couldn't hurt her. A man like Bill was who she needed to marry.

Wasn't he?

Polly rolled out biscuits in the kitchen and smiled to herself as she waited while the other line rang. A ham baked in the oven, scalloped potatoes bubbled, peas with pearl onions next to that, and baked beans simmered on the stove.

"Hello?"

"Olivia, hon, how are you today? I was just calling to double-check that you liked ham."

Liv stuttered and it made Polly smile even more.

"Oh for dinner tonight? About that, I hadn't really…"

"You are coming, aren't you? I've made an awful lot of food and I'd be so disappointed if you didn't come. You said you would last week or did I get it wrong? I'm getting old you know, sometimes I suppose I misunderstand but I was just thrilled you said you'd come."

Liv sighed and Polly barely held back a laugh.

"Oh no, you didn't misunderstand. Of course I'll be there. I love ham. Can I bring anything?"

"Now you're just insulting me. Just yourself, honey. See you tonight." Polly hung up, chuckling to herself.

Her boy wanted Liv Davis, he'd have her. It helped that she and Edward adored Liv and she was already considered a member of the family. But what mattered to her most was another one of her children realizing what it meant to love someone. Truly love her.

Liv was wary and Polly couldn't blame the girl. After all, even Polly knew about Marc's reputation and that had to scare any woman. And after the thing with Matt failing, Polly knew Liv's heart would be wounded and she'd be careful of a man like Marc. And the girl had lost a lot in her life. Her mother at a young age, her sister had been a handful and her father had up and left to Florida ten years before. Aside from Maggie, Liv had been alone a lot.

Family meant everything to Polly and she'd pull out all the stops to make Liv part of theirs.

"The woman is diabolical," Liv muttered as she pulled up next to the curb out front. She should have begged off, she knew that but it wasn't in her to refuse Polly "the amazing steam-roller" Chase.

Marc had sent her an email the evening before. She'd ducked his phone calls but curiosity made her read the email. He'd just been checking in on her and he repeated that he wanted her for the long term and that he wasn't giving up or walking away.

She wanted to believe him but it scared her to contemplate trusting anyone that way. It was a huge risk. *He* was a huge risk. She'd be a fool to trust a man like Marc Chase when he said he wanted something long-term.

He opened the front door and strolled down the front walk to meet her. She didn't even have time to give a surprised squeak when he grabbed her and laid a hard, long kiss on her out there in front of God and the neighbors. Not that she resisted, it felt too good after all her thinking. Eased the tension of fear in her gut. Replaced it with warmth and a pulsing, simmering desire. Again with the pushing of her buttons.

"Good evening, Olivia. This is a lovely outfit. Is it new?" He stepped back, leaving her slightly breathless but keeping an arm around her waist. Which was a good thing because her knees were rubber. She couldn't take her eyes off his thumb as it cruised over his bottom lip, clearing off her lipstick. She licked her lips in response and he got that wicked grin.

"Uh, yes. New. Just got it last week when I drove into Atlanta with Cassie for beads. Thank you."

He escorted her into the house and before she could gather her wits, half the family saw him with his arm around her and her lips kiss-swollen.

"Well, it's about time." Maggie laughed and kissed Liv's cheek. "Must have been some picnic. Don't think I don't know you've been ducking my calls. You're going to tell me every last detail," she murmured into Liv's ear.

"Uh."

Marc squeezed her, pulling her closer, and kissed her temple. "Everyone lay off. Miz Liv here is wary about me, and rightfully so. So if you rib her about this you'll be making my job harder."

Matt chuckled and kissed Liv's forehead. "It's going to be weird hearing all the details about my brother the way you shared about Brody. Although frankly, it's a big step up for you."

"Don't patronize me, Matt Chase." Liv narrowed her eyes at him and he chuckled more.

"Okay, sweet stuff. You got it. Although, you're fun to patronize, you have to admit."

"I'm gonna kick you in the junk," Liv muttered and shook Marc off, heading toward Cassie who accepted a hug and a kiss on her cheek without comment.

"Let's go into the sitting room and have a beer, shall we?" Maggie said brightly. "Well, you all can have a beer and I'll have a root beer." She sent a dark look back at the brothers gathered behind them. "No boys allowed."

Marc walked up and kissed her again, bold as you please, before heading into the living room with his brothers to watch whatever game was on the nine hundred channels' worth of sports Edward had.

"Well! Okay, come on." Cassie pulled Liv into the sitting room. "Before Polly gets in here, she's on the phone, spill!"

Liv cracked open a beer and took several long swallows before tossing herself into a chair. "I am so in trouble."

Maggie laughed. "Looks like the best kind of trouble."

Liv told them about the picnic and afterward, ending with their fight the morning before.

"Give him a chance. What have you got to lose?" Cassie sat back, one eyebrow raised.

"My heart."

Maggie waved a hand around. "Olivia Jean, if you don't think I can't see you've already lost it, you're out of your mind. We've been friends a very long time. We've been through a whole lot together and you've been there for me when things were so dark I wasn't sure if I'd survive. Why don't you let me be the one supporting you for a change, okay?

"I can see it on your face, can hear it in your voice. You have deep feelings for Marc. It's way more than sex. You're falling in love with him. Why resist?"

"Look what happened when I didn't resist Matt."

Cassie sighed. "I wasn't here for that so I can't say what it was like for you at the time but I've seen both of you since and Liv, while you have occasionally looked like you wanted to take a bite out of Matt, and who doesn't, the boy has a set of abs that makes me all tingly every time he parades around shirtless in those damned cutoffs. You know, the ones that hang a bit low on his hips so his belly shows all the way down to…oh, well, where was I?"

Maggie burst out laughing and Liv joined her.

"Oh yeah, so anyway, you haven't been pining for Matt. You've been pining to belong to something bigger than yourself. And heaven knows I felt that way too. But Marc? The way you talk about him, the way he looks at you, touches you, Liv, you're not alone in your feelings. He may be, have been, a huge flirt and skirt chaser, but he's honest. I've never known him to be deliberately hurtful and I've never heard a single one of the women he's dated say one negative thing about him. And you're a goner already. You're in love with Marc. It's not like you can unlove him. Give the guy a chance already."

"Oh for cripes' sake! I just had sex with him one time. Okay, uh," she paused, thinking, "five, no, six times. But still, that doesn't equal love. I have plans. I'm not going to give up on my plans for the future because I had some awesome sex. I have a date with Rancher Bill next week. I'm moving forward."

Maggie just shook her head. "You're a hardheaded woman, Liv. Always have been. I hope you know Marc isn't just going to let you run things."

"I've noticed his tendency to be domineering, yes. But he doesn't get to run me. I've given him my terms. He can accept them or not."

Marc smiled as she tried to maintain her distance from him at dinner. His mother had placed the two of them side by side so she couldn't avoid that. The whole family had just accepted her as his girlfriend no matter what she tried to say and she'd finally let it go in frustration.

"You know, if you gave her the illusion of cooperativeness with this so-called plan of hers, you'd probably sneak in past her defenses." Edward took a sip of wine when Marc came back inside after he'd laid one hell of a goodbye kiss on Liv at her car.

Marc loved the difference between his parents. Polly just spoke whenever a thought occurred to her, good or bad. But Edward didn't waste words so when he said something, Marc always listened.

"Go on, Daddy," Marc urged as he rocked back and forth in the old rocker near the fireplace. His brothers were sprawled through the room, all listening to their father.

"I see a lot of people in tense situations. A hazard of the job I suppose. But in the thirty-nine years I've been doing this, I've learned a lot about people when they're feeling threatened or are emotionally exhausted. They fight anything and anyone that offers a real depth of feeling or experience. Because it's frightening to give yourself to something bigger than you are. So they resist and resist and drive people away. Liv is the kind of woman who knows what she wants. In theory."

"I think she knows, Daddy. And I want to give it to her. She wants a white picket fence and a couple of kids, marriage, a mortgage. I've never wanted any of that stuff and she makes me want it with her. What I don't know is how to get her past her fears that I'm not real."

"What I mean, Marc, is that wanting marriage and love

and a family is one thing. But truly opening yourself up to those things is another. In order to really love someone, you have to make yourself very vulnerable. So she's loved people who haven't been capable of loving her back in the way she deserves. It's sort of a self-defeating cycle but certainly not unique. It ensures her hurt, yes, but not the depth of hurt she'd suffer if she truly loved any of these men. And I don't mean to be hurtful, Matthew, but you're the same way. You seek these women who you know on some level aren't right so you don't have to risk truly loving anyone and getting your heart broken.

"If something is worth having, it's worth losing. But that's scary. You're a brave man, Marc. You're in love with her, aren't you?" Edward stared at his son with perceptive eyes.

Marc sighed and nodded. "I realized it Friday night. I've always liked her, thought she was pretty and funny, smart, successful. All the things I admire in a woman. But I think the love thing has been growing as I got to know her better. I'm sorry, Matt, I hope this is okay with you."

Matt shrugged. "It hurts a little. But really only because I couldn't feel what you do for her. She deserves to be loved and I know you'll treat her right. I want that too, you know, I really do. I just haven't met the right woman yet."

"You will." Edward winked at Matt before turning back to Marc. "So here's what I think about you and the lovely Ms. Davis. You say she's got this plan to find Mr. Forever?"

Marc snorted and nodded. "I am that guy!"

"Of course you are, son. And she knows that too. I saw the way she looked at you, the way she responded to your touch. But as I said, she's afraid to really risk herself so she'll want to pursue the easy man who'll never challenge her and try and keep you out of her heart. Let her." Edward put a hand up to silence Marc. "Let me finish. Let her go out with these bland men in her search. She's not going to find anyone, because you're it. And in the meantime, you get right under her defenses and by the time she figures it out, it's too late.

You have nothing to fear from the likes of Bill and other men like him. Liv Davis needs to be taken in hand. Your momma needed that too."

Edward laughed at the sight of his sons' faces.

"What? I'm not *that* old, boys. Your momma is a willful creature and needs lots of space to do her thing. Needs a man who'll let her be herself and love that about her. I do. But she also needs a man who won't take any nonsense and pushes back when she gets cranky. Liv is that kind of woman and our Marc, although he tries to fool everyone with that easygoing smile, is that kind of man. Aren't you, boy?"

Marc chuckled. "To be honest, Daddy, I never thought of it that way. I've never felt any compunction to be like that with a woman before I met Liv. But yes, I've learned a few things about myself in the last months and that's one of them."

"The truth is, not every woman is worth the effort. You've found your woman, Marc. Let your Liv think she's on the search for Mr. Right when you're right there under her nose. Give her a few weeks to get the picture and then close the trap. It'll be hard to let her go like that, but you know, I get the feeling it's all going to be a big charade for her. She's not looking for anyone but you. Patience and you'll win this through."

"You're more diabolical than Momma. How come I never figured that out?" Kyle asked.

Edward chuckled. "If I have to tell everyone how diabolical I am, how diabolical could I really be?"

Chapter Seven

"Okay, you and I are going out for coffee when you're done tonight. We have some talking to do," Marc murmured as Liv came out of the locker room to stretch and warm up.

"I don't suppose I get a say in this?"

"Nope. Now get working."

The infuriating man actually sauntered off to help another one of his clients while she warmed up.

It helped that she was distracted while she worked out. Sort of. Marc's presence was nearly overwhelming. He leaned over her and touched her like he had a right. At one point he even brushed his lips over her temple surreptitiously.

She went through her workout quickly and efficiently. He shadowed her, making sure she did everything right, adding some reps and extra weight to a few of her machines.

Liv saw he was speaking with another client when she'd finished her warm-down and hurried to the back to change clothes. She really didn't want to talk to him. She was weak, she'd missed him and had looked forward to seeing him that evening. He'd also left a mug on her desk with some of the tea she often drank at The Honey Bear. How did he know? It touched her way more than she wanted to be touched. No one ever did that sort of thing for her before. He noticed things like that, little things, small things but things about who she was.

When she came back out he was locking the front door, standing next to the other one. He turned and crossed his arms over his chest. "Going somewhere?"

"I have work in the morning."

"Mmm. It's only seven. We can even have coffee at your place, save some time." He grabbed his bag and waited for her.

Sighing, she took his outstretched hand and they left.

"What did you want to talk about?"

"Your ridiculous idea of boundaries."

"Ridiculous?"

"Look, it's a crock and you're using it to hold me back. Okay, fine. Here's what I'm willing to do. You and I will continue to see each other, naked and clothed. I will continue to show you that *I* am this forever guy and you will date bland-oids like Bill. At some point, you will have to admit you and I are it, and this silly charade can end. Then we can move forward with a relationship."

"And you?"

"What do you mean, sugar? I'll be pining away while you're out on the town." He winked.

"You're such an ass." She was unable to stop the upturn of her mouth into a smile. He was infuriatingly adorable. And very accommodating. It made her nervous.

He took her keys from her hand and unlocked her door, following her inside.

"I *am* an ass. But in this I'm right."

"And I suppose you'll be dating all the twinkies in town while I continue my serious plan to find love." It hurt even to imagine it.

He laughed. "Do you want me to? Liv, sugar, I don't like Twinkies. I far prefer pie and cobbler. In any case, no, I won't be dating anyone with creamy filling but you. Because I only want yours."

"You're such bad news." How could she resist? He was funny. He made her laugh and what did she have to lose anyway? She could keep him and keep the plan in place. And a small part of her wanted to believe his claim about wanting a relationship with her. Okay, a big part. The part that beat then, just for him.

"I am. I'm very bad. And so are you. I think you need a little discipline." He waggled his brows at her.

"Oh man. I'm in trouble," she mumbled just before sprinting out of the room with him on her tail.

Laughing, he yanked her clothes off when he caught up to her.

"Bathroom. I need to shower. I'm all sweaty." She tried to fend him off, giggling.

"I could lick you clean. You taste mighty fine. But we haven't showered together yet so I'm all for firsts. I'll lick you dry."

He pulled his clothes off and she sighed happily, turning around to run the water.

"Nice bathroom you've got. That's some tub. Next time I foresee a long bath together. I do like you wet."

Those blue-green eyes went to deep, dark green. Shivering, she took in the long look up and down her body he gave her. His cock was hard and standing at attention. He pulled the door to the enclosure open and she stepped in, leaning back to get under the spray.

His hands, slick with soap, began to explore her body and she fell back into his spell. With his hands on her, she couldn't think about anything else but him so she stopped fighting and let go. It seemed with him, there was nothing but to let go.

Fingers rolled and tugged her nipples, over and over in a slow, sensual rhythm. The wall of his chest felt sure, strong as she leaned into him.

"Just an appetizer before the main meal," he murmured before nibbling her ear.

Still rolling and tugging, Marc moved his other hand down to find her clit, swollen and ready. With the same leisurely rhythm, he brushed his middle finger over it, building the pleasure bit by bit until she was blind with it, aching for release.

Pleasure sucked her under as she gasped. Climax roared through her body as her back bowed.

Muscles still jumping, she dimly registered movement as he turned off the taps. Warm and lazy, she dried off, watching the water roll down his body in rivulets over the hard-packed muscle.

"What's that smile for? Where's the bedroom?" He took her hand and she sashayed past, naked and satisfied, drawing him toward the end of the hall where her bedroom lay.

"The smile is because you look so good. And this is my bedroom."

Marc looked at her, bathed in the yellowish light of the streetlamp out front, dark hair wet and plastered to her head, only emphasizing the sexy shape of her eyes. Her body was mouthwateringly beautiful but what was most alluring was her comfort with her shape and size, the way she owned her sensuality and had no shame as she stood naked before him.

Her room was a lot like her. Simple, strong and straightforward. Deep blues accented by lighter blues colored the walls and bedding. No frilly stuff anywhere. Black-and-white photographs hung framed on the wall, Southern landscapes if he guessed correctly.

A laptop sat on a desk in the corner and in the other corner a single, overstuffed chair, flanked by a low table with a lamp and an open book. The space smelled like her. Minty but also—he paused, thinking as he had so many times trying to identify it…coconut?

"Liv, sugar, what perfume do you wear?" he asked her as he nuzzled her neck, rubbing the entirety of his naked body against hers, walking her backwards to her bed.

"I don't wear perfume."

He liked the way her breath hitched before she could answer him.

"What's that smell then? Mint and is that coconut?"

She laughed as he pushed her back onto the bed. "Oh, that's the stuff I put on my skin. Coconut and mint. Smells delicious doesn't it? Oh, my!"

He teased the entrance to her pussy with the head of his cock. He'd never wanted to plunge into a woman without protection as he did at that moment.

"Condom? Please say you have one in here or I have to go back into your bathroom for my pants."

Stretching her arm out, not leaving his embrace, she opened a drawer in her bedside table and rustled around, holding up a foil package in triumph.

Within moments he sheathed himself and sank into her body with a groan. When he was inside her, it felt like home. It felt so good there, deep within her, he wanted to yell it out to the whole world.

Each breathy gasp, every moan and sigh and squeal she made shot straight to his cock. He made her feel that way, no one else. And no one else would.

He had no problems telling her she could date these other guys while she figured out he was the right one because he knew, despite her attitude, she wouldn't be with anyone else but him. No, what they had between them wasn't simply sex, not only sex, but the sex was part of it and she'd know it. Deep inside the way he touched her, the way he made her come would be there no matter what she did or who she was with.

It was a matter of seducing her heart because her body was his.

When he looked deep into her eyes, their faces just inches apart, he felt as if he were drowning in her. He kept returning to kiss her lips as he slowly thrust into her pussy over and over, taking in her breath as he captured her lips.

"You feel amazingly good," she gasped out.

"Yes, oh yeah. I feel good. You feel like heaven around my cock, Liv. I was made to be here, inside you."

He changed his angle, rocking back to push her knees up, opening her to his thrusts. He knew he had it perfect when he swiveled a bit, grinding himself over her clit.

"Ah, you've got another one in you, don't you, sugar? Give it to me." He wanted to give her pleasure, wanted to make her happy and fulfilled. And right then he was. He felt the first tense and flutter of her inner walls around him and her nipples hardened. A low moan tore from her.

"Come on, Liv, come. I can't until you do and I want to. I need to." He felt climax build and build, threatening to over-flow and take over his system.

Arching her neck back, she rolled her hips to meet his thrusts and cried out as she came, pulling him down with her as he let go and orgasm rushed through him.

He continued to thrust until he was soft, finally rolling to the side.

Moments later, he pulled her into the curve of his body and kissed the top of her head.

Liv woke up, warm and safe. Before she opened her eyes she knew why. Marc lay curled around her. As she wasn't fully awake she could admit to herself that it felt good.

Waking up with Brody never felt like that. Waking up with Matt never felt like that. Before thought fully returned, she snuggled into him, breathing in his skin, listening to the slow beat of his heart as she laid her ear against his chest.

He made her want to melt, made her feel feminine and soft. Vulnerable in a way she hadn't imagined she ever could. And yet, all that outer stuff was stripped away. She was who she was, no artifice, no bull and he stayed.

How long would that last? How long would he be all right with her dating other people and how long would he not do it too? He'd use her dating as an excuse to see other women too.

And he'd be right to, after all she was. God, she'd built in her own damned self-destruct for this thing. When it went bad, there'd be a reason, one she could accept.

She would just ride it out between them until she found the right guy and Marc was ready to move on. Hopefully, she'd find the right guy first because she was pretty sure her heart would break when he walked away.

She eased away from his sleeping body, standing next to the bed to look at him before she jumped in the shower to get ready for work. His face was partially hidden by strands of his hair. A morning shadow of beard covered his chin and cheeks, making him look sexily disheveled instead of messy.

Reluctantly she turned to go into the kitchen, start coffee and head to the shower.

He was sitting at her kitchen table, reading the newspaper when she came out, dressed for work.

"You look nice today." He smiled.

As the only thing he was wearing was a patch of sunshine across his shoulders, she thought nice was a relative term for what he looked.

"You look mighty sexy, Marc." His hair was wet and combed back away from his face, only highlighting the lines of his face. He had the kind of good looks that could sell men's sportswear and casual clothing. Boy next door with a healthy heaping spoonful of sin twinkling in his eyes.

He stood and kissed her, careful not to smear her lipstick. "Are you late for work or anything?"

He shook his head. "Nope. I have a client in about forty-five. I go to her place though."

Liv took a sip of coffee and said nothing, although silly jealousy ran through her. She hated jealousy. It was a useless, base emotion and she should be above it. However, right about then all she wanted to do was let this mysterious client know Marc woke up in her bed that morning. *Hmpf.*

Marc smiled as he watched her face change. Ah, jealousy.

And not the petty kind that he'd experienced from women before. She didn't pout or throw a tantrum. But she had started to think of him as hers on some level. *Good.* He sure as hell knew she was his.

She was so beautiful and sexy, watching her move through her kitchen, getting herself breakfast—after asking if he wanted any—and that pretty, bright red dress floating around her legs made him crazy. He wanted her. No, he *needed* her. Thinking that other men would see her and have naked thoughts about his woman made him edgy. He'd never actually been jealous before. It was another indicator that he loved and adored this woman. Or something.

"What's that smile for? Makes me nervous." Liv sat across from him and ate her oatmeal.

"It should make you nervous. I was thinking about waking up next to you on Christmas morning with my mother yelling up the stairs for everyone to get their lazy butts out of bed and get downstairs for breakfast and presents."

Okay, so he shouldn't have enjoyed her reaction to that so much but it did make him chuckle. Because she *would* be there for Christmas, next to him, opening presents and eating breakfast with his family. She belonged with him and there was nothing else that could convince him otherwise.

"You're skittish. Like one of those little dogs. Never know when you're going to go off and snap at me. My client this morning is Lula Parsons. She's heartier than her seventy years, yes, but you're way hotter." He winked, just to poke at her more.

"Marc Chase, I do believe you enjoy fucking with me."

"I enjoy fucking you, yes. A lot. More than I've enjoyed anything. Ever. It's not generally what I mean when I say your insides are beautiful, but that's part of it."

She blushed, touching him deeply. Had no one ever really complimented her? Made her feel special? It wasn't like Matt to not treat the woman he dated with extra care but clearly she seemed uncomfortable and unused to it. Maybe it was him. He'd need to think on it more, watch her reactions. But he planned to put Liv on a pedestal and treat her like a queen because she deserved it.

She stood and put her dishes in the sink. "I'm going to get on. Lock up when you're ready to go."

"Oh hang on, let me walk with you."

She leaned against the sink, watching him as he pulled on his clothes.

"Wait a sec." She went into her bedroom and came back out a few moments later. "I can't help you with underwear. Not that I want to, I like knowing you're naked under there. But here's a pair of gym socks and a clean T-shirt. It's way too big for me but it should fit you."

Smiling, he took the shirt and pulled it over his head and got the clean socks on. The dirty stuff went into his bag. He hadn't the heart to tell her he had clean shirts and underwear in the messenger bag. He liked wearing something of hers. If they were hers.

"Hey, whose clothes are these?"

"Mine, silly. The shirt was some contest win and they just gave everyone extra-larges. And everyone has gym socks don't they? Do you think I'd be so tacky as to give you some other man's clothes?"

He laughed. "No. I don't think you're tacky. I think you're fabulous."

They walked hand in hand to city hall and parted ways at the front steps with a quick kiss. He liked that she didn't shy away from the public affection and he really liked the sway of her ass as she took the steps toward the front doors.

"Saucy." Grinning, he turned and jogged toward his place.

Chapter Eight

Friday night some weeks later found Liv staring at him as he played pool. And the damned little chickies who seemed to follow him around everywhere.

"It sucks. Just get used to it now."

Liv looked back at Maggie. "What are you talking about?"

Maggie snorted. "Puhleeze. Girl, don't you play coy with me. I've watched this thing blossom between you and Marc. You're watching him with hungry eyes right now. But you see the fan club too. Chase brothers come with a fan club. You're going to have to accept it. If you let it agitate you, you're going to be agitated all the time."

"I'm not agitated."

"Yeah, I can tell. Olivia Jean, you have got to stop lying to yourself or this is never going to work. All these women can do is look. He's not doing a thing to lead them on, not giving them any attention other than a how-do-you-do."

"Don't you let this silliness hold you away from something real with him. Speaking of silliness, how'd the date with Rancher Bill go?"

Liv turned to Cassie, ready to be upset but just let out her breath in a sigh. "Fine. I don't think we'll have any more dates."

"What? I mean aside from the fact that you're in love with Marc and all?"

"You're on a roll tonight aren't ya, California girl? Sheesh."

"It's July again. I freaking hate July in Petal. It's so *hot*. Makes me pissy."

Liv laughed. "Not as hot as August."

"I hate August even more than July. But there are plusses to August. Nice parties. Thank goodness we have good air-conditioning. Back to Rancher Bill?" Cassie's face was amused as she munched on her fries.

"He's a nice guy but he's not right for me. He doesn't do anything for me physically. It's not like he's bad or anything, he's just got no moves."

"You had sex with him?" Maggie's mouth dropped open.

Liv's eyes went wide, offended. "No. I'm having sex with *Marc*. I'm not a skank. Jeez. But I wasn't even tempted. I mean, he can't be Mister Right if I'm not even tempted can he? I don't think so."

"Is that the new standard then? If you feel like tossing Marc out of bed for him, that's the dude? Sounds pretty crass, Liv. Oh, I know! How about you just stop this and admit Marc is Mister Right?"

"A few years in town and you're suddenly all uppity," Liv grumbled into her beer.

"I was uppity before I came to Petal." Cassie laughed.

"It's why I like you so much. Anyway, Bill and I had a talk at the restaurant."

Maggie's eyes widened. "Really now? What about? He didn't ask you to marry him?"

Liv laughed. "No."

As a matter of fact, she and Bill had been sitting there at dinner, drinking some wine and listening to the piano music when he'd looked her straight in the eye and said, "This can't work, you know."

"What do you mean?"

"Liv, I like you an awful lot and you're nice to me. Sweet. I like your laugh. Sexy even. But you're in love with Marc Chase. Any fool could see it."

She'd nearly choked on her wine then. "What? He and I are friends. We date. I'm not in love with him."

Bill laughed then. "Olivia, one of the most attractive things about you is how straightforward you are. Blunt. You're take-charge, you don't play games like other women do. But if you can't see you're in love with the man, you're not as straight-forward as I thought. Or maybe you're defending your heart so hard you can't see your nose to spite your face. Is that it?"

Liv wished then that she'd been attracted to him. He was compassionate and smart. But not Marc. Damn. He was right.

He'd waited, watching her as she scrambled to process what he'd said, trying to deny it.

He smiled a bit sadly. "I do wish you and I had something because you're going to make Marc a fine wife. He's a lucky man. You're beautiful but scared aren't you?"

"I'm a big girl. I am, however, sorry if I led you on. I truly wanted it to work. You're attractive, smart, good. You're a very good man. But I don't know if I can overcome my really questionable taste in men. I seem to have a terrible addiction to men who are never going to make a commitment to me."

Raising a glass to her he shook his head. "As much as I'd like to run Marc down, I've seen the way he looks at you. The man is in love with you, Olivia. You're not like the other women he's squired around. But if he hurts you? I'll be here. After I kick his ass."

He'd taken her home and she'd cried herself to sleep.

But she didn't tell Cassie and Maggie any of it because she was afraid to say it out loud. Afraid to believe it could be real.

"He knew we weren't right for each other. He was very nice about it. But as I keep telling you both, this thing with Marc and me is just a nice fling. He's a wonderful friend and

I like him a lot. The sex is amazing but we all know he's not the forever type."

"No matter how many times you say that, Liv, it's only you who thinks so. I watch Marc with you every Sunday, every Friday and I think he looks an awful lot like a man who's invested in forever. I've never pegged you for a woman who would go out of her way to avoid happiness. It's sort of annoying because you're damned smart." Cassie looked over and her face lit up as Shane waved. "That's my cue. I'm going to go kick their asses at pool. Maggie, honey, you're looking pale. Go home and rest." Cassie kissed Maggie's cheek.

"My due date isn't for two weeks now. I don't want to pull Kyle away from his game."

Liv rolled her eyes at Cassie who shook her head. "You're full-term now they said. I didn't go to all those birthing classes and watch those films of women squatting while giving birth to have you ignore your health."

"The shower is tomorrow anyway. A full day with Polly, you'll need the sleep." Cassie winked.

"You're right. Okay."

"I'll send Kyle over and I'll see you tomorrow," Cassie called over her shoulder as she headed back.

Marc watched his sister-in-law approach. "Damn, Shane, your wife is something else."

Shane smacked him on the head with his cue. "Knock it off."

Cassie stood on tiptoes to kiss Shane and looked around him to Kyle. "Take your wife home. She's exhausted and the shower is tomorrow."

"Is she okay?"

The panic in Kyle's voice tore at Marc. Loving someone that much, so much that you worried for their health and now the health of the life she carried used to scare him. But despite the fear, Marc saw the glow about his brother too.

Cassie touched Kyle's arm gently. "She's fine. But she's

thirty-eight weeks pregnant, hon. It takes a lot of energy to gestate and it's hot. Take her home, have her put her feet up and make sure she keeps drinking water. I'll see you tomorrow."

Kyle put his cue away and said his goodbyes. Marc watched him scoop his wife up with gentle arms and a smile on his face.

An ache built inside him and suddenly this whole thing with him playing along with the looking for Mister Forever seemed utterly stupid. He wanted to be with Liv full-time.

Rocking back on his heels a moment, he zeroed in on the object of his thoughts. "Well, lookit my girl over there. She'll be all by her lonesome soon. I best get on over and give her some company." Marc looked at Liv and when her gaze met his, he felt the connection to his toes.

"So she believe you yet?" Matt asked.

"I'm working on it. I hear she had a date with Bill on Wednesday. Worked out with me, even let me kiss her good-bye and went on a date with that dullard." That hurt.

"Marc, she didn't even let him touch her. She said there'd be no more dates with him. She broke it off. This whole thing is stupid. I've never seen her like this but she's afraid. So afraid."

Cassie reached out and touched his cheek. "I'm amazed you're doing this, I truly am. And I admire that you're giving her this space. But when Maggie asked if she'd had sex with Bill, Liv got pissed. Said she was having sex with you and what did Maggie think she was?" Cassie kissed his cheek. "Hang in there. She'll see. It's right in front of her face and for what it's worth, you've got no competition. This thing with Bill was just a way to keep from admitting it to herself. But he's out of the picture now as an excuse."

"Oh hell, I know that. I just don't like her lying to herself. I want to be with her. This is all a waste of time."

Cassie shrugged. "If she's worth it, you'll wait. Only you can decide if she is or not. Everyone has their limits."

He looked back over at Liv as she blew a kiss at Maggie,

smiling. She was worth it. God he loved her. Okay, a little while longer.

"Night, all," he called over his shoulder as he walked through the restaurant toward her. She turned to see him coming toward her and stood, waiting.

"Hi there, handsome."

Without a word, he pulled her to him and kissed her. Hard and possessive. Satisfaction settled into him as she melted into his embrace, opening her mouth to him.

He took his time, knowing that people watched them. Wanting them to all understand how it was. Liv Davis was his woman.

When he was finished he dropped a small kiss on the tip of her nose and each eyelid. "Hi yourself, gorgeous. You ready to let me rock your world?"

Great googly moogly. He'd been rocking her world since he dropped that kiss on her in April. Hell, she'd been an independent woman in charge and she could only manage to hold on to him as he'd turned her knees to rubber as he did every time he touched her.

"Let's hit it, shall we?"

He snared her with his gaze and she let herself be swept up, nodding. Grabbing her hand, he drew her outside. Down the block he paused and pulled her into an alley. Pushing her back against the wall, he ducked his head, his mouth finding hers again.

The wall, still warm from the sun, scratchy against her skin, dug into her back as he plundered her mouth. Deep in the shadows, his hands roved her body as her mind spiraled. She should not be doing this! But it felt so good. It was dark, no one could see and all he was doing was kissing her. His tongue, clever and carnal, slid along hers, his teeth nipped her bottom lip.

The humid evening air cooled the sweat on her skin as he

pushed the bodice of her dress open and his hands found her breasts.

"No bra. God, what you do to me," he murmured, lips against the skin just below her ear.

Her hands slid down the wall of his chest to the waist of his jeans, unsnapping and unzipping them. She took him in her hands, sliding her grip up and down and he groaned.

His fingertips found the loose material of her dress and slowly pulled it up, exposing her thighs, and then he reached up the last inch and slid his fingertips into her panties.

She froze a moment until he brushed her clit and all thought left her. A rhythm of rolling hips, of thrusts and moans caught them, slowing time, taking them to another place where it was just the two of them.

"You're so damned sexy, sugar. I need you to come for me."

She whimpered softly as her thighs began to tremble. His cock in her hand was slick from the heat and the pre-come at the slit.

"Fuck. I'm so close. One touch and I'm halfway there with you. What do you do to me, Liv? So much, so much to me. You're so hot, so wet. I'm going to fuck you standing up when we get back to your house. I want to look in your eyes," he murmured into her ear, the heat of his body on her neck.

Liv had to bite back a scream when he pressed two fingers inside her and caught her where shoulder met neck, between his teeth. Orgasm came then, quicksilver, and she felt his warmth on her hand as he came as well.

With a soft kiss he rearranged her panties and let her skirt fall as his other hand pulled her bodice back together.

"Wait." She dug in her purse with trembling hands and pulled out a handkerchief, passing it his way.

He put it into his pocket when he finished. "I'll uh, get this back to you later in the week."

Smiling, she tucked his cock back into his jeans but let him button and zip to avoid any injury.

She should feel bad. He'd just made her come in an alley. But she didn't feel cheap, she didn't feel bad. The way he touched her was always respectful, he made her feel beautiful. The frenzy made her feel desirable.

"You make me lose control, Liv."

They continued to walk down to her house.

"Seems to me you have plenty of control, Marc." She laughed. "You're the most in-control man I've ever been with. Usually I'm the one in charge. You shoot that all to hell with your dirty talk and your swagger. You make me melt."

Holy crap, did she just say that out loud?

He turned to her, putting his arms around her shoulders. "Sometimes I feel like I'm a fool to keep chasing you. And then you give me a glimpse inside and I know you're worth it."

"Why do you say stuff like that?"

"Because I want you to know that I care about you. This isn't a casual thing for me, Liv. I don't know how many other ways I can say it to you."

He scared her. What she felt for him scared her. But she wasn't willing to let go just yet.

"Come on inside. I think you made a promise to me back in that alley that I need fulfilled."

The next morning she awoke to find him up already. Sleepily, she shuffled into the kitchen to find him there, drinking juice and looking out the window.

"Morning, sugar." He turned and moved to kiss her.

"You off somewhere?"

"I have a client this morning. I'll see you this afternoon at the end of the shower when I'm told men are allowed. Not that I'm in any great hurry to guess baby food flavors and hear labor stories."

Liv laughed. "You think *I'm* in a hurry to hear labor stories? Dee's gonna be there and she and Maggie talk of little else. But I can't wait for Maggie to see the quilt I made for her. Took me six months."

Marc's eyes widened in surprise. "You quilt?"

"Why do you look so surprised? I can quilt, knit and cook quite well. When my mother was alive, she taught me all the things she thought a Southern woman should know. I can make a cobbler, mighty fine pie crust, scratch biscuits, embroider, quilt and a most excellent gravy."

"You're full of surprises, Liv. Wonderful surprises," he added quickly. "I'm impressed. I didn't know you were making it."

"It's something I do in the late evenings when I can't sleep and sometimes on my lunch hour I do the piece work. I just finished it a few days ago. You can see it this afternoon. I had Cassie wrap it because she's a pro at that stuff. My presents never look all crisp and pretty like hers do."

"I'm sure Maggie will love it."

"I hope so. Maggie is special to me. She's been my best friend since kindergarten. Not many people have relationships that last that long. She's always been there when I needed her."

He reached out and ran his fingertips through her hair. "From what I've seen, you've done the same for her. And Cassie too."

She rolled her eyes. "I don't bake for the elderly and teach kids to love history. I'm an administrative assistant."

Marc's chest tightened for a moment. He knew what it was like to love people who were all overachievers. His father the town lawyer, his brother the sheriff, the other brothers men the community looked to and admired. He was the baby. The always-smiling man-about-town with an eye for the ladies.

"You're so much more than your job. And from what I see, you're the mayor's right hand. You seem to be better briefed than he is on things at town hall and city council meetings. And don't think I haven't seen you volunteering at the soup kitchen and food pantry. You're a good person and a wonderful friend and I'm more fascinated by you every day."

Leaning in, he brushed his lips over hers.

She blushed and he grinned. "Thank you. Is this a new client? You're doing really well these days. Can I make you breakfast? I'll even scramble egg whites for you."

Why that made him want to propose to her he wasn't sure.

"I am doing well. I'm at the point where I have to stop taking one-on-one clients just now. I'm working six days a week and the studio is full all day and into the evenings. And sure, I'd love some eggs."

She turned and began to assemble the eggs. He watched as she moved efficiently through the kitchen. He liked her house a lot. It was comfortable and lived in. He didn't feel wary about sitting down or using a plate or cup.

Her kitchen was bright and sunny from a large garden window over the sink. The scent of fresh herbs laced the air and he realized that it was a cook's kitchen. He'd cooked very simple fare for her a few times and she'd done sandwiches and salads but neither of them had made a dinner for the other yet.

"Will you make me dinner tonight?"

She tipped the eggs into the skillet and turned to him, smiling. "Sure. I'd love that. I can't believe we haven't yet. But it can't be tonight. Kyle and Maggie are having a barbecue at their place, remember?"

"Oh yeah. Okay. Well, can't be tomorrow or my mother would hunt us down."

They agreed on Wednesday of the following week and he left after eating the eggs and some fresh fruit she'd sliced up for the both of them. Her kiss tasted like peaches and sunshine and he hated to have to go.

On the other hand, he was even more sure he loved her and that they belonged to each other. It strengthened his resolve to keep on with his plan.

* * *

Liv showed up at Cassie and Shane's a few hours early to decorate for the shower. Smiling. Man oh man did waking up to Marc make her happy.

"Wow. That must have been some night last night." Cassie came back into the living room after she'd shooed Shane out of the house. "Spill. Polly will be here in a few minutes."

Liv laughed as she reached up and pinned the end of the twisted streamer. "You think they'll all figure out it's a boy when they see all the blue?"

Cassie took up her end and pulled it taut before pinning it across the room. "Maggie said that's what she wanted and I have no problem throwing her ass in front of me if Polly flips out."

"Man, you two have one of the best mothers-in-law ever. But you wouldn't want to cross her."

"She's wonderful and we *are* lucky. She's a good woman and she cracks me up. Nosy as hell and protective of her family. Can't complain about that one though."

They moved furniture and put out the cute little decorations they'd picked up the week before.

"Let's put the food over here and hello, you did not tell me about why you're smiling. You're sneaky all the sudden. With Brody you would not shut up about the details but with Marc it's like pulling teeth. I figure that means he's the real deal."

"Boy you're on that tune again. Okay here's the deal, Marc is special. I feel way out of my element and in over my head. I think…"

"Hey there, girls! I've got the cake."

Cassie threw her hands up in the air. "Hold that thought. Don't think I won't be back to it," she called back over her shoulder as she moved to the front of the house where Polly had just entered.

The cake was gorgeous and the day was hot. They'd set

up inside but had chairs and umbrellas on the deck as well if people felt up to it.

Polly helped them put the finishing touches around the place just before the guests began to arrive. Many faces, friends and family filled the room, laughing and preparing to share the day with Maggie, who was set to arrive at any moment.

Liv directed people to the present table and to the food while Polly took in the blue decorations with a serene smile.

Kyle yelled from the front door when he dropped Maggie off. He'd been told to go away by Polly, who escorted Maggie into the room.

Dee had arrived earlier and was firmly in charge of the shower games. Liv just did what she was told and handed out clothespins and carried the baby food jars on a tray for the smelling game. She sucked at both but it was fun anyway.

"Hey, Maggie, you want to go outside?" Liv asked a few hours in. "We've set up some shady seating areas."

"Girl, I weigh nine hundred pounds and have a nuclear heater in my belly. I'm not going outside until after the birth except to move to another air-conditioned place," Maggie replied from her seat on the couch, her feet up and a smile on her face.

"Nine hundred pounds. Yeah, you're not overstating or anything. Can I get you some more juice?" Liv called to her as she moved to the table where bottles of juice nestled in ice.

Maggie sighed. "Between you and Cassie, I'm having to pee every five minutes."

"You need the liquids. You're a big baby. Go on and hit the bathroom and when you come back we'll do presents and you can have more juice." Cassie winked and Liv laughed. Having friends like the two of them meant so much to her.

Liv helped Maggie up from the couch and bustled around to get the presents ready for opening.

The room erupted in squeals as Dee took the clothespin from Cassie's sleeve. "You said the forbidden word!"

Liv had lost her clothespin an hour before and she couldn't guess any of the green baby food flavors. Truth be told they all stank to high heaven and Liv wouldn't have blamed any baby for refusing to eat it.

Maggie came back into the room and Liv pressed a fresh glass of juice in her hand before putting her in the present chair that happened to be a glider rocker, a gift from Matt.

"This is like the one I want for the nursery. Make sure to show it to Kyle when the boys get here."

"The boys are here," Kyle said as he entered. After looking around the room he glanced at Maggie with a raised eyebrow. "So you want to tell me something?"

"It was her idea," Cassie said quickly and Shane bent to kiss the top of her head.

"You're so eager to toss me under the bus, Cassie," Maggie said with a laugh. "You said I could tell you when I was ready. I'm ready now."

Kyle grinned. "A son it is apparently. I guess it won't be Sophia then, hmm?"

"Not this time."

Marc came in with Matt and made a beeline for Liv. The man certainly didn't hesitate to lay sugar on her in front of the entire room.

"Hi. You look pretty today."

He was utterly incorrigible and it worked for him. It worked for her too. She kissed the cleft on his chin. "Sit down, it's present time."

"Where are you sitting?"

She pointed to her chair and he pulled one next to it. She couldn't deny how flattered and pleased she was.

"Okay first of all, you don't need to show Kyle the rocker so he can buy one just like it. That's Matt's present."

Maggie laughed delightedly and held her hand out to Matt who came to kiss her and deliver a hug.

"No standing," Liv admonished Maggie. "Everyone has to

come and give Maggie kisses like the princess she is. In fact." Liv bent and pulled out a tiara from behind the couch, meeting Cassie's amused eyes for a moment. "Here." She put the tiara on Maggie who simply grinned like a happy fool.

"I hope you all know I'm going to wear this all the time. Now presents!"

Liv laughed and she and Cassie began to bring presents to Maggie. There was much oohing and aahing over each little pair of pants and shoes, every little rattle and educational thingamabob. Polly, who'd been delighted instead of angry about finding out the gender of her first grandchild, would show Maggie and Kyle the nursery at her house the next night at dinner. Of course she couldn't resist just a few little things. Which turned out to be a three-foot-high pile of outfits, booties, hats and other baby gear.

Penny arrived late, apologizing for the delay. They'd hit a huge traffic jam. She'd brought Ryan and baby Laurel.

"Grab some food and have a seat. We're nearly done with presents." Liv kissed their friend and that sweet two-month-old baby girl. "I call dibs on this baby when I'm done handing out presents."

Penny laughed. "You got it. I'll try and hold Polly off."

Liv handed the last package to Maggie after Penny got settled. "This one is from me."

Maggie tore into the beautifully wrapped package with glee and stopped when she saw the quilt. Carefully she pulled it out and looked it over.

"Oh my goodness. Liv, you made this. For me, for my baby." Maggie's voice was thick with emotion as she looked at the blanket.

"I did." Smiling, Liv pointed to the corners. "These two corners are made from Kyle's baby clothes and the top are from yours. Your daddy actually braved your mother to go and get them."

Tears in her eyes, Maggie stood and hugged Liv tight as

she cried. "This is the most beautiful present I've ever gotten. Our son will sleep with a bit of his parents keeping him warm. And part of his Auntie Liv too."

Kyle hugged her as well. "Thank you, Liv. This is amazing."

"Stop it now, you're going to make me cry. Oh, there's a patch on the other side."

Maggie resettled back in the chair and turned the quilt over. The patch had the date it was finished and a little inscription. *Never doubt you're loved.*

"Sweet heaven, you've reduced an entire room to tears." Marc stood, putting his arm around her waist.

"I would have put his name there but I know you'll change your mind after delivery so I left that off. I'll add it later." Liv knelt beside Maggie.

"You're the best friend anyone could ever ask for. I don't have a very good biological family but I do have wonderful sisters of my heart in you and Cassie and soon," she rubbed her stomach and took Liv's hand, placing it over the place the baby kicked and squirmed, "another person to love. I'm so lucky."

Liv smiled, happy that Maggie had loved the quilt as much as Liv had loved making it for her.

Marc helped Liv up and Polly had Edward and Matt load all the loot into the car. Liv gave Maggie a piece of cake before turning to Penny and grabbing the baby.

Laurel had her daddy's coloring, pretty, big brown eyes and a shock of brunette hair. Her warm little body snuggled into Liv's and that sense of soft happiness stole over Liv. She may not be able to tell the difference between green beans and peas in a jar but she knew without a doubt she wanted this for herself.

Liv walked around and visited as she gently swayed back and forth with Laurel in her arms as Marc just watched.

"You want that." Polly handed him a soda and kissed his cheek.

"I do."

"With Olivia?"

"Without a doubt."

"Well, get working. I saw the way she looked at you when you came in. The way she leaned into your hug. That girl loves you."

"And I love her."

Polly grinned. "Have you told her?"

"Not yet. I'm afraid to scare her away."

"Too late for that. Go make me some more grandbabies."

Marc laughed even as he felt the pull in his balls as he watched Liv holding that baby. It matched the pull at his heart.

He moved to her even without realizing it, wrapping his arms around them both, pressing a kiss to her neck.

"Hey there, Laurel Ann," he said softly, loving the way the baby's eyes moved from Liv's face to his. "This baby sure is a pretty one. You and Ryan done good." He winked at Penny, who blushed. Marriage looked good on her. He knew she'd been devastated when she lost her first husband but she'd moved on and found a new life with Ryan and this baby.

"Your momma keeps sending me looks, I'm gonna have to give her up soon." Liv leaned her head into his shoulder.

Oh how he wanted to say that they could have their own baby, but he didn't want to spook her. That afternoon he'd put a stamp on their relationship in a public way in front of their friends and family and she hadn't resisted. That was a huge step. He'd save the baby talking for after he told her he loved her.

He loved how she tended to her own people. How she took care of Maggie, making sure she rested and kept her feet up. The quilt with Maggie and Kyle's baby clothes had nearly done him in. She'd given Maggie and his brother a piece of her heart to cover their child in. She'd reached out to Cassie in the aftermath after her ex-husband had turned up in town and tried to kill her. Liv still cared about Matt even though he'd broken her heart. She was good people and he couldn't love anyone better.

He also knew his newest client had come from her referral. Several of his clients had. She took care of him, too, in her own way. With her referrals and scrambled egg whites. She kept nonfat milk in her fridge and berry sorbet instead of ice cream. She understood that his feelings about fitness weren't based on vanity but a desire to help people live healthy and long. She got him. No, not his love of her, she had a blind spot there but he understood why more and more each day. But she saw what was special about him, made Marc understand himself better and that was more than he could say about just about anyone else he knew.

"You're incredible," he said into her ear and she smiled.

"Thank you. Where did that come from?" She turned to him, still swaying with Laurel in her arms, the baby's eyes drooping heavily with sleep.

"You just being you. Can I give you a ride over to Kyle and Maggie's later?"

"I drove here but if you want to follow me back to my house, I'll ride with you from there."

He touched his forehead to hers. "You got it. Now give that baby to my momma before she explodes."

Liv rolled her eyes and snorted. "I know, I know. She's shown a lot of restraint actually. I suppose I should reward that."

He watched as she moved to his mother and handed the pink bundle over, catching sight of one bare foot as Laurel settled into his momma's arms.

"So does Liv know you love her?" Penny asked.

"She'd have to be blind not to," Ryan added.

"I haven't told her yet. She likes to pretend she's convinced I'm just Mister Right Now and she wants to find Mister Right. But she's not taking that very seriously anymore. I'm with her five nights a week. She doesn't have much time to date." He snorted.

"She'll come around. Her heart's had some major beatings to it. Makes a girl scared of something real." Penny shrugged.

"I know. I'll be there when she finally figures it out."

"That's the kind of love any woman would be proud to have, Marc." Penny kissed his cheek.

Polly looked up at Liv as the girl finally handed that baby over. It made her heart skip a beat when she'd seen Marc standing close to Liv while she'd held the child. A vision of their future for a brief moment. Another one of her children had found his heart.

"Stingy is what you are." She winked. "Although with this little sugarplum, it's easy to be. Don't you just love the way they feel? Mmm, I miss holding babies. I can't wait until my grandson comes along."

"By the looks of Maggie's belly, that's going to be soon."

Polly chuckled. It was so easy, bringing these women into her family where they belonged. "True enough. You and Marc are going to make some pretty babies too. You do want babies don't you?"

Liv blinked several times and swallowed. Polly knew the girl couldn't overcome how she was raised and politeness was a weapon Polly would use without hesitation.

"Well, sure I want children someday. I don't know if Marc does but we're just dating casually. It's early to talk about children."

"Casually." Polly rolled her eyes. "Girl, you think I'm blind? I see the way you two look at each other." She waved it away. "You keep lying to yourself but it's plain to me and anyone else with eyes. My son cares about you. It's about time you stop this silly charade that only hurts you both."

Liv sighed but didn't try to argue. She was tired of arguing when she knew everyone else was right. She wasn't dumb, nor did she have much talent at self-denial. But damned if she knew what that meant.

She cleaned up in a daze but her heart knew exactly where Marc was the entire time.

Kyle and Maggie left for their house to get the barbecue going. It would be Maggie's way of thanking everyone for all they'd done although Liv had no idea where she'd put any more food after eating so much at the shower.

Back at her place, she changed while Marc replaced the lock on her back door. The key had broken off in it a few weeks before and he'd insisted on fixing it when he found out about it.

"I like you here, fixing things in my house," she said from the doorway before she thought better of it.

He turned and looked at her warily. "I like it too. This is a nice house. I like being here. It's impressive that you own your own home."

She shrugged. "I don't have any debts but this place. I have a decent income. My car was a frivolous impulse buy three years ago but I worked overtime to pay it off in three years instead of five. I can't see paying rent if I can pay to buy instead."

"What if this mythical Mister Right doesn't want to live here?"

She took a deep breath and leapt into the scary abyss. "Well, I can be flexible about living arrangements. But I don't think an apartment above a shoe store is better than my house."

A smile broke over his face as he moved to her. "You saying what I think you are?"

"I don't know. What do you think I'm saying?"

"That you finally believe I'm Mister Right and I'm here for the long haul."

"Do *you* believe that?"

He brushed his thumb over her lips. "I've believed that for months."

She took a deep breath. "Yes. I believe it. I'll pull my profile from the computer dating services today. Not that I have time to date when I'm with you all the time."

"You found time to date Bill."

"I'm sorry if I hurt you. I am. And it means so much to me that you didn't just walk away when I insisted on continuing to date. I don't even know what to say other than that I had to believe it, Marc. Bill was never a threat to you. I never even kissed him after you and I started up."

He kissed her softly. "It was hard, Liv. I know he wasn't a threat. If I'd believed otherwise I probably wouldn't have agreed to wait while you finally took me seriously. Still, I was worried you'd never see me and my intentions as genuine. What finally convinced you?"

She shrugged. "I don't think it was one thing. More a combination. Today at the shower your mother was the dozenth person to tell me that I was blind if I didn't see how you felt about me and I realized she was right. I was being willfully blind and stupid to ignore it. But I was afraid."

"We can deal with the fear together."

"Yeah."

He kissed her then, like he should have. It felt like something from a fairy tale, his hands on her hips, his mouth covering hers.

Chapter Nine

She'd been sautéing the garlic when her phone rang. Turning everything off, she'd left a note on her door and rushed to the hospital.

Kyle was in a state when she'd arrived, pacing and freaked out. Liv put her arms around his waist. "Hey there. I want you to focus, all right? She needs you to be calm just now."

"I can't. I'm trying but I keep thinking of worst-case scenarios. What if something happens to her? To the baby?"

She kissed his cheek. "Everything is going to be all right, Kyle. Women do this every day. She's here in a hospital. She's healthy. The baby is healthy. She needs all of us to help. You don't have the luxury of shutting down and freaking out. She loves you and she needs you, so get your act together."

Polly came around the corner and Liv handed Kyle off to his mother and went in to Maggie. They'd just changed Maggie into a gown and hooked her up to a machine that echoed the baby's heartbeat through the room.

Relief showed clear on her face when she saw Liv.

"So, how's it goin?" Liv let the same fears Kyle had pass through her. She wasn't good at death, especially when it concerned the people she loved. Still, there was no time for fear in front of Maggie.

"I'm apparently having a kid and my husband is apparently having a nervous breakdown."

Liv moved a chair next to Maggie's bed.

"He loves you. None of this is in his control and he's freaked. He'll get it together. His mother is whipping him into shape now."

Maggie laughed and then winced. Liv reached out and took her hand, holding eye contact through the contraction.

"We've been through a lot you and me. We'll get through this too and at the end you'll be holding your precious baby son."

"You're the best. I'm so happy you and Marc finally found each other."

"I love him." Liv took a deep breath. "I finally admitted it to myself and I'm taking it from there. I'm scared all the time anyway, may as well be scared while I'm with him. Do you want to walk or use the ball? You tell me what you need."

"Good for you, Liv. I knew you were strong enough to handle this. I expect the whole damned Chase family has gathered out there. I can deal with visitors just now but I want to make it clear that I do not want an audience *or* cameras in here when the big moment comes. Pictures before, pictures after. No money shots."

Liv laughed. "Got it. No pictures of Maggie's hoo-ha with a baby emerging. I'll go let the hordes know you're available for visits."

Before too long, the room had filled with family and it had become a festive place. Whatever Polly told Kyle had calmed him but he didn't move more than an inch from Maggie's side.

They all took turns walking with Maggie through the halls as she labored.

On a break, Liv leaned into Marc, who massaged her shoulders. "Sorry about dinner, sport."

"I'll grab a rain check. This is more important. Have you eaten though? You want me to go and grab you something?"

"Not right now, but why don't you go and get something with Kyle? He needs a break and the nurse said Maggie has several more hours to go."

When the guys left, Liv turned down the lights and she, Cassie, Polly and Maggie all sat quietly. Maggie's pain had ramped up considerably and she finally opted for an epidural so she rested, staring at a television movie while Liv watched Cassie make jewelry.

It was right that they all sat in the room, the generations all together as a new life prepared to make an appearance. By the time the men returned with food for everyone but Maggie, who waved away any apologies for not being able to eat, Liv wanted to simply snuggle with Marc until the sun rose.

Who knew that love would make her so content? But it had. Content and the restlessness was gone. Everything felt like it was supposed to be. She'd never felt so settled and happy and she refused to entertain any of those *oh no, what's going to happen to end this* thoughts. Well, they were there in the background but she could beat them back.

Everyone but Liv and Kyle went to rest or nap in the waiting room when the labor nurse came to check on Maggie. She told them Maggie was just at four centimeters and they expected it to be several more hours before she'd be fully dilated.

Liv kissed Maggie's forehead. "You've got a ways to go. Rest for now. I'm going on a walk with Marc. I have my phone and I won't be far but you need to sleep. You won't if I'm here." She turned to Kyle. "Stretch out in that chair, it converts into a bed. You sleep too. She will if you will."

Kyle hugged Liv and she went out and found Marc waiting just outside the door.

"I need to walk, get some air. You want to come with me?"

"Of course. I wouldn't miss it." Marc took her hand as they went to inform the nurse's station that they'd be going on a walk for a while and to call if there was anything Maggie needed.

Once they'd gotten outside, Marc turned to her. "What do you need? You've been taking care of her all night, running interference, making sure no one pushed her too much."

She laid her head on his chest, listening to his heart. "I love you," she whispered, her voice trembling.

"Oh, sugar, I wanted to say it first. I love you too. I want this with you, you know."

"You do?"

"I do what?"

She laughed. "You love me?"

"Woman, have you not listened to a damned thing I've said in the last months? Yes. Yes, I love you. It'd be impossible not to."

She smiled. "Oh. Good. And what is it you want with me?"

"So many ways I could go with that question. But being serious instead of lascivious for a moment at least, I want a family. A life like Kyle and Maggie, Shane and Cassie have."

"Marc, the age difference…"

"Stop it with that!" He pushed her back and shook his head. "That does not even matter. It's six years, not even quite six years. You act like it's twenty years. It seriously pisses me off."

"It pisses me off that you think it's nothing."

He wrinkled his nose. "Please. You're so full of shit for a woman who looks so good. I'm over twenty-one. And what difference could it make? Come on, sugar, it's six years. When you get old, I'll be old too. It's not like anyone is going to think I'm marrying you for your fortune because you're so old and hideous."

She laughed. "Stop that. I'm serious."

"So am I. Liv, tell me what difference our ages have to make in our relationship."

"You have time left to get out there and sow wild oats. I don't want you to settle down if you're not ready."

He snorted. "Olivia Jean Davis, girl, you are crazy. I've

sowed 'em. Lots and lots of them. I don't have any more I want to sow except with you."

They walked a while longer as Liv let herself believe in what they had together and it grew inside her until it filled every cell. Almost every cell. The fear still crouched, small and nearly defeated. She could be loved by someone like this man, damn it. She would do it because he was worth it.

Liv walked out of Maggie's room, face bright with tears. "He's here. Nicholas Edward Chase is now ready to see two people at a time. Maggie is tired but she knows you all want to meet him. Polly, why don't you and Grandpa go first?"

Liv collapsed into a chair next to Marc and he hugged her. "You okay?"

"Oh my God. I've never in my life seen anything more amazing. Maggie deserves a medal. And Nicholas is the most beautiful boy. Looks an awful lot like your dad." She stood. "I need to call Dee and Penny. Maggie's dad is on his way here from the airport. I bet he's kicking himself for having to take a business trip when Maggie had the baby."

"Can I help with the calls?"

She smiled at him. "Thank you, darlin', but I need you to be the gatekeeper. You'll need to wrestle your parents out of there in about five minutes. Then Cassie and Shane can go in. Hopefully I'll be back but I need to go outside to call. Only two people and only five minutes. She needs to sleep. They all do."

She made her calls in the early afternoon heat. Smiling and crying as she relayed the details to Penny and Dee. Maggie would be so happy to see the flowers her students were going to send and Kyle's employees would take care of their accounts for the next two weeks so he could focus on Maggie and the baby.

It was then she saw Lyndsay Cole walking out of the building across the street from the hospital. She looked up and flinched when she saw Liv. Liv expected to feel fury but she didn't. Instead she just felt sad that anyone could be so cold as Brody had been and Lyndsay deserved him.

Liv had just been in the room to help her best friend deliver a new life into the world. No silly skank could ruin that. Not when she had Marc Chase in her bed and her heart.

She turned and went back inside.

Chapter Ten

Liv swayed in Marc's arms on the dance floor. The Honky Tonk on a Friday night and the place was packed. The Dixie Chicks played and Marc was lazily propositioning her in her ear. Shivers ran up and down her spine as he described in great detail just how he was going to make her come.

They'd forgone pool and beer at The Pumphouse and had gone on an actual date instead. Liv saw Shane and Cassie nearby and Matt sat with Amy Jackson at their table.

"What do you say?" Marc pulled away from her ear to look into her face.

"I'm not sure that's even physically possible but I'm up for it if you are."

He laughed and she felt light and dizzy with happy. Could have been the lack of sleep because Marc had slept over the last two nights and she'd been over at Kyle and Maggie's several times to check in. She wanted to bring by food but Polly had prepared enough food to keep them fed until Christmas.

"Okay. But a beer first to fortify me. Plus you realize this is our first actual out-on-the-town date now that we're an official couple?"

"You mean all the times you came over to have sex didn't count?" Liv winked at him.

"Well, now yes they did. They did very fine. But this lets all these dimwits know you're mine. So no more sniffing around you every damned time you're out in public." He frowned as he led her off the dance floor.

"Me? You've got to be kidding. Marc, a stream of women follows you by scent. Everywhere you go there's some bimbo nearby fluttering her lashes and thrusting her boobies at you."

"Boobies?"

"Yes, that's how I think of them when their owner is twenty-two."

He blushed and it was her turn to laugh.

"Olivia Jean, are you jealous?"

"I don't like it, no."

He stopped right in the middle of the aisle they were walking on. "Do you think I'd do you like Brody?"

"No. No I don't. I wouldn't be with you if I did, Marc." She shrugged. "I didn't accuse you of cheating on me. You made a comment about men sniffing around and I countered with your harem. Every Chase brother comes equipped with one apparently. You asked if I was jealous and I answered you honestly. Don't ask a question if you don't want to hear the answer."

He relaxed and kissed her lightly. "I'm sorry. You're right. I just hate that you might compare me to Brody."

"I can understand that. But I wasn't. I don't like it that I have to wade through a bunch of women to get to you all the time."

"Doesn't signify. The only woman who matters is you." He took her hand and tucked it into his arm and continued to walk her to the table. When they got there, he pulled out her chair, enjoying the view as she plopped into it.

"Nice jiggle." He sat and poured her a beer from the pitcher.

"Hmpf. Hey, Matt."

"Hey, Liv, how are you tonight? Looking mighty fine." Matt winked and Marc growled.

Matt just laughed. "It's payback for all you've done to Kyle and Shane."

"Just wait. You're the last one." Marc drank his beer while drawing circles on the back of Liv's neck with the other hand, loving the way she shivered in response. He noted the stares that Liv attracted but also the way she ignored it.

Until Brody came in with Lyndsay.

Everyone at the table froze except for Amy who waved and called out Lyndsay's name.

"No." Matt shook his head and put his hand on Amy's. "Neither of them is welcome at this table."

Amy looked confused and then her face changed when she caught sight of Liv, blushing. "I'm sorry. I didn't think."

Liv shrugged. "It's okay, Amy. I know you're friends with her."

"I know, but I wouldn't want her at my table either if I were you. Even though I think you got a way better deal." Amy smiled tentatively and Liv laughed.

"I know I did."

Lyndsay had been on her way over with Brody until she saw who else was at the table and froze. Brody saw Liv and paled. Marc narrowed his eyes at them both. He was thankful Brody's stupidity drove Liv to his arms but he hated the bastard for hurting her.

Shane and Cassie came up behind them and Marc noted with some amusement that Shane used a bit more of his body than was necessary to push past Brody. Cassie just stared at them like she smelled something nasty. Brody and Lyndsay moved to the other side of the dance floor.

"Asshole," Cassie muttered as she sat down.

Marc grinned as he looked around the table. His family was hers now too. He loved that she was so close to Cassie and Maggie. His family was important to him and she was already a part of it.

"It's a small town. We're bound to see each other. I'm surprised this is the first time I've seen him since the end of February." Liv took a sip of her beer.

"I'm sure he's been laying low. Everyone knows what he did. I told him what an ass I thought he was when I ran into him two months ago at the hardware store." Marc thought Brody should have been glad the running-into-him part wasn't with Marc's truck.

"You didn't tell me you ran into him." Liv raised an eyebrow at him in question.

Marc shrugged. "It didn't matter enough to mention. He's a punk and he's lucky I didn't put my fist in his face."

"Damn right," Cassie said.

"Marc and I are going to be getting out of here. He's got an ambitious new workout routine he's promised to show me."

Choking on his beer a moment, Marc stood with Liv and waved to everyone else as he dragged her out.

In the parking lot, he backed her against the side of his truck. "You're playing with fire, Liv." To underline his point, he rolled his hips, grinding his cock into her, inflamed even more when she half closed her eyes and moaned softly.

"You okay to drive?" Her hands skimmed over his shoulders and back as she writhed against him.

"I only had three sips of my beer before you dangled kinky sex in front of me. I'm as sober as a parson. If we don't get going right now, I'm going to do you right here in the parking lot."

"As tempting as that is, the family watching us through the window of the diner across the way might not appreciate it."

He stepped back and opened the door. She climbed up and in and he smiled, catching the flash of bare leg he got as she scooted across the seat to her side.

"My place is closer." He fastened his seat belt quickly and put his keys in the ignition.

"Cool. I like having sex in your monument to bachelorhood."

"Where do you get the stuff you say?"

"I'm naturally gifted that way." She lifted her shoulders nonchalantly.

He drove safely but quickly to his apartment. Parking somewhat haphazardly, he dragged her up the stairs, pushed her inside and kicked the door closed behind him.

"Clothes off. Now."

She took a deep breath and undid the ties at the shoulder of her dress. It fell to the floor, pooling in a spill of deep blue at her feet.

"You had no panties on that whole time." He swallowed hard.

She shook her head. "Not a stitch."

"Damned sexy. And oh so naughty." He stalked toward her, yanking his shirt over his head, toeing his boots off when he reached her and tossing them back with the shirt.

"I have this recurring fantasy." He looked down at her, liking the way her mouth turned up at the corner when he said it.

"Oh? Do tell."

"It involves you, on your knees."

She dropped to her knees and he sucked in a breath.

"Like this?" She looked up at him.

"That'll do nicely. And then you suck my cock. Afterwards, we make love nice and slow. This after I go down on you of course."

She reached up and unzipped his jeans, freeing his cock. "Of course." Her tongue darted out to lick around the ridge of the head. Swirling her tongue around him as she took him farther and farther into her mouth. The heat built in him. Her mouth, hot and wet, surrounded him fully as her nails lightly scored his balls. Pleasure so intense he had to lock his knees to keep from crumbling burst through him.

Liv thought she was pretty darned good at oral sex. Because she loved it. Loved making him squirm and groan, loved the feel of his cock in her mouth as it got harder and harder. There was power there, even on her knees, because it was her and no one else who made him feel that way.

Over and over again, she took him into her mouth, rocking back and sliding forward on him, keeping him wet and the pressure even. Every few passes she added a flick of her tongue just beneath the head.

His hands squeezed her shoulders, guiding her movements. No other man would have been allowed to do that but with him it seemed natural. Not overly aggressive or controlling in a negative sense but more like he couldn't resist because he needed her that much.

"You feel so good, sugar. I don't know what I did to deserve a gorgeous creature at my feet, sucking my cock, but I'm thankful to the powers that be for you. Fuck. Fuck. I'm close."

She hummed her approval around him and he cursed under his breath before he groaned low and long while he came.

He sank to the carpet beside her, bringing her to lie across his body as he caught his breath.

"Yeah. Better than the fantasy. Not that it'll stop me from having more fantasies about you or anything. Now I'll have more fodder."

She laughed and he rolled her over onto her back, looming over her. "That was spectacular, Liv. Now, I think it's your turn."

"Like I'm gonna argue?"

Marc looked down at her, lying there beneath him, naked but for some seriously sexy heels. The look in her eyes made his heart sing. Trust. Love. Openness.

The long line of her neck called to his lips and he didn't resist. Leaning in, he licked from shoulder to earlobe, loving the way she arched into him, giving him more of her neck.

No shy miss here. She widened her thighs and rolled her hips. Her fingers dug into his shoulders, urging him on.

Taking his time, he meandered over the hills and curves of her body, licking across her collarbone, laving his tongue through the warmth at the hollow of her throat. His fingers kneaded her muscles as he moved down, kissing the curve of her breast until he reached the nipple, swirling his tongue around it and sliding the edge of his teeth across it until she gasped.

"You like that?"

"Yes, oh yes. More, please, Marc."

"Since you asked so pretty." He continued to kiss down the bottom slope of her breast, over each rib, down the soft plane of her belly, pausing to dip his tongue in the sweet well of her navel.

Her low moan of encouragement made him grin as he sat back on his heels. Grabbing her ankles, he pushed her knees up and pressed them wide, opening her up to him completely.

She gasped and caught her bottom lip between her teeth.

"You need to keep your thighs wide for me. If you move them I'll stop. Can you do that for me, sugar?"

She blinked rapidly, licking her lips before managing a nod.

Satisfied, he slid his palms down her thighs and pulled her labia apart just before lowering his mouth to her and taking a leisurely lick. He felt her thigh muscles tense under his hands but she relaxed, keeping her legs open.

Sliding his tongue through her pussy, he reveled in the pleasure he brought her. He loved her taste, the way she responded so totally to him. The fingertip he'd had circling her gate slowly pushed into her and he closed his eyes against the way her body clasped around him.

A second finger followed the first and she arched her back. He paused and she moved her legs back in place.

"I find it quite erotic to control you, sugar. The way you just got even hotter and wetter says you do too."

She exhaled around a soft whimper and he got back to work, his tongue swirling and flicking around her clit over and over as he fucked into her with his fingers.

Her clit bloomed against his tongue as she cried out softly, her thighs wrapping around his shoulders as she came.

Finally she went lax, her thighs falling open, and he put his head on her belly, looking up the line of her body at her face, a relaxed smile on her lips.

He kissed her belly and stood, holding a hand out to her. She took it and he helped her up.

"Condoms in my bathroom. Just bought a new box today. You keep me very busy." He pulled her down his hallway but she stopped at the doorway when he went inside.

He saw her reflection in the mirrors over the sink, saw the mirrored doors on the closet and realized the entire room was walled by mirrors. He smiled. "Come on in here." He patted the counter. "I think this is the perfect height."

Shucking his jeans and socks, he hoisted her up on the counter, stepping between her thighs and going in for a kiss.

"I like this view. I can see your ass and the muscles in your back. You have a very sexy behind."

"Why thank you, ma'am. I do try." He winked, sheathing himself quickly and testing her for readiness before slowly pushing himself into her.

Liv watched him make love to her from every angle, really appreciating the mirrors on the closet door fully. Watched the clutch of his glutes as he pushed his cock into her, the flex of his shoulders and down the long line of his back.

She caught sight of her body wrapped around his, the paler skin of her legs contrasted with the more golden hues of his. Her eyes, slumberous, lips parted. They were beautiful together, linked.

It was almost as if she watched someone else there in the mirror. Perhaps through his eyes? In the mirror she was confident and trusted him completely as he stoked her desire that he'd just sated scant minutes before.

His body was made to fit into hers and he did it so very well. His cock, wide with a blunt head, brushed over her sweet spot

over and over. He knew just where it was and took great care
to give it attention. That's how their sex was. Mind-blowing,
yes, but because he *wanted* it to be. For her.

"I like seeing you from all these angles. So pretty." A fingertip traced around her nipples, featherlight. "These are luscious. When I see you my mouth waters to taste them."

His head bent then, the warmth of his tongue sent shivers up her spine as he flicked over the nipple quickly, in time
with his thrusts.

How he did it she didn't know but it was a form of erotic
torture and he devastated her with it time and again. Each
flick was followed by a sucking pull that brought a throb from
her clit.

"I love the way your pussy flutters around me when I do
that. Such sensitive nipples."

"For you."

He looked into her eyes then, pausing. "I love you, Liv."

She felt it to her toes and blinked back tears. "I love you
too."

His free hand found her clit, squeezing it lightly between
slippery fingers and she arched, grinding herself into him, into
his thrusts as yet again, climax washed through her body, leaving her helpless to do much more than hold on and ride it out.

"There you go, sugar. Give it to me," he said, voice hoarse
as his thrusts deepened once, twice and a third time before he
pressed as deep as he could and came.

And as if she weighed nothing, he picked her up and carried her to his bed, laying her there carefully, gently.

"Rest up now because we're going another round or five
when I get my breath back."

Laughing, she reached up and traced the line of his jaw.
"Even if my legs were working I wouldn't want to escape."

Chapter Eleven

Liv stood under the tree the large blankets were spread beneath for the annual homecoming picnic. Nicholas, two months old now, stared up at her, wide-eyed with a gummy grin on his face.

"Aren't you just the most handsome little man?" Liv smooched his chubby cheeks and smoothed down the patch of bright red hair that normally stood straight up on the top of his otherwise bald head.

"Handsome? Well, certainly he's got a lot of character but with that hair, I don't know." Matt grabbed a bare foot and kissed it, making Nicholas emit a breathy laugh.

"A man with character is handsome, I'll have you know." Polly stood there, moving from foot to foot, and Liv finally took pity on her and handed the baby over.

"You're greedy with him." Polly never took her eyes from Nicholas as she teased Liv. "You should have one of your own and you can hold him. Well, every once in a while because he'll fit just fine here on my other hip."

Marc laughed, a little distracted. He'd run into one of his old ex-girlfriends the day before and she'd come on to him. Strong. It wasn't so much that he was interested but there'd been a moment when part of him panicked at the thought of never being with another woman again. It passed quickly enough as he'd realized he didn't want to be with another woman. Liv was everything.

He'd considered talking to her about it but he'd been concerned that he'd hurt her or make her think he was having second thoughts. He'd worked so hard and so long to gain her trust, he didn't want to endanger that. But he felt like he was hiding something from her because they normally shared everything.

"You okay?" Her head cocked, hand on her hip, she looked so beautiful it made his chest hurt a moment.

"Yeah, fine. Hungry? We've got a lot of food here and I can see Momma has left us all to fend for ourselves now that the youngest Chase has stolen her attention."

Liv sat next to him on the blanket and began to make plates and pass them down to everyone. Cassie sat across from them, leaning against Shane while Maggie looked up at Polly as Polly sang silly songs to the baby. It was good there with the people he loved.

Since Nicholas's birth, he and Liv had gotten closer and closer. He practically lived in her house and saw her or spoke to her daily. She'd become a regular at all Chase family events and dinners.

He loved waking up to her, feeling the warmth of her body next to his. They'd cooked together, side by side, and he'd enjoyed the feeling of familiarity and comfort. Their sex life had remained active, exciting and very frequent. But it wasn't just sex, every time he was inside her he learned something new about her and himself. She saw into him. There was a time he'd have been freaked out by that, but instead, it made him feel whole.

He didn't want to do anything to screw that up and so he'd keep the thing with Nancy to himself because it had meant nothing anyway.

* * *

Liv knew there was something Marc wasn't telling her. She'd known him long enough to tell the difference between the way he was acting then and his normal behavior.

She didn't like it. It felt familiar. Before the end with her other lovers it had been like this. Smiles and assurances that nothing was wrong and then the end. Her insecurity ramped up.

All afternoon and into the evening it sat at the back of her mind, worrying her, nagging at her. Finally, as they were packing Nicholas and all his gear into Maggie's car, her friend turned to her, touching her cheek.

"Is everything all right? I feel like I've not paid a lot of attention to you these last two months. Nicholas takes up so much of my time but I want to know what's going on with you. I care about you."

Liv gave Maggie a tight smile. "I'm fine. I think. I don't know." She sighed. "It's Marc. Since yesterday afternoon when I came into the shop to work out he's been acting odd. I don't know, like he's not saying something."

"Are you two having problems?"

"No. Things have been going great. He's totally present in this relationship, you know? We talk all the time, share everything. I've never felt this way before. He's good to me, you know? He cares about me. But I'm afraid." A sob tore from her and Maggie hugged her.

"It's okay. He loves you. He does. I've seen the way he looks at you. I've heard how he talks about you. I'm sure it's stress or something silly like that."

"I'm afraid he's going to leave me." Liv felt like the words tore a part of her to say. Like everyone she loved left. Sooner or later it happened.

"Oh honey, don't cry. I'd give everything I own to bet on Marc loving you. Just give it some time. I'm sure he'll relax and all this will seem silly in a few days."

Kyle approached with Marc and Shane, all holding stuff

to load into the cars, and Liv quickly dried her eyes and stood back.

"Call me tomorrow, okay?"

Liv nodded. She leaned down to kiss Nicholas's head as he slept in his car seat. "Night, sweetie."

Kyle looked at her, a question in his eyes but she shook her head and he moved his gaze to Maggie who shrugged.

"Everything okay?" Marc asked as he took Liv's hand.

"You tell me."

"Okay, what the hell is going on?" Kyle asked.

"Nothing, hon. Liv, you call me tomorrow, you hear? Marc, good night and make sure you take care of our girl." Maggie gave him a stern look and got into the car.

"Liv, honey, have you been crying?" Marc touched her face gently.

"It doesn't matter. I want to go home."

He helped her into his truck and drove back to her place.

"It does matter." He turned to her once he'd pulled into her driveway. "Tell me what's wrong."

"You're the one who's not telling me what's wrong, Marc. I can tell there's something up but you won't say and that makes me wonder just what it is you're hiding."

"Sugar, I'm not hiding anything. I love you. You believe that, don't you?"

"I want to."

Marc's heart began to pound at the desolate sound of that answer. God, he'd made her so upset without even trying to and now if he told her it would make it even worse. She'd think he was hiding it because it meant something instead of just a stupid thing that he didn't say anything about and now had snowballed.

He moved over to her side and pulled her to him, holding her tight. "I love you, Olivia. More than anything. I swear that on my life. I'm just stressed, honey. It has nothing to do with how I feel about you."

Nodding against his chest she hugged him back. "I need you to tell me stuff, okay? I can't bear thinking that you're having second thoughts or something and not telling me."

He tipped her chin up, kissing her lips. "I love you. I don't doubt that for a moment. Now let's go inside, okay?"

Things had gotten back to normal pretty much and Liv relaxed. Maggie had been relieved that everything was all right and Liv realized that things were going the best they had her entire life. Her plan had actually come to fruition and loving Marc Chase had been everything she'd imagined true love to be and more.

A spring in her step, she walked toward the studio a bit early on a Wednesday. The heat had finally edged away and fall was in the air. She'd picked up a few brochures for a bed-and-breakfast down on the coast. She thought a nice weekend away would be just the thing for them.

Pushing open the front door of the studio, Liv halted. The smile on her face froze and then slid off as a pain so sharp she wasn't sure she'd survive it sliced through her gut.

Marc was there on the floor, on top of another woman, Nancy Ellis. Nancy's thighs were spread and wrapped around him.

Nancy, laughing, looked up and caught sight of Liv as Marc pushed away and scrambled up. When he turned and saw her he went as pale as a ghost.

"Sugar, it's…"

"Not what I think?" She felt totally empty, as if there was nothing inside her at all, which she supposed was better than the searing pain she'd felt just before.

"You made me think I was imaging things." She took a step back and he took one forward. "Don't. Don't you fucking come near me. Not ever again. Don't call me. Don't come see me." She pressed a fist to her gut to keep from screaming as the pain came back, filling her from her toes up to her ears. She would not cry. She would not give him the satisfaction.

Turning, she left and he was on her heels.

"Liv, damn it, wait!" He grabbed her arm and she spun, kneeing him square in the balls, smiling with savage satisfaction as he crumpled to his knees.

"Don't you touch me. You fucking bastard." Turning again she ran as fast as she could.

Knowing he'd probably go to her place, she grabbed her car and got the hell out of there.

Marc had been busy with one of his clients when he'd turned to see Nancy walk in. *Great.*

"Hey, Nancy. What brings you here?"

She put her hand on her hip and gave him her sexiest smile. "I came for a workout."

His other client had been cooling down and by the time she'd gone, it was just Marc and Nancy.

"Well, I told you that I'm with Liv Davis and I meant that. If you'd like to work out without any sex involved, I'd be happy to help. I'm not taking one-on-one clients just now but I have a wait list. But you can use the facilities here without a personal trainer."

She'd appeared to take the news well and had gone back to change and he'd filled out enrollment papers and gotten her signed up. He should have known it was too good to be true when she'd said she was having trouble with one of the machines. He'd bent over her to help and she'd pulled him down, laughing, wrapping her thighs around his waist.

Pissed off beyond measure, he pushed himself away from Nancy and to standing when he'd heard a gasp. A sound that constricted around his heart. He'd turned, knowing she was there but that knowledge hadn't been enough to prepare him for the look on her face.

Her voice, flat, empty, didn't fit with the pain glittering in her eyes. He had plenty of time to relive the entire event as he lay there on the sidewalk after his gloriously pissed-off woman had kneed him in the balls and taken off running.

He limped back into the studio where Nancy stood, fully dressed and looking upset.

"Oh goodness, Marc. I didn't... I'm so sorry. Is she all right?"

"I don't know," he said, voice strained as his balls throbbed. "What the hell were you thinking?"

"I was just flirting. I didn't mean for that to happen. I may have wanted you back and wanted to test to see what your commitment to Liv really was, but I'd never, not ever in a million years want to hurt her like that. Or you. I'm so sorry." Nancy wrung her hands anxiously. "Do you want me to talk to her? Tell her what happened?"

"Not for now. Maybe later. Fuck." He pushed a hand through his hair. "I have to go find her." He put up the closed sign and Nancy left, promising to be available to talk to Liv if he needed her to.

Maggie opened her front door and her warm greeting died in her throat. She reached out and pulled Liv inside.

"My goodness, honey, what is it? Is everyone okay? Who got hurt?"

"Marc," she gasped.

"Marc got hurt? What happened? Where is he?" Kyle came into the room.

"Marc cheated on me." Liv crumpled to her knees as she wept as if her heart would break.

"He what? No. No, he wouldn't!" Maggie sank to scoop Liv into her arms and rock her slowly. "Honey, you must have misunderstood."

"Two weeks ago he was h-hiding something and tonight I found him on the floor with Nancy Ellis. He was on top of her, her legs wrapped around him. She was l-laughing."

"This can't be right. Liv, honey, my brother adores you. He would not do this to you. I know it." Kyle looked helplessly at Liv as he brushed a hand over her hair. "Did he explain?"

"Explain what? Do you think I'm a moron? Or some desperate woman who'll buy a bunch of lies to hold on to a bigger lie?"

"Let's get you up and on the couch, all right? Kyle's gonna go and make us some tea and we're going to talk after you finish your cry." Maggie raised a brow at Kyle who left the room quickly.

"I love him so much. My God this hurts more than anything I've ever felt before. This is not right. Why would he do this? If he wasn't ready he shouldn't have pushed me. I was... I had a plan! Damn it, I had a plan and he promised he loved me and I fell in love with him and he sucks. Oh he sucks and I hate him and I hope I did permanent damage when I kneed him in the sac. That fucker."

Maggie sighed heavily, not knowing what to do but hoping like hell Kyle picked up her hint and was tracking down his brother to find out what was happening.

"I tell you something, Olivia Jean, if Marc has cheated on you, I will personally skin him alive. I swear it. I've got your back. But let's not be hasty here. Let him explain."

"Explain what? Maggie, he was on top of another woman with her legs wrapped around his waist! What is there to explain about that that isn't totally obvious?"

"Okay so it sounds pretty bad." And boy how it did. What the hell did Marc do? "But..."

Liv stood. "No buts, Maggie. I never should have allowed myself to get close to him. I should have listened to my head and not my freaking vagina. I have been such a fool. This probably isn't even the first time."

Kyle came into the room and put a tray down on the table with a pot of tea and some mugs. "I'm going to go check on the baby. Should I make up the guest room for you, sweetie?"

"No. No. I need to go. Be alone. I have to think."

"I don't think that's a good idea. You should be with people who love you right now. Stay here, please. You know Nicholas adores his auntie. Stay here tonight and we'll have pancakes tomorrow morning."

"Oh, I'm having biscuits and gravy and six slices of bacon tomorrow morning. Maybe a cheeseburger for lunch. But I don't want to be around Nicky in this mood, it's not good for him to see me this way. I'm sorry, I shouldn't have come."

"Of course you should. Liv, you're my best friend. You've been there for me when I've needed you for thirty years. Please, let me be there now." Maggie took her hands, aching at the pain on Liv's face.

Liv kissed Maggie's cheek. "I love you for being my friend, I truly do. But I know Kyle called Marc when he was in the kitchen and I don't want to see his face. I can't." She moved to the door. "I'll call you when I'm ready."

She turned and left and Maggie stared at the door with tears in her eyes.

"He's on his way but he was at her house when I called so he won't make it. Let me call him back."

Maggie turned to her husband. "And tell him what? She didn't tell me where she was going because she didn't trust me not to tell Marc. Kyle, I've betrayed her today just like your dumbass brother did."

Kyle took her in his arms. "You didn't betray her. You wanted to help her and make this thing right. He says it was all a stupid misunderstanding. That she walked in at the wrong moment."

"Clearly! I'm sure he was hoping to finish up by the time his *girlfriend* walked in on him between another woman's legs."

"That isn't what it was. Or it is but not what it looked like. Maggie, damn it, I love Liv. I would not cheat on her." Marc walked into the room. "Where is she?"

"Gone. I don't know where. But you'd better have a damned good explanation."

Marc sighed and sat down heavily on the couch, telling them everything.

"Do you know where she is?" Polly asked, pacing.

"She left a voice mail for Cassie saying she didn't want her to be put in the middle between her friends and her family but she was okay and would be gone for a while," Shane said. "Cassie's all torn up over it. She's upset that Liv is alone right now and didn't think she could turn to her or Maggie."

"I could just knock the spit out of that Nancy," Maggie said, patting Nicholas's back.

"If I could just get her to talk to me, I know I could get her to see some sense," Marc said heavily. "I've left her messages and notes at her house. She's not gone back there since Wednesday night. They told Maggie, Liv took a week's vacation from work. No one is talking to me. I wouldn't cheat on her, I swear it. I know it looks bad but I'm not that man. Not now and I wasn't even a cheater before I fell for my girl. God, I hate thinking about her out there believing I'd betray her like that. I just want to hold her and love her."

Polly squeezed his shoulder and kissed his cheek. "Honey, this will be all right. We've got to find her and let her know she's loved by all of us."

In Atlanta, Liv sat, eyes closed, relaxation à la white wine and a facial.

"Just relax here for a while longer. The deep cleansing mask will be done in about ten minutes and your hands will be ready to come out of the paraffin," the disembodied voice of the beautician told her.

"Mmmm. Thanks," Liv mumbled, settling deeper into the chair.

"Oh girl, you're a sneaky one."

Liv sighed, knowing it was too good to be true that she'd remained unmolested for the last week.

"What are you doing here? Where's Nicholas?"

"What the hell is on your face? Nicholas is right here in my arms if you'd opened your eyes to see."

"What are you doing here?"

"You already asked that and your eyes are closed still. Don't you want to see your godson? He's missed you, you know. Gone for a week without a damned word. I mean really. I ought to sic Polly on you."

Liv cracked an eye and turned her head. "Hi, lumpkin, how are you, sweetie?" Nicholas cooed at her and reached toward her voice. "In a few minutes, bubba. Right now Auntie Liv's hands are wrapped in wax. I know, silly, aren't I?"

"Not as silly as having that green crap on your face."

"Deep cleansing mask with milk and chamomile. Are we here to trade beauty tips?"

"Lookit you with that smart mouth."

"Look, Maggie, what do you want?"

Just then the beautician came back to clean off her mask, put on some moisturizer, remove the wax from her hands and massage them.

"I'll skip the manicure today, Sarah. My godson here is sensitive to smells."

Liv paid her bill and left a tip, not looking at Maggie as she went toward the doors.

"You are so not going to just walk out on me, Olivia Davis. Thanks to Dee and Penny, I tracked you down. We've all been worried as hell about you. How dare you not keep in contact?"

Liv spun and glared at her oldest friend. "I would say something very unladylike right now but Nicholas is watching so I'll just tell you to mind your own beeswax. I've been looking at apartments here. I've gone on two job interviews. I'm moving on, thankyouverymuch. I haven't kept contact because you have other allegiances now as does Cassie. I thought I could trust Dee and Penny but I guess I was wrong. Give me that baby."

Maggie handed Nicholas over who giggled and reached up to touch her face. "Hey, lumpkin." She kissed his tiny face, missing the way he smelled.

"What the heck does that mean? Other allegiances?"

"You know what it means. Where's Marc? Hiding some-where ready to jump out? With his new girlfriend at his place?"

Maggie sighed. "Okay, this is what we're going to do. You're not going to take this attitude with me. Other allegiances my ahh—booty." Maggie looked at Nicholas. "Then you and I are going to your hotel and we're going to put the baby down for a nap. You're going to tell me about this fool plan to move away from Petal and I'm going to knock you out if you go through with it. And then we're going to order room service and talk about Marc over a few beers."

"Do I have any choice?"

"My next step is to call Polly Chase. She's more agitated than I am over this so she'll drive out here like a shot. You decide." Maggie folded her arms over her chest.

"Straight to first-strike nuclear war." Liv shook her head. "You've gotten vicious in your old age."

"Exactly. What'll it be?"

Sighing, Liv handed Nicholas back to his mother. "Fine. I'm sure you know what room I'm in."

Stalking off, Liv headed for her car and the hotel. When she arrived, she waited for Maggie in the lobby.

Maggie looked surprised when she saw Liv waiting. "What's the problem?"

"I figured you'd have a bunch of baby gear and would need help carrying it."

"Tough guy. Total marshmallow in the center." Maggie smiled and handed Nicholas to her along with his baby bag. "Take him on up with you, I'm going back to the car to get his porta-crib."

"Come on, you, you're the best man I've taken to a hotel room ever." Liv kissed his forehead and took him upstairs.

She'd changed a diaper and was singing him some Aretha Franklin when Maggie knocked on the door and moved to set up his crib.

"I'm going to nurse him down. Order me something good to eat and settle in. We have a lot to talk about and I'm staying over."

"Bossy."

"Damned right. Get to it, I'm hungry."

Twenty minutes later, Nicholas was sleeping in the bedroom and the food arrived. Liv cracked open a beer and sat back, looking at Maggie. "So? Go on, tell me."

"You tell me. What kind of stupid shit is this? Moving to Atlanta? Why? Over a stupid misunderstanding with your boyfriend? Even if he had cheated on you, which he didn't, why would a woman like Liv Davis let anyone chase her out of her own damned town?"

"Because that woman can't keep a damned man, Maggie. I don't want to be her anymore. I don't want to be there anymore. I'm making a clean break and starting over here. A new city and a new outlook. I'll find the right man here and I won't have to see Marc Chase's face ever again."

"He loves you, damn it. What you saw was Nancy acting a fool. I talked with the stupid cow a few days ago. She faked a problem with her machine and when he leaned in to help her she grabbed him with her legs. He'd just pushed away from her when you walked in. He was ready to rip a hank off her hide. He's sorry you're hurt. He knows it looked bad but it only *looked* bad. Honey, he loves you. He's been miserable since you've been gone."

"Oh boo hoo. What about me, huh? I couldn't even go to my best friend without her calling Marc. I couldn't talk to my other best friend because she's married to that fink's other brother. My best guy friend is his other damned brother. And I'm in a hotel an hour and a half away and my other two friends finked me out as well. Why does Marc get all the consideration here?"

"I'm sorry! Liv, honey, I am truly sorry I hurt you. I just wanted to help. I know he loves you. I know you love him. I didn't mean to drive you away." Maggie took her hand and squeezed it. "Of all the people in my life, you've been there for me the longest. When no one else loved me, you did. When no one else cared about how I was feeling or how I did on an exam, you did. When no one else remembered my birthday, you did. It breaks my heart that you feel you can't count on me. Please forgive me. Honestly, I can't bear it that you feel you can't trust me."

Liv sighed. "I understand why you did it. I just needed to be alone. I needed to think."

"Well, you haven't been thinking at all if you think moving away is a logical way to deal with this. Do you think Marc is just going to let you walk away? Liv, haven't you heard anything I've said about that night?"

"I have. I heard it from him too via voice mails."

"And?"

"And I don't know. I've been thinking about it and wondering if I believed him but really I suppose the problem is that I have to think about it to begin with."

"What does that mean?"

"I mean if I really trusted him and if he was truly trustworthy, would I have had to think on it for a week? Would I doubt him at all?"

"Liv, you know, I can't do this for you. I can tell you my opinion, which is that Marc is telling the truth. That he loves you. That he's worth trusting. I can also tell you that you love him. But there's something else inside you that you never quite share with me. Doesn't mean I can't see it though. Fear that you're not good enough."

Liv shrugged, feeling the shame of it roil in her gut.

"You act so tough. So in charge and confident but there's

something always in the back of your mind, isn't there? Telling you that you don't deserve forever. So you're going to jump on something like this to keep from taking a big step with a man who is your match. And he is, Liv. These other men, Brody, Matt, you've enjoyed them and had long-term things with them but they weren't your equal. Not the way Marc is. You can't manage him or keep him walled out and that scares you."

Liv chewed her bottom lip, blinking fast to hold back tears. "I want forever. I do."

"I know you do. And you *deserve* it too. But in order to have it, you have to risk your heart and really trust yourself as much as you need to trust Marc. Trust that you deserve to be loved. I had to risk that, risk my heart and take the leap when Kyle came along. I was scared shitless but hell, look at us now. A mortgage, a kid, a mother-in-law who fills my house with so much baby gear I can barely walk. I figure if you marry Marc, she'll spend some of her energy on you and I'll get a break."

"I don't know if I can. If I take him back and he cheats, I don't know if I can survive it. When I saw him there with Nancy like that… I've never in my life felt that kind of pain. Not even when I lost my mother did it feel so awful, so hopeless. I don't want to experience that again." Liv toyed with the food on her plate but didn't eat anything.

"Up until the homecoming picnic, I've never seen you happier. It felt good didn't it? Right?"

Liv thought about it. Had been thinking about it for the last week. "Yes. Yes it did. I felt whole for the first time in my life. But that changed at the picnic because then I began to panic that there was something wrong and he'd dump me any day. I hate feeling like that. It was that way with Matt, just waiting for the other shoe to drop. I want to feel safe. Secure in my relationship. I don't think it's too much to ask."

Maggie nodded. "It isn't too much to ask. Why don't you talk to Marc about all this? See what he says?"

"Because he lied to me, Maggie."

"I told you, he didn't cheat on you."

Liv held up a hand to cut her off. "I know that. I'm pretty sure of it anyway. It was a public place. Plus if he had and I'd busted him, he'd have stopped trying to lie about it after a few days and moved on to another woman."

"Then what are you talking about?"

"The homecoming picnic. There was something wrong and not something about his work. I don't know what exactly it was, but I know he lied about it and I let it go. I let it go because I was afraid and I know now I can't live that way."

"Give him a chance to explain, Liv. He's fallen apart this week without you. You have nothing left to lose. You're already in love with him. Don't run away from the best thing that's ever happened to you. I want you to be happy. You *are* happy with Marc. Don't let fear take this chance at a future with the man you love away from you."

Nicholas woke up then with a cry and Maggie went to get him.

"Does Marc know you're here?" Liv asked as Maggie settled back in to feed the baby.

"He does. He was so worried I wanted to let him know you were safe and that I was coming to see you. He agreed not to come and bother you until I'd spoken to you. Well, after Polly interceded and talked him out of rushing out here to grab you by the hair and drag you home."

Liv laughed. "Yeah, he does have that caveman thing going on. Surprising really. I'd never have suspected it. He always seemed the laid-back skirt chaser. But he's got an iron spine beneath that exterior."

"He's never had to fight for anything he wanted and stood to lose before." Maggie shrugged. "I need to call Kyle and let him know I got here okay. I just texted him when we got here earlier. He was uneasy to have me come to stay the night with Nicholas away from him."

"Go home, Mags. You'll be back in Petal by nine and everyone will feel better. Your husband wants you in his bed tonight and he wants to know that his baby is okay. That's his right and you want that too. I'm not running off again. In fact I'll be back in town by Sunday."

"Really? It's no big deal to stay here. I'm not far away. He knows I'm all right and I want to be here when you need me. I'm still pissed that you ran off."

"Honey, Nicholas is a precious little bundle of fabulous. Take that lumpkin home to his daddy. And tough. I did it for myself."

"You'll talk to Marc?"

"Probably. I don't know."

"But you'll be back by Sunday for sure, you promise?"

Liv held up her pinky. "Pinky swear."

She helped load them into the car and waved them on their way back home.

Chapter Twelve

On her way back from a small shopping trip, Liv stopped at the cemetery near the hospital. Heading to the back corner near the large oak tree, she walked from the car to the headstone.

Laying lilacs down on the marker, she knelt, brushing the dust off the letters that made up her mother's name.

"I have the urge to lay down and start singing a Madonna song, Mom." Liv laughed to herself.

"So there's this guy. Okay, *the* guy. I love him so much it's not funny. This is the same one I told you about the last time I was here and yeah, the time before."

Liv traced a finger over the purple explosion of flowers as she spoke, relating the whole story to herself, wishing her mom really had been there to hear the whole thing and give her advice.

People you loved left you. They died. They moved to Florida. They married and had kids. Things changed and change was scary. If you kept a part of yourself back, protected, it never got hurt. Did it?

Sighing, she arranged the flowers her sister had most likely left and arranged her own with them before standing. Brushing her pant legs off, she walked back to her car, wondering what the price of that little bit of safety was and whether it was worth it.

Head down, bearing packages, she walked down the hall to her hotel room, thinking about all that had happened.

"Let me help you with your burdens."

The caramel drawl made her stop in her tracks and look up. Marc stood in front of her door.

Her eyes took a lazy tour from the toes of his battered cow-boy boots, up the faded denim covering the powerful legs, the deep blue sweater she'd given him on a whim, the face, the handsome set of the jaw, those gorgeous green eyes and the tousled hair. Beautiful. The man was flat-out beautiful.

He held out a hand and gently tugged on the bags she held and she let go, letting him take them while she unlocked the door and held it open for him.

He put them down and turned to face her, saying nothing but his gaze took her in hungrily.

"Oh, sugar." He reached out and traced the curve of her bottom lip with the pad of his thumb. "I've missed you. And here you are with an ache in your eyes that tears at my heart. Will you talk to me?"

"Marc…"

"Olivia Jean Davis, I love you. Damn it, please. Are you going to make me beg? I will. But I'd prefer to ask you and have you agree to talk to me, hear me out."

"Sit." She waved at a chair. "I need to put the bags in the bedroom. I'll be back in a minute."

Marc waited until she'd left the room before heaving a re-lieved sigh. She looked tired and thin and he wanted nothing more than to scoop her into his arms and take care of her. He doubted she'd let him at that point though.

Instead he grabbed the room service menu and flipped through it. Cobbling together an order, he called down and arranged to have it brought up.

She may have looked tired and thin but she was still the

most beautiful thing he'd ever seen. She was there and he was there, at least he'd gotten that far.

Maggie had called to say she wasn't staying over in Atlanta with Liv and Marc had gone over to their house to wait for her to get an update. She didn't tell him a lot and he knew that part of it was that she didn't want Liv to feel betrayed. But she did tell him she thought he still had a chance to make things right between them.

He could have waited for her to come back by Sunday like she'd told Maggie she was planning to. But he didn't want to. He wanted to go to her and lay it all out. They'd hammer things out once and for all and leave together on Sunday morning or he'd leave alone. Okay, he'd leave alone and then work to get her back after trying to convince himself he didn't need her for a few weeks. But they had to work it out, the last walls had to come down between both of them or they'd never be able to move forward.

She came out a few minutes later, having changed into the soft yoga pants she thought he hated. In truth, they made her look even sexier with the way they lovingly hugged her ass and long legs.

Gracefully, she folded herself into the matching chair across from his. "Are you hungry? I haven't eaten since breakfast. We could order up some food if you'd like."

"Did you even eat breakfast? Liv, sugar, you look like you haven't been eating much at all."

She shrugged. He didn't like the dull look in her eyes.

"I took the liberty of ordering us up some dinner and a bottle of wine while you were in the other room. It should be here in a few minutes."

"I'm going to order some chocolate cheesecake. I've been having a slice or two every day." She moved to grab the phone.

"I already did."

"You did? It's got like eight thousand calories in it."

He laughed. "Oh I see. You're trying to agitate me, is that

it? Well, too late, I'm already agitated. You haven't been taking care of yourself. That agitates me. A slice of cheesecake isn't going to kill you. And if you've been eating it daily, it doesn't show."

Snorting, she rolled her eyes.

"I didn't cheat on you."

"I know."

He jerked his head back, surprised. "You know?"

She shrugged.

"What the fuck is that shrug? If you knew I didn't cheat on you why the hell did you bolt?"

"If I want to shrug, I'll shrug. Don't you tell me not to shrug. I'll shrug if I want to." Her chin stuck out defiantly and he fought the ridiculous urge to grin at her. "And I didn't decide to believe that you hadn't cheated until yesterday."

He moved toward her but she put a hand out to stay him. "What? If you know I didn't cheat on you, why aren't we making up right this moment?"

"Because that's not everything and if you don't know that, we're worse off than I imagined."

Room service arrived and set up while she looked out the window. He signed the receipt, tipped the guy and put out the *Do Not Disturb* sign before closing and locking the door.

He moved to stand behind her, lightly resting his hands on her hips, relieved when she let him. "Liv," he laid his head on her shoulder, "I love you. It's killing me that there's this wall between us. Let me in."

"Do you know who first called me Liv?"

He took the opportunity to wrap his arms around her waist and pull her closer. "No. Maggie?"

"My mom. She was Olivia too, you know?"

"I remember that. I don't remember much else about her though."

"My dad, he loved her so much it was like my sister and I barely existed if she was in the room. Anyway, she started calling me Liv to give me something separate from her name, to set us apart a bit."

"How old were you when she died?"

"Thirteen. She got sick when I was eight."

"I'm sorry. It's got to be hard. I can't imagine."

"It was. Anyway, she told me once that her favorite thing about my father was her ability to trust him totally. That she could rely on him no matter what."

Ah, there it was. He'd been wondering why she'd chosen that moment to share that story about her mother.

"Nancy faked a problem with one of the machines and when I..."

"Yes, yes, I know." She moved away and he felt her absence acutely. "I told you, I believe you didn't cheat on me. Believe me, Marc, if I thought you fucked Nancy you'd be coughing up blood right now. Whether or not she'll find herself in that situation if I catch her ass in town is another thing."

"I'm lost, sugar."

"No you're not. And this is seriously pissing me off."

"What the hell are you talking about, Liv? If you know I didn't cheat on you, why are you pissed off?"

"Because I can't trust you, that's why. And you need to get the hell out of here right now if you're going to play stupid."

"You're going to sit and eat and we're going to talk right now." Clenching his jaw, he stalked back to the table and began to uncover dishes.

"You need to cut that bossy shit out right now." She sat and put a napkin on her lap.

"Shut up and eat."

She narrowed one eye at him and he felt better at seeing her spark back, even if it was directed at him.

"I could just say I'm sorry to end this argument but I'd rather know what I'm sorry for."

"You. Lied. To. Me." She took a rather vicious bite of her fish and washed it down with a sip of red wine.

"When did I lie to you?"

The growl she emitted would have been cute if her eyes hadn't looked so dangerously angry.

"On the night of the homecoming picnic. There was something wrong. I *know* there was and I know it wasn't about your stress level like you said. I know it was about me. But I let it go and I shouldn't have. I was a coward because I didn't want to rock the boat and lose you. But the doubts were worse than losing you. You lied to me, Marc."

He sat back, wiping his lips.

"I did. But it wasn't important and it only would have upset you."

"Please go. When I come back to Petal, just leave me alone. It'll be easier if we make a clean break."

"Whoa!" He put his hands up. "What the hell? I'm not leaving and I'm sure as hell not making a clean break. I told you it wasn't important. It wasn't."

"We'll make one if I say so." Her jaw clenched and panic ate at his insides.

"What is it you want, Liv? Tell me and I'll give it to you. I love you, damn it."

"I want your *honesty*, Marc. We're supposed to be partners and you're hiding things. Lying to me and when you're busted you have the audacity to sit there and tell me it was for my own good? It wasn't important enough for you to tell me the truth? Is that what I'd have to look forward to as your girl-friend? Honesty when you decide it's important?"

Oh crap. He was in a corner and it was of his own making.

"The day before the picnic, I bumped into Nancy in town. She came on to me pretty strong. There was a moment, just a moment, when I panicked. Felt a bit smothered and had a bit of a 'man I'm only going to be with one woman for the rest of my life' moment. But it passed in a few minutes and I realized I didn't want to be with anyone else but you for the rest of my life."

She jammed a piece of bread into her mouth, clearly angry. She watched him as she finished off her glass of wine and got herself another glass.

"And when you saw how upset I was that night you told me it was nothing. You didn't think I'd be happy to hear you'd faced a moment of fear and realized you wanted to be with me?"

"I didn't want to spook you! I've been walking on eggshells not wanting to scare you off. I didn't tell you because I wanted to be with you." He shot up and began to pace.

"You lied to me and it's my fault?" She stood up but he pushed her back into her chair.

"Eat, damn you. You can be furious with me *and* eat some food."

"You can't tell me what to do, Marc Chase," she grumbled but forked up another bite of fish and some rice.

"You talk too much," he murmured more because he wanted to poke at her than because he thought so. "It *is* your fault partially. No, sit your pretty ass down. What I mean is that worrying about your reaction to things made me pull punches when I should have just shared. I see how that upset you and made you feel like I wasn't being honest. I was about what really mattered but you're right, honesty is important. But you haven't been totally honest with me either."

"About what?"

"Your doubts. Not the ones at the beginning but your feelings that there was something else and you kept quiet because you didn't want to rock the boat. Is that what you think? That my love for you is so thin that a question would break us up? I'm here, begging you to take me back. Is that what happens with a man who's so shallow he'd break up over a question?"

"And am I so fragile I can't bear hearing the truth?"

"Touché, sugar. So where do we go from here?"

"I don't know. Marc, I love you but at long last I've figured out a few things. I need love from a man who's worthy of me.

And I need him to trust me enough to share all of himself and be honest. Even if he thinks I may not handle what he has to say well. There's got to be trust that the love is strong enough to bear the bumps."

He sighed. "Okay. That's fair. Here's what I propose because you and I are at a stalemate. I can tell you I'm that man and that I'll change and be totally honest from now on but it's clear words alone won't be enough. So let's try this. Give me today and tomorrow. Walls totally down. Complete honesty from each of us. If, when we wake up Sunday morning you don't believe I'm the right man, I'll leave you alone and let you move on."

His heart raced as she remained quiet, finishing up her dinner and mowing through the cheesecake.

He wanted to groan at the sight of her licking the tines of the fork when she'd polished off the last of the cheesecake but relief came when she nodded.

"All right, you have a deal."

Moving to her, he grabbed her wrist and pulled her up against his body. "Well then, if you're finished eating your way through Atlanta, let's get started."

Her gaze met his and he fell in, leapt into her with open arms because she meant everything to him and he wanted her to know it. He sensed her hesitation but she straightened her spine and opened her gaze. The shadows fell away and he saw her fear, her uncertainty and more importantly, her love.

Licking her lips, she exhaled and cleared her throat. "I worry that what you're really attracted to is the novelty. You know, the woman who didn't fall into your bed, thighs wide and begging you to fuck her. The woman who walked away first. Knowing you felt that bit of temptation but realized what we had was bigger, more than what you were giving up, means something to me."

Touched that she'd shared something so intimate, he gave in and kissed each eyelid before replying. "I love you, Liv.

Enough that it's changed me in so many important ways. That day with Nancy, the one I didn't tell you about, it wasn't even that I *was* tempted. The fact is I haven't been tempted by anyone else but you since before I kissed you in April. It was just a moment when I realized that it was us. You and me. And it was forever. You weren't a passing fancy or a novelty. And you did so beg me to fuck you."

She grinned. "You're bad."

"I am. You make me that way."

She snorted. "You were born that way."

"Okay, partially. But you're the key. You unlocked part of me I didn't realize existed until you came along. I never ordered a woman to hold her thighs open while I went down on her or I'd stop. You make me crave pushing you in bed, seeing what your limits are."

"That was pretty hot. I can tell you if any other man had said the same thing to me I'd have held his head with my thighs until he suffocated."

Throwing his head back, he laughed. "There's no one like you, Olivia Davis." And there wasn't.

Need rushed through him. Need to be with her, to share intimacy, to touch and taste her in ways no other man would again. The need to re-establish their bond and connection.

Chapter Thirteen

If he didn't start the sexin', and soon, she'd wither and die. Liv needed him so badly she'd be begging him within moments.

He touched her. Deeply and with a rawness that was both intimate and scary. She wanted these two days to be real, to see the truth of his commitment because she meant what she said. She'd move on with her life because she'd wasted enough time on the wrong men for the wrong reasons.

But she wanted this man. Younger or not, he was the man of her dreams. And she wanted to dare imagining forever with him. But first, she wanted him to fuck her six ways 'til Sunday.

Arching her upper body away from him, she writhed until she got her long-sleeved shirt up and off, tossing it behind her.

"Oh. Well now." His cocky grin made things inside her tingle and then tighten. "It's like that is it?" His shirt followed and in three quick movements her bra was gone. He crushed his upper body to hers, skin to skin. The pleasure shot through her and out her mouth as a groan. Her nipples were diamond-hard, throbbing in time with her clit.

"You feel unbelievably good. I've missed this. I slept every night hugging my pillow but it wasn't the same." Liv's emotion thickened her words but she knew he needed to hear them as much as she needed to say them.

"Girl, I love you. No one ever said anything like that to me before. It disarms me," he murmured against her temple as he pressed hot kisses down her face, over the edge of her jaw to her mouth.

When he finally kissed her, after over a week of absence, she came home, felt the shape and form of a future she'd dared not imagine. His lips covered hers. No gentleness, only barely leashed passion as she opened to him in a gasp and his tongue barged in, taking what was his, had been his for months. He possessed her mouth, ate at it, devoured her, nibbled, licked, nipped and sucked.

Heat shot through her as his tongue flicked against hers, seductive. She'd missed his taste, the way his mouth felt against her own like he was made to be there.

Frissons of heat and pleasure flickered, sparking as his fingertips played at the small of her back, tracing over the indentations on either side of her spine and then along the top of her pants around to her belly button. She groaned as shivers of delight racked her body. He wrecked her, utterly. Small touches and caresses reached into her heart and captured it.

She swallowed his moan when her thumbs played over his collarbone, down the lightly haired chest to his nipples. He arched into her when she scored his nipples lightly with her fingernails and came back to flick her thumbs over them back and forth.

A slight roll of his hips and his cock pressed, hot and hard, against her body. Needing him with great intensity, her hands traced down each ridge of his abdomen and upon reaching his jeans, jerked them open.

One hand at the back of her head, holding her to the kiss, he yanked his jeans off. She heard the dual clunk of his boots and felt the breeze of movement when he threw the jeans over her shoulder. Quick, clever hands shoved her yoga pants down and she stepped out of them, kicking them away. Impatiently, he yanked her panties off. They stood pressed together a few moments, still.

He backed her toward the corner of the room where the small couch stopped her movement.

His mouth left hers and cruised down the column of her throat, across the sensitive skin of her collarbone and down to her nipples. First one and then the other.

With a frustrated sound, one-handed he pressed her breasts together and bent to them, using mouth, teeth and tongue to pay them so much attention she felt orgasm began to build.

Reaching around his body, she grabbed his cock in a sure grip and pumped a fist around him. He thrust hard and the wetness from his pre-come slicked her grip.

Impatient to feel him inside her, she angled him, hiking her thigh around his hip.

"Shit!" He looked into her eyes as he thrust into her waiting heat, naked. His chest heaved. "Oh, sugar, that's so good. No. No don't move. If you move I'm going to come and I'm not wearing a condom."

Taking a deep breath and leaping into the void, hoping like hell he caught her, she writhed provocatively against him and watched as beads of sweat popped out on his forehead. "We're tested, I'm on the pill. If this is forever, make it forever."

"Are you sure?" She saw the toll of his self-control while he made sure she was really okay with it.

Nodding, she tightened her inner muscles around him.

"Damn! That felt good with a condom on, without it you're going to make me come in three seconds. This is a gift, Liv. Thank you." Drawing out of her body nearly completely, he slowly pushed back in, setting a slow, deep rhythm. "Back, let's get you against that wall behind you."

He helped her hop backwards to the wall where she leaned back for purchase while he resumed his pace.

"Your pussy feels so hot and tight. I'm going to have you

so many times it'll burn anyone else out of your brain. Out of your body."

One of his hands cradled her ass while the other did naughty things to her nipple.

"Marc," she let a sob come, "there hasn't been anyone else since you kissed me the first time." Tears rolled down her face and he kissed them away.

"You wreck me. I adore you, everything about you, the good, the bad and the complicated. You're the most beautiful creature I've ever clapped eyes on."

This only made her cry harder as he continued to make love to her. It wasn't gentle or soft, it was unrestrained need unleashed and she felt like a goddess for edging away his control.

One of his hands moved to cup her throat gently, his thumb tracing back and forth over the skin beneath her jaw.

The length of his cock stroked over her clit each time he thrust into her pussy, sending ribbons of hot sensation through her, drawing her closer and closer to orgasm.

"Open your eyes, Liv. I want to see that moment when they blur and I lose you just a bit when you come. You're close, I can feel your pussy flutter around me. It's so good."

She dragged her eyes open and met his gaze, snared, helpless to do anything but feel as he stroked her closer and closer, the pleasure growing sharper and sharper with each moment.

Her breath grew shallow and suddenly it swallowed her whole, the wave of climax that had been building. Mouth open on a hoarse gasp of his name, her gaze was still locked with his even as her vision blurred a bit and she fell away, letting the rush of endorphins sweep her up and ride her.

Moments later, she blinked and found him smiling at her. "Beautiful. Now me." His fingers dug into the muscle and flesh of her ass as he pressed hard and deep and came, his gaze still with hers.

The depth of connection, of intimacy at staring into his eyes as he came clutched deep, pulled at her, tied her to him in ways she hadn't imagined. Seeing him in a moment of emotional and physical vulnerability and having him give it to her freely swelled her heart as she loved him more than she thought possible.

Breaking their gaze, he dropped his head to her shoulder as he caught his breath for a few moments.

"Right. This is a pretty swanky hotel. Is the bathtub big enough for two?"

She laughed. "I don't know. I hadn't thought about it. Let's go see."

Marc went back out into the living room to grab the wine. He'd never experienced a sexual interlude so intimate before, not even with Liv. She gave him everything without holding back.

And being naked inside her had been earth-shattering. He'd never been inside a woman without a condom before and her trust in him, in giving him such a gift, was unsettling. But in a good way.

He realized she was serious about letting the walls down and he had to give it back to her in equal parts. He knew how to seduce her body but he had to remember part of this was in showing her he loved every part of her, not just the sex part.

Grinning, he picked up the phone and called the concierge desk.

She looked up at him from her perch in the rather large tub, naked and glistening. He honestly thought his brother Matt was the biggest idiot ever breathing to let this woman go.

He handed her a glass of wine and put his next to the tub as he climbed in behind her and pulled her back to his chest. "How you could have not seen this bathtub as a sex spectacular is beyond me."

"I wasn't thinking of sex when I came here."

"I'm sorry. I'm sorry that my not telling you about the Nancy thing led to all this complication."

"I'm sorry you felt like you had to walk on eggshells, Marc."

"That wasn't entirely fair of me to use that. Yes, I did feel hesitant about sharing it for the reasons I told you but I can't argue that you didn't have reasons not to be wary. I'd just worked so hard to prove I was genuinely in love with you, I didn't want to give you any reason to doubt that."

She turned and wrapped her thighs around him, pulling close.

"This is nice. You're very limber. I admire that in a woman."

Laughing, she took a sip of her wine before setting it on the side of the tub. "I'm going to have a 'come to Jesus' talk with Nancy when I get back to Petal."

Marc chuckled. "You won't be the first. Cassie got hold of her first, then Maggie, I think Matt and Kyle too. Oh and my momma."

Liv winced. "I almost feel sorry for her for that. Almost."

"Don't. She thought she'd *test* my commitment to you. She's sorry but it's not enough."

Liv grinned and leaned in to kiss his chin.

"What was that for?"

"You didn't take her side."

He laughed at that outright. "Do I look crazy? Sugar, she nearly broke us up because she acted like a selfish bitch. Her being sorry doesn't erase that. I almost lost the best thing that ever happened to me. I nearly kicked her butt myself."

"Hmpf."

"I like this side of you."

"The side where my goodies are?"

Lord how she made him laugh. "Well, that too. But I meant the possessive, slightly feral side. Not that you have anything to worry about. You don't. Liv, I'd never cheat on you. In the first place, I love you. In the second, I have honor."

"Well, I have to deal with an awful lot of female attention your way. Which sucks. I mean, it was bad with Matt but you're worse. You're a very flirty man. Women, some women, tend to purposely misunderstand that and take it for an invitation. I don't like it but I don't think you're fixin' to cheat on me. Let me just tell you, a knee in the junk is the least that'll happen to you if you really do cheat on me."

He winced but couldn't deny the viciousness in her eyes was a turn-on. Man he was sick.

"Liv, sugar, I'm going to make a real effort not to be so flirty with other women. I don't want you being bothered by it and I don't want you to feel disrespected, nor do I want to send the wrong signals. It's something I do on autopilot. This is all sort of new to me, the being-hopelessly-in-love-with-the-most-beautiful-woman-in-the-world thing. I'm learning as I go."

"I don't want you to give up who you are."

"You think flirting with women is who I am?"

She rolled her eyes. "No. But I don't want to change you. I just want to try and find a way we can be together without either one of us having to give up who we are."

He soaped a washcloth and began to minister to her, enjoying the way she arched into his touch like a cat.

"Olivia, woman, you are exasperating sometimes. Just when I think you're doing one thing, you go and do or say something that shows me just how unselfish and giving you are. You have such a tough exterior and it's all bullshit. You're a marshmallow, aren't you?"

"I am not. I am a hard-assed bitch. Ask anyone."

He pushed her back playfully and she ducked under the water and got to her knees to return the favor and soap him up.

"I have asked and that's not anyone's impression of you at all. Well, except the mayor and that's good. He should be scared of you. Maybe his crush on you will wear off. I have to deal with male attention your way too, you know."

He watched as she stood and grabbed a towel before stepping out. "He's just lonely, that's all. And I don't come equipped with a harem but if you see me flirting or you feel uncomfortable about the way I interact with anyone, please tell me. I'd hate for you to feel bad."

Standing, he got her wet again as he embraced her.

A knock sounded on the door and he held a hand out. "I'll be right back."

"What are you up to?" she called out.

"Hold your horses."

She got dressed in the bedroom and peeked out to see what he was up to.

"Nosy. Come on out and bring a blanket."

"What?" She grabbed a blanket and skipped toward him.

He caught her, laughing, picking her up and she wrapped her legs around him. "Now that's the kind of leg wrapping I approve of."

He kissed her quickly and put her down on the couch.

"I had them bring up some DVDs and some snacks."

"You did?"

"Yeah. The *Matrix* movies and those weird chocolate things with the white stuff you like."

"Sno-Caps? Where? Gimme!"

He put in the first movie and came back to the couch, handed her the box of candy and settled in beside her.

"You remembered I liked Sno-Caps. That's one of the sweetest things anyone has ever done."

"It's candy, sugar, while I'm content to hog up credit that'll get me laid later, it's not that big a deal." Smiling, he put his arm around her shoulder and tucked the blanket around them both.

But it was a big deal. He noticed something small and seemingly inconsequential. They'd only gone to the movies once and she'd gotten the candy there. And the movies he'd gone to the trouble to get? She had just a teeny celebrity crush on Keanu Reeves.

The sex had blown her mind but the movies and the chocolate had shown her he'd noticed more about her than her bra size. It occurred to her she needed to be more mindful of what he liked too. She hadn't been as aware of things as she should have been, or at least she hadn't shown him. If they were to make a go of their relationship it was up to her to do her part as well.

As she snuggled into his side, she let hope settle into her bones. Hope that just maybe, Marc was more than her future, *they* were the future.

Breathing heavily, Marc rolled off Liv's sleep-warm body and onto his back beside her. With a feline smile, she stretched, leaning over to kiss his chest over his heart.

"That was a very inspired good-morning, Marc Chase."

"What can I say? You inspire me," he gasped out.

"Don't you need to get back to your clients? I feel bad that you're here when you have a business to run."

"You're more important to me than that. I couldn't have waited until tomorrow for you to come back to town. I wanted you to know I didn't betray you, wanted you to know how much I love you. One of my buddies from my old gym has taken my clients until Monday so that's not a problem." He cocked his head. "But thank you for asking, for thinking of it."

"I love you. Your business is important to you so it's important to me. Now get up. We're going to breakfast and then I have somewhere I'd like to take you."

They quickly got up and dressed and headed out, hand in hand. She drove him out of the city center, to a greasy spoon the likes of which she'd rarely seen anywhere else. But an older hippie couple owned and ran it so she knew firsthand they had healthy offerings too. When her mother had been in the hospice during those last seven months, she often snuck away to come to this place to get away from the pain and death. Every time she came to Atlanta in the twenty years since, she'd stopped in and it had become a part of her in a sense. A refuge.

He gave her a skeptical look when she pulled in.

"Stop. Trust me."

He took her hand and they walked in together. "I do. With all my heart if not my cholesterol."

"Livvie! How are you, darlin'?"

"I'm well, Rain. And you?" Liv kissed the cheek of the bird-thin woman with short white hair.

"Pretty darned good. And who is this fine-looking specimen?"

"This is my boyfriend, ugh, that's such a weird term for an adult woman to use, anyway, this is Marc Chase. Marc, this is Rain Scott. She and her husband Pete own this place."

Smiling and turning on the charm, Marc shook her hand.

"Boyfriend huh? That's nice to hear. Well, let's get you to a table. Coffee will be up in a moment." Rain handed them menus and they sat near the windows overlooking a side vegetable garden.

Liv watched him through her lashes as he opened up his menu and his face changed.

"Sneaky." He grinned her way.

She shrugged. "I knew you'd like it. The food here is really good."

"And healthy. Thank you."

"I like to eat healthy too, you know."

He took her hand and kissed her knuckles. "I like you. How did you find this place? It's sort of off the beaten path."

She told him and noted that he was touched.

After breakfast, she took him to the cemetery. "I know this is sort of weird but when I'm here in Atlanta, I come by. My dad buried her here. The hospice she spent the last year of her life in is just across the way. She'd look out the window at these big oak trees and say that's where she wanted to rest. I don't think he ever denied her anything. I wish she was in Petal but he's bought the plot next to hers and my sister lives here now anyway." She got quiet, looking off into the distance.

Marc stopped and stared at her, turning her chin so she

faced him. "I don't know what to say. I'm amazed that you'd share this with me."

"You are? Have I been so selfish with you?"

Marc felt the gulf between them again but determined to push through it. "No. It's not that. But you've kept a lot of stuff to yourself. I guess I'm just seeing how much I didn't see, didn't know."

"Okay. That's fair I guess."

Her shoulders dropped and he felt like an asshole. He hadn't meant to make her feel bad. In fact, he was touched she'd brought him there. But she hadn't talked about her mom much before and he realized there was so much he didn't know about her.

"Liv, I'm sorry. I didn't want to make you feel guilty or lacking."

"You feel how you feel."

He sighed. "Eggshells here, Liv. I'm just expressing my surprise. I want to be able to be honest with you but I'm going to hold back if I hurt you."

"I don't want to do this here. Let's go."

He stopped her, grabbing her hand. "Honey, this is going to be a work in progress. You know that. We can't make things right if you just give up. First things first. I'm honored, truly, that you'd share this with me. Let's go and visit your mother and then we can talk." He tried to show her how much he loved her, wanted her to see it in his eyes.

Keeping her hand in his, he followed her across the quiet grass to the flat, pale stone. They knelt together and he nearly gasped when he saw the name. He *knew* it was her mother but seeing Olivia's name on a headstone gave him a start.

"I know. It's odd isn't it? My father told me shortly after my mother died, that it was hard for him to come here because he thought of me every time."

Her voice was quiet, soft, and he put his arm around her shoulder.

"She was only thirty-five when she died. So young." A shiver ran through him again at the comparison.

"I'm now older than she was when she died. She passed two days after her birthday. And yet she had two children and a marriage when she died. I have none of that."

He remained quiet. Not because he didn't have something to say about that but because her mother's grave wasn't the place to say it.

"Lilacs and lilies. Pretty." He indicated the flowers there.

"My sister is most likely the source of the lilies. I brought the lilacs. They're out of season but I know this little florist not too far away and I call ahead and he orders them for me. My mom loved them. She wanted to name my sister Lilac." Liv laughed. "I know. Well, Susan lucked out I think."

"She was the year behind me in school so I don't know her very well. Not well enough to really get a feeling about whether she'd be a Lilac or not. But she doesn't seem like one." In truth, Liv's sister had been pretty wild back in the day. They hadn't run in the same circles but she'd gotten around quite a bit, partied pretty hard, got into trouble.

They stood and walked back to the car, driving back to the hotel quietly. He realized just how complicated his woman was. She was so confident on the outside but each layer he uncovered showed him a wounded heart. It began to settle in that this issue between them was bigger than the Nancy thing. He was also pretty sure Liv herself hadn't realized it just yet. He'd have to confront it and make her see it. It wouldn't be easy, he had the feeling there'd be more tears before the breakthrough, but he needed to be steadfast so they could build their future. He meant to have her as his wife and the mother of his children and that meant she had to accept he wasn't going anywhere.

She spoke then, pulling him out of his thoughts. He looked at her as she walked through the room, the grief on her face.

"She's not. A Lilac, I mean. She's had a lot of problems but in the last few years she's straightened herself out. I suppose you know that, as you two were in school together the way you were. Getting away from Petal was good for her. She's here in Atlanta now. Got married two years ago, has two kids."

She sat on the couch and put her feet up.

"You're not close." It was hard for him to imagine not being close to a sibling.

"We are in our own way. Susan was young when our mom died. Seven. It was harder on her because pretty much all of her memories of our mother were of her being sick. I had her for longer, it affected me differently. And I had Maggie. By that point neither one of us had a mother. Hers wasn't dead but may as well have been for all the attention Maggie ever got from her. My dad sort of checked out. Gave up expending emotion. He never neglected us, we had a nice place to live, he came to our plays and school stuff. But when he moved to Florida ten years ago, it wasn't like there was much of a difference in my life. He's happier now I think because the memories are farther away."

"I'm sorry. I can't imagine not being close to my family. But I'm glad you and Maggie had each other." And he began to understand her more with each bit of her life she exposed. "So, why haven't you shared any of this before now?"

She sighed heavily. "Marc, it's not like I was hiding it. But I don't just take my dates out to the cemetery ninety minutes away to show them my mother's grave. I've never shown anyone her grave. It doesn't matter, she's been dead over twenty years. I shouldn't have taken you today, it was a stupid impulse."

"What? Stupid? For you to open up to me? Is that what you think? Sharing with me is stupid?"

"Oh get off your fucking self-righteous high horse, Marc. Here's a clue, I'm not perfect. And here's another, neither are you. I don't come from some perfect, *Leave It to Beaver* life. My mom didn't greet me at the door with cookies when I got home from school. My sister was a drunk by fifteen and my mother died when I was thirteen. I don't have family dinners every Sunday and hang out with my family on purpose."

"Stop it. I'm on to you, Liv. You get all bitchy when people get close to keep 'em back. It's not going to happen with me. I'm in this with you for the long haul. And yes, you do have family dinners every Sunday. With my family, who are now your family. And you're going to have to deal with that. You can get close to people, Liv."

She winced and he knew he'd hit home on that one. "Oh man, is this going to get all *Oprah*?"

He knew her game and didn't let her get to him. It was all a front.

"You can't love on your terms, you know. That's not how it works. Love, real love, makes demands. You have to give, compromise. You have to let yourself be vulnerable."

"Oh man. And what about you? Mr. perfect family and well-adjusted emotions, what do you have to give up? Your pussy buffet? If you're so fabulous why've you been fucking your way through every female in town for years?"

He waved that away. "Sharp-tongued bitch. You don't scare me, Liv. I've seen your underbelly. And I love you anyway. Do you hear that? I love you. I'm not leaving. Stop it. Let it all go because I'm not going to walk out that door because you're not perfect. And death isn't desertion. She couldn't help it and you didn't give her cancer. Your father was weak but he's human. You survived and you're a strong woman worthy of love and respect. I love you. Maggie loves you. That baby adores you, Liv. He lights up when he hears your voice. My family loves you. Your friends love you."

Tears ran down her face as she stood and began to pace. He watched her from his chair, wanting to go to her but realizing they needed to play this out until she let it all go. This was the issue, not his omission of the thing with Nancy, not his flirting, not his former skirt-chasing ways. Those things were part of it, yes, but it was her flat-out terror that everyone she loved she would lose because she wasn't worthy. That was a huge burden for one person to carry and he planned to knock it off her shoulders, even if he made her cry to do so.

"I'm not a charity case, Marc. Is that it? The novelty of fixing me?"

"You'd like to think so. That way you could blow off what's between us and continue to hold yourself back or keep hooking up with men you can control and never commit to fully." He shrugged. "You can't control me, Liv. I'm your equal. Snuck in there, didn't I? I didn't quite get that until I was way too far gone in love with you. I suppose I have my own share of emotional shit to shovel."

Her hair stuck up from the way she kept running her hands through it and tugging at it. She looked like a pretty porcupine. It made him smile and she made a distressed sound. "What? What are you smiling at, Dr. Phil?"

He chuckled. "I love your sense of humor. I was smiling because I like looking at you. You're cranky when you're on the ropes."

"Oh man, now you're going to be patronizing on top of judgmental and self-righteous?"

"I'm not judgmental, Liv. I'm in no position to judge you, even if I wanted to. And I'm not self-righteous. I understand you. Drives you nuts too. We're going to fight you know. It's part of who we are. But fighting won't change how much I love you. You can blow your top and throw a tantrum and I'm still going to love you." His father's advice some months back really hit home, then.

"Matt and I never fought."

"Yeah, and that turned out well, didn't it?" Ruthlessly, he had to push past his need to soothe her to keep going. "Come on, Liv. Putting Matt between us isn't going to work. He doesn't want to be there, first of all. Which is his mistake because losing you has to be the most asinine thing he's ever done and believe me, I've known him my whole life and he's done a lot of asinine things. And secondly, I'm not threatened. What you and I have is *real*. It's messy and complicated and frustrating, but that's what love is. You fucked my brother for a while. And the fact that he didn't love you isn't about you being lacking. It's about his own shit and your total incompatibility outside of bed. You're a rock star in bed, Liv. I know you know that. But so what? It's not everything and you know it. So after a while, people fall away because you can't live on fucking alone. Brody is a douchebag and never was good enough for you and all the others have been the same. But I'm not them and you can't hide from that."

She stared at him, openmouthed, and he leaned back in his chair. "You can't work me, Liv. I know you're a bitch, I know you're cranky, I know you're loving, I know you're smart and funny, I know you're giving and generous. I'm not walking off because you're not flawless. I don't want a diamond, I want a wife." He smiled when she paled.

The man was infuriating! Liv snorted and resumed pacing. "You don't want a wife, Marc."

"Yes I do. I want you to marry me. Normally, I'd ask you on Christmas, it's a family tradition, you know. But instead I'm asking you right now. We can get married on Christmas instead. Yeah, the more I think about it, the better it sounds. What do you say?"

"You're asking me to marry you in the middle of a fight? Are you out of your mind?" Her heart thundered as hope warred with terror.

"Liv, I lost my mind when I kissed you on Founder's Day. We've established that already. That night when I first touched your lips I knew. I fought it for a while but it was useless so I gave in. And I didn't want to resist you anymore anyway. It's funny but I don't think I truly knew just how much I loved you until today when you took me to your momma's grave. Because not only did you share that with me but it opened up that last barrier, the big one. People you love leave you."

Grief, rage, fear and the ember of hope he'd stoked burst through her and a sob tore from her lips. "You don't know anything!" But he did. Damn it, he did. How is it that he did and she didn't?

Is this what people meant when they referred to a moment of clarity? Everything fell away then as she stood, weeping, letting it all rush through her. Jesus. He was right. Maggie was in her heart because they'd been friends before she lost her mother and how could she not love Nicholas when he came from the sister of her heart? But even Cassie and Dee she'd kept from loving fully. Matt, sweet wonderful Matt, had never been right for her but he hadn't been a challenge to be with. In the end she'd left because she knew he'd never love her but holy crap, she'd never really loved him either, not totally. She'd thought she had but as she compared it to the way she felt for Marc, it was a shallow, pale thing.

How is it that she never really confronted this? How could she not have known? She knew she had a basic fear when people around her got sick but this was huge. Man, like self-help book huge. And Marc saw it. He saw it and he confronted it and he fought it. For her.

Dimly, she realized she'd slid to the floor and he'd moved closer, his hand on her thigh. "Let it go, baby. I'm not going to leave you. I love you. I adore you. You're worth everything, don't you see that? I didn't leave you. I came after you. I will always work for you, for us. Because, Liv, that's what real love is. I can't guarantee I won't die." She caught his shrug through the veil of her tears. "That's beyond my ability to promise. But I'm a healthy guy, I work out, I eat right, I wear sunscreen and I want decades of happiness with you. All things that are in my favor long-life-wise. And being with you will keep my mind sharp because you're a pain in the ass. A beautiful pain in the ass and worth it, but crotchety, cranky, defended, defensive and sulky sometimes too."

"Is that supposed to be flattery?"

"Nope." He kissed her forehead and pressed some tissues into her hands. "It's honesty."

In a rush, she threw her arms around him, clutching him tight. "I love you so much, Marc."

He stood, still holding her tight. "And I love you, Liv. You gonna make an honest man out of me? You haven't said anything about my proposal. I don't have a ring. I've been looking but I planned on asking you in a few months at Christmas. We'll get right on that. Well, after we have sex, because that's necessary."

"Sex first." Fear still lived in her heart, even as she tried to beat it back.

"Nope. I'm not some floozy who'll just sleep with any old gal. I need a promise of marriage first. For my honor and all."

She laughed and the fear loosened its hold. Taking a deep breath, she looked him in the eyes and defied the fear of losing him. "Okay. You can't dump me when I get old though. I forbid it. You made your bed by marrying an older woman."

"Deal. Wow, you've made me a very happy man." He started walking toward the bedroom.

"You saw it all, Marc. You saw inside me, past the bullshit and you loved me anyway." She started crying again.

"Because you're the best thing that's ever happened to me. And you know my flaws too. Yeah I did fuck my way through every woman in town. I do have some issues about living in the shadow of the Chase men. Trying to act like it doesn't matter so I never really treated myself like I mattered. Not emotionally anyway. You knew that about me and you loved me anyway. How lucky am I?"

"Not as lucky as you're going to get in a few minutes."

Marc sat back on the bed and looked her up and down. "Absolutely the most beautiful woman I've ever seen. Inside and out. Take your clothes off for me, sugar."

She toed off her shoes and socks and then stood straight, her gaze on him. Sliding her hands up her torso, she smiled when his eyes widened as she paused to trail her fingertips over her nipples. Slowly, she slid each button loose until the front of her sweater was open and she let it drop.

"I love that bra. You need a dozen more."

A quick flick and she popped the catch between her breasts and let the bra follow the blouse.

"Now, I don't normally get crass in the presence of such a fine lady and all, but your tits are fabulous."

She chuckled and traced the nipples, round and round until her breath hitched and his eyes widened, glued to her movement.

"Hoo boy, that's hot." His hands convulsed a few times on his thighs like he wanted to touch her.

Catching her bottom lip between her teeth, she moved her hands to her jeans, lowering the zipper and bending forward to pull them off.

She turned to grab a chair and moved it to the foot of the bed. A quick yank on each side of her panties and the ties loosed and they fell away, leaving her totally naked.

In for a penny. She sat, hooking a leg up on the arm of the chair. His aroused groan emboldened her and she met his gaze.

"Go on then, sugar. Show me how you like to be touched."

"First, take your clothes off. I want you to have your cock handy."

He took a slow breath and got to his knees to get rid of the sweater and then shimmied out of jeans, socks and underwear. Reclining, he put some pillows behind his back and raised an eyebrow at her. "Your move."

Liv couldn't believe she was going to do this in front of him but she felt so sexy she couldn't stop. He made her feel wanton and she liked that a lot.

Wetting a fingertip with her tongue, she moved back to her nipples pinching and rolling them until her breathing grew shallow and she felt her pussy slicken in response.

"Touch your pussy, Liv. I can see how wet you are. I want

you to know while you're doing it that my tongue will be there later on. I'm going to eat you until you can't come anymore. Over and over again. I love your taste."

Wow. Her entire body tightened at that. She knew he'd do it too. And boy did she look forward to it.

One hand slid down her belly, her fingertips lightly grazing her labia, teasing them both until she could no longer stand it. She slid her fingers into the wet flesh, finding her clit swollen. Without even meaning to, her hips lurched forward when she touched it. She wouldn't be long, she wanted him too much and was already very close.

He crawled off the bed and knelt on the floor between her thighs. "Keep going. I just wanted a better view." He laid his head on her thigh and reached out to hold her wide open.

She was too far along to be shy so she covered her clit with her thumb and slid two fingers deep. Both of them moaned softly as she began to roll her hips.

Closer and closer, her clit hardened and her pussy grew wetter, hotter. He blew over that humid flesh and she cried out, sliding her thumb back and forth over her clit as she climaxed.

The muscles in her body were still jumping when she found herself picked up and dropped into his lap, pussy sliding down onto his cock as he'd sat where she had in the chair.

"I know I said I'd go down on you, and I will soon. But I had to be inside you right this minute. I've never in my life seen anything sexier. I'm so damned close I thought I'd come while I watched you. But I'd rather come inside you. Just an appetizer to take the edge off. Ride me, sugar."

Squeezing her knees between the outside of his thighs and the chair, she rose and fell on him. Electric pleasure arced up her spine each time he filled her fully. Her hands rested on his chest for balance and his roved her body, played with her nipples, kneaded her thighs and shoulders, caressed her face and ran through her hair.

She tightened herself around him, adding a swivel each

time she took him into her completely. She knew he wasn't lying when he said he was almost there, his thighs trembled. Satisfaction that he'd been so aroused by her so completely roared through her.

Bending to him, she kissed his upturned lips. "I love you, Marc. For seeing all of me and loving me anyway." She increased her speed. "And for saying I was a rock star in bed."

His laugh died into a gasp of her name as she felt him come, his fingers tightening on her hips just this side of pain.

Standing, he took them both to the bed and they collapsed in a heap. "I can't do anything else but love you, Liv. I was meant to do it. Born to."

Chapter Fourteen

Liv and Marc walked into the Chases' front foyer the next evening. They hadn't told anyone they were back and they'd had a few errands so they'd returned from Atlanta the day before to finish them.

Polly came around the corner, distracted, reading glasses perched on her nose. She stopped when she caught sight of them both. "Oh! You're back. Honey, welcome back." She rushed to Liv and hugged her tight.

"Thank you. It's okay that I'm here?"

Polly frowned a moment. "I can't believe you'd ask that. Of course. It's more than okay. You're supposed to be here. It's Sunday night and that's family dinner and you're family." She grinned at Marc. "I'm going to go add two more places to the table. Go on through, everyone's in the living room."

Marc winked at Liv as they walked back and into the room where the rest of the family had gathered.

Maggie called out a pleased hello and Liv was engulfed by hugs from Shane, Kyle, Edward, Matt and Cassie. Nicholas made piercing cries, demanding her attention, and she got to all fours next to where he'd rolled over and pushed himself up on his blanket.

"Dude, you're an amazing little genius aren't you? Rolling over and pushing up! Pretty soon it'll be eating your first Cheerio and sitting up. Then college."

He grinned at her as he lost his balance and rolled back over. Sitting up, she picked him up and rained kisses all over his face.

"I think I'm jealous," Marc said as he dropped a kiss on the top of Nicholas's head. "She likes you more than me, kid."

"Uh, Liv?" Maggie moved closer.

"Don't, not yet. Wait until Polly gets in here or there'll be hell to pay," Liv murmured.

Maggie just kissed her square on the mouth and grinned.

"Wait, can we see that again?" Matt said and Edward bopped him with a pillow.

"Lamb? I think you need to come on in here," Edward called out.

Polly click-clacked into the room and smiled at the sight. "What is it, Edward? The potatoes are done and I was getting ready to smash them."

"You were supposed to tell me so I could do it, Mom." Cassie frowned at her.

"Oh I was right there. But you can now." Polly laughed.

Liv handed Nicholas to his mother and let Marc pull her to standing.

"We have an announcement to make." Marc put his arm around her waist. "Liv and I are engaged."

Polly whooped so loud Nicholas began to cry but only for a moment as every adult within reach swooped in to kiss or comfort him. Assured he was the center of the universe again, he calmed down.

Polly hugged both Marc and Liv to her tight, followed by Edward and then everyone else.

"I can't believe I didn't even see that ring," Polly sniffled and looked at the pretty diamond engagement ring on Liv's left hand.

"We just got it this afternoon. I moved into Liv's house

last night. Well, mostly. I figured you all could help with the big stuff."

"Into our house you mean."

Marc smiled at Liv and she felt like a princess.

"When's the wedding?"

"Christmas Day. I know it's an odd day but I like the connection to tradition and I'll never forget our anniversary that way." Marc laughed.

"Christmas? That only gives us eight weeks!" Polly looked aghast.

"We want it simple, Momma. We'd like to do it here if that's okay with you. Just family, like we'd do anyway. We don't need catering except for the cake because we'd have dinner here as it is."

"Is it okay? Of course it's okay! My goodness, congratulations to you both. Olivia, welcome to the family, honey. And Marc, you've done well." Edward nodded at his son.

"I owe it to you, Dad. You raised me right and gave me some great advice."

"He did, did he? And what advice was that?" Liv grinned.

"To never share his advice with my fiancé."

After dinner when the women were all chattering about wedding details, Marc sat with his brothers and his father, watching a football game.

"You chose well, son. I mean that. Olivia is a good woman. She'll be a fine wife and keep you on your toes."

"Thank you, Dad. I think so too. I hope you know I'll be coming to you for advice lots and lots."

Edward laughed. "Marc, I still go to my daddy for advice about your momma." He looked to Matt. "You're next. I had a dream about you last night."

Matt looked surprised. "Well, is it going to be one of their exes? Because we sure do seem to find women for each other in this family."

"True. But I don't know who it'll be. I just saw cookies and not in a euphemistic sense. Actual cookies. Damned if I know what that means."

"Maybe Matt needs to hang out at The Honey Bear because his future wife is a baker." Shane laughed.

"Or a Girl Scout troop leader." Marc stood and stretched. "Well, gentlemen, I have to take my fiancée home. She has to go back to work tomorrow, as do I. Shane, don't forget that we're upgrading your workout on Tuesday."

Liv met him in the hallway and for a moment there was nothing else but her face and the way she looked at him. She grinned and he laughed, grabbing her and jogging out the door into the night full of possibilities.

* * * * *

Making Chase

Author Note

Hey there, all you lovely reader friends!

Way back in 2006 I got an idea that I knew I couldn't sell to the publisher I had been with at the time, so I took a chance on a new publisher and a new editor with my small-town contemporary romance.

Twelve years later, the Chase Brothers series has been reissued, but with the same beloved editor, Angela James, who continues to kick my butt and make me a better writer.

I've done very little to change these books. Some grammatical stuff here and there, but though I like to think my writing has come a long way in those intervening dozen years, I wanted to keep these the way they were. The heart of the stories is unchanged. The heart of this group of friends and family is unchanged.

The Chases remain a personal favorite of all the books I've written and it's always a pleasure to see them reach new readers even now. If you're a new reader to the series, welcome to Petal! I hope you enjoy your stay. If you're returning, welcome back!

Either way, I'm glad you're here.

Lauren

Chapter One

Tate Murphy sat in the comfy chair at her station, sipping coffee and looking out the window. It was a Saturday in the very beginning of February. Winter had been cold but spring was beginning to imagine itself. The trees carried buds, heavy with leaves, and the air wasn't quite as chilly as it'd been even a week before.

All in all, a lovely day. Soon to be even lovelier. One leg crossed over the other, foot slowly kicking back and forth, she waited for her morning visual donut. Matt Chase.

Ah, there he was. *Hot damn*, her body lit up when he pulled his truck into the lot adjacent to the salon. Hopping out, he hefted a duffel bag over one shoulder and loped across the street.

"Good Lord the man looks good enough to eat," Tate murmured as she took a drink of her coffee. Faded jeans showed off long legs and a nice, trim booty. A hoodie sweatshirt fended off the cold but didn't stop her from seeing the work-hard body beneath. He was in dire need of a haircut and she had no trouble admitting she'd love to get her fingers in it. A bit shaggy, it curled up just around his ears and touched the back of his collar. A color like burnt sugar.

Although he had on cool-looking sunglasses, she knew the

eyes beneath were a light green, fringed with chocolate lashes. Mmm. Mmmm. Mmmm.

"Ah, I see his hotness has arrived." Anne, co-owner and her next youngest sister, stood beside her, leaning into the chair.

"Kinda makes me want to set a fire," Tate said, one corner of her mouth lifting.

"Um, I smell something burning already. Your panties perhaps?"

Blushing furiously, she spun, laughing at Anne's outrageous comment. "I'm gonna light a candle for you. Three."

Anne joined her in laughter. "You just about raised me, I expect I need all the help I can get."

"Hey, divas, did I miss him?" Beth, the last owner and next youngest sister after Anne approached to refill everyone's coffee cup.

"Yeah, he just went inside. But there's always lunchtime." Sated for the morning, Tate stood and began to get all her tools in order, making sure her station was stocked and ready for the day.

Four years before, Tate and Anne had decided to buy the run-down old house at the far end of Main Street and renovate it into a hair salon. They'd scrimped, saved, worked multiple jobs and got the down payment together and then had spent months doing the renovation work themselves. Luckily, they had a large, and free, workforce. With eight Murphy kids and two spouses to help, they'd been able to paint, knock out walls, drywall, replace the plumbing, landscape, and apply for all the proper permits and licenses. Hell, they'd even put up a new roof. A few months after Anne graduated from beauty school, Tate left her old salon in Riverton and they opened the doors to Murphy's Cuts and Curls.

Two years after that, Beth came in as part owner and ran the business end of things. The salon was a family affair. Beth had been helping out with the books when she'd offered to buy in at a smaller share. The place would wither and die without her to, well, do everything that needed doing. Not only did she handle the books and deal with ordering supplies but if someone needed a shampoo she could do that too.

Truthfully, Tate had wanted a fancier name but their youngest sister, Jill, who was getting her degree in marketing, told them that if they kept the name folksy but not too cutesy, it'd make people more comfortable.

Jill must have had something, because from the moment they'd opened, they'd done a brisk business. Women stopped leaving town to get their hair done. Tate and Anne offered everything from the giant hairspray helmet the women like Polly Chase preferred to the stylish razor cuts her daughter-in-law Liv currently sported. It made Petal seem a friendlier place to Tate, who always had felt an outsider there.

Tate made a decent living. Enough that she'd been able to help Tim and her other siblings pay tuition at the University of Georgia for their two youngest siblings. Before that, she worked to pay for her younger brother Nathan's college and master's in teaching. They'd all worked together to help out when the others had needed it and that's what counted.

"Anne, your first client of the day is a color, I'll send her over to Tate for the cut," Beth announced as she made another pot of coffee.

Tate looked at the place she and her sisters had built from the ground up and pride swelled her heart.

Matt tossed his clothes into the hamper with his name on it and headed toward the showers. He'd been up for sixteen hours and was dead on his feet. Too bad he didn't have the luxury of sleeping, one of the other guys at the station had been injured at the fire they'd just put out and Matt needed to fill in for him.

As he quickly cleaned up, the scent of freshly brewing coffee cut through the steam, waking his senses. When he stumbled out into the main living area on the second floor of the firehouse, he saw his older brother Shane waiting for him.

"I heard about Tony getting hurt." Shane's voice was gruff as he handed Matt a cup of coffee. Matt knew it was Shane's way of making sure he was unhurt.

"He'll be all right. Jim had some smoke inhalation so he's at the hospital too, just to get checked out. I wasn't in the part of the house where the beams collapsed so I'm lucky."

"Here, Momma sent this over. She wanted to come herself, you know how she is. But Daddy intercepted her and I promised to bring it." Shane quickly covered his grin with a pathetic attempt at hunger as he handed a series of sealed containers to Matt.

"Come on, get that hangdog look off your face. I'm sure there's enough for five of us." Matt put the containers on the table and pulled out plates and utensils as Shane popped the lids off and made sounds of approval.

"Smothered pork chops, mashed potatoes, dang, she even sent over cornbread. Cassie's gonna kill me for spoiling dinner but I can't resist."

Matt snorted as he filled his plate. "Yeah, 'cause Cassie's such a fine cook and all."

Shane couldn't stifle a laugh but shook his head. "You're a bad influence on me. She may not be able to cook worth a damn but she makes up for it in other areas. Speaking of hot sexy women, how're things going with Melanie?"

Matt shrugged. "Eh. She's..." he paused before sighing "...vacant. Yeah, she's pretty and has a great body. She's good in bed and all, but she doesn't make me laugh. We don't *talk* about anything real. She doesn't seem to care about anything. Honestly, I want to have what you guys have. But the right woman hasn't come along yet."

"I used to think being married was being tied down and trapped. But Cassie, being with her changed me, changed my life. Even after being married a year and knowing her two, I haven't found myself bored yet. The woman is a roller coaster." Shane chuckled.

"Well, I'm a lucky man. My sisters-in-law are all firecrackers. I want that too. I'm wondering if I'll find her. I'm thirty-two, I've dated a lot of women within a thirty mile radius of Petal. Maybe she's not out there. Maybe I fucked up with Liv and I'll never get another chance."

"You didn't want Liv. You still don't. She's meant for Marc. All I can say is your woman is out there. I know it for a fact. I think you're looking in the wrong places. If you want a deep woman you can laugh with, stop going out with women like Melanie. Break the pattern, Matt."

Matt sighed as he ate. "Women like Melanie are familiar territory, you know?"

"I do know. I was you, Matt. Okay, better looking, but still, look at the women I kept ending up with. Except for Maggie, and we all know that was doomed. It wasn't until I clapped eyes on Cassie that I *knew* what I wanted. Her. Forever. It took Kyle a few months and Marc a few years of knowing their women. You? I think you're more like me. You'll see her and you'll know and it'll be right."

"You know, everyone in this town thinks you're such a hardass. If they only knew what a sensitive person you were deep inside. I'm not being snide, I mean it. Thanks. Thanks for checking in on me and for the food and for caring."

"You're my brother, Matt. And my best friend. Although if you told Kyle or Marc, I'd have to say I love you all equally and crap because I'm the oldest and all."

Matt snorted and popped his brother one on the arm.

Chapter Two

"What brings you into my bookstore today, young man?" Cassie moved from behind the counter to kiss Matt's cheek and give him a hug.

"I just had lunch at The Sands and was on my way back to work so I thought I'd stop in to say hey." He turned at the sound of his name as his other sister-in-law came in. "I'm surrounded by Chase women. How are you feeling, darlin'?"

Liv accepted his kiss and gave one to Cassie, who rubbed Liv's stomach.

"I'm fine. That damned brother of yours and his super sperm. Who'da thought he'd have knocked me up so fast." Liv patted the barely perceptible swell of her belly.

"You said you wanted a husband and a family. Well, there you go. No April Fool's for your ovaries." Cassie winked.

"And all within four months. Marc moves fast." Matt was thrilled for his brother and Liv. Another grandchild for his parents and another niece or nephew to join Nicholas.

"Yeah, like honeymoon fast. Cassie got a tan on her honeymoon, I got a fetus!"

Suddenly, the screech of tires and screams sounded from outside. Matt turned and saw a car accident through the windows of the store. "Call 911!" he yelled as he headed toward the door.

He saw a woman lying in the street and his heart sped as his professional side took over.

"Everyone needs to back up. An ambulance is on the way." He knelt next to the woman, who groaned and put her hand up to her face. A trickle of blood oozed from a cut on her forehead. "Miss, how are you feeling?"

Her eyes fluttered open, bright blue eyes, and widened for a moment before she tried to sit up.

"No, stay still. I don't want you to move until I know more." Quickly and efficiently, he skimmed his hands over her. She'd received some abrasions on the backs of her arms where the pavement had ripped her shirtsleeves.

"I'm all right. Really. He wasn't even going that fast."

"What happened?" Shane jogged up as the ambulance arrived.

An elderly woman who'd apparently seen the accident came forward to explain as Matt and Shane helped the paramedics. "Charlie pulled away from the curb and Tate here got jostled. Bunch of boys from the high school on skateboards. Rushing to get back to school I'd wager. Anyway, looked to me like they rushed past and she got pushed out into traffic. He couldn't have been going too fast."

"Those boys need to be put in jail!" one of the gathered people called out.

"No, no, they didn't mean to hurt me. Honestly. They're just silly kids doing silly kid stuff. I'm just a bit scuffed up," the woman, the witness had called her Tate, said from the gurney.

"Miss Murphy, I'll send someone to the hospital to take your statement. Just get yourself over there and get checked. Don't worry about anything else just now," Shane reassured her and Matt closed the doors to the ambulance and stepped back.

"I've got to get back to the station. I'll talk to you later. I didn't see anything but if you need a statement, you know where I'm at."

* * *

No freaking way did Matt Chase rub up all over her while she lay sprawled in the street like a drunken hobo! Tate couldn't believe her luck. The closest she'd ever been to the man and of course she had to have a torn shirt, bleeding face and her back-of-the-drawer panties. *Special.* Well, okay, so he didn't see her panties or anything but *she'd* known they were on. And she'd noticed, as Tim had insisted on driving her home, she'd spilled something or other on her shirt.

"Tate, honey, I doubt he noticed the stain on your shirt." Anne laughed as Tate regaled her with the story the following day.

"Well, I suppose I should be glad I didn't toot or have a giant booger or something."

Anne snorted. "I can't believe you got hit by a car. What's the world coming to when teenaged boys shove a woman into the path of an oncoming car?"

"Drama much? They didn't shove me into the street and Charlie Wilks was doing five miles an hour tops. Which is only two miles an hour slower than he drives at full speed. He's a hundred-and-fifty years old, I'm just glad he stopped instead of thinking I was a blonde-headed speed bump."

"I still think you should have pressed charges."

"Their parents made them come to my house and apologize. Really, Anne, they were sorry. And Tim scowled at them extra hard. You know that face."

"One of the only helpful things any of us got from Dad," Anne mumbled.

"I don't suppose either one of them bothered to call," Jill called out from her perch in the window seat, looking up from a book.

"Good Lord, go back to school already." Beth bustled past and put towels at everyone's stations. "You know they didn't and thank God for that. Mom is off with some dude in Dallas and Dad is in the bottom of a bottle. I doubt they even know Tate moved out much less got hit by a car."

"Children, please." Tate sighed as she shook her head. Jacob and Jill had come back to town immediately when they'd heard about the accident. Jacob was out working with Tim for the day at his plumbing business and Jill was doing some studying.

"Ahh, my ten o'clock is here." Anne turned and smiled as Polly Chase came click-clacking into the shop. "Good morning, Mrs. Chase! How are you today?"

Polly patted her hair and smiled. "I'm good, sugar. I've got a bit of a dent here in the back so I need a good, solid re-do from you. My roots may be in need of a bit of TLC too." She winked and Tate grinned. If there was a person who could resist Polly Chase, Tate hadn't met them yet.

"Good morning, Tate, honey. I hear you had a little run-in with Charlie's front bumper yesterday. You all right?" Polly's cheeky mood softened into concern. Tate was nearly as short as Polly so it wasn't hard to let herself get pulled into a hug.

"Oh, I'm fine. Just a bump on the head. Both your sons were there to help though."

Polly brightened. Tate did love that about Mrs. Chase—the way she doted on her family. What she wouldn't have given to have a mother like her instead of what they all got in Tina.

"Shane's the one who told me, but I haven't seen any of my other boys."

"Matt helped until the ambulance got there. He was very gentle." And he smelled really good.

"He's a good boy. They all are. I'm glad you're all right, honey. I would have called you right away last night but Maggie said she talked with Nathan and all your siblings were on the job. If you need anything at all don't you hesitate to ask." Of course, Nathan, Tate's brother the teacher, worked with Maggie and would have told her all about it. Small town gossip moved fast.

"Thank you, Mrs. Chase. I appreciate that."

Anne helped Polly to the shampoo station. Draping her to protect her clothes, she got to work while Beth went to mix the color they'd need.

Tate had several cuts right in a row and kept busy for the rest of the day, in between her siblings dropping by the shop to check in on her.

At two-thirty she swapped out her teal-blue kitten heel slides for a pair of sneakers. "I'm going to pick Belle, Sally and Danny up from school. I'll be back in a few."

"Let me do it," Jill piped up.

"Look here, missy, you have an exam you need to study for. You shouldn't even be here. I can walk the four blocks to the grade school and pick them up and take them to William and Cindy's. Same as I do every Wednesday."

"You will not." Anne came into the reception area. "William is picking the kids up. I told you that this morning. Tate, you got hit by a car. A. Car. You can cut yourself a one-day break."

"I made a commitment. They expect Aunt Tate to pick them up every Wednesday. Just as Uncle Nathan picks them up on Tuesdays and Auntie Beth on Fridays and mommies and daddies on other days. That's what family does. We keep our promises and we don't let each other down."

Anne pulled Tate into a hug and said softly into her ear, "You're not drunk or passed out in some hotel room with a stranger and they're not starving. Tate, honey, your family never doubts for a millisecond your commitment to them. We know. Belle, Sally, Danny and Shaye know you love them but got hurt yesterday. Let us help *you* for a change."

As she'd done many times in her life, she let her family make her feel better.

By the end of the day she was glad she'd listened because her muscles ached and her head hurt. The doctor had said she'd most likely have some soreness and a headache for a while on and off. She took some pain reliever and hoped for a quiet night for a change.

Jill drove her back home and Tate spent the last bit of nagging time to convince her sister and brother to get back to Atlanta and to school.

"After dinner though." Jill grinned.

Tate was good at three things—cutting hair, dancing and cooking. She was so good at it her siblings, even as adults, could be found at her dinner table any given day of the week. She took great pride in these things. It was a good thing to have skills that made you happy and people could always use a meal, a bit of dancing and a trim. It wasn't rocket science but it made Tate special.

The driveway already had two cars in it and Tate smiled, the tiredness ebbing as she found comfort in those people she loved most. Except for Tim, her siblings were almost like her children and rather than feeling burdened by it, it buoyed her, anchored and strengthened her.

Her house, a neat little bungalow in that area of town that hovered between decent neighborhood and neighborhood in decline, was her proudest possession, even more than the shop. It wasn't much. Just two bedrooms, a small living and dining room, but the kitchen was big and the bathroom was too.

She'd decided on a pretty butter yellow with light blue trim on the shutters. She was no green thumb though so William, a baker and gardener extraordinaire, took pity and did all the planting and managing of her yard.

It was her oasis from the world and was quite frequently teeming with Murphys. Luckily, while the house was small, the lot it sat on was gargantuan. She had a big, fenced-in backyard so her nieces and nephew could come over and play any time they wanted. Which was often enough she had a toy box in her living room and a play set out back.

"Looks like you're not the only one who wants to eat at my table tonight."

Jill laughed as she pulled Tate's car into her spot closest to the house. "Duh. You feeling okay? We can get takeout too. It's really just that I'd like to spend some more time with you before we go back tonight."

"I'm good. I just had a headache but it's going away now. I expect some food will help."

The scent of freshly baked bread greeted her when she walked inside. Nathan smiled from the kitchen. "Hey, sweetie. William brought several loaves of bread by. He said he'd see you tomorrow and to call if you need anything. I told him Jill and Jake are going back tonight and I'm sleeping over here so he didn't have to worry."

Nathan looked like he'd be the most laid-back of the whole Murphy crew but in reality, aside from Tate, he was the most tenacious. She knew he'd sleep on her porch if she didn't give him the guest room so she didn't bother arguing.

"Thank you, Nate. I don't need it. I'm fine, of course, but as no one is listening to me, I'll save my breath. And yes, Jill and Jake are going back after dinner."

Beth wandered in and absently pressed a hand to Tate's forehead. "You're warm and you look tired. Why don't we get takeout?"

"Yes. I'm calling right now. China Gate I think." Jill pulled out a menu and began to consult with Nathan. Tate just shook her head.

"Fine. Get extra egg rolls. I *am* going to bake some cookies though. Chocolate chip with walnut and oatmeal peanut butter chip I think."

"Dang, I think so too." Jacob walked into the living room, hair still wet from the shower. "Don't worry, the car is packed. I know you're kicking us out after we eat. But I wouldn't look amiss at some cookies to take home." He sent her puppy dog eyes.

She changed clothes and got started on the cookies. It didn't take long, she tended to have a basic mix in her fridge or freezer to add extras to because she baked so often.

Her siblings cleared the dining room table and laid out plates as she changed out baking sheets and cooled the cookies.

"Wow, you're sending that many home with us? You rock."

Tate rolled her eyes at Jacob. "No. You can have a third. Nate can take another third to his class, you said they had some kind of math-olympics thing, right? And the last third is a thank-you for the firefighter who helped me yesterday after the accident."

They ate a big dinner and saw Jill and Jacob off clutching enough food for the next few days. Beth left for her apartment a few blocks away and Nathan bunked down in her guestroom.

Tate sat in bed and stared at the television for a while, letting the cherished silence settle in around her. She had a very full and satisfying professional and personal life with her family. And yet, something was missing. She saw Anne with her boyfriend, Tim with Susan and William with Cindy and she wanted that too. She wanted a man to come home to. She wanted children of her own.

Would she ever have that? Would a fluffy girl like her be able to find a man who'd want the whole package? So okay, Tate knew she was a big girl and most days she was okay with that. She didn't really have problems being fat. She didn't even have issues with the word *fat* unless her father was the one using it. Using it to slap her, to punish her for not breaking, for helping the others survive.

But it wasn't just the abundant curves, it was the seven siblings, two sisters-in-law and their children.

It wasn't like her family was meddlesome so much as they were all very involved in each others' lives. Tate didn't have many friends she wasn't related to. Some men she'd dated had a problem with that. They'd felt like they didn't fit in or that she didn't drop everything for them. When she thought about the man she wanted to share her life with, she knew she wanted to share her family with him too. Wanted him to think those things were as important as she did.

She yawned so wide her jaw popped but at least it shook her out of her thoughts. Gawd, clearly the accident was making her maudlin. Time to go to sleep.

Chapter Three

Matt opened up the box and the heady scent of cookies greeted his senses. Mouth watering, he read the note, ascertained the cookies were from Tate, the woman he'd helped out earlier in the week after the car accident. He vaguely remembered her from school. Perhaps a year or so behind him, definitely not from his circle though.

Knowing she wasn't a terrorist, he gave in and shoved a chocolate chip cookie in his mouth. And moaned. Holy shit, that was the best thing he'd ever eaten, even better than Maggie or his momma's cookies though he'd never admit it to them. An oatmeal cookie followed. Nope, *that* was the best cookie he'd ever eaten. Peanut butter chips in oatmeal cookies? Fabulous. Thank goodness she'd been okay after she'd gotten whacked by that car. The world couldn't live without this cookie-baking goddess.

Looking at the outside of the box, he realized the address was the beauty salon just across the way. He'd have to go and thank her in person.

He'd saved some folks, helped at quite a few accidents and emergencies and fought fires in and around Petal for the last decade. Still, he could count the number of times he'd received a thank you note on one hand. It felt good to be appreciated.

Finishing up in the late afternoon, Matt grabbed what was left of the cookies, knowing he'd have to work out extra after the dozen or so he'd scarfed down since the mail came. He'd had to hide them from the rest of the weenies at the station who'd have swiped them if they'd known. And with cookies as good as the last five in the box, he wasn't gonna share.

He'd never been inside the beauty salon though he'd seen it just about every day for years. He had a vague idea that the women in his life got their hair done there, but that was the extent of it.

When he opened the door, the jingle of pretty wind chimes greeted him first, followed by the pleasing sound of feminine laughter. Oh how he loved the sound of a woman's laugh.

Smiling, he headed toward it. He saw her before she saw him. Her hair was the prettiest blonde he'd seen on a woman and unless he was mistaken, she came by it naturally. It hung in a high ponytail and still cascaded down her back in a long spiral curl. Those wide blue eyes of hers were set off by some floaty-looking blouse that was a sort of pinkish-orange. He was sure they had a name for it, women always had names for colors like that. He'd say that Nicholas had light green walls in his room but Maggie had told him they were sea-foam green. He'd just looked at his brother over her head and Kyle rolled his eyes back at him.

She was short. Like really short. And all curves. Her musical laughter cut off when she caught sight of him and then began to choke.

Dropping his things on a nearby counter he rushed to her, concerned as she waved him off, her eyes widening as she backed away.

"She's all right," one of the other women said.

Tate recovered and turned a shade of red he was sure they had a name for too, but it was clear she'd either injured herself or was mortified.

"Fuckety fuck," she muttered as she tried to catch her breath.

"Are you all right?" He touched her arm.

Her blush deepened as she nodded, sending her ponytail swaying. "Fine. Um, can't breathe and swallow at the same time. Apparently I forgot that."

He grinned. "I'm Matt Chase. I just wanted to come by to thank you for the cookies."

"Oh…oh, I'm glad you got them. I should have just brought them over but I didn't know when I'd get the chance to get away and my family was sort of trying to steal them and if I hadn't wrapped them up they'd have ended up at the University of Georgia with my kid brother and sister."

He couldn't stop grinning. The woman was like one of those little dogs with all the energy. "It's fine. They're really good. Like criminally good. In fact, and if you repeat this, I'll deny it, they're the best cookies I've ever eaten. You missed your calling you know. You should have opened a bakery."

"Her cookies are a drop in the bucket. She makes a peach cobbler that'll bring tears to your eyes and the most perfect scratch biscuit you ever tasted. That's until you try her chicken paprika," one of the women, clearly a relative, told him proudly.

"Stop it now. I already said you could have Saturday off." Tate winked and the other woman laughed. "Oh, my manners! I'm Tate Murphy. Aside from bleeding all over you the other day, I figure we haven't been formally introduced."

He shook her hand, still wearing a stupid grin.

"This is my sister Anne and the sister just younger than her, Beth."

He nodded to all of them and noted they all had the same nose but they were redheads with green eyes while Tate had blue eyes and blonde hair. She was also a lot shorter than the other sisters, who were at least five-seven or so.

"Nice to meet you all. I think I know your brother Tim. He

and I were just a year apart in school. We had a few classes together. Redhead right? Green eyes? Freckles?"

"That's our brother." Tate grinned.

"He's a nice guy. Tell him I said hello. Well, I don't want to keep you all. I just wanted to thank you for the cookies."

"Well, thank *you* for helping me. A few cookies are nothing in comparison."

He liked her smile. Wide, open.

"I'll see you around then." And he realized that he'd never bumped into her at all around town. Which was sort of silly considering they worked right across the street from each other.

"Night, Matt. Nice to meet you. Your mother talks about you all the time."

He stopped as he'd reached the door and heard her laugh. "You knew that'd get me, didn't you?" he said, looking back over his shoulder at her.

Her eyes widened in mock surprise. "Me? I have seen you naked though. With a cowboy hat on even."

He groaned, knowing the picture. His momma did love to show that picture of him at about eighteen months old, naked as a jaybird wearing a cowboy hat.

"Are you imagining me naked now?" he teased back and she blushed bright red again. He toyed with asking her what women would call that shade of red but decided against it. He winked and waved. "See you around, Tate Murphy."

He whistled all the way to his truck.

"Fuckadoodledoo. I cannot believe I nearly choked to death on my own spit when I caught sight of the man in my own shop." Tate fell into a chair and put her face in her hands.

Beth chuckled. "He's so handsome I'm surprised you could talk. Nice too. And clearly, he liked you, Tate."

"Oh yeah, 'cause I'm totally his type." Tate rolled her eyes.

"Stop it," Anne said harshly.

"What? Come on, Anne. You've seen the women on his arm. What do they have in common with me other than like, having skin and hair and basics like that? You know what the Chase wives look like."

"I won't hear you speak about yourself in his voice, Tate. I won't, damn it. You are the best woman I know. Period." Anne was so vehement it took Tate back a bit.

Tate stood and hugged her sister. "Hey, I'm not putting myself down. I swear to you. But I'm being realistic. Anne, there's a place between Dad and being totally delusional. Matt Chase dates tall, strikingly beautiful, *thin* women. I am none of those things. Oh, now let me finish! I'm attractive in my own way but I'm five foot one and not thin and while I wouldn't crack mirrors, I am not strikingly beautiful like Jill or Beth."

Beth snorted. "You're the best of us, Tate. I don't know a woman more beautiful than you are and that's the honest truth. I do have very nice knockers though not as big as yours."

They laughed, the tension broken by Beth's silly comment.

"We on for Martini Friday?" Anne kissed Tate's cheek and squeezed Beth's arm.

"Hell yeah. My place in two hours. No boys allowed. I picked up vodka yesterday and I've been marinating the chicken and shrimp all day." Tate grinned.

Tate went home and tried not to think about what an utter lameass she'd been in front of Matt Chase. Choking, blushing, making that stupid crack about him being naked and then his question. If she'd known him better she'd have told him the truth. Hell yes she'd been imagining him naked. Had done for years now. It was her daily pastime. She got bored? Picture Matt Chase nekkid and at her beck and call. Waiting for the dentist? Imagine Matt Chase having her be naked and at his beck and call. Oh so many variations on such a fine theme. Matt Chase naked. Yep.

Every Friday her sisters and sisters-in-law all congregated at one of their homes without husbands and children and had

Martini Friday. Sometimes, usually during the summer, it would be Margarita Friday instead but the idea was to gather, blow off the week, eat tasty food and have some drinks.

Tate changed and started the broiler before grabbing the ingredients she'd need from the fridge and cabinets. She loved the time just before people came over. That effort in preparing things for others, in sharing her food with them, in making her house comfortable and inviting.

Once she'd made the salad and pulled out the mini appetizers she'd prepared the night before, she dropped the chicken onto the broiler and moved into the living room to light candles.

PJ Harvey on the stereo singing about New York City made Tate sway a bit as she took the glasses from the cabinet and put them on a tray. It'd been a while since she'd had a date over for dinner. Cooking for dates was an odd thing. Some men liked it and enjoyed it but others, well, their feelings about her weight transferred onto any event with food and made her feel self-conscious. She hated that. Her father made her feel that way and she didn't want anyone else to ever do that to her again.

She'd known why Anne got so angry earlier. They all knew Tate had continually redirected his attention onto herself so her siblings could be spared their father's emotional abuse and Tim had done the same with the physical abuse. Her siblings were fiercely protective of each other and most especially her over her weight. It was a thing, a wound they all shared because of how cruel her father had been about it. While Tate truly wasn't bothered by it most of the time, they all took great umbrage when anyone ever made a flip or unkind remark, even Tate herself.

Talking on the porch lifted her out of her thoughts. She greeted her sisters with a smile.

Like he did every Friday, Matt got together with his brothers at The Pumphouse for a few games of pool. He was the last single brother, a fact that every woman in town seemed to take up as a challenge. Free beers came his way multiple times a night, women traipsed past and bent over with come-hither looks.

"I hate to admit it, but all this is tiring." He took a shot and missed.

Shane chuckled. "I figured it'd be hard on the last single Chase brother."

"Well, and now that Liv is pregnant, it's like blood in the water. Women not only throwing themselves at me but wanting to talk about babies too."

"Let yourself be caught then," Kyle said, grabbing one of the beers that'd been sent over.

"Hey, I will when it's the right woman."

"The right woman isn't gonna send over a beer and lean over so you can see her hoo ha," Shane grumbled.

Marc laughed. "What was that Daddy said back last year? Something about cookies? You hang out much at the Honey Bear lately?"

"Hardy har har. Speaking of cookies, do any of you know Tate Murphy?"

"Tim was in my year. Nice enough, I think. He was out a lot. He's a plumber here in town now. Damned good one. You know those roots on that oak in our backyard? Totally screwed up our laundry room plumbing. He came in and fixed it all. Nathan, he's one of the younger ones, he teaches at the high school with Maggie. You should ask Momma, she knows all that stuff." Kyle studied the table before taking a shot.

"Why?" Shane looked at his brother across the table.

"You know I helped out the other day when Charlie hit her? She sent me some cookies and I went in to thank her today. She's sweet. I was just wondering about her. Seems silly that in a small town I don't know someone so close to my age."

"I doubt she moves in the same circles."

"What's that supposed to mean, Marc?"

Marc drew back, surprised at the edge in Matt's voice.

"Nothing. She's just not at The Tonk that I've ever seen, or here. Never seen her at the places we seem to hang out. So it's not a stretch to think she moves in different circles. What's your problem? She do or say something to upset you?"

"No. No, I'm sorry. I just took it the wrong way."

"Like how?" Marc leaned on his cue.

"She's, well, she's sort of heavyset and if I remember correctly, Tim always had messed-up clothes and was working on the side."

"You thought I meant since she was fat and poor she wasn't our kind?" Marc narrowed his eyes at his brother and Kyle put a hand on Marc's arm.

"No, I think Matt likes her and is feeling protective of her. Like you'd be of any one of your friends. Right?" Kyle asked Matt.

Matt nodded. "And she's not fat. Don't say that."

"I was being sarcastic." Marc sent him an agitated glare.

Matt put his cue away. "Whatever. I need to go. I'll see you all on Sunday."

Shane frowned and motioned to Kyle and Marc to stay back while he followed Matt out the door.

"Hey, asshole, wait up," Shane called out and Matt stopped, his shoulders drooping.

"I want to go home. Why are you pestering me?"

"Take your attitude down a notch or five or I'll have to kick your punky ass, Matt. What's going on with you? You're all over Marc tonight."

"I'm just—I don't know what I am. I suppose I just felt bad for them all the sudden. The Murphys. Anyway, it's been a long week. I'm going to go talk to Momma and then go home. I'll see you later. I'm all right, really."

"You know where I am if you need me, okay?"

"Yeah. Thanks, Shane."

Shane squeezed his brother's shoulder and let him walk away. Matt drove over to his parents' house. The lights were on so they were still up. He tapped on the back door and his mother looked out the window, frowning as she opened it.

"Well, come on in, boy. Why did you knock?"

He kissed her cheek and waved to his father, who sat in the breakfast nook, a steaming cup of tea at his right hand and the newspaper spread on the table before him.

"I didn't want to barge in and wake the baby up. It's after nine."

She rolled her eyes. "Sit down. I just made some tea and got Nicky down. He loves being with his Nanna and Pops." She smiled at the mention of her grandson, who'd be turning a year old in just a few short months.

"Pretty soon you'll have another one to spoil." He grinned and she did too. His father chuckled as he put the newspaper aside to drink his tea and visit with his son.

"It's a happy time around here, isn't it? What brings you to my kitchen?" She poured him some tea and put a slice of coffee cake in front of him.

"Momma, do you know much about the Murphy family? Tate?"

She smiled, the way she did when she thought of someone she liked, and relief settled into him. "Tate's a sweetie pie. She was just telling me you and Shane helped her the other day after Charlie whacked her with his car. I tell you, I know it's a sin but I was relieved it was someone else's bad driving that got them in trouble for a change."

Wisely, Matt avoided his father's gaze so neither man would laugh. He knew his mother would pick up the story so he ate the cake and waited.

"Anyway, Tate and her sisters own the salon where I get my hair done. Liv goes there regularly and Maggie from time to time too. Anne, the sister, she does my hair but Tate does all that newfangled razor cut stuff and the color jobby with the aluminum foil strips." Polly shrugged. "She's a nice girl.

All those kids turned out so well. Especially considering what they came from."

Edward sighed and patted his wife's hand.

"What do you mean?"

"The father, um, Bill, yeah that's right, total drunkard. Lazy fool. Those kids went hungry a lot, I think. We tried to think on ways to get them food but the father…" She shook her head. "Refused any so-called charity. We did manage to get the kids free lunch at school. That Tate, she's something else."

"Why do you say that?"

Her very perceptive eyes narrowed, homing in on him. "Why are you asking?"

"She sent me cookies today for helping her after the accident. I met her when I went to thank her. She seemed nice but I realized I didn't know much about her. Kyle suggested I ask you."

She harrumphed. "Tate Murphy is a nice girl, Matthew Sebastian Chase. She and her older brother are the ones who raised the rest of those children. Eight in all. The mother, she's worse than the father. Kept having 'em and running off again with some new man who blew through town. I saw Tate with babies on her hip when she was in kindergarten. They didn't have the same kind of child welfare services then. But from what I've seen and heard over the years, every single one of those kids went to college if they wanted to or some kind of trade school and they all pooled together to pay for it. Tate and Tim being the oldest have done the lion's share."

"How come I never saw any of this?" Matt felt shame that all this happened to people his age and he never knew.

"Oh, they lived over in the trailer park on Ash. Not like you had much call to get out that way. You were lucky children to have your lives free of that sort of thing." Polly clucked.

The other side of the metaphorical tracks. That part of town was ramshackle and dark. Not the tree-lined stately homes of his neighborhood or even the nice residential flavor of the majority of Petal. That side of town had more burnt-out cars and trucks up on blocks than oak trees.

He stayed and visited with his parents for a while longer and went home. But Tate's wide, friendly smile stayed with him even after he'd turned off the lights.

Chapter Four

Matt saw her everywhere once he'd actually noticed her the
first time. That bright shock of white-blonde hair was a bea-
con along with the vivid, colorful clothes she always wore.

Somehow, it fit and he loved the retro vibe it lent her. Quite
often, she wore dresses that made him think of the fifties.
Flared skirts and tight bodices in bright red or blue. Always
shoes to match. The woman could probably give Cassie a run
for her money in the shoe department.

Two weeks after he'd gone into her shop that first time, he
saw her sitting on a bench at city hall. It was early May and
the day was clear and warm. Her hair gleamed in the sunshine.

He plopped down on the bench next to her and began to
unpack his lunch. "Hey there. This seat taken?"

Her surprised jump made him glad she wasn't eating or
drinking anything after the first choking incident. "Hi. No.
No, sit down. I was just having my lunch."

Looking between his sandwich and whatever the heaven-
in-a-bowl she was eating, made his stomach growl. "What is
that? Looks way better than a turkey sandwich."

She held out a forkful to him and without thinking he took
it. Instantly, his taste buds lit as the flavor rushed into his
mouth.

"It's green curry with tofu."

"That's tofu? No way. Tofu tastes like, well, nothing."

She laughed, that sweet, musical laugh. "Tofu will soak up the flavor of whatever you cook it with. This has garlic, basil, eggplant and tofu in it and I like to add mushrooms just because. The green curry is spicy and the coconut milk is sweet. All together it just works doesn't it?"

"Yeah. I'll never wrinkle my nose at tofu again."

She curled her lip at his sandwich. "Is that *pressed turkey*?" Her tone made it seem like he'd been eating dog poop.

"Um, I don't know?" He shrugged. "I get it at the market, in those baggies where the cheese is. Is it bad?"

"Tell me something, Matt Chase, does your mother ever serve turkey that tastes like that?"

He recoiled in horror. "Never!"

She handed him the curry. "Good Lord, eat this. And go to the deli to get your turkey there next time. You know what a tomato is right?"

Obediently he ate and nodded. "But it makes the sandwich soggy."

"Keep the slices in a separate baggie until you're ready to eat the sandwich." She peeled the bread and looked at him accusingly. "Is this processed cheese? The kind that comes in little individual plastic sleeves?"

"Yeah. Hey, I like that stuff!"

"No you don't."

She sounded so sure of it, he started to doubt himself. Instead, he ate the food she'd given him. "What are you going to eat?"

She pulled out another container and two small containers. "I have marinated tomatoes and mozzarella with crostini."

"Huh?" He leaned over and nearly drooled when she pulled the lid off the container and the scent of olive oil and basil hit him along with the sweet acid of the tomatoes. "No way."

Grinning, she popped a tiny ball of cheese into his mouth

and he groaned. "You can't have it all but I'll share some of it. I usually give my leftovers to Beth. If she hunts you down later, don't blame me." She pulled several little toasts out of a paper sack. "This is crostini. Just little pieces of toasted bread with olive oil or even plain. You put things on it, olive spread, tomatoes, cheeses, that sort of thing. My brother William works at the Honey Bear. He bakes the bread and tempts me with it even though fresh sourdough bread is the last thing I need every day."

"I go in there all the time. I can't believe I haven't recognized him. Does he look like you?"

"He starts work at four in the morning and he's off by two most days. You wouldn't see him, he bakes in the basement. All of my brothers and sisters are redheads with green eyes except me and Nathan. Nate's got brown hair. William looks like a younger version of Tim, my older brother."

He'd started to chide her about the bread thing until she spoke about her coloring. He remembered back to his momma's comments about Tate's mother's behavior.

Tate cocked her head and he actually saw her openness evaporate. "Yes, I'm aware of my mother's reputation, it's well deserved but you won't catch poor white trash by sharing a fork with me."

"Whoa!" The hurt in her words nearly made his eyes water. Putting the bowl down, he reached for her hand. "I would never think such a thing. Tate, I don't think that about you."

"I saw your face change when I described my coloring to you." She tried to remove her hand but he wouldn't let go.

"Yes. Yes, okay, I did think about what I'd heard about your mother. But that has nothing to do with you. I don't even know your mother. For all I know, your dad has blond hair and blue eyes."

"Both my parents are redheads with green eyes, Matt. Don't think everyone in the world didn't notice me and Nathan and that we don't look a damned thing like my father. Don't think my father failed to notice and make us pay."

He stilled. "What do you mean?"

She began to pack her things up. "I need to get back to work."

Reaching out, he touched her arm and she stopped, looking into his eyes. "Wait. I'm sorry. I didn't mean to pry. If you leave I have to give your food back." He grinned tentatively and she snorted.

"Ugh, another man after my food. I have to beat you all off with a stick. Really, it's difficult to be objectified that way."

He laughed but he saw her humor as a way to deflect the conversation away from her comment about her father.

They stayed for another twenty minutes or so before she had to get back to the salon.

"I'll walk back with you. I need to get to work too. I can't believe we work across the street and I've never really hung out with you before." He helped her pack up. "Wow, what is this little lunchbox thing?"

"Cool isn't it? It's a Mr. Bento. I got it at this cookware store in Atlanta a few months back."

They walked companionably through the early May afternoon toward their end of town.

"I take it you like to cook?"

She nodded. "It's a great stress reducer. It's a way I can do something for my family."

"So you cut their hair and make them curry?" He grinned, liking that a lot.

"I do. Although Anne is really good with hair too. We're all pretty handy in the kitchen but it sort of turned into my place to be the house everyone comes to for dinner." And they all knew her cupboards would never be bare, ever. Once she'd moved out, that was her promise to herself and she'd kept it. No one she loved would ever be hungry if she could help it.

"Do you do men's hair? I think I need a cut." Absently,

he ruffled a hand through his hair and a surge of giddiness rushed through her. Thirty-one years old with a crush, wasn't that special.

"We don't get a lot of men in the shop. Men in Petal tend toward the barber shop on First. But we get a few and I'd be happy to do you. Um, do your hair that is." She blazed bright red.

He laughed. "You blush easily don't you?"

"It's a curse of very pale skin I suppose." They stopped just outside the salon. "Give a call to check the schedule. I'll be glad to fit you in and trim you up." She brushed the hair away from his neck and tsked. "And I'll get your neck too."

"Okay, I'll do that." He paused before waving and crossing. On the other side of the street he called out, "Thanks for the curry. I'll talk to you soon, Tate."

"Hoo boy," she mumbled, watching him as he went back into the stationhouse.

Matt found himself in Tate's company several times a week. He liked Tate Murphy a lot. Liked her cooking, liked her sense of humor, liked the shape of her eyes and the smattering of freckles on the apple of her cheeks. Her voice was low and scratchy, totally unique, just like the rest of her.

He found himself thinking about her when he wasn't with her and making excuses to try and bump into her around town.

About a month after that first lunch with Tate, Kyle had invited himself over to Matt's apartment with Nicholas and the three of them spent the afternoon watching NASCAR and building block towers. Nicholas was quickly approaching a year old and Matt had babyproofed his living room and kitchen to make it safe for his nephew's presence. Still, the boy was fast as lightning.

Kyle jumped up to grab Nicholas when the doorbell rang. He opened it with Nicholas under his arm, laughing.

"Oh, I'm sorry. I thought this was Matt's apartment."

Matt perked up at the familiar voice. He looked around Kyle's body and saw Tate standing there holding a duffel. "It's my place. Kyle and Nicholas are hanging out today. Come on in."

She hesitated and Kyle stepped back, allowing Matt to take her arm and pull her inside before she could bolt.

"I-I'm sorry to interrupt. I was in the neighborhood and I remembered you saying you lived here." That pretty blush crept up her neck.

"You're welcome to visit any time. Is this a social call or...?"

Nicholas jumped out of Kyle's arms and before either of them could move, Tate had effortlessly dropped the duffel and grabbed Nicholas and held him to her. Face close to his, she grinned and kissed his nose. "Hey, you, the ground is lots harder than you think. Let me help." She lowered him carefully but he didn't take his eyes from her. Instead, he held his hand up and took her finger, tugging her over to his block tower and began to babble about it.

Kyle's eyes widened as Tate sat down and began to babble back and forth with Nicholas and work on the tower.

"Not a social call, not purely," she said over her shoulder.

Matt stood still for a long moment, looking at this woman who took joy from building a tower with his nephew. She wasn't faking it to seem attractive to him, he'd seen that one and it burned him up every time. No, Tate Murphy genuinely liked Nicholas and was having fun with him. How cool was that?

"Can I get you something to drink? Oh and that's Nicholas there and his daddy, my brother Kyle. Kyle and Nicholas, this is Tate."

Kyle moved to the place where Tate sat with Nicholas and joined them. "Hi, Tate. Nice to meet you."

"I've heard a lot about you. Your mother and sister-in-law Liv come into my shop a lot. Sometimes Maggie too. And you, Mister, are a very good builder. I'm very impressed. I haven't built block towers in a few years and I'm a bit rusty, thank you for helping me."

Matt brought her a glass of lemonade and swallowed hard. Holy shit, yep, Tate was…well, yeah. He liked her. *Liked* her liked her. When did that happen?

"What were you doing 'round these parts?" Jealousy stabbed through Matt as Nicholas reached up and petted Tate's hair. "Not that I'm complaining, it's nice to see you."

"I was just at the assisted living house a few blocks away. I go on the first Sunday of the month with Anne and we do the ladies' hair. It's hard for them to get out like they want to, so we go to them. And the last several times we had lunch together you kept telling me you needed a haircut and as I was in the area and had my stuff with me, I thought I'd make a house call."

"You're good with kids and the elderly too? You're running an animal shelter at your house aren't you?" He grinned.

"I'm horrible with animals! We didn't have pets when I was growing up and I have to admit dogs scare me and cats don't seem to like me. I'm also a terrible housekeeper and I'm late all the time. I have many flaws." She laughed. "I can come by another time for the cut since you're busy."

"No. Please. Today is the first Sunday in over a month I've not been working or at someone else's house. The wives are all out baby shopping, that's why Kyle and Nicholas are here with me." Did he even breathe through any of that?

"Would you do my hair too?" Kyle asked and Matt wanted to pop him one.

She stood. "Of course. When Nicholas is ready, you let me know. I do children's cuts too."

"You can do it today if you like. I mean, he needs it." Kyle picked Nicholas up.

"Oh no. There's no way I'd cut a baby's hair without his momma there. You'd be in big trouble with your wife, I'd wager, Kyle. But oftentimes, if it's a first cut, kids feel better in familiar places so I'd be happy to cut his hair at your house or wherever."

Abashed, Kyle smiled. "Yeah, you're probably right about Maggie. She's touchy about that sort of thing."

Tate pushed Matt toward a kitchen chair she'd placed by his window. "That's not touchy, silly. She's his mom, a first haircut is a milestone, she'd want to be there. I do love his hair though. My nieces and nephew have red hair too."

Matt allowed her to direct him into the chair and she put a fabric drape over him and one on the floor to catch the hair. He zoned out as she touched him.

"First thing, let me shave your neck." Gently, the clippers trimmed and shaved his neck. Her hands were easy as she worked and the soft scent he'd come to recognize as uniquely hers wafted through the air.

She'd nearly finished with his cut when a group of women showed up at his door.

"I've come to gather my men," Maggie said, waltzing into the apartment, stopping when she caught sight of Tate. "Tate, how are you?"

His gregarious Tate suddenly got shy. "Hello, Maggie. I'm fine, just cutting Matt's hair. I should be going though."

She started to move away but Matt grabbed her arm. "No, not yet."

Kyle grinned at them both. "You said you'd cut my hair too."

Blushing, Tate cleared her throat, her eyes widening and looking to Maggie. "Well, I'm sure you'll want to be with your family now."

Maggie laughed. "Oh, hell no. I've been after him to get a trim for weeks. He goes to the barber shop and they always cut it too short and then he waits until it gets shaggy."

Liv came into the room with Marc and seeing Tate, she smiled. "Hey, Tate. You do house calls?"

"Hello, Liv. I hear congratulations are in order." Matt noticed her shyness got even worse with Liv's presence. He

wondered if it was that they used to date or if there was another story.

"Thank you." Liv touched her belly and then her hair. "I'm
in dire need of a cut but I'm a total worrywart about the chemicals and smell in salons."

"It's okay, I understand. I can come by your place if you'd
like. That way you wouldn't have to worry."

"Really? Oh that would be fabulous. Do you have time
today?"

Tate blushed and nodded.

Matt just watched the interplay and let it settle in. He'd
been startled by the revelation but now, he realized, it'd been
happening since that first visit at her salon. Damn, she was a
good woman, a genuinely nice person.

She ended up cutting Kyle's, Marc's and Liv's hair as well
as giving Nicholas a trim. Maggie sat and watched the whole
thing and Matt knew he'd hear from his sisters-in-law after
Tate left.

"I should go. I'm having dinner with my family tonight."
Tate cleaned up, aided by Matt.

"Ah. I was going to see if you wanted to have dinner with
me."

She froze, blushing again. The best thing about her was that
he could tell what she was feeling by her skin tone.

"I'll be at our bench tomorrow. You can have lunch with
me then."

He pulled his wallet out and her eyes widened again. "How
much do I owe you?"

"Do you think I go door to door hustling haircuts on the
weekend for extra cash?" Her hands fell to her hips.

"I...uh, no. But you're a hairdresser, you performed a professional service. I certainly don't think you'd do five haircuts
for free." Matt looked to Maggie, who shrugged, also uncer-
tain how to proceed.

It was Liv who broke the stalemate by shoving money into

Tate's hand. "Shaddup. Take the money. I need you to come and do my hair in six weeks at my house and Marc's too while you're at it. I feel loads better already. You're a whiz with the scissors. If Kyle did your lawn or Marc designed a workout, they'd expect to be paid too."

Tate nodded shortly and put the money in her pocket. "Right then. Listen, I was just in Atlanta to see my brother and sister last weekend. Have you been to Lullaby Rose?"

Liv shook her head.

"I went in to get some stuff for my niece, she's turning three. Anyway, they're having a huge sale right now. I know you were out today but they have a lot of great stuff. It's near the convention center. I'm sure they have a website too."

Liv's eyes lit up and Maggie leaned in. "They have boy stuff too?"

"Oh yeah. Newborn to age six. All sorts of stuff."

Matt hefted her duffel when she readied to leave. "I'll walk you out."

"Okay then." Getting to her knees she accepted a hug from Nicholas. "I'll see you later, Nicholas." And said goodbye to everyone else.

At her car, Matt tossed the duffel into the passenger seat. "Thanks for today." He touched his hair and she shrugged.

"No problem. I'll see you tomorrow."

He'd wanted to try and smooch up on her but she got into the car before he could make a move. All he could do was wave as she pulled away from the curb.

Back inside, he moved to the couch. "Before anyone asks, yes, I'm into Tate. She seems utterly clueless though."

"Into? Yeah, that's a mild word for a man who stared at her like he wanted to devour her." Liv chuckled.

"She's not your usual type, Matt." Maggie bounced Nicholas on her knee.

"What do you mean?"

"Stop being so damned defensive about her already,"

Marc grumbled. "She's *not* your usual type. She's a very nice woman, no doubt. But," he shrugged, "she's not the perky cheerleader beauty queen you normally date."

"What was that thing about the money?" Kyle asked.

Liv snorted. "You guys all grew up so sheltered. Tate Murphy is a hardscrabble girl. She came up the hard way. Struggled, worked for everything she has. She's defensive because of what she comes from."

"And how do you know? You grew up pretty well."

"I did, yes. And I'm lucky. Tate's sister-in-law Susan was tight with my sister. When they ran wild together anyway. Susan mellowed long before my sister did. Anyway, I know Susan pretty well and through her, I know a bit about the Murphys. It's going to be hard for you to get her to let you in, Matt. She's been hurt, a lot. And, I'm going to say it because it's my place to say things everyone is thinking but no one says—the looks thing is going to be a problem."

"What looks thing?" Matt thundered.

Liv waved it away. "I've known you a long time, Matthew. Don't play games. You go out with women who are drop-dead beautiful. Even I was intimidated when we dated. She's a beautiful person, that goes without saying, but she's not like the others."

"Are you saying she's ugly? Because that's fucked up, Liv, in addition to being untrue."

Liv snorted and put her hand on Marc's arm to keep him from speaking. "*I'm* not saying she's ugly. I know her. Not as well as I'd like to, she seems much more reserved around me than with other people. But enough to know I think she's beautiful. But here's what they're going to say, Matt—she's short and fat and from the wrong side of town. She's after your money and your name. You're tall, handsome and you come from money and an influential family." Liv shrugged.

"You have to be prepared for it, Matt. You have to protect her and yourself by accepting it up front and understanding how to deal with it. If you mean to make something with her, you're going to have a lot of hurdles. Other people may pretend that's not a problem but I'm not other people and I love you too much not to say what everyone is thinking."

Marc chuckled. "My fragile flower. So shy."

"I never thought of it that way. Well, I don't care what people think. I only care what I know. All my life people have just assumed I'm shallow. Kyle, he's the sensitive one, Shane is the gruff one, Marc's the happy-go-lucky one and I'm the pretty one no one thinks much of. I've gone out with dozens of women. I've been able to have a decent conversation with maybe three and only one has ever had the same feeling about family I have. I've gotten to know Tate. This isn't sudden. She's the one. She doesn't judge me, she doesn't look at me and think about how much money I might inherit or how much my family name can do for her. She doesn't look at me and think that grabbing the last Chase bachelor would be a feather in her cap. She just sees Matt. No one else does. Do you know how special that is?"

Marc looked at Liv and then back to his brother, nodding. "I do. If you want her, you know you have our help and support."

"You know Momma will be in your corner. If anyone says a word about it in her presence they'll rue the day." Kyle and Maggie looked to him. "I'm looking forward to getting to know Tate and making her part of our family. You've got our support."

Matt looked at them, the people he loved, and smiled. "Thank you. Looks like I might just have a job and a half ahead of me. Good thing I've never shied away from a challenge."

"That's putting it mildly." Kyle winked.

Chapter Five

"Are you absolutely sure you want to do this?" Beth looked to Tate as they stood just outside the trailer.

"Sure? Fuck no. I *know* I don't want to do this. But Jill and Jacob are in there and they need our support. If Mom and Dad don't sign those papers, it'll be hard for the kids to get their loans. We can pay for most of it but without those loans, it's awfully hard. Plus, damn it, with their signatures they can keep getting state grants too. They deserve at least that from those two worthless assholes. So we do this once a year and thank the heavens it's just that rare an occurrence." Tate took a steadying breath and reached out to Anne on one side and Beth on the other. It fell to them because Tim, William and Nathan couldn't be in the same room with their father without violence breaking out. They all played to their strengths and worked together. Dealing with their parents was her cross to bear.

The door opened up and Jill stood there, relief on her face. "Hi, guys, come on in." Her eyes sparked a warning and Tate steeled herself for the inevitable.

Once she walked up and through the creaky door, the assault of her entire childhood plagued her like it always did.

The cloying stench of stale sweat, cheap perfume and alcohol assaulted her. God, she hated that smell.

Her mother raised a hand in halfhearted greeting from her place on the tattered sofa. Tina Murphy had a drink in the other hand. Her hair was currently platinum-blonde with three inches of red growout at the roots. No matter that her daughters were excellent hairdressers, no, Tina had killed her own hair with repeated home dye jobs that rendered it to straw.

Bracing herself, she bent to kiss her mother's cheek. "Hey, Mom."

"Hey, honey. I like that color on you." In her own way, Tina was closest to Tate. What passed for love in Tina's world was a scarcity but she did seem to care about Tate when she could be bothered to come home.

"Too bad orange isn't slimming. Those shoes are hideous. Trying to take the focus off your fat ass? You're late as usual, Tate. Stop at a drive-thru on your way over? Let's eat, we don't know when your mother will decide to cat off somewhere else." Her father's words had already taken on a heavy slur.

Jacob started to speak but Tate shook her head once, hard. If anyone engaged with their father, it would make matters worse. If you just ignored him, he gave up after a while. Or he passed out. Either way, he'd shut the fuck up before she gave in to her urge to smack the shit out of him with a frying pan.

"Good evening, Dad." She walked past him toward the tiny eating area. Her mother may have a lot of faults but when she concentrated for long enough she was a pretty good cook.

It was just a matter of holding out through dinner. Just finish, make nice and get the hell out of there before anyone cried.

"Did they sign the papers?" she asked Jill in an undertone.

Jill nodded imperceptibly.

Only one more year.

"Don't pass the potatoes by lard ass. I told you to make her a salad, Tina."

"Bill, shut the hell up already."

Tate drank her tea and kept her head down. Finally, after bickering back and forth, her father shut up. She didn't bother eating, it would only prolong the evening.

After strained small talk they all made an exit.

"Come back to my place?" Beth hugged Tate tight.

Tate shook her head and hugged Anne, Jill and Jacob too. "I need to be alone for a while. Shake this off. I'm not good company."

"Yes you are. Honey, don't do this alone." Anne kissed her forehead.

"Look, I give you all most of myself but this is mine. I'm going to go and eat dinner. Alone. Please."

"We're going to stay at William and Cindy's tonight. We still on for breakfast tomorrow before Jacob and I go back?" Jill asked.

Tate nodded. "Of course." She needed to be alone, damn it. Quickly, she got into her car and headed back into town.

At The Sands, Ronnie was there with a smile and a cup of coffee, ushering her to a corner booth. It was already half past eight on a Sunday night so the place was pretty uncrowded.

"Evening, Tate."

"Hey, Ronnie." Tate opened her menu.

"Hey, fancy seeing you here."

She looked up into Matt Chase's face and only barely resisted taking a long glance down the rest of him. His face was enough of a treat. Made her feel tingly when all she'd felt just moments before was numb.

"Can I join you? I've been on a call. Warren and Pearl Jervis's place. I wish they'd leave each other, but they won't. He set fire to their couch tonight. Made me miss dinner at my folks'."

"Sometimes it's because they don't know any other way. Other times, it's because they don't give a shit about anyone else and can't be satisfied until they bleed their misery on you."

"Wow, sounds like there's a story there. I'm sorry for bringing you down. You can tell me. Or, I promise to entertain you with happy stories if you let me sit with you."

She rolled her eyes and laughed. "Sure, have a seat."

Instead of sitting across from her, he slid into the booth beside her, stretching out his long legs next to hers.

"I'm absolutely convinced that Polly Chase will have a plate set aside for you in the oven as we speak," she said dryly to hide the tremor working through her at his nearness.

He grinned. "Probably. But I'd rather be here with you."

She narrowed her eyes at him but Ronnie came to take their order. "I'll have the roasted chicken with the rice and a salad. Vinegar and oil please, Ronnie."

"Give me the pork chops and mashed potatoes and a salad with ranch, and a beer."

"Oh yeah, that sounds excellent. Beer for me too, please."

Ronnie smiled at them both and sauntered back to put their order in.

"Rough night?" Tate looked at him, liking the way his nose looked from the side.

"Why do you say that?" Matt asked warily.

"Because you had to go on what amounted to a domestic call, which can't be much fun. But you're here and avoiding your mother's cooking, which I hear is legendary. Is something up?"

He chuckled and took a long pull off the beer Ronnie dropped off along with the salads. "Polly is a mighty fine cook, yes. And I don't know how Shane does it. These domestic calls are awful. I don't have to deal with them often but when I do, it's hard to take, you know?"

"Yes, I do know."

He turned and their faces were just inches apart. She could see the beginnings of a beard on his cheeks and chin.

"Too close to home?"

"I really don't want to talk about that right now. Until about

five minutes ago, I was having a very crappy night. It's looking up so don't screw with that."

"Tell me about your night and why it's been so bad."

"Dinner with my parents."

Matt nodded, wanting to know more. He'd only heard bits
and pieces around town and from his mother. He knew the old
man drank and the mother kept running off.

"I won't pretend that I don't know a little bit about your
history. That's not who I am and it doesn't seem like who you
are either. He been drinking?"

"Is that a rhetorical question? I'm sorry. I shouldn't be dis-
respectful of him. And it's not just him." She shook her head
and waited while Ronnie put the food onto the table.

"Once a year I have to endure dinner with them. It's for
my youngest brother and sister. Because they're still young,
they need my parents' signature on their federal financial aid
forms. We pay for most everything, my siblings and I. But
it's expensive and they can get loans at reduced interest and
grants. Anyway, it's just once a year. I go over there to check
on him, my dad, every month or so but dinner there is just the
worst. I sit and don't eat, for an hour, and we all dash out the
back door and run for it."

"You don't eat?"

"So, how did you end up as a firefighter anyway?" she asked
with a grin as she changed the subject.

He allowed it, for the time being. "I considered being a cop
like Shane but the police academy was not my cup of tea. One
of the instructors there suggested I try firefighting instead.
I did." He shrugged. "I like it and the people of Petal. Well,
most of them anyway. It's nice to find something that makes
you feel fulfilled, you know?"

"Yeah, I do know. When I first got out of high school, I did
all sorts of odd jobs to pay the bills. Tim and I got an apartment in town, big enough for everyone. After a time, I got into
beauty school and I realized I'd found what I was good at. It

isn't police work or anything, but I like making people feel better about themselves. So many women have crappy lives or bad days or never get a chance to feel pretty or special. It's amazing what a bit of hair color and a nice cut can do. Makes you walk out of the salon like you're on air." She smiled as she said it and Matt felt it like a blow to his gut.

"You have such a pretty smile."

She blushed charmingly. "Thank you."

They finished up and he ordered a slice of pie.

"I should go. I have an early breakfast with my family to-morrow morning. It was nice having dinner with you, Matt." She scooted out of her side of the booth and stood.

"Wait, have some pie with me."

"Oh, I can't."

"Can't? You allergic to peaches? If so they've got cherry and lemon meringue too." He grinned.

"No, I can't do pie. The crust goes straight to my butt and it's big enough as it is." She laughed but it sounded brittle.

"Tate, I happen to like your butt. In fact, it's pretty darned stellar. Come on. I know you want to," he sang out softly. He loved her shape, soft and lush, all curves and dips.

"Look, I have bad enough self-control as it is, don't tempt me," she whispered and he stood. Thank goodness she had on some spiky heels or he'd have towered over her.

"It's just pie. It's supposed to be tempting." He grinned.

"I said no! It's easy for you. Stop it. I'm not laughing." The vehemence of her voice was laced with something else, pain and shame. Matt did not like the way it sounded one bit.

Tate let out a surprised gasp when Matt stepped to her, banding her waist with his arm, hauling her close. "Let me tempt you with something better then," he said in a near growl, so low it strummed along her spine. Her nipples pebbled against the front of her blouse and every other part of her called to attention. The heat of him buffeted her, nearly made her sway with want.

"Wh-what would that be?" Confusion swallowed her. What was he doing? This felt distinctly sexual and even more mutual. But it couldn't be. Matt Chase could not be...holy shit was that his cock poking into her belly?

"...a movie? Watch it at my place? Your place? Any place?"

"Huh?" God, he'd been speaking and she missed three quarters of it. The grin he sent her in response was so wicked an involuntary moan slipped from her lips.

"Would you like to come back to my apartment now? Have a drink or kiss? A lot?"

"Don't tease me like this, it's not nice." She tried to push away from him but he wouldn't let her go.

"I'm not teasing you, Tate. God, you have no idea how much I want you." He rolled his hips. "Here's a little clue though."

"I don't know."

"I do. Come on. Your place. Your rules. I promise to behave. Or well, to not push but I don't want to leave your company just yet and I'd really like to be alone with you." His lips skimmed over hers briefly and her resistance melted.

He reached into his pocket and tossed a wad of cash onto the table before all but pulling her outside into the warm June air.

At her car he stopped and spun her into his embrace, watching the way her skirt swirled around her legs. "I love this dress. And this color, it reminds me of orange sherbet. I do so love to eat orange sherbet."

She swallowed and felt like Alice fallen down the rabbit hole. Was Matt Chase rubbing his cock on her and inviting her to make out? She must have hit her head or something. It had to be a dream.

"I...this is a bad idea. You can't really want to hang out with me. You just feel guilty or something. Why would you want me like this?"

Matt exhaled in frustration. His damned cock was so hard it throbbed. It sure as hell didn't feel guilt. He wanted to fuck her so badly he was just barely holding himself together. Grinding his cock into her body, he felt triumphant when her eyes partially closed with pleasure. "I want to. I feel several things, Tate. Turned on. Hot for you. Desperately in dire need to kiss you. I want to touch you and be alone with you. I really truly do. Guilt isn't on the list of things I'm feeling for you." He grinned and she gave him a small smile in return.

She paused for long moments and finally nodded. "All right. You can follow me home then."

He'd been driving to his parents' from that fucked-up scene and her hair caught his eye as he'd spotted her through the windows at The Sands. A brief phone call to his mother to say he wasn't going to make it and he'd headed toward her. It wasn't like he could have done anything else. She called to him.

Feeling like a teenager, Matt's hands shook as he drove to her house. Not a bad neighborhood. Not fabulous but solid working class. He knew which one was hers even before she turned into the driveway. The little bungalow was unique, just like she was.

He parked and tried not to shove her to her front door and pin her to the first available surface. Instead he took her hand, smiling at her that she'd waited at her car for him.

"It's a bit of a mess. I left in a hurry earlier today." She fumbled with the lock and her scent hit him hard when the door swung open. He couldn't even pinpoint what she smelled like, it wasn't perfume, she seemed too much a ball of raw energy to take the time to dab a bit of scent behind her ears. It reminded him of earth, not dirt, not musk, but vibrant, essential, heady.

"I like it. It feels like you in here. Colorful." He looked around and took the place in. Bright framed prints hung on her walls. "Frida Kahlo right?" He motioned toward one of the prints.

She nodded with a smile. "I love her stuff. Her husband, Diego Rivera, got more attention but I think her art is startling and disturbing as well as just plain gorgeous."

"I don't know much about art. Do you know Cassie? Shane's wife? I think you'd like her. Your tastes are similar." If what Matt suspected about Tate's childhood was correct, Cassie's experience as a victim's advocate might be really helpful as well. If anyone could understand Tate's perspective, Cassie would.

"I don't. I mean, I've seen her around town. Who could miss her?"

"What do you mean?"

"Uh, hello? It's not like you can miss a nearly six foot tall woman who looks like Cassie. I'm as straight as they come and I think I have a crush on her."

Matt laughed. Cassie was startlingly beautiful but the woman he was with right then was a thousand times more precious and she didn't even know it. "She's a pretty woman, yes. I'm sure you'll meet her soon. Come and sit down here. I can't kiss you if you're all the way over there."

He plopped down onto her couch and she stopped, looking at him, surprised. "What?"

"Yeah, not so good with the woo, am I? I'd love for you to come here and sit with me."

Tate didn't know quite what to do. Matt Chase flustered the hell out of her. A sense of unreality settled into her. The guy, the donut of her dreams, sat on her couch and wanted to kiss her? Did she hear him right?

"Tate? Did I say something to upset you? I want more than a kiss." He stopped and shook his head. "What I mean is I want to take you out too. This isn't just some fun way to spend my Sunday. Although, I'm certainly enjoying being with you. God, I'm usually more smooth than this," he mumbled and she laughed, kicking off her shoes and moving to the couch.

"I don't know what to say."

Scooting so that his body pressed full against hers, he put a finger over her lips. "Then don't say anything just now. I really need to kiss you, Tate. So I'm gonna."

His hand slid up her arm and cupped her neck, holding her, tipping her chin up. Before she had much of a chance to register anything but the delicious heat of his palm, his lips found hers.

Slow. Incrementally building up the heat, he gently led her to open up to his tongue. She'd never been really crazy about kissing but she realized it was just that she'd never been kissed by someone who knew what he was about before. All the difference in the world lay right there.

He didn't jam his tongue in her mouth and down her throat, he teased her with it, tasted her, tickled her with the tip. His teeth joined the action, coming in to nip her bottom lip from time to time until she nearly panted with wanting him more.

The heat of his mouth moved from her lips, skating along her jaw to the hollow just below her ear. A gasp ripped from her gut when he sucked there, the wet, warm sensation shooting straight to her nipples and then to her pussy, flooding her with moisture.

Needing more of him, she adjusted, sliding her hands up into his hair.

Matt had never wanted a woman more than he did as the taste of her rushed through him. She was soft under his hands, smelled right, felt good. These little sounds kept coming from her, little moans and sighs of need, and it drove him crazy. He didn't want to scare her but if he didn't get inside of her sometime soon his cock would explode.

Before he knew it, her hands had slid from his hair to his chest and she was opening the front of his uniform shirt. Hesitantly but with some strength, she pushed him back enough to get on her knees and part the front of his shirt. When she leaned down to brush kisses over his collarbone before moving to flick a tongue over his nipples, he jumped, breathing her name like a prayer.

Her hair was like silk over his superheated skin. Needing

to see it all, he reached back and undid the clasp holding it up. It tumbled down in a sweet-smelling wave.

When one of her hands slid down his belly and her nails scored over his cock he moved back into action.

He took her arms so he could see in her face. What greeted him, passion-glazed eyes and kiss-swollen lips, made him suck in a breath. Holy shit she was beautiful.

"Tate, I want you. Are you with me?"

Swallowing, she nodded before licking her lips.

"Bedroom?"

She stood, held out a hand and led him toward the back of the house. He felt her tremble a bit, but as he was shaking too, it was hard to tell where he began and she ended.

Her room was messy and it made him smile.

"God, I'm sorry. I...well, it goes without saying I wasn't expecting to bring a man back here." She motioned toward her unmade bed and turned out the light he'd turned on.

For some reason, that comment only made him want her more.

"Good." He used his body to push her toward her bed until she fell back and looked up at him, her hair a brilliant corona around her head. "Tate, I want to see you." He turned on the bedside lamp before moving to unbutton the bodice of the dress she wore.

The blush was back and she put her hands over his, stilling them. "Turn the light off, please."

"But I won't be able to see you that way. Tate, I've been fantasizing nonstop about your body for weeks now."

"I can't. Matt, please."

Instead of turning the light off, he lay down on the bed and pulled her to him. "Tate, are you changing your mind about making love to me?" She shook her head but he saw the glimmer of tears in her eyes. "What is it, sweetness? Am I scaring you? Moving too fast?"

She buried her face in his neck and he burrowed through her hair to hold her. "I don't want you to see me naked."

"If you're not naked, how can I be inside you?" That's when it occurred to him he didn't have any condoms.

"Just leave the lights off!"

"Tate, I want to see you. Would you deny me that pleasure?" He pulled his head back to see her face, hoping she'd smile, but he got confusion, anger and a bit of embarrassment too. What the fuck? "Tate? What is it?"

She pushed at him and jumped up, pacing in front of the bed. "I'm not one of the women you're normally with!"

"I know."

She stopped and sneered.

"I mean," he added quickly, "yes, you're not like them. And that's a *good* thing. Tate, you're important, special."

"Matt," she sighed, sounding impatient. "Are you going to make me spell it out?"

"You'd better, sweetness, because I have no fucking idea what the issue is."

"Dolly, Melanie, Lisa, Kelly—what do these things have in common and what do I not have that they do?"

"They're vapid and shallow and you're not?" Standing and going to her, he kissed her lips quickly, tossing his shirt to one side blindly.

"Okay, well, you have a point there. Although what the hell were you doing with them if so?" The air left her lips in a soft whoosh when he pushed her gently back down to the bed.

"Well, you have a point there too. We can talk about the ramifications of that later because it's totally getting in the way of me putting my cock into your body. And speaking of that, we're not getting naked again why?"

"Because you go out with women who are drop-dead gorgeous and I am not! They're all tall and thin and *cheerleaders*. I am, aside from having breasts and a vagina, nothing like them."

He tried not to laugh, he really did but she was hilarious.

"What are you laughing at?"

He rolled and pinned her to the bed with his body, raining kisses down her chest, over the fabric of her dress. Pulling her skirt up, he traced the soft skin of her thighs with his fingertips.

"I'm laughing at you, Tate Murphy. I've never heard anyone but Maggie say cheerleader like it was some sort of disease. Frankly, I find it hard to find fault with women jumping around in tight sweaters and short skirts but I don't think it has a damned thing to do with why I'm dying here for you and not with anyone else. I'm here because *you're* here. I don't want them, I want you. I want to see your body, I think you're beautiful."

"I can't concentrate with the lights on."

There was so much panic and emotion in her voice he let it go. Reaching out, he turned out the light.

"Better?"

"Yes."

He found her mouth again and she relaxed, melting into him, hooking one of her thighs around his ass, arching her back to bring her pussy into contact with his cock.

Busy hands found the buttons on her bodice and made quick work of them, exposing her bra to him. He wished he could see more in the dim light that came from the open bedroom door but there'd be time for that later.

There wasn't a catch between her breasts so he helped her to sit up to get the back hooks undone.

Sweet mercy, her breasts, even what he could see in the low light, were beautiful. Large, heavy, juicy, dark nipples.

While she sat up, he helped her get the dress off and tossed his pants, socks and boxers before returning to her. She'd slid under the sheets, which agitated him, but he began to really understand some of what Liv had said a few weeks before about what some people might think about Tate. Apparently Tate herself felt some of those things too. Well, that'd be next, showing her just how damned beautiful she was—cheerleader or not.

When their bodies came together, skin to skin, he thought he'd lose consciousness it was so deliriously good. Fuck! Condom.

"Tate, uh, I have a problem. *Shit!*" She grasped his cock, giving a few slow pumps with her fist.

"What is it?" She nibbled on his ear and he lost his train of thought for long moments until she smeared her thumb over the wet slit at the head of his cock.

"Condom. I don't have one. Please, please tell me you do." He caught a nipple between his lips, swirling his tongue around it.

"I, ohgod, I don't. I don't bring men back here for sex."

He rested his forehead on her chest a moment, disappointed but not in her comment that she didn't bring men back for sex. "Okay, well, I'm not leaving to go get one either. We'll just work around it. We can do other things for tonight."

"Other things? Oh, yesss."

His fingers found her pussy, wet and swollen. He kicked back the sheets and kissed his way back and forth between her nipples as his fingertips teased around her swollen clit. She was slick and ready and he needed more.

Kissing a trail south, he marveled at the soft swell of her belly as he insinuated himself between her thighs. He felt her muscles tense but before she could object, he spread her labia and took a long, deep taste of her and they both sighed.

She was sweet and savory all at once. Her clit bloomed under his tongue and he realized he was quickly becoming addicted to making Tate feel good.

Tate could not believe she was in her bed with Matt Chase's mouth on her pussy. Naked. Naked! She wished it weren't so dark so she could see his body, she knew it would be gorgeous. She certainly hadn't had a complaint when she grabbed his cock and found him nice and thick.

No condom, fuckadoodledoo. She added a trip to the drugstore after breakfast to her mental to-do list. She wasn't sure there'd be a part two to this interlude but if fate was that kind to her again, she'd be ready.

Oh, almost there, just a bit… "*Fuck* me!" she exclaimed as he sucked her clit into his mouth and pressed two fingers into her pussy at the same time. Orgasm hit her hard, stealing all speech but a long hard exhale.

Moments later, he kissed the inside of her thighs and moved to lie beside her. "I'd love to fuck you, by the way," he murmured into her ear and she laughed.

"Sorry, I have a fuck habit. That's to say I say it too much."

"I haven't noticed it." He kissed her shoulder and she pushed him back and kissed down his chest.

"I've been trying to watch my mouth around you."

"Something I hope will end right about now," he groaned as her tongue traced his navel.

The man had the hardest, flattest belly she'd ever licked. He smelled so good she wanted to take a bite but resisted, being so close to his cock and all.

A cock that by any indicators she'd been acquainted with, was quite pleased at her presence. Especially when she ran the flat of her tongue across the head and around the crown.

Sliding her hair over his abdomen and thighs, she took him into her mouth—all she could—and pulled back only to suck him back inside again.

"Tate, oh, yeah, right like that. You're…holy…oh."

Triumph and pride bloomed within her. She'd reduced Matt Chase to incoherence. Her, Tate Murphy, the girl most likely to not be remembered by anyone. It wasn't like she'd given a thousand blow jobs or anything, she just wanted to please him and she couldn't get enough of him.

She'd never considered fucking without a condom but damn she wanted him badly. Still, she'd seen the results of thinking with one's pink parts. Tate did not want to end up like her mother. Or her father, whoever the hell he was.

Matt's thigh bunched and flexed beneath her palm as she loved him with her mouth. Her nails lightly traced his balls as they pulled tight against his body. He made a small sound at the back of his throat and then said her name as he came.

Sometime right after, he pulled her up and encircled her with his arms. "Condoms. Next time there'll be condoms."

She laughed, totally happy.

Until her phone rang. She picked up the receiver and looked at the caller ID window. "I'm sorry, it's one of my sisters." She hit the on button. "Yes?"

"Are you all right?"

"Beth, I'm busy. I'll talk to you tomorrow. I'm fine."

"You know, you can't run off after these dinners, the twins blame themselves."

"Beth, I don't want to talk about this right now." She sat up and grabbed a robe from the nearby chair and pulled it on as she stood and headed for the hall.

"Tate, you take the brunt of dealing with them and then you run away. We all feel guilty about that. Why don't you let us help?"

"Beth! For fuck's sake! Let it go. You can't have everything. I give you all ninety-nine percent but I'm allowed to have my own feelings about dealing with them. I wouldn't do it if I didn't want to. I'll see you in the morning but I'm warning you, don't bring it up again."

"Tate…"

"Good night, Beth. I'm hanging up now. I love you." She hit the off button and turned off the ringer. When she turned, Matt stood there in the doorway to her bedroom and yep, he looked better naked than in clothes.

"Is everything all right?"

"Yes. Family." She shrugged. "I expect you know what I mean."

He moved to her, pulling her into his arms. "I do indeed. Can I help?"

She laughed, tossing the phone on the couch. "I think you've done your part in my stress relief."

"Well, come back to bed, I've got a few more tricks up my sleeve."

"Sweet talker."

He'd stayed until nearly two but as both of them needed to be up early, she talked him into going home. Not that it stopped her from sleeping on the side of the bed he'd been in, loving his scent.

Not only that, but he'd asked her out on a real date for the following Saturday night and she'd agreed.

She headed into town to the Honey Bear where her siblings were all meeting for breakfast before the twins headed back to Atlanta. They were taking summer classes to finish school early.

Ignoring Beth's frown, she kissed everyone and took the seat they'd been saving. A full house, so full they'd had to push two tables together to fit all eight siblings, two spouses and four children.

They had coffee and talked around the dinner the night before. Things had eased up by the time they'd all eaten and headed their separate ways. Anne, Beth and Tate all walked to the shop to open up.

"I had sex with Matt Chase last night."

Anne, who'd been cleaning her scissors, looked up, surprised. "You did?" Plopping into Tate's chair, she put her hands on her lap. "Do tell. And don't dream of skipping a single detail."

"What's going on?" Beth wandered past.

"Tate was just going to give me all the details of her sexual encounter with Matt Chase last night."

"What? That's what busy meant? Shit, I'd have hung up on me too. Tell us."

"I didn't hang up on you. I told you I was hanging up."

Beth rolled her eyes. "Details I don't care about. Matt Chase, naked, in your bed? That I care about."

Tate made sure the place was empty and told them all the details, including their plans for a date that Saturday.

"It's about time. He's only been looking at you like a hungry puppy for the last month."

Tate looked to Anne. "What do you mean?"

"Tate, you're so clueless. He shows up where you're going to be as many days a week as he can. You two have lunch together what? Three days a week? He calls here just to say hey. You make enough food for two when you bring your lunch. He likes you. And that's no surprise to me."

"He's out of my league, Anne. So far out of my league I've made a pact not to think about it overmuch until it comes crashing down around my ears."

Anne looked angry. "Damn you, Tate. Why do you have such a low opinion of yourself? Why do you let Dad make you feel this way?"

"Okay, we're done now. I have a client in about five minutes." Tate shooed them all away from her station and looked out the window at the fire station across the street, wondering if Matt was inside.

Chapter Six

"Beth, I'm throwing myself on your mercy. Please go shopping with me." Tate showed up at the front desk at closing time on Thursday night.

"Come to my parlor said the spider to the fly." Beth chuckled. "You're in luck. You don't even have to go shopping. I know how much you hate it so I went shopping last night and picked up a few things for your date. Come to my apartment and try them on."

They drove over to Beth's place and Tate sucked it up and tried on the outfit, undergarments and shoes her sister had bought.

"Since you're going to The Tonk, I thought this might suit best." Beth held up a black dress with a full skirt, covered in red roses. The bodice was tight, with three-quarter sleeves. "I think it'll give you lots of movement when you're dancing. And let's face it, Tate, no one dances like you."

Tate liked the dress immediately and even got over feeling exposed by the deep vee of the neckline. It didn't make her look like a supermodel or anything, but it showcased her better features and camouflaged her not so good ones—namely her thighs. With a pair of pretty heels and her hair done just right, she'd do in a pinch. Okay, more than that, she looked pretty and what woman didn't like to look pretty?

"Thank you, Beth. It's perfect."

Beth grinned. "It does look really lovely on you. By the way, we're going to The Tonk Saturday night too."

"We?"

"Me, Nathan, Anne and Royal. What? You think we'd just throw you to the wolves over there?"

There was a reason the Murphys did their drinking and dancing at Reba's over in Riverton instead of The Tonk. The Tonk wasn't their place, was generally filled with people who had made fun of them when they were younger.

"Well, I could pretend to be annoyed but you'd see through me. Thank you." Tate hugged Beth. "I appreciate the backup."

"Tate, I don't say this enough, but I've always got your back. It's not that I feel like I owe you for raising me. You're my sister and my best friend and I love you. We're family and that's what family does. If anyone says one wrong thing I'm planting a boot in their ass."

Tate laughed. "Well, I'd pay to see that one."

"You ready for your date tomorrow?" Marc took his shot as he spoke to his brother.

"It's not like I've never been on a date before."

"Not with *the one* you haven't. Liv's all worked up." Marc grinned and his eyes gravitated to his wife who sat at the front of The Pumphouse at her usual table.

"You shouldn't bring her. It's smoky in there. It's not like you have to protect me from Tate Murphy. She's barely five feet tall." Matt chuckled.

"You say that as if I have a choice in what my beautiful wife does. She assures me we'll get a table near the back doors which are open during the summer."

"They're all planning on something," Shane rumbled as he looked at the table.

"Count on it. Maggie's the ringleader no doubt. She wants to be sure we get there early so we can welcome Tate properly. And she warned me about *those stuck-up bitches* I used to date and how I'd better be sure to make Tate feel more welcome than she felt." Kyle grinned.

"For a little thing, your woman is scary."

Kyle laughed. "And now yours is even smaller. What's Tate? Like five-one?"

"She claims five-two but I think she's fudging a half an inch. There's a lot to her."

"Well, I'm looking forward to getting to know her better. I have to say I heartily approve from my time with her at your place a few weeks back. When are you going to tell Momma and Daddy?" Kyle asked.

"I'm trying to get her to come to dinner on Sunday. I figured I'd talk to Momma tomorrow afternoon. I need to pick up some stuff they're donating to the firefighter's auction. I'm sure adding another plate won't be a big deal."

Marc laughed. "No big deal? Yeah, you keep thinking that."

Matt couldn't believe his eyes when Tate opened her door. She stood there in a black dress covered in big red roses. Bright red lips, silver hoops in her ears. She'd done something to her hair so that it hung in smooth, pale waves around her face. She looked like a fifties movie star.

"Holy shit. Tate, you look gorgeous."

She blushed and he couldn't help but kiss her on her neck.

"Thank you. It's Beth's doing. She picked it out. You look very nice too. I haven't seen you dressed for dancing."

He kept an arm around her waist and pressed another kiss just beneath her ear, up the side of her face and over her brow. "You taste good."

"My, you're very fancy with the compliments. By the way, a few of my siblings are going to be at The Tonk tonight. I hope you don't mind."

He escorted her to his truck and helped her in.

"Of course I don't. My brothers and sisters-in-law will be there too. They're all anxious to get to know you."

"Yeah, 'cause that won't make me nervous or anything."

"They're all very nice people. You already know Liv and Maggie."

"Sort of. It's not the same, working for someone. It's not like I'm friends with them or anything."

He nodded, chewing over that mentally as he drove. "Well, okay, if you say so. It's hard for me to know and all, they're part of my life so I just think of them as friends."

"Liv was your girlfriend too, right? For a while a few years back?"

He laughed. "Yes. Odd isn't it? She married my little brother and she's going to have his baby in September."

"Odd, yeah that's a word for it."

"Does it weird you out?" Admittedly, he hadn't thought of that, of how the woman he'd want to be with would feel about Liv.

"Well, I don't really have a place to be weirded out. It's just a date."

"Tate, it's not *just* anything. I don't want you to feel un-comfortable being with me when we're out. There's nothing between me and Liv, hasn't been for years now. She's one of my best friends and my brother's wife, that's it."

"This *conversation* is making me uncomfortable."

He laughed. He liked it when she got prim and sort of prickly. They pulled into the parking lot of The Tonk and he hopped out, heading around to her door to open it.

"What is it with the men in this town and these damned trucks? Can't you all have cars that aren't fifty feet off the ground?"

He helped her get down and tried not to smile. "You're just a bitty thing, I'll have to get a ladder for your side. Not that I don't like helping you in and out but…"

"My God you talk a lot."

He looked at her, surprised, but her grin brought a matching one back to his lips. "You're kinda spunky for someone so small."

She took his arm and *hmpf*ed.

Tate was nervous as hell. She'd never been to The Tonk but was thankful that through the sea of people she sighted her sisters and brother across the room. They appeared to be sitting with a bunch of Chases. God, they all looked so pretty. There she was, a dumpling in a dress and everyone else was pretty. Figured.

Still, the music caught her within moments. The way it always did. And she didn't feel so much like a dumpling anymore. She felt graceful and a little bit sexy.

"Looks like you're a girl who loves to dance. Which is lucky for me, 'cause I'm a guy who loves girls who love to dance. Fate is a beautiful thing." He spun her into his arms and swayed a bit. "I like the way you feel against me."

"My word you're quite the flatterer." So much so it made her all giddy and weak-kneed. "I love to dance. Always have. We go to Reba's every other Saturday."

He kissed her and spun her again, leading her through the crowd toward the other side of the club where their family awaited. Only the disbelieving stares directed toward them made Tate uncomfortable and pissed off.

"Hi, honey, you look beautiful." Nathan stood to kiss Tate's cheeks, sensing her distress.

"Thank you. You all look fetching as well." She grinned at her sisters and Anne's boyfriend, Royal, before turning to the Chases assembled there. "Hi, everyone."

"I think you know most everyone. Kyle and Maggie, Liv and Marc were at my place a couple of weeks back. The big lunk there is my oldest brother, Shane, his wife Cassie. Guys, this is Tate." Matt pulled a chair out for her and she sat down, feeling very grateful for her family there.

"Nice to meet those of you I haven't met before. While we're introducing folks, this is my brother Nathan, he teaches at the high school with Maggie. My sisters Beth and Anne and Anne's boyfriend, Royal Watson."

"We've all introduced ourselves but we hadn't met Matt yet." Nathan squeezed her hand briefly.

"Tate and I have an appointment with the dance floor. When our waitress comes by can you order me a beer? Tate, sweetness, what would you like?"

"Oh, beer is fine."

Matt stood and escorted her through the crowd down to the dance floor just as the music changed to something slow. He pulled her close against his body and eased her into the dance. Right off they matched. Their rhythm was the same, and everything else but the music and his pale green eyes on her fell away. She studied his face in the low light. He was the kind of handsome that was nearly pretty but not quite. His nose was just a little bit crooked but it's what took him straight into masculine handsome. High cheekbones defined his face and a light beard covered his chin and edged the line of his jaw. All in all, it made everything inside her go gooey.

Dangerous to let him make her feel that way but she couldn't seem to grasp her caution with him so close. Swaying there, their bodies moving as one, she might almost believe he could love her. And even if he didn't, it didn't matter. He treated her with respect, made her feel sexy and funny, there was simply no reason she could see to not enjoy him.

"You're so beautiful, Tate. Have I told you that lately?" he murmured, dipping his head to kiss her temple and then her lips.

But *that* bugged her. It was like he said it just to say it or something. Beautiful was Cassie Chase or Liv. He'd run through his share of beautiful in his lifetime and his flattery, comparing her to them, just made her mad.

"I don't need that stuff."

"What stuff? And why are you so pissy?"

"Pissy?"

"Yeah, you're cute with your chin jutted out and all but I like it when you're snuggled up to me even better."

"Look, I don't need compliments. Other women you're with may expect it, but I'm not them. I don't want empty flattery."

He stopped and pulled her out onto the back deck, past their families. Once outside she yanked her arm away from him and took a step back. "Don't ever manhandle me again."

Matt felt like she'd punched him in the stomach. What a fool he'd been. "I'm sorry. I didn't mean to make you feel unsafe with me. I just wanted to talk to you out here."

"Just ask me. I'm not a pet. Don't just yank me around like I've got no will of my own."

He couldn't help but be charmed, touched and really turned on by the spark in her eyes.

"Of course. I didn't think."

She relaxed and he did as well.

"Now, repeat this bullshit about empty flattery, please. Because it sounded to me like you called me shallow."

"What? I'd never say that." She reached out and touched his cheek and he saw the sadness in her eyes. "I'm sorry. Did I make you feel that way?"

"We're both kinda touchy, huh?" He grinned. "Yeah, I felt that way. Why are you upset that I complimented you?"

"Look, I don't need that, okay? I'm all right that I'm not all supermodel gorgeous. I have eyes. You have eyes. I'm not Liv, I can't even knock on the door of the kind of beauty your brothers' wives have. Don't shit me because it insults me. We're here, I'm fine. I'm not some bimbo who needs to be massaged. You're totally in, right? You know you're getting some, so spare me the lubrication with the flattery."

Did she not know? He backed her against the railing and caged her with his arms. "Yes, my sisters-in-law are lovely women. But there's more than one kind of beautiful and none of them can hold a candle to you. You *are* beautiful. I'm not making that up. Although, it's nice to know I'm in later." He chuckled. "Tate, when I look at you, I see a beautiful woman. Curves in the right places, beautiful eyes, lips that call to me, your smile melts me. I don't say things I don't mean. Especially not to someone I care about and respect."

Because he couldn't resist, he leaned down and kissed her. It started slow but built until he was on fire for her.

"Well, now. Did you hit your head or can a real woman get in on this action?"

Stunned, Matt broke the kiss and looked up to see Melanie standing there, wearing a smirk.

"Slumming on the wrong side of town, Matt? Trust me, I'm better than she is in bed and my dad isn't an alkie and my mom's not a slut."

Not quite comprehending that anyone could be so cruel, Matt stepped in front of Tate to shield her from Melanie's verbal assault. But he should have known she wouldn't take being shielded that way. She stepped around him.

"Opposed to slumming on your side of town, Melanie? My goodness, is this what they're growing here on the pretty side of town these days? Hmm, big mouth, I can see the appeal. Too bad her brain's so small."

Matt put his arm around Tate's shoulder and saw her brother come out onto the deck.

"Everything all right out here?" Nate's face was guarded and Matt got the feeling this sort of thing wasn't unusual for them. It made the nausea he felt even worse.

"Just throwing out the trash. God, Nate, how is it you can stand being related to this fat bitch? You lucked out, you're not like the rest of them. Why do you associate with this scum?" Melanie turned to speak to Nathan.

Nathan blinked several times and Matt gasped. Tate was the only one who seemed unsurprised.

"Just when I think people can't get any worse, you go and

lower the bar, Melanie." Nathan shook his head as he moved toward Tate. But Matt was going to protect Tate, not anyone else.

"We all have our crosses to bear. Matt, I'd like to go." Tate's voice was remote, flat and it sent a chill down his spine.

"We're not going anywhere. You and I are here to dance. Nate, I think you and I need to share a beer when your sister and I are done dancing." Matt guided Tate back into The Tonk, keeping his body between her and Melanie at all times.

Melanie grabbed his arm. "Remember what you come from, Matt Chase. She's a fat nobody, you come from better. *We* come from better."

He shook himself free with a sneer. "You could have fooled me, Melanie. You best be aware that Tate's my girlfriend, I won't tolerate any nonsense." He continued past her and back toward their table.

He felt sick and saw Maggie watching Melanie with narrowed eyes. Cassie leaned in and spoke to Beth, appearing to hold her back. Anne had a look on her face that scared the hell out of him but luckily she stayed seated. Liv whispered in Maggie's ear and he worried all hell would break loose any moment. Not that Melanie deserved to be spared the wrath of every angry person at the table, but he didn't want Tate to feel any worse than she already did.

"What just happened?" Beth demanded and Tate shook her head. Nathan told them and gasps sounded around the table.

"I can't believe that bitch!" Maggie hissed.

"Oh I'm gonna smack a bitch down," Anne growled but Tate reached out and touched her sister's arm.

"Please don't do this. I don't want to make a big deal out of it." Matt hated that she sounded so resigned to the treatment she'd just received.

"Tate, when I first came here with Kyle you should have seen the way some of them reacted. I know how it feels. We're on your side. People like her aren't the majority and even if they were, they don't count." Maggie shook her head vehemently as she spoke.

"Tate, I'm sorry you had to be subjected to that kind of thing. Melanie is—" But Tate interrupted Matt before he could finish.

"Just saying what half the women in here are thinking. I really don't feel well and I'd like to go. I can catch a ride with Beth if you want to stay here." Tate wouldn't meet his eyes.

He took her shoulders gently. "Don't you go away on me. I don't give a crap what anyone else thinks but my family and you. You got me? You don't let these small-minded idiots chase you off. Please, stay here with me. Let's dance."

"Tate, don't let the Melanies of the world ruin this. Matt is here with you. She's jealous. Show her you're better than she is," Beth said softly.

"Listen to your sister, sweetness." Matt kissed her.

Tate sighed. "Okay, okay. Let's get dancing then."

Relieved, he stood and helped her up before leading her to the dance floor.

She was graceful and sexy as she moved. He'd never seen a more natural dancer than Tate Murphy. He loved the way she lost herself in the music.

After another couple of hours he leaned over and whispered in her ear, "Sweetness, I'm dead on my feet. Do I still have that in? Because I have condoms and after a cup of coffee, I'll be ready for you."

She threw back her head and laughed and that simple thing filled him with joy.

"Let's go then. I have condoms too."

They said their goodnights and headed out into the evening. He didn't fail to notice the sneers and outright hostility some of the people showed toward Tate as they left.

"If we go to your place do you think I could squeeze breakfast out of you in the morning? You're a damn fine cook as well as being mighty lovely to look at."

"I've never met a man more full of it." Tate shook her head but could only barely stifle a smile.

"Does that mean yes?"

"I suppose so. You don't have to sleep over you know. I wouldn't be insulted if you wanted to go."

"Tate, you don't know me all that well so I'll excuse you this one last time. I'm gonna repeat, I don't say things I don't mean. I wouldn't have angled for breakfast if I hadn't wanted to stay over."

She drew a breath and nodded. "All right."

"That's my girl." He pulled into her driveway and escorted her to the door. She bustled around, kicking off her shoes before padding into her kitchen.

"I'm starting a pot of coffee," she called out and he wandered in, smiling at her.

"You look good with your shoes off. I like it. I like being here. Your house is nice, comfortable."

She smiled. "Thank you. I wanted to build a home. I..." She trailed off, turning quickly to open the cabinet and pull down two mugs.

"You what?"

"Do you take sugar?"

He put his hand out to stop her movement. "You what? Tell me. Share with me."

"I didn't grow up in a home. I grew up in a place where I slept. Sometimes. A lot of the time I didn't sleep because I wanted to be sure my brothers and sisters were okay. I saw this place and I knew I wanted it. I knew I could make it into a place where I could sleep safely. Where my siblings could come and feel safe too. God, Matt, you should go. We are so different it's not funny."

His stomach clenched. "Tate, why would I leave? We aren't that different. Not really. We both think family is important. We're close to the people we love. We're so much alike."

"Tell me, what's your memory of your eighth birthday?"

He smiled. "My dad took me and my brothers out to the lake. We went camping and I caught this piddly little catfish. He skinned it and cooked it up like it was the biggest fish ever caught. He tells people about it to this day. You'll like my dad, he's a good man."

"I bet he is. You know what my eighth birthday was like?"

He shook his head warily.

"My mother left the night before my birthday. Beth was a year old, so tiny. But I was already more of a mother to her than ours was. My father went on a bender after he beat the hell out of Tim for protecting me from the intended beating. I had to stay home from school on and off for two weeks to take care of Beth, Nathan and William, none of them were in school yet. Tim and I traded off going to school back and forth to keep the welfare workers away."

Matt swallowed hard. He couldn't imagine.

She put her hands in front of her face a moment and then pointed at him angrily. "Don't. God, don't look at me with pity in your eyes. I didn't tell you that for pity, I told you to underline the differences between us, Matt. Other kids had it worse. At least I had a bed to sleep in. I have a good life now. I own a business, a home. I don't need pity."

He looked down at her, small, her hands fisted at her sides. Damn, when did he start feeling so protective of her? Need welled up then as he reached out slowly to cup her cheek.

"I don't pity you." He bent to kiss her but when she was barefoot, he had to bend his knees to reach her. Instead, he picked her up and sat her on her kitchen counter, making a space between her thighs to get to her. "Give me your mouth, sweetness. I need that."

Tate didn't quite know how to handle it when he did that. He heard the bad stuff and still wanted her. Not out of pity. It unnerved her. And yet, she still wanted the hell out of him. Giving in to her desire, she reached up, sifting her hands through his hair and fisted, grabbing him and pulling him to her.

His kiss was eager and passionate. A moan of approval came from him as his hand swept up her neck to cradle her head while he continued his sensual assault on her lips.

He broke away long enough to speak against her mouth. "You taste good enough to eat, Tate. I think I need a snack to tide me over," he murmured as he moved up to nibble on her earlobe. Tate gasped as he ran his tongue around the outer edge and dipped it inside.

Waves of warmth headed down her neck, over her nipples, straight to her pussy. She melted, molding her body to his.

The coffeemaker beeped that it was done and he sighed softly, stepping back and helping her down off the counter.

"Let's take that into the bedroom, shall we? We can sip between smooches."

Blinking quickly, she gulped and poured two big mugs, adding sugar whether he liked it that way or not.

She took both mugs and led the way down the hall to her bedroom. He watched as she placed them on the small table in the corner and turned shyly.

She laughed. "You sure you don't want to run away?"

He got serious and shook his head. "I don't want anything but to be inside you, Tate Murphy." He paused. "You don't have any idea what you do to me do you?"

"I don't understand it. Why me?"

Remaining there in the doorway, he knew she was nervous. She picked up the mug of coffee she'd just put down and took a sip. He didn't fail to notice the slight tremble of her hands as she did.

"Sweetness, I want you so much I think I'm going to have a stroke. All the blood in my body is now in one spot and I'm slightly dizzy from it," he said with a rueful grin as he motioned toward his cock. "Can I show you how much I want you? What you do to me? Again? Because if you recall, we were in a similar situation last weekend. Only now we've got condoms."

She nodded, staying silent. He took one step and then another and another until he reached her. He switched on the light and took a sip of the coffee. "Ahh, nice and sweet like a proper Southern woman knows how to make it." He winked.

She smiled, shaking her head at him.

"I want to see you," he said, coming to stand in front of her. Finishing the last of the coffee, he got down to business, popping buttons on her dress one by one.

"Turn off the light," she whispered.

"No, I won't be able to see you if I do that. I want to see your curves, sweetness. We did it your way last time. Let me see you."

"But…" She blushed and he paused to quickly pull his own shirt off, tossing it in the nearby chair.

"See, I'll go first."

"Yeah, like that's a comparison," she grumbled but he couldn't help but love the way she stared at his body. It wasn't that he hadn't been sized up by the fairer sex before. But this was different, this was Tate looking at him like he was the best thing since Christmas morning.

"Sweet holy fuck. Oops, sorry, my fuck problem again. You're beautiful. Matt…" she hesitated, wringing her hands "…I'm not…my body isn't like yours."

He chuckled and kissed her quickly. "I should hope not. Not that there's anything wrong with that." With a grin, he took her hand and put it over his cock. "This is what your body does to me. I'm not lying when I say you're sexy."

He got back to work until the last button on her dress slid free. Slowly, gently, he slid the dress back, letting it drop. She stood there for a moment, blushing, her eyes screwed shut tight.

Reaching out, he drew a fingertip down the curve between her breasts, right along the lace of the sexiest red lace bra he'd ever seen. Her panties matched, high cut on her hips. She was a little Venus there, delicate and yet larger than life.

"You still with me, sweetness? You're so damned beautiful,

so sexy. I can't believe you wanted to hide yourself in the dark. Your skin is amazing, flawless." He smoothed his palms over her arms, down her stomach and around to cup her ass briefly.

Her eyes opened a little bit but she still looked dubious. He'd have to change that. Tracing the lace of her bra, he reached around and undid the hooks, letting it fall and join the dress.

Such pretty, alabaster-pale skin. He saw the faint tracery of blue veins just beneath. Her breasts were large and heavy in his hands, nipples hard and dark pink. They hardened further when he brushed his thumbs across them. He looked up to see her catch her lip between her teeth. Still, nervousness vibrated through her and he could tell by the way she stood she wanted to cover up.

Murmuring softly, he lay her down on the bed and eased her panties off. A triangle of closely trimmed pale curls shielded her pussy. She moved her hands to cover herself but he took them, kissing each one and putting them down on the bed.

"Please don't try and hide yourself. You are so damned beautiful and sexy I can't wait to be inside of you," he growled, pulling off his pants and shorts.

Her eyes widened as he stalked toward her and he was pleased by the look of hunger on her face.

He got to the bed next to her and she smiled up at him. "Now, where was I?" He waggled his brows.

Taking a deep breath, Tate sat up on her heels. "You'll have to wait," she said and took his cock into her hands. He slid his palms up her arms and into her hair but when she took him into her mouth, his head lolled back.

"Ahhh, you're so sweet. Heaven on Earth," he murmured, caressing her scalp. Her hands stroked the length of his cock when it wasn't in her mouth, palmed his sac, ran over the muscles of his thighs and dug into the flesh there with her nails, pulling him closer to her, deeper.

He watched as that pale, sunny hair slid forward, hiding her and revealing her in turns. She may have been shy but she certainly wasn't shy about making him feel good. He loved that. They were far more evenly matched in bed than he'd first imagined they'd be and the surprise was a good one. He knew from the weekend before that she was tireless and inventive and tonight was no different.

And yet it was. He felt like it was the very real beginning of everything he wanted to have with her for the future. She'd let him in just a bit. Told him some about her childhood and she was there, naked with the lights on. That trust in him was as much an aphrodisiac as anything ever had been.

He'd wanted her too much in the last days to hold out very long. When orgasm hit, he groaned and shuddered, her name a sigh on his lips.

Moments later, she moved away from him and he settled in, bringing her body close to his. "Give me a few years and I'll be right with you," he mumbled into her hair and she laughed softly.

Stroking the velvet skin at her hip, he marveled at how she felt. Coming back to himself, he kissed her face, her lips, her jaw and down the line of her throat. He tasted her thundering pulsebeat as he moved down her chest and kissed over the curve of one breast. When he sucked a nipple into his mouth she sobbed out a gasp.

"Responsive, perfect. You're perfect," he said with approval and he raked his teeth across the sensitive tip and she shuddered. He rolled the other nipple between his fingers and she writhed beneath him. He slid his hand down her stomach and through her curls and found her hot and wet as he stroked her.

She smelled sweet and spicy and the heat of her skin drove him wild. He kissed down her chest, rimming her belly button with his tongue.

"Hmm, I've been here before. I like it." Scooting down, he settled between her thighs, putting them on his shoulders. She sobbed out again, arching off the bed when he dipped his mouth to her sex.

Tate was sure she'd never in her life felt more desired, more desirable. He ate her up with his gaze, with his hands and his mouth. He took the time to learn her, find what made her tick, what made her writhe and beg.

There with him in her bed, with the pale light of her bedside lamp on her nakedness, she felt all right. He didn't look at her with distaste, he looked at her with longing. She knew she wasn't comparable to Liv, but at the same time he desired her and that made things all right.

With his mouth on her pussy, he pushed and pushed her toward coming. With him it was easy, she'd been halfway there just smelling his cologne as they danced at The Tonk. But his very talented fingers and tongue devastated her.

A nearly feral groan came from deep in her throat as she shuddered. He hummed his approval, sending the vibrations up through her clit. He lapped at her and learned all of the things that drove her wild and finally, after making her beg for it, pushed her over and made her come.

"Don't go anywhere," he whispered as he leaned over and rustled through his pants, holding up a condom with a triumphant smile.

"Even if my legs worked I wouldn't leave my bed with you there."

Cocking his head, he looked at her, his smile softening.

"So you gonna moon at me all night or get with the condom application so you can do me?"

Startled a moment, he laughed and ripped the packet open to quickly roll the condom on.

"You know, you look like butter wouldn't melt and then you open your mouth. There's a smart-ass living inside you, Tate. I like that. A sex goddess and a smart-ass."

He said it as he moved back between her thighs, which she happily widened to admit him. He probed her entrance, teasing her with the head of his cock, but she wrapped her legs around him and grabbed his ass. She needed him, it'd been a

very long, very frustrated week. Surging her hips up and pulling him toward her with a handful of his ass, she brought him
into her with one hard thrust.

She felt the intrusion of his cock straight up her spine. She'd
never felt so full before. It wasn't like he had a king-sized
penis, it was good, did the job quite nicely. But it was made
for her.

Suddenly, she felt a lot more exposed than just being naked
with the lights on. She pushed it all away, all the emotions
that weren't just about how good he felt. There'd be time for
panic later on.

"Jesus!" he gasped out. She was scalding hot and really
tight. It'd been a while for her or she did those exercises to
make her pussy tight. He doubted those worked this well
though.

Trying to concentrate and not come two minutes after he got
inside her body, he stopped moving. Instead, he leaned down
and flicked his tongue over one nipple and then the other, al-
ternating as he felt like it. She made tiny, gaspy, needy sounds
that eroded his control even more.

He began to slowly move inside of her, sliding almost all of
the way out and then inexorably back in again. She met him
thrust for thrust, his hands at her hips, tracing the curves there,
her strong legs holding him to her—*as if there was another
place on earth she'd rather have been.*

So this was making love. This was the intensity of connection with the person you cared about more than anything
else. "Tate, I..." He broke off, it was a bad idea to tell someone you loved them during sex wasn't it? "I feel so good, *you*
feel so good."

He teased her with short, shallow, slow digs of his cock,
delighting in how she writhed and tried to get more from him.
He loved teasing her, drawing out her pleasure and being the
one to deliver it to her.

She tightened her inner muscles around him, making him gasp.

"Oh man, that felt good," he said with a groan.

"I'll do it more if you just let me come," she panted out, doing it again, causing his balls to nearly crawl back into his body.

"Deal." He picked up his pace, moving a hand to where they were joined. Her hips jutted forward when he flicked a finger across her clit. He thrust and she tightened, he flicked and she rolled her hips until she bowed off the bed, a deep, earthy moan breaking from her.

Her pussy clutched at him, pulling at his body as if she couldn't bear to let him go. He tried to ride it out but she pulled him under. He pulsed as she did, his head back, muscles taut.

He fell to the side and they both lay there panting for a few moments. He got up briefly and came back to her. She'd gotten under the sheets and he joined her, snuggling against her body.

Long after she'd felt him drift off into sleep, Tate lay awake, listening to the tick of the hallway clock as the minutes slid past.

She'd moved past panic and into terror and back to unease with her feelings about Matt Chase.

She wasn't a virgin. She wasn't super experienced or anything but she'd been with several men and had good times in bed with almost all of them.

But what she'd experienced with Matt Chase that night was more than a good time. What she'd experienced was a huge leaping sprawl into holy-fuck-I-may-love-this-guy territory.

And she could not love Matt Chase. She was a Murphy. He was a Chase. Buildings in the town were named after his family! He was beautiful and charming and came from an ease and privilege that she'd have resented a few years before. Still made her uncomfortable. He was a man who never had to fear being hungry or being hurt by someone he loved and was supposed to be protected by. She'd lay odds he'd never seen either one of his parents drunkenly angry.

There was a whole universe between her world and his and

she'd never fit in. He'd come to see that in time and he'd find some suave way of dumping her and she'd go back to her side of the street and he to his.

She could not love Matt Chase and she couldn't let him make it happen either.

Chapter Seven

The next morning they'd had a nice breakfast but Matt could tell she was holding herself back from him and he didn't like it one bit. And he had no plans to let her get away with it either.

"So I sort of told my mother you're coming to dinner at their house tonight." He sipped his coffee and sopped up the gravy on his plate with a biscuit. She was the best cook he'd ever met, even better than his mother. If the woman hadn't been everything he'd ever wanted otherwise, he'd still have wanted to keep her for her skills in the kitchen.

She jerked her head back and put her fork down. She'd eaten fruit and just one biscuit, much to his consternation.

"What? Why would you have done such a thing? I'm having dinner with my family here tonight. We do every other Sunday."

"My momma's gonna be so disappointed."

"Matt, I'm sorry but I have plans with my family."

"Can't you break them just this once? Have dinner with them tomorrow night? My parents are expecting you and you know my mother, she'd take it awful hard if you didn't come."

Her eyes widened and he knew he'd gone too far.

"In the first place, I would *never* ask you to dump off a family commitment for me. In the second place, I would never dump a family commitment for something like a sneak dinner invitation that you didn't even bother asking me for. I have nieces and a nephew, they have school during the week so I wouldn't interrupt their weeknight schedule just to suit your whim. In the third place, my family is very important to me and I don't appreciate you treating it otherwise. Lastly, don't you ever try and guilt me with your mother like that."

Knowing he'd been rightfully busted he put his coffee down and reached out to take her hands. "I'm sorry. You're right, I shouldn't have asked you to choose like that. It wasn't fair. Next Sunday will you come to dinner at my parents' house? Assuming you don't do dinner with your family in those off Sunday nights?"

"I don't know, Matt. This is moving so fast. I…"

"Fast? We've known each other for a few months, that's not fast. Come on, Tate, look, let me just go ahead and put it all on the line and be totally straight with you. I really like you. I enjoy your company and I want to be with you. I want us to continue dating and I want to see where this can go. This is not a casual thing for me. I'm old enough to know what I want and you're it, Tate Murphy."

"You can't know what you're saying." She pushed back from the table and began to pace. The silky red shortie robe she wore fluttered around as she moved.

So on the ropes, his little Venus. He grinned. He knew then what had to happen. He'd helped every single one of his brothers with the wooing of their future wives so he had enough experience. Clearly Tate was caught up in their supposed differences again and he'd have to drag her, kicking and screaming, hopefully in the throes of orgasm, into love with him.

He leaned back in his chair and watched her. "I know exactly what I'm saying, Tate. I'm well on my way to being in love with you."

She spun, sputtering. He had to bite his cheek to keep from laughing.

"Love? Fuckadoodledoo! You've had sex before last night, right? I've heard enough stories about your prowess to know you have. I promise to let you in my bed again, you don't have to tell me you love me to get back in."

"Little Venus, gorgeous, I know I don't have to tell you I love you to get back between those silky, pale thighs of yours." His voice lowered and he winked at her, loving the way she blushed and fanned herself briefly. "But the truth is, I do love you." He shrugged.

"Matthew Chase! You can't love me! I'm a fat little nobody from a horrible family from the wrong side of the road. You're meant to be with a woman who knows how to use all the right forks, a woman who knows how to pick linens. A woman who has buildings named after her family."

He stood and moved to her, so angry he barely remembered moving. "You will not talk about yourself like that." He took her arms and kissed her hard. "You are someone. You're Tate Murphy. You work hard, you built your life from nothing and I couldn't possibly care less about forks or linens. You don't think much of me if you think I'd care about all that stuff more than what's inside a person."

"What's inside? Matt, you have no idea what kind of genes I'm carrying."

"You don't scare me, Tate. We're not the sum of our parents you know. You aren't. None of your siblings is from what I can tell. You're not his anyway, even if I was concerned. Isn't that what you told me?"

Her eyes widened and he raised a brow. "What, think you can scare me away with rough talk? Not. Going. To. Happen."

"This is just crazy talk."

He nodded. "It is. Now will you come to dinner next Sunday and can I come over here tonight after I finish up at my parents'? I'm not going to let you push me away. The cooking's too good and you're hot in bed."

She shoved her hair back away from her face, frown lines

etched into her forehead. "You don't love me, Matt. This can't be anything more than some fun evenings."

"Tate, don't tell me I can't love you. It's too late and it already is more than some fun evenings. If I didn't know you were so scared, I'd be offended and thinking you just wanted to use me for my great big penis."

She fought a smile and he realized the warmth in his chest was her, the way he felt about her. Love. He'd never felt it before but he knew he never wanted to be without it again. She made him whole.

"Your penis is just fine, Matt. But just what exactly do you envision this being?"

One arm banded around her waist, he pulled her back to the table and down into his lap. "Don't want this to get cold," he said, picking up the remains of his bacon. "Damn, you're a fine cook. What I foresee this being, Venus, is we date and date and have lots of sex and you get to know my family and I get to know yours and then I ask you to marry me and we get married and have a passel of kids and our house will always be full of busybody relatives."

She closed her eyes. "Marriage and kids? We've been on one date, two if you count that first time at the diner. That's not fast?"

"Every single lunch from May to now was a date."

"This can't happen. Look, let's just date, have fun. Leave the marriage talk out of the equation."

"Are you saying I'm only good enough to fuck?"

"Just go. Get your stuff and go." But she said it with no conviction at all and he waved it off.

"I'm not going anywhere, Tate Murphy. Not in the way you're suggesting. You need to know that right now. I don't give up when there's something worthy of working for. You may think I'm some soft, shallow guy who doesn't know what it means to struggle and maybe that's true in a lot of ways. But damn it, I'm worthy of you."

"What the fuck are you talking about? This isn't about you! This is about me."

He stood, setting her on her feet gently before kissing her forehead. "I'm going to get going. Not because I'm going for good but I need to help Kyle do some work in my parents' yard this morning."

"I'm… I don't want to hurt your feelings, Matt. I don't think you're soft and shallow. God, I don't even know where you get that. You're wonderful and handsome and funny and sweet. And you're not for me. Can't you see that? Can't you see how wrong I am for you?"

"I'm not arguing with you over that point, Tate. It's a stupid fucking point and I'm not discussing it." He shrugged into his shirt and sat to lace his shoes. "I'll be here tonight after dinner with my parents. I hear you make excellent dessert."

"Matt, are you listening to me?"

He stood, pulling her to him, and brought his mouth to hers and kissed the hell out of her. "Of course I am. But you're wrong. I'll see you later. And I'll be back between those thighs again too, Tate. Don't think you can hold yourself away from me. I want you, you want me. It's that simple."

He strode out the back door and she stood in the kitchen, the morning sun shining through the window as she heard him get into his truck and go.

"I am in big trouble."

Polly Chase watched Matt tear through his meal. *Good Lord, finally.* "You have someplace else to be?"

He sighed explosively and put his fork down. "Okay, Momma, I need your help."

She sat back and smiled at him and then at his father who chuckled. "Tate Murphy?"

"How'd you know?"

"Son, she's a witch. Didn't growing up with her as your momma teach you anything? You can't hide it from her." Edward amused himself entirely too much. Polly winked at him and frowned a moment. The scamp was utterly unrepentant and winked back, taking her hand and kissing it. She married him for a reason and she'd collect her payback after everyone left.

"Matthew, you asked me about her. I've seen you in town with her a few times. I heard you took her to The Tonk last night." She laughed, seeing his surprise. "Honey, who do you think the gossip about the last single Chase boy comes to first? I know you eat lunch with her three times or more a week. I know you ate dinner with her last Sunday night at The Sands. I know you slept at her place last night too." She raised an eyebrow at him. "I've just been waiting for you to ask me. I take it she's holding herself back? Telling you she's not right for a Chase?"

Maggie looked up and Polly laughed again. Young people! All one needed to do was keep their eyes open and their ears ready. People weren't that hard to read.

"Yes. Stupid isn't it? I told her I loved her this morning and she told me she just wanted to have a good time."

"What? She thinks she's better than you? I say you're better off without her then!" Liv snorted.

Polly hid a smile. Liv was a smart girl.

"No! She just said it to blow smoke. Stupid woman said a bunch of stuff about linens and forks and me needing to be with a woman with buildings named after her family. She thinks she's, and this is her words, *a fat nobody from the wrong side of the road.*"

Liv winked at Polly before turning back to Matt. "And you said?"

"I told her she *was* someone and not to talk about herself like that. I also said I didn't care about any of that shit. Uh, stuff, sorry, Momma. I want to marry her."

"Wow, that was fast." Shane put his napkin down and looked at Matt. "You sure?"

"I've been sure since I watched her building block towers with Nicholas last month. I know it here." He pressed the heel of his hand over his chest. "I'm old enough to know the difference between liking a woman and loving one. I sure as heck haven't ever loved one before."

Polly shrugged with a grin. "Well then, we'll bring her into the fold won't we? And her brothers and sisters too. You know you won't just be getting a wife right?"

"That's what I love so much about her, Momma. All the women I've been with haven't ever thought about family the way I have." He quickly looked at Liv. "Well, Liv but that was different. Anyway, she has such a love and commitment to them and they to her. So protective of her. You should have seen them at The Tonk when Melanie said a bunch of stuff about her. I thought we were going to have to hold her sister Beth back from taking Melanie out."

Polly's smile was nearly feral. Matt wanted Tate and so that made Tate hers too. Anyone who meant harm to the girl or her family would have to deal with the consequences and that meant Polly.

"I heard about Melanie." Polly waved it away. "She'll need a talking to. But, cookie, you know you're going to have to deal with a lot of the same, right? Tate *does* come from the bad side of town. Her parents are awful people and she's not as comely as the other women you've dated. Not that she isn't beautiful, don't you give me that look, Matthew. But I didn't raise you to pretend the obvious doesn't exist and if you don't confront it, it'll hurt her. Love isn't about a dress size, neither is beauty and it certainly isn't about a bank account. But it's gonna be said so we have to be ready for it.

"Each one of my daughters came to me in her own special package but one thing they all have in common is that they're stunning women. Without even knowing them, you look at them and they make your heart beat faster. Maggie had to deal with some jealousy issues but frankly, Tate will have it the hardest. You're going to have to be very up front and very vocal that Tate is your choice."

Matt nodded and Polly began to plan.

"Thanks, Momma."

"Of course, cookie. That's what family does. I take it you're eating your food at three times the normal speed to go to her? Why didn't you invite her here?"

"I started to talk to you about it earlier this week but I got busy with work. I invited her this morning but I sort of tried to guilt her into it." He told her of what he'd done that morning and Tate's reaction.

"Matthew, I'm appalled. I am happy to see the girl put you in your place after that. Things have come very, very easy for you. Too easy I think. You've never had to struggle. Always top marks in school, top of your class at the academy, you've always excelled at whatever you put your mind to. And never had to break a sweat to do it. Now you boys know I love you all equally but Matt, you're the handsomest one of the crew. You grin and flutter your lashes and the girls have always bent into pretzels to please you. This one is skittish, you need to be blunt and up front with her at all times. Yes, be charming and handsome, it's who you are, but don't rely on that to do the work. *You* do the work."

"I thought I was the handsomest," Shane grumbled.

"Shane, you're the biggest and bravest. Kyle is the kindest and most compassionate. Marc? He's the sweetheart charmer. All of you are handsome, you know that so don't try and play me. But Matthew here? Ahh, he's nearly pretty he's so handsome. Smart too, but handsome has done the work for him. He's just realizing that now and he's feeling a bit bad about it. Don't feel bad, cookie. You're a good man, a lot better than you give yourself credit for. You've found your special girl, that's everything. You'll build a life with her and she'll be part of us and you'll be part of her kin. Our family will get larger by eight, or fourteen because there are wives and children. Ahh, more grandchildren for me." She smiled.

Matt wanted to put his head in her lap. No one understood him better than she did. He shouldn't have waited so long. It felt so *good* that she knew him so well. He looked around the table at the family he loved and who had his back. Damned lucky.

"Go on. Tell her she's invited here next week. Invite them all. I hear she's a good cook. That so?"

Matt nearly choked on his tea, he wasn't going there. "Sure. I won't go hungry."

"Better baker than Maggie?"

"Okay on that note, I'm going to get going. Thank you for the support." He got up and kissed his mother's cheek while his father chuckled.

"I'll walk you out."

His father walked to the door with him. "Nice one. She's really better than Maggie or your momma?"

"Daddy, I've never eaten biscuits that I'd have sold my soul for until this morning. And she made them while she did three other things."

Edward laughed again. "Look, Matt, her daddy, I didn't want to say anything in front of the others, Shane may know it though, being sheriff and all. Her daddy is a thug and a violent one. Keep an eye out. He's a wastrel too. I wouldn't be surprised if he hit you up for cash. Watch yourself. And her too, it can't be easy on her coming from that when she's such a good person."

"It isn't, I can tell. But the rest of them are good people."

"Course they are. You wouldn't have loved her elsewise. Don't rush up on the girl. Let her know how you feel but she's a person who's been abandoned and disappointed and lied to by people she should have been able to trust. It's gonna be a bit like she's a wounded animal, I know that's not entirely an accurate comparison but it's close enough for you to know what I mean."

Matt's father didn't hand out advice right and left. He knew people better than most because he listened more than he spoke. Kyle was a lot like him, Matt realized.

"It's hard. I want to scoop her up and protect her."

Edward smiled and squeezed his son's shoulder. "I know. That's why you know this is real, the fear of losing it or her."

"You're pretty smart for an old guy."

"Smart-ass. Now get on out of here. If you promised her you'd stop in, do it. Keep your promises to her, no matter what."

"Thanks, Daddy."

"That's what I'm here for, boy."

"Why don't you call him?" Nathan asked her softly as she looked to the front door for the hundredth time.

"I don't know what you're…oh fuck me, he said he'd stop in after dinner. It's not like it's a date. He probably just forgot. It's not a big deal." Tate knew it was useless to try and lie to Nathan.

The house had been loud and chaotic and filled to the rafters with Murphys but now with bellies filled and coffee making to go with the cherry pie she'd baked earlier that day, things had quieted down. The kids played out back in the twilight.

"Tate, if the man made a promise, he's meant to keep it. If he doesn't, he's not worth caring about."

Tate put her head on Nathan's shoulder a moment before Tim noticed. If Tim saw her in any distress at all he'd go into protective mode right away. So far that evening he'd been on kid duty so she'd been spared his usual close monitoring of her moods.

She moved into the kitchen when the coffeemaker beeped. Beth followed along with Anne to slice pie and get coffee for everyone. Tim came in to get milk and pie for the kids.

Tate smiled, her life was good. When she was Belle's age she'd never have imagined her life would be so wonderful as an adult. Matt Chase or not.

But when she made her way back into the dining room with a tray of plates with pie, she caught sight of the man she'd been trying so hard not to think of come in through her front door.

He grinned as he caught sight of her. "I see I got here just in time. Do I smell cherry pie?"

She smiled back before she could even think about it. "There's enough for you most likely. Have a seat there." She indicated a chair with a tilt of her chin and he rolled his eyes, approaching to take the tray from her and place it on the table.

"Thank you."

"I don't suppose I need to even ask if this is scratch pie."

Nathan snorted and grabbed a plate and a mug of coffee. "Better grab a slice now, there won't be a flake of that crust left over in about three minutes."

Matt sat and she smirked, pushing a plate to him following that with a mug of coffee. "It's decaf."

The kids came screaming into the house but got quiet when they caught sight of Matt sitting at the table. Tim gave her a subtle eyebrow raise and Susan chuckled quietly.

"This is Danny. Danny, this is Matt Chase." Her nephew took a bowl of ice cream and pie and sat at the small table kitty corner to the larger one. He eyed Matt carefully, making sure the stranger wasn't going to snatch his pie. Nodding his head in a very fine imitation of his father, he got down to eating.

Matt nodded solemnly, eating his own pie.

"And this is Shaye." Three-year-old Shaye waltzed into the room wearing a tutu and clutching her bowl.

"I don't like cherries. Tate made me peach pie 'cause I'm special. And you can't have none either."

Matt stifled his smile. "Pleased to meet you, Shaye. I promise not to steal your pie."

She re-introduced him to everyone else and explained that William and Cindy were home with their sick twins or there'd have been four more people there.

"Sit down, sweetness." Matt patted the chair next to where he sat and she did. He looked around the table and she knew what was coming next. "Hey, let me go and get you a slice of pie."

She put a hand on his arm to stay him. "No, I don't want any. I'm having coffee."

He narrowed his eyes at her and held a forkful of pie toward her mouth. "Take a bite of this pie and tell me why you aren't having a slice. Because I've never tasted better."

"Don't bother," Tim mumbled. "She won't."

"Don't interfere," his wife, Susan, murmured.

"He's right. Why we all sit here when she does this is beyond me. Tate, take a bite of the pie." Anne glared at her and Tate widened her eyes and then narrowed them, sending a nonverbal *back off* to her sister. One her sister ignored with a snort.

"Because *she* doesn't want any pie. Why are you all talking around me? I don't want any pie. It's not a national tragedy that Tate Murphy isn't having pie. Let it go." Shame and anger roiled in Tate's head. This wasn't something for outsiders. She hated it enough when it was just them but it didn't concern Matt and she didn't want him in the middle of her damned business. She'd have told them to shut up and fuck off but Danny and Shaye were there a few feet away and she didn't want them involved.

"Is this a regular thing? The not eating of pie?" Matt asked Tim.

"My father made us all messed up in our own special way." Her older brother looked at her totally unrepentant. Triumphant even that he'd gained another ally in his war against her refusal to eat dessert. It was stupid.

She crossed her arms over her chest and glared at them all. None of them seemed to care, which only made her angrier.

It was her damned body, what she chose to do with it was her business. She didn't let her father control it and she wouldn't let anyone else either. If not eating pie pissed anyone else off, too bad. It had taken an awful lot of years to be okay with her shape and her size and she was! She didn't deny her own issues, she knew she had them, but they were hers and she'd deal with them in her own way.

Matt felt her tense up next to him. He glanced at her, noted the blush and looked at Tim. Relieved, he saw the concern on her older brother's face before remembering the moment in The Sands and her reaction to the pie there—her comment that she didn't eat dinner when she was around her father. His heart ached for the wounds she'd been dealt by her own damned father. Instead of railing about it, he sighed and thought about how he'd handle it.

"Tate took the brunt of it all for us. To protect us. He did the worst to her." Nate kept his eyes on his pie as he spoke and a chill worked its way down Matt's spine.

"Nathan, Tim, stop it now. You too, Anne. We don't need to relive it. *I* don't need to. All of you stop talking about me like I'm not here! While you're at it, remember the children are listening to everything we say."

"Well then, you talk to me." Lowering his voice, he turned to her, seeing her eyes spark but feeling enough spark of his own. He'd be damned if he let her asshole of a father abuse her when he wasn't even there.

"I don't want any fuh…freaking pie." She looked quickly at the children, who happily ate their pie and ice cream, before turning back to him. "That's all. I'm full. I had dinner and I sampled when I made it. It's not like I'm in any danger of wasting away." She made a frustrated motion at her body.

"And you're not in danger of exploding if you have a bite of this heaven on a fork either." Matt danced the fork in front of her but she was not amused.

"You need to stop this now, Matt," she told him softly and he reluctantly pulled the pie away but not before he saw the look of approval on her siblings' faces. Well, they liked him and were on his side in this thing.

"Fine. For now."

He finished as he visited with her family, getting to know them all, liking them tremendously. There was a great deal of familiarity there and he approved. They loved each other, made jokes and took care of each other. Tate would fit into his family just fine, and he would hers.

Everyone helped clean the kitchen and Matt didn't fail to notice Tate kept busy, avoiding being alone with him. Silly woman. She couldn't win when he wanted something. And he wanted her.

Tim and Susan left first with the kids and everyone else followed. Matt ignored her looks suggesting he go each time someone else left and he liked seeing her siblings ignore the hints too.

"Alone at last." He flopped back onto her couch, putting his feet up on her coffee table.

She bustled into the room and pushed his feet off with her bare one. "Get your feet off my table."

He grinned. "Sorry. Come sit here with me. I'm lonely and I've wanted to kiss you all night."

"Matt, I'm so tired."

He saw the edge of fear and panic on her face. She needed comfort and didn't want to need it. She broke his heart sometimes. God how he loved her.

Standing, he moved with purpose to where she stood and encircled her with his arms. "I know, sweetness. Let me. Let me ease it for you. Lean on me." He spoke, lips against the pale, cool silk of her hair.

"Why are you doing this?"

"I told you. I love you, Tate. Let me love you."

"You can't love me. You don't love me. You just feel sorry for me."

He sighed and walked her to her bedroom, turning off lights as he went.

"You talk too much about stuff you can't possibly know about. I know what I feel, Tate."

"I need to be alone, Matt."

"No you don't. You need to be held. I want you, yes. But tonight, let me hold you. I want to sleep with you against me. Will you let me stay here tonight?" He searched her face tenderly, loving the surprised and slightly confused flutter of her lashes.

"I don't know…"

"I do. Please, Tate." He'd never actually begged a woman to let him sleep in her bed, not even to fuck her, before. He needed her as much as he knew she needed him.

"All right. All right. I can't argue with you over it. I don't want to."

He smiled, leaning down to kiss her gently.

Damn that Matthew Chase! Tate couldn't help but smile as she pushed her cart through the grocery store several days later. No matter how much she tried to push him away, he was there. Always there.

So thoughtful too. She'd come home two nights before to find a new flower bed dug and planted. He and Kyle had spent part of their day doing it. All because she'd told him how she kept planning to do it but never had the time.

Reaching up, she touched the small silver Venus pendant he'd brought to her that morning at the shop. Said he'd seen it and it reminded him of her, wanted her to wear it against her skin and think of his lips there.

A shiver of delight headed up her spine.

All her delight evaporated as she turned the corner and saw

Melanie standing there with Kendra Fosse and some other twit, Dolly somethingorother.

Melanie caught the cart as Tate attempted to steer around them.

"Go on then, say your piece and then move." Tate glared at Melanie.

"I shouldn't need to point out to you that you're in over your head, you gold digging whore."

The look on Melanie's face was pure hatred and Tate had seen it more than once. She could never quite figure out why Melanie Deeds hated her so damned much. But they all treated the Murphy kids, especially Tate, badly. Because they could, she supposed. Where most of her siblings were tall and thin, her sisters were gorgeous and her brothers all hale and handsome, Tate was short, pale and fluffy. That made her otherness the biggest target.

"Excuse me? I take it this little scene is sour grapes because Matt and I are seeing each other?" Short, pale and fluffy or not, she wasn't about to take any guff from the likes of a snotty bitch like Melanie and her little cabal of mean girls. Mean girls way past thirty. She snickered.

"Seeing each other? Is that what you call it?"

"Get to the point, Melanie, the shrillness of your voice makes my teeth hurt and your fake tan is giving me a headache. Oh and do your roots for cripes' sake." Hee! That hit home. Melanie's pretty face crumpled on even more ire. Tate hoped she got a wrinkle Botox couldn't clear up.

"You keep your cheap, fat ass on your side of town. Matt Chase isn't meant for the likes of you."

Tate raised an eyebrow, a naturally blonde eyebrow. "Ahh, that's what this is about. Can't take it that he dumped you and came to me. Oh, that must sting that shriveled up, black heart of yours. All the money and good shoes in the world can't lure Matt from my bed to yours. I may be fat and cheap but I'm the one getting laid by Matt Chase. Guess you'll have to find some other guy because Matt is taken."

Melanie pushed the cart but Tate was stronger than she was and she pushed back, making Melanie step backward.

"Don't you push me, Melanie Deeds. You said your piece now get your ass out of the way or I'll run you over and smile while I do it."

"We'll see how funny you think this is when me and my friends boycott your ratty little salon."

Tate whipped her head around. "Oh no you did not just insult my salon! Look here, you stupid bimbo, you'd better have a salon visit somewhere in your future because your roots are so bad you look like you'd be at home next to my old trailer." She turned to Kendra who'd been smirking at Melanie's little tirade. "Although I'm sorry we can't help you. We don't do Botox."

"You slut! Just like your mother. You're not good enough to be a Chase, you just remember that. Matt Chase will get tired of you soon enough and you'll run back to your tacky little house and your cheap, buy-one-get-one-free life with your cheap shoes and knockoff bags. You're a nobody, Tate Murphy. A *fat* nobody who doesn't even know who her dad is." Melanie's face was red but Tate was the one who saw red.

"Get. Out. Of. My. Way." She shoved the cart menacingly and Melanie finally moved aside. "I'm Tate Murphy and I'm better than a thousand of you, Melanie Deeds. You know it too. If money bought worth, I'd still be better than you."

She blew past them and managed to finish her shopping instead of running out the doors in tears like they'd wanted her to.

Still, there'd been several cancellations for the rest of the week. It'd cost the shop several hundred dollars. But not her pride. Never, ever her pride.

Chapter Eight

Matt chuckled to himself as they approached his parents' front door. They were a sight to behold, Tate and Matt along with three of her siblings. His momma would be in hog heaven.

Add to it the bonus of having Tate be more comfortable because her family was with her for that first dinner at the Chase household. And it was a big night, they were celebrating Kyle's birthday too. In another three weeks Nicholas would be a year old.

He remembered back to July of the year before, Maggie was heavy with pregnancy and Liv was just about to admit to herself that she loved Marc.

It'd hurt then. Just a bit. To see his brother finding love before he had, and with the woman Matt had been with a few years before that. But part of the hurt had been Matt's frustration that he just hadn't ever loved Liv, even though he'd wanted to. He'd wondered if he'd ever find what his brothers had found and here he was, his arm around the shoulder of the woman who made him whole.

Not that she made it easy. The woman was a pain in the ass. Skittish as hell. Defensive and so damned strong. He loved her so much and he knew she felt deeply about him too, figured it was love even. But she was scared and he couldn't do much more than ease her into life as his woman.

Thank God for her siblings who'd supported his relationship with her totally.

The door opened before he could reach the knob and his mother stood there, a great big grin on her face. Rushing onto the porch, she pulled Tate into a hug.

"Hey there, Tate. Don't you look pretty tonight?" Polly stood back and Matt realized his mother and Tate were roughly the same height. He stifled a laugh but looked up to see his father making the same discovery as he stood in the doorway.

Tate blushed. "Thank you so much for having us, Mrs. Chase. I know it's a family occasion and all. I told Matt we should come on a different night but he insisted."

Polly waved a hand at that. "Pshaw. Piffle even. Come on in. Hello, Anne and Beth, it's nice to see you two. And you're Nathan, right? We've met once at a town hall meeting about the new high school. Come on in!" She shooed everyone into the front hall.

Edward looked at Matt and then down at Tate, his face softening. Matt wanted to sigh with relief. His father would temper his mother's enthusiasm and make Tate feel at ease.

"Hello, darlin'. I'm Edward, Matt's daddy. Welcome to our home." Edward took her hand and kissed it and damned if Tate didn't actually emit a girlish giggle.

Edward winked at her and Polly snorted. "Edward, don't you go trying to trade me in on a younger model."

Edward shook his head at his wife, smiling. "My darling wife, I'd never trade you in. But I do hear Tate's quite the cook. I was just hedging my bets."

Tate laughed and Polly grinned at Matt.

Edward introduced himself to her siblings and put Tate's hand in the crook of his arm, escorting her into the family room where the other Chase boys and their assorted wives were already seated.

Tate saw Kyle and handed him a present, wishing him a happy birthday. Shane moved to her with purpose, giving her a kiss on the cheek and a hug as Cassie followed in his wake. Matt loved that his giant of a brother was so gentle with her. He supposed part of it was Cassie's doing.

Nicholas saw Tate, squealed in delight and toddled over. She knelt at his level and within moments lay on the carpet, driving cars around.

"My sister is a good person. Kind, smart. She'd do anything for the people she loves." Nathan stood with Matt as the rest of the group mixed and chatted.

"I love your sister, Nate."

"I know. She's afraid of it."

"Why? I'd never hurt her. She has to know that. I've never been violent or even angry with her. I'm always gentle." It tore him apart that she'd fear him.

Nathan sighed. "Matt, that's not it entirely. She's afraid to truly love you and have everything that makes the two of you so different come back to cause her pain. She's afraid that once you know all of it, everything about our parents, how we came up, you'll reject her."

"That's silly. I don't care about any of that stuff. Nate, I don't care where you grew up."

"You don't. But others do."

"Who cares about them?"

"She didn't tell you." Nathan hesitated and Matt tore his eyes away from Tate and Maggie playing on the floor with Nicholas to face her brother.

"Tell me what?"

"She's going to kill me. She needs to tell you herself."

"Fuck that. Come on, Nathan, you opened the subject up, just tell me." Matt kept his voice down, not wanting to alert her.

"Melanie and her friends cornered Tate at the market earlier this week. Taunted her. Said she was a gold digger. Called her a whore. They're boycotting the salon. She's lost some business."

Matt blinked, disbelief clouding his brain as he struggled to understand. "What? Why would they do that? Is there some old battle between them or something? I broke things off with Melanie two months before I walked into the salon for the first time and met Tate. I don't understand."

"Matt," Nathan shook his head, "you're a good guy but you don't know what it was like to grow up the way we did. Melanie has *always* been this way about our family. Well, mainly Tate. Always Tate because she's different. She…" He broke off, pressing his lips together.

"She what? Please, Nathan, she won't tell me any of this herself. I want to understand her, I want to protect her and I can't if I don't know."

"She's already going to be pissed I told you this much, Matt. She's ashamed. We all are but she's the worst. She protected us all at great risk to herself."

Sickness roiled through Matt's gut at the thought of her suffering. Of anyone hurting her, including Melanie. He'd have a few things to tell her when he ran her to ground.

"Dinner! Come on, everyone." Polly clapped her hands to get attention and Nicholas copied her.

Kyle laughed, scooping his son up and heading toward the dining room.

Matt went to Tate, holding his hand out to help her up, and the smile she gave him as she took it melted any anger he'd had at her for not telling him right away.

Nathan cornered her after the cake, telling her he'd let Matt know about the thing with Melanie.

Humiliation and then a sense of betrayal rushed through her. How dare he? "You did what? How could you do that, Nathan? If I'd wanted him to know I'd have told him myself."

"He needed to know, Tate. He loves you. He wants to protect you."

She narrowed her eyes. "I don't need anyone to protect me,

Nathan. I can take care of myself." No one else ever had, she could count on herself, damn it. Melanie was a stupid bitch and Tate had handled her.

"You don't need it but you deserve it. I don't feel bad, honey, so spare me the look. It hasn't worked on me in ages."

"It worked on you Thursday, Nathan, when you were arguing with William."

He tried not to laugh but he couldn't help it. "Okay, okay, so it still works. Tate, I love you. You don't know how much. I'll never be able to put into words how much you mean to me, not in a million years. He wants to be part of your life, why hold him out?"

"What's going on?" Beth approached and Nathan sighed.

"Nothing." Tate waved it away. The last thing she wanted was to bring any drama to the Chases' grand living room.

"I told Matt about what happened with Melanie."

Tate gasped and then growled at him. He had the good sense to look worried.

"Well, good. I don't know why Tate hadn't before now."

"I'm not having this discussion. This is *mine*. It happened to me. Not you, not Nathan, not Matt. You don't own it and it's mine to share or not. You don't get to make my choices for me. No one gets to make my decisions for me but me. You had no right, Nathan, and you've made me look like a pathetic fool." He took something and used it against her. Matt would feel sorry for her and there was nothing worse than having someone feel sorry for you. Especially when she'd handled it and quite well she thought. Those women didn't make her feel bad, she meant it when she said she was better than they were. She was.

"Tate, you know I'd never…that's not what it was. I wanted him to know, to see you, to understand what you face."

"Damn you, Nathan! I'm not some pathetic little fat chick who needs crumbs from the table of anyone. I trusted you.

You've humiliated me and I don't know if I'll share with you so readily the next time."

Anger burning through her, she hardened herself against the way his face fell at her words. Instead, she spun and walked away, out into the hallway. And straight into Matt. Could the night get any worse?

"I hear you had quite the little run-in with Melanie earlier this week. You planning to tell me about it before the picnic day after tomorrow?"

"Don't start on me, Matt. It's nothing and it doesn't concern you." If he hadn't been so angry at her for not telling him about Melanie, he'd have been amused at the way her chin jutted out and her eyes narrowed at him.

He grabbed her hand and tugged her outside onto the front porch. Cassie and Shane sat snuggled on the glider swing on one side so he hustled her to the opposite end, pulling her into the large chaise with him.

"Tell me."

"Matt, I told you, it was nothing and I don't want to talk about it."

"Well, that's not an option. You can't not share with me. I care about what happens to you. When I track her down I'm giving her a piece of my mind."

She stood, moving away from him quickly. "You will do no such thing! It's handled. I handled it. I don't need anyone to fight my battles for me."

"You may not need it but I do. I need to help you, to be a part of your life." He stood and she backed up a step. He exhaled with frustration. "Don't do that. I hate when you do that."

"I need to go." She darted to the side, toward the steps to the front walk.

"Oh no you don't, Tate Murphy! You can't run from me every time I get close."

Out of the corner of his eye, Matt saw Cassie stand and

Shane rose shortly after that. Tate saw it too. Shane's size worked against them both in that situation.

"You going to stop me?" Tate's voice trembled a moment but steadied.

By that point several others had come out and at seeing Tate backed up against the porch railing and Shane and Matt looming over her, Nathan shoved them both aside until he reached Tate, pulling her into his arms.

"Get her things," Nathan said calmly to Beth who turned and went to retrieve their stuff. "Come on, honey, let's get you home. Why don't you stay at my house tonight? I'll even let you make me waffles tomorrow morning."

Cassie's hand caught Matt's elbow and pulled him back. When he turned to her, she shook her head hard, pain clear on her face.

"What the blazes is going on? Matthew, what have you done?" Polly came out and Beth moved around her, their stuff in her arms.

Matt hated that Nathan kept his body between him and Tate as he drew her off the porch and down to the sidewalk.

"I wouldn't have hurt her. I never..." Matt's voice caught.

"Matt, there's something so broken inside me. I know you wouldn't have hurt me but look how I acted. I can't control it. Just please, can't you see how wrong we are?" Tate's voice was thick with tears.

He moved toward her but Nathan shook his head and Cassie's fingers dug into his arm.

"Why are you holding me back? I can't let her go like this." He looked to Cassie, begging her.

"Look at her, Matt. Leave it. Let her get herself together. Let them help her. You can't fix her just now." Cassie's voice was thick with emotion.

Shane put his arm around Cassie and his cheek against her hair.

Polly looked to him and down at Tate. "Honey, please

don't go like this. This was all a silly misunderstanding. Matt wouldn't hurt anyone, least of all you. He loves you. Let us be your family too."

"I know he wouldn't hurt me!" Tate cried. "Can't you all see? I can't even have an argument without turning into some kind of freak. There's something so wrong with me. Just please, leave me alone." She paused, looking at Matt sadly. Matt felt a sob building in his gut. "Get away while you can." She turned and let Nathan guide her down the sidewalk and help her into the car.

"Tate, I love you. You're not broken, damn it. You're beautiful and wonderful and I'll call you tomorrow," Matt called out.

Anne and Beth got in the car on either side of Tate, both putting their arms around her.

Matt saw her body shake, knowing she wept. He had to lean against the railing to keep his knees from buckling as the car pulled away.

"Why the hell didn't you tell me she was abused?" Cassie asked softly.

"I don't even know the whole story! Bits and pieces is all I've heard. The dad is a drunk, the mom ran off a lot. They were poor, neglected. I don't know the extent of the situation. I know she's got major issues around eating because of whatever the hell the dad said to her and she took the brunt of a lot of emotional crap because she's not really his." Matt shoved a hand through his hair and began to pace. "I shouldn't have let her go. We could have worked it out."

"Matt, she was on the verge of losing it. Her family will know what to do."

"You have to help her, Cassie. Will you help her?" Matt pulled her hands into his.

She nodded. Cassie had been physically and mentally abused for several years by her ex, a man who tried to kill her twice. In the wake of a devastated medical career and no longer able to perform the complicated surgery she used to excel at, she'd become a victim's advocate.

"I'll try, honey. You've got to try and rein in your frustration when she flinches from you. It's not about you. She already knows it's bad, she knows it has nothing to do with you or how she feels about you."

Polly kissed Cassie's cheek before hugging Matt's side. "We'll all help her. She's a good girl. A smart one."

"Melanie started all this and I'm going to have a word with her about that." Matt wanted to shake some sense into his ex. How could she have been so stupid? And how could he not have seen what a horrible person she was while they dated?

"Melanie?" Polly's voice held warning.

He told them all about what Nathan had said and Polly was fit to be tied. "You leave that girl to me, you hear? The last thing we need is for her to spread rumors that a Chase boy threatened her. She and I will have a talk. Boycott my daughter-in-law-to-be's shop? I think not. Not if she wants everyone to keep shopping at her father's florist."

Edward laughed, the tension easing on the porch.

Matt was pulling on his shoes when his phone rang. He'd left multiple messages for Tate but she'd shied away from replying. He knew from Nathan that she was all right. Mortified by her reaction at his parents' house and trying to process everything.

He left her a voicemail telling her he'd be picking her up for the July Fourth picnic at two. He planned to hash things out with her for a few hours before they met their assorted family members at the park for food and fireworks later on.

Half expecting it to be her trying to dodge, he was surprised to see Shane's cell on the display screen.

"Hey there," he answered as he stood to grab his keys and head for the door.

"Matt, Tate's at the hospital."

Matt sat down again. "What? Oh my God! Shane, is she all right? What happened?"

"I don't know everything. It happened at her parents' trailer. She's got a head wound. I'm on my way to the hospital just now. She's unconscious. One of my deputies is asking questions at the scene. I thought you'd want to know."

"Yeah. Yeah. Thanks. I'll be there as fast as I can."

He ran out the door, calling Nathan and getting voicemail. Getting the same from every other one of her siblings he tried. He called his mother and she told him they'd meet him there.

He burst through the emergency room doors and the staff directed him upstairs. Rushing up the stairwell three steps at a time, he saw her family, Shane and Cassie there waiting.

"What happened? Is she conscious?"

"My father happened," Tim said, his voice tight and very controlled.

"Your father put her in the hospital?" A sense of cold, deadly calm slid through Matt then. He'd never been one for fighting, always a kind of laid-back guy, but at that moment he was sure he could have beaten the hell out of Bill Murphy.

"One of their neighbors heard an argument. Nothing new. He called Tate because it got pretty bad. My dad and mom were on the steps, screaming at each other. He kept threatening to kill her.

"Tate went because that's what Tate does. Tate fixes things. According to my mother, Tate arrived and tried to calm my dad down. Told him someone would call the cops if he didn't stop yelling. She went up the steps to the little landing where he was standing. He pushed at her, to get her away, and she lost her footing and fell back. She hit her head on the concrete pad the trailer sits on."

Nathan put his arm around his older brother and took up the story. It occurred to Matt that this probably wasn't the first time something like this had to be related to someone else.

"Head wounds bleed a lot. My mom saw it and yelled at one of the neighbors to call the cops. My dad took off."

"We were already on the way." Shane put his hand on Matt's shoulder. "Thank God, one of the neighbors had already decided things were too far gone and called 911. An ambulance got there right as we did and brought her here. We've got a warrant out for her father."

"Can I see her? Is she going to be all right?" Helplessness clawed at Matt, thoughts of her alone and hurt in the hospital bed filled his brain.

"She's unconscious but they said her vitals were good. I've had a few concussions. She's in for a long night of being poked awake every hour but Tate is strong, she'll be all right. Physically." Cassie smiled at him, squeezing his shoulder.

Matt swallowed and nodded. If he fell back on his professional training as well as the support of his family and his love for her, he'd be a bigger help to her.

"Where's your mother?" Matt looked back at Tate's siblings.

Nathan's mouth flattened and he shook his head. "She's at home. Apparently she told the cops she doesn't remember much about what happened even though what she told Tim was pretty detailed. Said she had to get out of town. She's more worried that she might have to testify and it'll put a kink in her social calendar than about Tate."

"I've got to see her." Matt had to hold it together for Tate's sake.

"Go on in." Tim nodded. "She needs you."

"Little Venus? Hey, gorgeous, time to wake up."

Tate opened her eyes and found herself staring into the most beautiful eyes she'd ever seen. Matt. Then the light brought a sharp new blast of pain to her head and she winced.

"What happened?" she croaked.

"Your father," he ground out through clenched teeth. "He was drunk and arguing with your mother. Threatening to hurt her."

"Oh that's right. I went up the steps to try and calm him

down. His face was so red, I thought he might have a stroke or something. He turned to me, screaming, his hands waving all around. He went to push me back and I lost my footing and slipped. Hit my head on something."

"Yeah, the damned concrete. He could have killed you."

"Is he all right?"

"You're worried about him?"

"He was so red. It's hot. He was drunk, really drunk. Is my mother all right?"

"She's fine." Tate may have had a head wound but she knew enough to understand his silence meant her mother hadn't bothered to show up. Tate wished it didn't hurt as bad as it did, still years later.

Matt brushed fingers up her arm. "Your dad left the scene. There's a warrant. Don't you feel sorry for him. Damn it, Venus. My brother has blood all over his uniform pants from where he rushed to you when he got there. Why didn't you call me?"

"He saw it?" She was horrified that Matt had been exposed to this part of her life and now Shane had been too? Great.

The doctor came in and pushed him out of the way to shine a pen light into her eyes and check her other vitals. Matt stood to the side, not letting her out of his sight.

"You're all right. Concussion. I told you the last time to watch yourself. Ms. Murphy, your father—"

"Yes, I know, Doctor." Tate cut him off before he could say anything else but she caught Matt scrubbing his hands over his face. *The last time* echoed in her ears and she knew he'd heard it too. Shame, sharp and acute, roiled in her stomach and she had to fight back heaving her breakfast.

"Well, you're going to have a shiner where the railing of the steps connected with your face when you went down. We're going to keep you here overnight for observation, you know the drill. Your eye is fine and the bruising should go away in a week or so. Your ankle on the other hand is sprained. You twisted it when you went down. You really shouldn't wear such high heels, they're murder on you."

"I like 'em and they're definitely murder on me," Matt murmured and Tate snorted a laugh.

Before leaving, the doctor said a nurse would be in within the hour and to ring if she needed anything. She did indeed know the drill.

Once alone she turned to him. "Oh fuck! Your family picnic. Go on, now and get going. I'm fine. I'll doze and be woken up repeatedly and you can call me tomorrow when I get home."

He shook his head and kissed her temple. "Tate Murphy, you are the dumbest woman I know. I'm not going anywhere. What kind of man would I be if I went to eat fried chicken and watch fireworks when my girlfriend was in the hospital? Plus, there's plenty of fried chicken here. Your whole family and mine are all in the waiting room. I doubt they'd let us picnic in here but I promise once I make sure it's okay, we'll get you a plate and you and I can snuggle and have our July Fourth lunch right here."

She started to cry. What had she done to deserve this man? He took the hand that wasn't hooked to an IV, alarmed. "Venus? Honey, what is it? Why are you crying? Are you in pain? Should I call the doctor?"

"They're all here and I'm your girlfriend?"

"That makes you cry?"

"It's a good kind of cry. Answer me."

"Woman, I told your blonde ass I loved you over a month ago. Of course you're my girlfriend. You think I'd let just any woman make me scratch biscuits and cherry pie with fresh whipped cream? And I hate to say this, Venus, but only a man who loves you would stick around after hearing you sing in the shower. You're my woman. My heart."

She nodded, wincing a bit at the pain but happy. So damned happy. "Good. Okay then. Matt? I love you too."

She did. She always had in some sense as a fantasy but the

reality of Matt Chase was beyond anything she could have imagined. Sweeter than her visual donut. He was special and there for her when she needed it. She'd have to worry about whether he'd bolt when he heard the full truth later. For the moment though, she let herself love and be loved.

At her admission, relief washed over him and he wanted to kiss her. Hell, he wanted to whoop at the top of his lungs, chide her for not saying so sooner, scoop her up and protect her forever and fuck her ten ways til Sunday all at once.

Instead, he sighed with a grin. "'Bout time you said so. I was beginning to think you were just using me for the sex. And where else would your family be? They love you too. And mine. As a matter of fact, they're all worried sick. Let me step outside and tell everyone you're okay. Your brothers and sisters are going to want to see you too."

"Matt?"

"Hmm?"

"Thank you for knowing they need to see me. Thank you for being okay with that."

"Honey, family is everything. It's one of the things I love most about you."

He walked outside and leaned against the wall, relief that she'd finally allowed him to love her and herself to love him warring with the rage he felt for her father. Bill Murphy would never hurt Tate again. Not while Matt had breath to draw.

Everyone looked up expectantly when he entered the waiting room. Marc, Liv, Kyle and Maggie had arrived. "She's awake now. The doctor came in and checked her out. She's got a shiner, apparently she whacked the railing with her face on the way down. A sprained ankle, you know the heels she always wears." He laughed, emotion still tight in his chest. "They're going to keep her overnight."

Shane put his arm around Matt's shoulder.

Tim and Beth stood. "Can she see people?"

"Yeah, I know she wants to see you all. They said two at a time."

"We've done this before." Anne sighed. "You guys go first. Nathan and I'll go next. Then William can go in. Jacob and Jill should be here in an hour or so. Go on, I'll call them and check in. Mom too, I suppose," she said. Tim and Beth nodded before going down the hall toward Tate's room while Anne headed outside to use her cell phone.

"You okay, son?" Edward asked.

"Yes, sure. No, no I'm not. Damn it. She could've been really hurt."

"Well, it's happened. You knew you loved her, but now you really *see* the power of what it means to love someone. A powerful thing, love. The power of the connection you feel but also the power of the fear of losing it," his mother said as she patted his hand. "Bend on down here and give your old mom a kiss. I'm proud of you. You have excellent taste."

Matt smiled and bent to hug and kiss his mother. "She told me she loved me."

Nathan grinned. "About time. I'm glad. You're good for her, Matt. But, you know this isn't going to be easy."

"Hasn't been so far. But it's been fun when I'm not scared to death."

"I'd like to see her too," Cassie said quietly, telling him with her eyes that she'd try to help Tate through the trauma if she could.

"Thank you, Cassie." Matt breathed a sigh of relief.

"We all want to see her. We'll wait for her kin and then we'll go in and let that girl know we love her too." Polly squeezed Matt's hand.

"Fine, that'll be fine, Momma. I'm here for the night," Matt said, distracted.

"You sure about that? You won't get any rest with them waking her up hourly," Nathan said. "We'll all be here if you need to get home for work."

"You think I'd leave her alone here? After what happened to her today? If she'd only called me before she went over there." He sat down, head in his hands. "Why didn't she do that?"

"Because, she's been handling my dad—and worse—for most of her life. She's ashamed," Tim said, after coming out of Tate's room to sit across from Matt.

"I'm going to go in now while Beth's still with her. Tell him. It's been a secret too damned long," Anne said softly. Nathan kissed her cheek as she passed him to go toward Tate's room.

"It's not her fault, why should she be ashamed?" Matt didn't like feeling helpless and he really didn't like it that she'd feel responsible for being hurt by someone else.

Tim started to speak but he seemed so angry he had to shake his head and point at Nathan.

"Look, you have no idea what it's like to live in a family like mine. Your parents are educated, you grew up with money and prestige. Yours is one of the premier families in this area. You were all loved and cherished.

"My family wasn't. My mother took off for weeks at a time, leaving us with my father. It's no secret that he's a drunk, a mean drunk. He didn't work much so Tim and Tate had to take care of the rest of us. You can look at Tate and see she's not his, he knows it too. She embodied my mother's infidelity, a slap in the face every time he saw her."

Beth and Anne came out and Nathan stopped the story. "I need to see her. I'll be back in a few minutes." William joined Nathan as they went to Tate.

Matt heaved a sigh and Polly dabbed her eyes.

Beth settled in next to Tim and Susan.

Tim took a swallow of his coffee and continued. "So I'm big. Big like he is and after a few memorable knockdowns with my dad, he left me alone, physically anyway. But Tate is small. I had to work, to bring food in for the others. She stayed at home for the kids, to take care of them that way. So the only way she could keep safe was to fade, to stay unnoticed. Other than me, she had no one who could protect her. She had to keep her focus on the little ones, he wasn't above hurting them to hurt her.

"I've seen your house at Christmas, by the way. All lit up with sparkly lights, that big tree in your front window. My house, our trailer, wasn't on the Petal Christmas lights map. You think Tate's reservations about your differences are silly, I know you do. And I know it's because you don't know any better. But at our trailer Christmases were hell. Any excuse to drink more was a disaster. We didn't have a big shiny tree with loads of presents. We had one tree and my mother set it on fire to get back at my dad for something.

"My senior year in high school I only went enough to get my diploma. By then I worked two jobs and Tate did house-work on the side for different families around town to bring in the money. I moved out and we brought all the kids with us. Tate finished school the best she could but worked every spare moment. Then she graduated and Anne did it, Nathan after her." Tim's voice broke.

Anne took over the telling and Matt realized what a unit they all were, with Tate at the heart. "We tried but we'd have fallen apart if it weren't for Tate. She missed a lot of school, didn't go to dances, didn't date. She dumpster dived for clothes even though it got her teased. But let me tell you, none of us missed school. She wouldn't allow it. She worked nights for Doctor Allen in Riverton so we could have healthcare." Anne worried her lip with her teeth. "Tate isn't heavy because she eats for stress or whatever, she's always been curvy, and our father would use that like a bludgeon. The stuff he says to her, it's repugnant."

"This isn't her first concussion," Cassie broke in gently.

"No. I told you, she was, is, his favorite target. Most of his abuse was verbal and emotional along with neglect. But when he got really drunk and if she was around…" Anne paused, taking a breath. Her hands shook and Tim ran a hand up and down her arm. "He broke her arm when we were in elementary school. She's had two concussions. He knocked her into a door when she shielded Nathan, she was like fifteen maybe? And another time, right after we'd moved out. Technically, Tim and Tate had no right to take us. She paid him to let her bring us with them. She doesn't know we know that, it would kill her with guilt if she knew. She was late with the payments and he beat her pretty bad."

Anne put her hand over her mouth, unable to finish. Nathan rejoined them with William at his side.

"That's a shame, Matt. Living with secrets, living with people who'd shake you down for money, people who harm you because you're the face of their failures. So no, she didn't call you. We were raised to hide it. Tate has lived her life for all of us, even for my asshole of a father and my waste of a mother. It's not that she didn't trust you to protect her, it's that no one has ever protected her ever. She's only had herself."

"She never said. I've asked her about it but she wouldn't talk about it. I knew it had to be sort of bad, but why didn't she tell me?"

"Jesus man, have you not heard a thing we told you? She's *ashamed* of it! She's afraid you'll judge her, the way people have judged us all our whole lives. Deal with it. How does one tell someone they've been abused anyway? Is it appropriate between courses at dinner? After a picnic? How should she have told you and how would you have reacted? She's afraid of letting anyone in, because people hurt her or they ignore it when she's hurting." Nathan shook his head sadly.

"Good Lord," Polly whispered, holding Edward's hand.

"If you're going to leave her over this, please do us, do her a favor and wait until after she's recovered and home," Beth said.

"You think I'd walk away from her because of this? God, what kind of man do you think I am? I love her. I wasn't making that up. She's...in the months we've been together, she's become so much to me. I would never hurt her, especially not over something that wasn't her fault."

"We'll be her shiny Christmas mornings," Polly said quietly. "We've got room around our tree for fourteen more."

Matt kissed his mother, fighting back tears. "Thanks, Momma. Why don't you and Daddy go to see her while I get myself together."

His parents nodded and headed down the hall. Matt stood and faced her siblings. "Thank you for trusting me to tell me this and for helping me to understand her better."

"We trusted you with the story because you seem worthy of her. Please let us be right." Anne stood and hugged him.

"I love Tate with all that I am."

His siblings and their wives surrounded him, hugging him.

Shane looked into his face. "You gonna be all right? We've got your back."

"Yeah, but thanks. Thanks to all of you."

"It's gonna be hard to make charges stick if the mother won't *remember* anything. If he says it was an accident they may not go forward. It's not my choice, I want you to know I'll do all I can, but you should be ready for that eventuality."

Matt sighed, swallowing hard. "We'll handle it if it comes along. Maybe the mother will do the right thing."

Shane's face told Matt just how dubious he was at that idea.

Matt's head spun. He didn't quite know how to process all he'd heard. He felt a deep, murderous rage toward Tate's father and bottomless tenderness toward his own woman. He knew he couldn't show her any pity or she'd be hurt. Knew she didn't want it, just his love and respect.

Tate looked up to see Cassie Chase come in. Deep, bone-deep exhaustion settled into her. She wanted to be that cultured, that beautiful and graceful, and that wasn't going to ever be. She'd never be tall and beautiful like Cassie.

"Hi, Tate, how are you feeling?" Cassie sat in the chair next to the bed and kicked off her shoes.

"Been better." She smiled weakly.

"Yeah, worse too, haven't you?"

Tate stilled as Cassie looked at her through alarmingly perceptive eyes. "I don't know what you mean."

"Yes you do. Takes one to know one, Tate. I've been there in a hospital bed after a man gave me a concussion. More than once as a matter of fact. I know the bitterness of shame in my gut too. I know what it is to hide it and think people will judge. Do you know my story?"

Tate shook her head. "I know someone tried to hurt you a few years ago."

"My ex-husband. Tried to kill me actually. For the second time." Cassie told her the story of her years of abuse and of how her ex skipped out on his sentencing and then came to Petal to try and finish the job he nearly succeeded in before.

Cassie held up her right hand, the middle finger was bent at an odd angle. "This is what he did with the hammer. I'll never be a surgeon again. Funny how life works. Still, it drove me here to Petal, which brought Shane into my life and I realized what happened to me wasn't my fault. Wasn't my shame to bear and it's not yours either, Tate."

"I can't...how did you know?"

"I saw how you reacted after dinner the other night. I saw myself in your eyes. Heard more from your family just now."

Tate felt the heat of her blush, replaced by the familiar coldness of the shame. "They told you? All of you? They told you all of it?"

Cassie reached out and took Tate's hand. "I'm sure there's more. Years of shame. They told us enough that I know you were abused and still are. Enough that I know what an amazingly strong woman you are for stepping in with your younger siblings. You have a family with them. Your father tried to destroy it but you didn't let him. You win, Tate. That's what he hates so much. He can't break you."

Tears rolled down Tate's face. The wall of shame, the barriers that'd kept it all back were gone and it rushed out in wave after wave of emotion. Cassie got in the bed next to Tate, putting her arms around her.

"You win, Tate Murphy. Don't you see? You're worthy of all the people who love you. And let me tell you, your brothers and sisters love and respect you so much it made me proud to know you. And Matt, he loves you, Tate. It's not charity. It's not pity. He loves *you*. All of you, flaws and alcoholic father, neglectful mother, everything. Let it go and stop letting him get to you."

"That's so easy to say," Tate sobbed as Cassie continued to hold her. Wanting with all she was for it to be true.

"It is. Now. It wasn't just a few years ago when it was me in your place. I was a successful vascular surgeon, Tate! I had a good family who loved me, privilege, all the advantages in life and I ended up with a man who raped me and tried to kill me. I didn't deserve love. I didn't deserve a man like Shane. I didn't want a bossy, pushy control-freak cop who barely fits through doorways without having to turn to the side."

Tate couldn't help but laugh.

"I know. He's huge. Heh, yeah, that way too. But I digress. Listen, you, Polly is on the case so just give in. The woman will stop at nothing, do you know that? Matt loves you, you love him. He wants you and she'll stop at nothing until she helps him get you. And since you want him too, why fight it? Stop letting your father control you. Stop going over there. If neighbors call, call the damned police. I promise you your father won't be shoving Shane around. You are not responsible for your mother and the life she's created for herself. You are not responsible for your father's pain that you're not his. It is not his right to harm you. Stop letting him control you. It's the only way you're going to heal and be free of it. And your siblings will follow your lead. They look to you for guidance."

"I have to eat with them at least once a year. For Jacob and Jill's loan stuff."

"Fuck that. Come on, Tate. Look, there are six of you and all the Chases too, we can come up with alternatives. It's one year. Don't let him control you this way. Let the people who love you help."

Could she believe it? Grasp the hope that she could have a normal relationship with Matt?

Matt tapped on the door, poking his head in. Seeing the state Tate was in, he rushed to her bedside, alarmed.

"Honey? Cassie, what did you do?"

"She just helped me. It's okay. Really."

"You're feeling better?"

"No. I have a horrible crying headache to go along with the concussion headache. My messed-up childhood has been exposed to my boyfriend and his family without my permission and I've had a very emotional discussion with someone who knows where I've been. But I only have up to go, there's no more down at this point."

Cassie got up, hugging Tate carefully. "Please, give me a call or stop in at the bookstore if you want to talk. I'm trained as a victim's advocate but more than that, I'm your friend. I like you, Tate. You have excellent taste in shoes, I'm not sure if I told you that before or not."

Tate smiled. "Thanks. For everything."

"That's what friends, and family, are for." Cassie kissed Matt's cheek and headed for the door as Jacob and Jill burst in.

"Easy!" Matt grabbed Jacob before he jostled Tate.

Jacob winced. "Sorry. You okay? Tateness, I told you to stop going over there. Let the cops sort them out." Jacob kissed her forehead gently and Jill moved around to the other side, taking Tate's hand.

"If you just let them kill each other, we'd all be better off anyway," Jill mumbled.

Tate sighed. "Don't. Don't let them make you bitter. You're better than that. Now what on earth are you doing here? Jill, I know you had plans today with that new guy you're seeing."

"Shut up! My God, Tate, he could have killed you. You think making out and watching fireworks is more important to me than you are?" Jill looked offended but Tate saw the tremble in her bottom lip and knew she was about to lose it.

"I do think it's more important, Jill. Yes, I do. Damn it, they've disrupted our lives enough. I don't want him to do it anymore. Now get your butts back to Atlanta. Make out, watch fireworks. Use a condom!"

"I don't need a condom to kiss for cripes' sake! I've only known him a few weeks, he's not getting any just yet."

"Enough information, thank you very much. Tate, you're out of your mind if you think Jill and I are leaving before you get home from the hospital." Jacob crossed his arms over his chest and glared.

The nurse came in and frowned. "Too many guests. She needs to rest and you all need to let her."

"I'm staying." Matt stayed at her side.

Tate looked up at him and wondered why his voice sounded that way. Was he trying to be alone to dump her? That was probably it. Loving a woman with some family problems was one thing, now that he knew the whole story surely he'd see how impossible it was for them to be together.

"Go on, guys. I need to talk to Matt and then I need to nap. You have the key to my place. There are leftovers in my fridge and clean bedding in the guestroom."

Jill kissed her cheek. "We'll get it ready for you to come home to. I'll stop by the library to grab you some books."

Jacob followed, kissing the other cheek. "We'll be back tonight. Rest. Love you."

"Love you both too."

They left and Matt settled into the chair next to the bed. Reaching out, she touched the softness of his hair for a moment and he leaned into her hand.

"They told you about my father."

He nodded. "Yes. God, Tate, I don't know what to say it's so awful. I'm just relieved you're all right."

A tear rolled down her cheek. "I'm sorry. I didn't know how to tell you, it was embarrassing. You…you don't have to stay here anymore. I understand."

His eyes widened and then narrowed. "Good God, Tate, what do you take me for? Have I given you any indication that I'm that shallow a man? I love you, damn it. Not your father. You. I want to be with you and continue to build something with you. If you weren't suffering from a head injury I'd be offended."

"Matt," she sighed, "I worry that you'll regret this."

He cocked his head. "Why would I regret loving you? You don't seem to understand and that's my fault I suppose. Tate, I'm old enough to know what I feel. Old enough to know this is very different than anything I've ever felt before. It's you. You and me and it's right. Surely you can feel it."

"We come from very different worlds."

"So you keep saying. And I keep saying—so? Seriously. Yes, you had a fucked-up childhood. One I can't even begin to imagine. But that doesn't mean we don't have a future together. Sometimes I'm going to do something stupid and thoughtless because I don't know any better. I'm a guy, it's what we do. And sometimes you're going to react in ways I don't understand and it's going to piss me off or confuse me. We'll get through it."

Tate put her head against the pillow and closed her eyes. He was fooling himself to ignore the real fact of the situation. People in town were going to talk. They already were talking. He'd always been on the inside, how was he going to take it when he risked that to be with her? Still, she was too damned tired to deal with it right then. And she didn't want to.

"Rest now, Venus. I'll be right here. If you wake up and I'm gone, I've just nipped out to get something to drink or to make a call to fill in your family or mine."

He kissed her forehead gently and she let herself fall into sleep.

By the time they were ready to release her the next morning, his normally good-natured Tate was a very grumpy woman. He didn't blame her, they'd woken her up every hour on the hour and she looked dead tired.

He'd slept in her room all night, which meant he woke up every hour on the hour as well. And every three hours a new one of her siblings showed up and stayed in the room with them.

Shane had gone to Matt's apartment and packed him a bag, bringing it by the hospital. They'd found Tate's father and arrested him sometime overnight. Her mother had gone off to Dallas after trying to borrow some money from Tim, who'd refused.

Once the release papers had been signed, Matt and Tate got into a heated argument. He'd wanted to carry her to his truck and she'd looked at him like he'd lost his mind.

"I'll do the wheelchair thing like I'm supposed to but you're not carrying me." She slapped his hands away as he'd tried to pick her up.

"Why not? Tate, honey, let me help you."

"You're insane. You can push the wheelchair."

He growled at her and she raised a regal, white-blonde brow at him. Sighing, Nathan pushed his way into the discussion.

"As fascinating as it is to watch you two argue over stupid shit like this, let's motor. Matt, push the damned wheelchair, she doesn't want you to pick her up because she thinks she's too heavy. You, Tate, sit your ass down and shut up."

Tate did that cute little *hmpf*ing thing and Matt thought

about arguing over how stupid it was that she thought he couldn't pick up a bitty scrap of a woman like her. He could carry two hundred pounds on his back up a ladder during a fire for God's sake, but she really was cute when she made that sound.

They got her settled in at her house. He tucked her into bed with some magazines while one of her sisters made tea. His mother had wanted to come over but already Tate's little house was bursting at the seams with Murphys so Polly agreed to bring over some food later that day.

Tate had fallen asleep by the time the tea had steeped so he left her to rest in the cool, darkened room and snuck quietly out to the living room where her family waited.

"Is she all right?" Beth asked, putting the tray with the tea on it down.

"She's asleep." Matt fell onto the couch.

"You need the sleep too. Do you need to go home? To work?" Tim asked from across the room.

"I'm good. I took the next three days off. I planned to stay here. Are you all okay with that?"

"More than okay with it. But one of us will stay here too." Anne drank some iced tea, rocking slowly. The house was shaded by several large willow and oak trees and the air conditioning kept it cool as well. Still, it was July in Petal and the heat rose from the pavement out front in dizzying waves.

"Mostly me, Anne and Nathan," Beth spoke up. "Jill and Jacob have summer classes so they need to go home and William and Tim have kids and wives."

"Hey, doesn't mean I won't do my duty here!" William grumbled. "She's mine too, damn it."

"William, we know that. She knows that. But you know how she is. She'd worry about Cindy being alone with the kids and you being here. She'd worry about you not being at work. She'll worry about Susan at the shop and Tim's business if he's not there. You can come by in the evenings. Back me up when I insist she take the rest of the week off."

"She can't mean to go back to work just yet anyway!" Matt looked at them all.

Tim snorted. "She'd have gone back today if we'd let her. Tate views any kind of illness or injury as a weakness. She's the hardest worker I know. We'll have to wrestle her to keep her from going to the shop this week, crutches and all."

"She's going to do no such thing. She's got four stitches on the back of her head, she had a concussion, she doesn't need to cut hair just yet."

Beth waved it away. He recognized the gesture from Tate. "If you put it that way she'll go back just to spite you. Anne and I have worked the schedule out. We've got it covered until Monday. That gives us four days. Let us handle that part. Although I like that you put her first. I like that a lot."

Pride swelled through him that her family approved.

He excused himself, going into her room and closing the door. Quickly stripping to his boxers, he carefully slid into her bed, pressing himself against her before dropping into sleep.

Chapter Nine

Tate chafed at the way her sisters watched her so closely. Every five minutes someone shoved a glass of water or some fruit at her.

"I'm not made of glass!" she growled through clenched teeth but Anne clucked and continued to hold out the glass of iced tea.

"It's that mango green tea crap you like so much. Shut up and drink it or I'll tell Tim you're not taking care of yourself. You weren't even supposed to come back to work until Monday. We agreed to let you work today because you said you'd take it easy."

"Oh for heaven's sake!" She took it and sipped. "Thank you. Now go see to your client please, mine is coming in two minutes and I need to take a pit stop."

Tate hurried off but when she got back she recognized the lacquered blonde head sitting in her chair. Her eyes met Polly Chase's in the mirror and there was no escape.

"Hello, honey. How are you?" Polly turned to look at Tate better as she approached.

"I'm fine, Mrs. Chase. How are you?"

"Well, just worried sick about you. But your color is back.

You do have such pretty skin. I always wished mine was that creamy smooth."

Tate looked at the woman perched in the chair. Polly Chase was a total stunner for her age. Even with a hairstyle that predated computers. She was tiny but all around tiny. Petite little hands and feet, always wore perfect clothes. Tailored suits, pretty dresses, spiky stilettos. Her makeup was always flawless and her eyes, big and green, reminded Tate of late spring grass, vibrant. Tate would have bet her entire year's salary that Polly Chase never envied anyone's skin, much less hers.

"Mrs. Chase, I'm beginning to see where Matthew gets his gift with stretching the truth."

Astonishment showed on Polly's face a moment and then she laughed, delighted. "I sure do like you, Tate Murphy. Now come on over here and do my hair and we'll talk about my son. And you'll call me Polly."

Anne met Tate's eyes as she passed and they both had to hold back a laugh. The woman was totally incorrigible.

Beth gave Polly a shampoo and brought her back to Tate's station. "I'm going to go ahead and pretend I don't know Anne normally does this so you can grill me on my intentions with your son. Would you like some tea?"

"Yes please. And I do so love it when people let me boss them around. Makes a small woman feel mighty, know what I mean? Of course you do, you've pretty much raised your brothers and sisters. I see the way they are with you. A gift, having people love you so much, being part of something that means everything."

Tate felt something click inside her at that moment. Polly Chase understood her better than anyone had, more than Matt, more than her own siblings. She met Polly's eyes in the mirror briefly before beginning to towel and blow her hair dry. As she got the extensive backcombing and spraying process started, she had to wrestle back her emotions. Other than her siblings, when had an adult actually cared about her? Reached out the way Polly was doing? That broken little girl inside Tate's soul wanted to grab it, take the hand Polly held out because damn it, she needed it.

"It's all right, honey. What *are* your intentions with my Matthew then?" She knew. The amazing thing about Polly Chase was that she saw that little girl inside Tate and didn't run. She *wanted* to comfort her and know her.

Polly sat back and Tate began to talk about Matt.

As Tate worked on her hair, Polly absolutely fell in love with Tate Murphy. She loved all her daughters-in-law but none of them had ever really sat down and talked about her sons with her the way Tate did.

Tate loved Matt. Not his name, not his looks or his money, she loved his laugh, the way he pitched in when anyone needed anything, the way he took care of her after the hospital. So many people looked at Matt and saw a pretty boy who had it easy, they didn't see the rest of him, the compassion and love, the way he threw himself into everything he truly cared about. Tate saw that and Tate loved him for it. And Polly loved Tate for it.

The girl was fragile in many ways but she'd always be a good partner to her son. Polly would never tell anyone, but she'd always worried about Matt the most. He seemed so carefree and easygoing but he wandered around looking for something to challenge him. Women were easy, too easy. Which is why he never kept one very long. She'd had hopes for Liv, thought Matt was a damned fool for letting that one go at the time but now she knew Liv was for Marc. But Matt had started drifting again after Liv. He needed something to work for.

He did have it easy in other ways too. He'd been tested at school early on and scored off the charts, got that from his daddy. He'd never gotten less than an A in a class all the way through school, scored outrageously high on his SATs and then rejected college. Broke Edward's heart that none of his boys wanted to go into the law.

But underneath it all, Matt wanted to make his own way. When he'd started the fire academy, Polly had known it was the right choice. Yes, he'd been at the top of his class but he'd had to work for it. And when he was out on the job, he worked, he had to focus and give it his all and that made it perfect for him.

He'd been fulfilled by his career and it made her and Edward proud to see Matt come into himself as a man through his job. But still, no challenges in his personal life.

Until Tate.

Polly watched Tate as she worked on her hair and laughed, talking about Matt. Who'd have thought it would be this girl who stole her son's heart? Matt had squired some of the most stunning women in the area around. None of them had been right for him and Tate was beautiful in a different way but it wasn't apparent at first glance.

"So, tell me, has Melanie been keeping up with her nasty little campaign?"

"Blunt. What if I said I didn't want to talk about it?"

Polly thought about it for long moments. "Well, surely it's your business and all. But you should know right up front that no one messes with me and mine. Certainly no twitterpated piece of fluff like Melanie. And make no mistake, Tate, you're one of mine. All your brothers and sisters and their children are too. I don't take kindly to anyone threatening Matthew's sweetie. And I really don't like her attitude about you and your background." She met Tate's eyes straight on in the mirror. "Because money doesn't give you class or pride and your address or your parents don't make you better than anyone else."

"That's not true, Polly. You and Edward made your sons better men."

Oh. That tore at Polly because the girl meant it and that was a shot straight to her heart. Reaching up, she took Tate's hand and squeezed it. "I do believe that's the best compliment I've ever received."

"Melanie hasn't been back but several cancellations called up and rescheduled. Thank you."

"Don't thank me. I don't like that sort of play on class differences. It puts my back up. I wasn't raised that way, my boys weren't, it offends me. Girls like Melanie after my boy offend me. You are coming to dinner tomorrow night, right?"

"No, Mrs.....Polly, it's family dinner at my house this week. Last week at your house was pretty disastrous, I wasn't sure you'd want me back. I'm sorry. I didn't get a chance to apologize for making a scene."

Polly saw the girl go pink. "Tate, I understand there are reasons that made you react the way you did. Matt, like his brothers and his father, is a very protective man. He wanted to help you when he knew you'd been harmed. You know that, I expect, as well as you know he wouldn't ever hurt you or try to control you. We all have buttons, honey. Yours got pushed. It makes you human. Why don't you all come to my house tomorrow? I'll put an extra leaf in the table and we'll eat in the formal dining room. We've got room for an extra dozen. Your brothers and sisters and those children are always welcome."

Beth strolled past and waved hello. "Afternoon, Mrs. Chase. No offense or anything, but you're going to find it a hard proposition to talk a Murphy out of a dinner where Tate cooks. It's the highlight of the month, those Sunday dinners at her table."

"I'd heard you were a wonderful cook, Tate. Good enough to give me a run for my money even." She winked to let the girl know it didn't make her angry. "Tell you what, we can cook something together. How does that sound?"

Tate was quiet for a bit as she continued to do Polly's hair.

"Tate, honey, it's no secret my son loves you. He wants to be with you and eventually, our families will have to merge more. Why not start now? In fact, why don't we eat at your house this time, trade back and forth."

"Polly, my house bursts at the seams with fourteen as it is. But we can do something out back since the weather is so nice. It's a huge yard with lots of shade. Play equipment for the kids although Nicholas isn't quite big enough for most of it just yet. I don't want Liv to be outside in the heat, though, being as pregnant as she is."

The girl was really a miracle.

"Livvy loves the heat, unlike Cassie and Maggie." Polly chuckled. "But if we make it after seven when the sun is going down it'll be fine. I worry that you're taking on too much though so soon after the hospital. That's ten extra people."

Tate stepped back and looked at Polly's hair, making sure it was even. She patted it and handed Polly a mirror.

"You did a great job with that, honey." Polly spun the chair and checked out the back.

Tate wanted to offer her the chance to change it with a new look but women like Polly identified strongly with their hair-dos and Tate didn't want to upset that applecart. Polly Chase had a strong enough sense of identity that she could ask for something new if she wanted it.

Tate was scared shitless over the idea of having ten Chases at her house. Her little house. But Polly was right, Tate and Matt had gotten a lot closer since she'd returned from the hospital earlier in the week. Things between them were serious and if she meant to go on with him, they would have to bring their families together. It didn't make sense to keep them all apart when both Matt and Tate were so close to their families.

"Well, if you'd like, you could come over early and help me cook." Another woman in her kitchen, an alpha woman like Polly, would be a challenge but Matt was worth it. Family was worth it.

Polly grinned. "Why that'd be lovely! I'll come over at say, five? What are you planning to make? I'll bring over some of the ingredients. No, don't argue, you can do the same next week when you come to my house. Since you're such a fabulous cook we can share duties. If that's okay with you?"

Tate took a deep breath and let it out. "Sure." She told Polly her menu plans and the two of them worked out a grocery list and a schedule.

Tate got out of her car and froze as she saw who stood on her porch, leaning indolently against the railing.

"What are you doing here?" She stood by the car, not wanting to get any closer to the man who'd landed her in the hospital just days before.

"I'm out on bail. Seems the prosecutor believes my story that it was an accident. Your mother had a convenient memory lapse as well. I thought I'd come here to mend some bridges." Her father's smirk belied his words.

She leaned against the car, arms crossed over her chest. Nathan would be by in fifteen minutes but if she had to, she'd get in the car and drive away. She was done letting him hurt her.

"I'm not interested. Just go home. And don't call me to fix your problems with my mother anymore." Her voice shook a bit but it was a step.

"Well and see, here I was about to congratulate you for landing yourself a man at all, especially one with a wallet like Matt Chase." He took a step off her porch but she put a hand out.

"Stay back. Don't get any nearer."

He stopped and jerked his head to the side. "I didn't come here to touch you, *daughter.* I had no intention to have you fall down those steps. I don't care enough about you to harm you."

"Could have fooled me all those times you did harm me. Now what do you really want? We both know you're not here to mend anything."

"Money. You have it, I don't. Give me some."

A sick feeling twisted through her. "Ah yes, I should have known. I suppose a job is too much energy to give when you could drink all day instead? How about I pay for rehab? You know I will." She hated that she wanted to help him, he didn't deserve it but she couldn't make herself stop being concerned.

"I don't need a job now that my daughter has her own business and a rich boyfriend, now do I? The way I see it, Tate, is you landed him, God knows how looking the way you do. And I should benefit from that. I supported you and those other brats, I should be reimbursed for that."

Incredulousness rode her. "You did *what*? I'm not arguing with you. Nor am I giving you a cent. I work for my money and I don't take anything from Matt. I don't need to. We both *work* for a living. You ought to try it."

The thin veneer slid off his face then and the man she'd feared settled into his features. Nausea threatened but she held back.

"Let's put it this way then, Tate, since you're being so ungrateful and all. I'm thinking I'd love to be part of your new life. Turn over a new leaf. I'd love to get to know your new family. Since I have so much time and all, I thought I'd come over more often. Maybe stop by the firehouse and visit with my daughter's new beau." He shrugged. "Or you can give me a few hundred bucks and I'll keep scarce."

She sighed. The Chases seemed okay with her past but that was when they didn't have to confront it face-to-face. How would it be if her father just showed up at Sunday dinner, drunk and belligerent? How would Matt feel then? And how would her brothers and sisters feel when they'd finally had a good life?

She'd gone to the ATM earlier to give Nathan cash and her grocery list. She dug into her purse and pulled out three hundred dollars cash and thrust it at him.

"Take it and don't come back."

He took his time, leisurely coming toward her and grabbing the money. Tucking it into his pocket, his smile made her sick. "Thank you, *daughter*. Now I'll be on my way, not to bother you again."

Nathan found her rocking in her chair, still sweating from throwing up. He knelt in front of her. "Honey, Tate? Are you all right? Do you need to go back to the doctor? Is it your head?"

She shook her head slowly, wanting so much to tell him what happened. He'd understand. He'd hug her and tell her it would all be okay. But after that experience with the whole Melanie thing, she knew he'd also want her to tell Matt. Or worse, tell Matt himself. He'd also tell her to stop giving their father money and she couldn't do that.

She finally had something real with Matt and no one was going to threaten it. She was the only one who stood between the ugliness of her father and the beauty of her family. She had to protect them as she always had and now that Matt was hers, she'd protect him too.

"It's the heat. I'm all right now. I made you a grocery list but I forgot to get cash."

He waved that away. "Not a big deal. You never let us pay for anything and I'm bored with sneaking money into your purse when you aren't looking." He cracked a smile and she snorted. They all did it. She just put the cash aside and used it on the kids or to make special treats for them.

They were safe from their father. She could handle him and keep him away from everyone. She'd done it most of her life and she'd keep doing it now.

"Let me give you a check." She moved to rise but he put a gentle hand on her shoulder to stay her.

"I mean it, Tate. No. You don't know how happy it makes me that you're letting me do your grocery shopping. So let me. It's some groceries. Considering how much I eat over here, it's a bargain for me. I'll be back in a bit. Matt should be here in a while right? You want me to stay until he gets here?"

She smiled, love flooding through her. "I'm fine. I managed without a keeper before Matt came along. I need to call William about the tables and extra chairs anyway. Bring back something you want me to make for dinner. You can stay can't you?"

He laughed, dropping a kiss on her cheek. "What a question. I'd love to stay. I'll be back as soon as I can. I'll have my cell but I'm betting you'll have another Murphy or two over here before I get back anyway."

She wanted to tell him about their father but she couldn't explain how she knew.

When he left she called William and he promised to bring over a few extra banquet-size tables and chairs early the next afternoon.

Making up her mind, she called the police station.

"What do you mean they let him go?"

Matt heard Tate's voice rise and he hurried through her front door to see she was on the phone.

"Yes, yes, well, isn't that nice? Perhaps someone would have seen fit to call me, you know, the person who got a concussion and spent the night in the hospital? No! If someone had called me would I be calling now? Oh fuck me! Listen here, bub, do you think I give a rat's ass if someone in some other place should have called me? I didn't get called."

Matt exhaled sharply. They let her father out of jail? He pulled his cell out of his pocket and dialed Shane.

"Yes, I know, she's yelling at one of my deputies right now. I'm sorry, Matt, it's up to the prosecutor's office to call the victim and we didn't know she hadn't been informed," Shane answered before Matt even said a word.

"They let him go?"

Tate turned and saw him there on the phone, he stepped to her, kissed her briefly and they both went back to their calls.

"The prosecutor isn't going to prosecute. He said it was an accident and Tate wasn't that eager to testify. Matt, the mother is backing up his story."

Matt's stomach dropped as he looked up at Tate who was

apparently hearing the same thing. She mumbled her thanks and hung up the phone.

"Shit. I have to go." Matt wanted to make it all right for her, damn it.

"I'm sorry, Matt. I know where you are right now. Believe me. Come talk to me when you can, okay?"

Matt agreed and flipped the phone shut.

"They let my father go. They're not even going to prosecute him." Tate's voice as she spoke to him trembled slightly.

He embraced her gently, stroking his hands up and down her arms. "I know, I was just talking to Shane. I'm sorry, Venus."

"My mother is backing him up. And it was an accident. I don't think he deliberately tried to hurt me. He was gesturing all around. I yelled at that deputy. I need to apologize. It wasn't his fault."

A bubble of hysterical laughter hit Matt and he let it go. Only Tate would be concerned about that right now when the man who'd hurt her was out free.

She called and apologized to the deputy as Matt got them both some tea. He didn't like how pale she looked. Nathan came in with groceries some minutes later and Beth followed soon after.

Tate perked up as she started to make a chicken salad for dinner. She didn't even rely on the crutches much by that point as she hobbled around her kitchen. It seemed to him that merely taking care of other people made her feel better.

As they ate, she told him about the combined Chase-Murphy dinner the following night and he grinned. His mother never ceased to amaze him. Then again, neither did Tate. Twenty people was a big chore for a woman who'd just been in the hospital, but if his mother agreed to it, he knew she'd make sure Tate didn't overdo it.

After dinner, Beth and Matt did dishes while Nathan took out the trash and Tate folded laundry. He realized how normal it felt, being there with her in her little house. How quickly they'd moved to this level surprised him but he wasn't scared.

"You don't need to stay over, Nathan. I'll be here and I have tomorrow off so I'll help in the morning to make sure she doesn't overdo it." Matt looked around the corner where Beth helped Tate put clothes away before telling Nathan about their father and mother.

Nathan slammed a fist down onto the arm of the couch and Tate came rushing out. "Nathan?"

"I'm sorry, honey. Matt just told me about Mom and Dad."

So much for talking quietly and in private.

Beth's eyes widened as she demanded an explanation and she began to pace when they gave it to her. "She's out of her damned mind. Well, that's it. Tate, no more. Don't you dare go over there again. She's made her bed and so has he. You can't fix them and it's just going to hurt you. We don't need them anymore. We'll figure out what to do with Jill and Jacob. It's just one more year."

"Amen. Now, Tate needs rest. We'll see you both tomorrow afternoon." Matt ushered them both out and came back to find Tate pouring herself a drink.

"You want one?"

"You sure you do?"

She turned and sipped the amber liquid. "I'm not him. Yes, I grew up with a man who used alcohol as an excuse to be a monster." She shrugged. "I don't. It's not an excuse but it's not evil either. It's just a substance."

Drawing her close he pressed his lips to the top of her head and breathed her in. "You're a very wise woman, you know that, don't you?"

"Fuck me, Matt. Put your hands all over me. Make me come."

He stilled, wondering if he'd heard her correctly or if she was using an exclamation. He took her glass and placed it on the counter. A look into her eyes told him it was the former.

"I'm going to lock up. I'll meet you in your bedroom in three minutes. Be naked."

Hurriedly, he checked the doors and windows and moved toward her room.

He halted in the doorway and watched her move. Graceful and feminine, she was so beautiful. She turned and locked eyes with him as she reached up to let her hair fall like a pale spill of moonlight around her shoulders.

Moving to her, he undid the straps of her dress and let it fall to pool at her feet. Her bra followed and she stepped out of her panties. He loved that she'd lost her shyness around him with regard to her body. He was glad she'd accepted how damned sexy she was to him.

"Take your shirt off. I want to see you, Matt."

He heard the urgency in her voice and it disturbed him. He traced her jawline with his thumb and she bit the fleshy pad when he moved over her lips.

"Are you all right, Venus?"

"I *need* you, Matt. Please."

His clothes were off in record time before he backed her to the bed and she fell back to the mattress, looking up at him, eyes shining with raw need, with something else he couldn't quite define. So he did all he knew how to do, ease that need, meet it with the same desire he felt for her.

Sometimes you needed to make love and sometimes you needed to be fucked. Tate needed the latter, needed every muscle in her body to know she belonged to Matt Chase.

She loved him so much it scared the hell out of her but she couldn't not love him. That he loved her too continued to awe her but she was done questioning it. She wanted to be with him forever and if he wanted that too, who was she to argue?

At that moment though, she needed him to want her. Needed his desire, his lust and attention.

Reaching out, she fumbled through the box in the nightstand and grabbed a condom. "On you. Now."

He grabbed it, ripping it open with his teeth and rolling it on in record time. When his fingers brushed over her pussy and found her wet and ready, a strangled moan broke from him.

"God, so damned hot and wet. You're so ready for me."

She reached down and guided the head of his cock to her gate and rolled her hips.

"Impatient," he chuckled.

"Yes! Where have you been the last ten minutes? Fuck me, buster!"

His only answer was a long thrust into her body that made her gasp his name as he filled her.

His eyes bored into hers, seeing so deeply that she wanted to weep with it and run away at the same time. It meant something to be known, to be loved despite what she came from, because of who she was. Emotion, deep and overwhelming, swallowed her, bringing tears to her eyes as she let her love for him flow from her, through her.

"Venus? Honey, am I hurting you?" He stilled and she wrapped her thighs around his waist and squeezed, pulling him closer to her.

"No. No, it's fine. They're good tears. I'm sorry." She laughed because he was so good, so fine and she was so damned lucky to be loved by him.

Leaning down, he kissed the tears from her cheeks. "I love you, Tate. I don't know what I'd have done if something happened to you. Seeing you in that hospital bed nearly tore me in half. You're so strong but damn, you're a tiny thing. Fragile."

"I love you too, Matt. And I'm fine. Fine here with you."

She squeezed her inner muscles around him and winked, breaking the tension.

His lips skimmed down her neck as he whispered endearments to her. His body slowly entered and retreated. Not fucking anymore, he made love to her with exquisite detail, kissing her, caressing her, telling her he loved her.

There was nothing but the two of them and that was all

right. Better than all right, it was perfect and Tate couldn't remember another moment that was ever so perfect.

Matt hauled tables and chairs along with Tate's brothers and his own as they set up in Tate's backyard. He loved her house and the giant yard out back.

Tate's nephew and nieces played on the playset, yelling and laughing in the early July evening and he realized just how happy he was. Satisfied. Fulfilled.

In the kitchen overlooking the yard, the women who meant the world to him laughed and prepared a meal while the men chased children and set up the tables. What an idyllic moment.

Edward stopped next to him, putting an arm around his shoulders. "You're good with this girl, Matthew. I like what she's done for you. I like this place. I like seeing our kin mix with hers. This is right."

Matt's heart swelled with pride at his father's compliments. "I was just thinking that. I love Tate. I think I started falling for her with the first bite of her cookies. But I hate that her father is out and I hate that threat."

Shane approached. "I'm sorry about that, Matt. I truly am. It wasn't up to me. If it had been, the bastard would still be in jail. I'm doubly sorry she didn't find out about it before he got out. I chewed the prosecutor's office a new one over that."

Tate had come out into the yard and lit citronella candles all around and plugged in the colored lights she'd strung through the big trees in the back near where they'd lined up the tables. The children laughed and she did too. She was damned good with kids and she'd be a wonderful mother. He froze a moment and then eased. She would be. And he'd be a good father too. He wanted to be with Tate every day for the rest of his life.

"Just hit you, didn't it? Saw her with your babies on her hip."

Matt looked at his father and laughed. "You're pretty scary sometimes, Daddy."

Edward shrugged. "I have to be. Your momma keeps me on my toes."

The women began to flow from the house with heaping platters of food, piling them from end to end across the three long tables they'd set up. Matt loved the way they all sounded, soft and light. He heard Tate's scratchy low voice and her laugh as it married with the sound of his mother and Tate's sisters. The thought that someone had just put her in the hospital less than a week before made him clench his jaw.

She was so damned precious to him. How could he protect her from her father at all times?

"It's hard. Getting past all the hurt she's been caused." Shane looked at Matt for long moments before his eyes moved to Cassie. Matt had watched as Shane learned more and more of Cassie's past, watched as his brother suffered over the pain the woman he loved had endured. And Matt had watched as Shane grew and matured into a man he admired deeply.

"But you will. And you'll need to let her let you in. Don't try to manage her, Matt. Be there for her but don't push."

"Yeah, 'cause you're such an unassuming, sensitive guy. What if she needs Matt to help her through things?" Kyle asked as he joined them.

"She's thirty-one years old. She runs a successful business. She and her siblings have supported each other through school. You saw how she dealt with this whole thing, how her family rallied around her. How she bounced back. She's not a mess. I'm just saying. I've been there."

Nicholas toddled over to Tate and she picked him up, kissing both cheeks and putting her own against the top of his head as she swayed side to side. When she opened her eyes, she looked around and saw Matt and her smile was for him.

"Thank you, Shane. Daddy and Kyle, you too. If you'll excuse me, my woman looks like she's going to leave me for another man if I don't get over there."

Tate held Nicholas against her as he played with her hair.

Maggie laughed and said something to her right but all Tate was focused on was Matt. She smiled as he approached.

"Hey, you trying to steal my woman?" Matt asked Nicholas who just laughed and burrowed tighter against her.

"Mommy's getting jealous, Nicholas. Won't you come and give me some love?" Maggie held her arms out and Nicholas jumped into them.

Matt didn't waste any time, he grabbed Tate and hugged her before laying a kiss on those lips of hers. "I'm starving."

She laughed. "Sit down. Everyone, come on and sit down, dinner is ready," she called out and the seats around the tables filled quickly and food began to move around in an orderly circuit.

Damn his woman could cook. Matt sat back some minutes later and rubbed his expanded belly. "Woman, you're the best thing that ever happened to me."

He found her telltale blush charming even through the onset of food coma.

"I heard that. Tate, I have to tell you, girl, you're an awfully fine cook. That's not a compliment I give often." Polly put her head on Edward's shoulder, leaning into him.

Matt and the other men cleaned up while the women sat outside and watched the children play.

He felt like they'd taken a huge step with that dinner, one toward unifying all the things in his life that he held most dear.

Chapter Ten

Tate watched as Polly tucked a wayward curl behind Beth's ear as they sat around the table at the Chases' for Sunday dinner. The two women laughed together and while it gave her great joy that they'd all been pulled into the Chase family with such ease, it also made her ache just a bit.

Polly Chase had become something more than the slightly scary mother of her boyfriend. More than the town matriarch and a client. She called Tate to check in on her day, sent over recipes and asked for Tate's. She picked up scarves and little knickknacks she told Tate reminded Polly of her. Polly knew her favorite flowers and what kind of tea she liked.

More than that, she extended that maternal care to all the Murphys great and small. Her nieces and nephew were totally at home in the Chase backyard.

It was a revelation to Tate, that mothers like Polly existed. At the same time, it made her resent that she never had that. It wasn't like Tate to wallow but sometimes, at night in a small corner of her heart, she allowed it just a tiny bit.

As Liv's due date approached, Tate and her sisters were invited to the shower. It wasn't so much that Tate disliked Liv, in fact, Tate had always appreciated Liv's humor when she came into the shop. But now that Tate was with Matt, it was a reminder that Liv was everything Tate wasn't. And she'd been with Matt. Matt had seen them both naked and it made Tate cringe just thinking about it.

Being around Liv now made her distinctly uncomfortable. She didn't want to go to the shower but it was unavoidable. She was Matt's girlfriend and a pseudo member of the Chase family and it was expected. And more than that, she didn't want to hurt Liv's feelings.

So she let Beth drag her out shopping. They found the place Liv was registered at and picked her up a few things. Money had been tight, her father had come by the week before and demanded five hundred dollars. His price rose each damned time she saw him. Still she didn't want to skimp. Liv was important to Matt and so she was important to Tate too. Even if she hadn't liked Liv herself, Tate would have gone out of her way for her.

At least the shower was at Cassie and Shane's. Tate liked Cassie Chase a lot and had come to consider her a friend independent of her relationship with Matt. She loved the way Cassie handled her dominating, burly husband. She even liked Shane, despite the fact that his size took some getting used to. And Cassie understood her in a way most other people she wasn't related to couldn't.

They stumbled in, trying not to gawp like hillbillies at the beauty of the house as they put presents on a table with the others.

"Hi, Tate!" Maggie came over and gave her a hug. Cassie, carrying a tray of food, grinned in their direction and called a hello.

"Can we help?"

Polly chuckled as she click-clacked over and pulled Tate into a tight hug and smooched her cheeks. "Come on out onto the deck. Liv's got her feet up and a slice of cake and she's not moving. Everything's done already so just enjoy yourself."

Tate smiled at Liv, waving. As they came out onto the

deck she saw it was more than just Chases, there were several women she didn't know and a few she only knew by sight from school and town.

She felt fifty pounds overweight, three income levels too low and distinctly unattractive as the women sized her up.

"Hey all, this is Matt's sweetie, Tate Murphy," Polly called out to the crowd. She introduced Tate's sisters and she heard a lot of names and would remember a tenth of them.

Liv smiled up at her. "Hiya, Tate. I'm glad you're here. Come sit over here and let's visit."

Damn. "Sure." Tate sat and Polly shoved a glass of something pink into her hand and toddled off chattering and towing Beth in her wake.

"Why don't you like me, Tate Murphy?" Liv pushed her sunglasses up and looked Tate over.

Tate, startled, blinked quickly. "I… I do like you."

"I think you're the best thing that's ever happened to Matt. You're smart, funny, pretty, you care about him and his family. You're too good to be true but you don't like me much and it drives me nuts because I want you to like me. Is it that Matt and I used to be involved?" Liv motioned to her stomach. "Because as you can see, that's totally over."

Tate snickered. "Honestly, Liv, I do like you."

"Then what is it? You seem to get along with Cassie. Maggie, well, she's like a bumblebee in a jar, she takes getting used to but she's all right. Me? You sort of skirt around. Have I done or said something to hurt your feelings? I'm sorry, pregnancy is making me even more mouthy." Liv's grin told Tate she wasn't sorry at all but it only made her like Liv more.

Tate sighed and thought honesty deserved honesty. "Look, you're, well, jeez, look at you. Here you are, tall and gorgeous, you dress well, have a lovely house, your body, even when you're pregnant, is way nicer than mine. I can't compete with that. It's not that I don't like you. I do like you, it's impossible not to, which is intimidating in and of itself. It's that I'm *not* you."

Liv was quiet a moment as she nodded. "Well, the thing is, Matt doesn't want me. He didn't want me when he had me. Tate, he wants you. You. Thank you for the compliments, really. But maybe you don't see yourself clearly."

"You know what I like about people? When they don't bullshit me. I'm not all low-self-esteem girl, but I can look in a mirror okay? I'm good for what I am, but I'm not you. And I don't see any point in pretending anything else. I don't have the time to pretend anything else. So pretty is as pretty does, and being smart and funny and having a nice face—all those things are fine. I'm good with who I am, but damn it, every time I get near you that seems to fly away and I feel fat, short and totally out of my element."

Liv cocked her head. "Fair enough. Every time I see the way Matt looks at you—even though I adore Marc with every fiber of my being and I love him more than anything but this tadpole in my belly—part of me twists because he's never looked at anyone like that. And then I'm so totally happy because other than Marc, he's the male I'm closest to in the world and he's found *the one*. He's one of my best friends and I want you to be part of that too. He loves you, you're the center of his everything and since he's my friend and my brother-in-law and since I think you're pretty damned cool, I want us to be friends. Plus, damn it, I want you to like me as much as you like Cassie. I'm shallow that way."

Tate laughed. "A lot of things come to mind when I think of you, shallow isn't one of them."

"Oh, tell me more!"

Tate relaxed, even as she continued to catch a blonde woman about their age staring at her throughout the party.

"Who is that?" Tate asked Liv after the presents had been opened. She could hear cars pulling up and knew the guys had arrived.

Liv looked up. "Ah. Yeah. That's Sal. Don't sweat it. I wouldn't even have invited her but she works for Marc, takes on some of his clients who need nutritional consulting."

"And she's looking at me that way because she used to play naked with Matt."

Liv burst out laughing and the blonde looked at them again. "You know that's something you'll have to deal with, right? The ex-girlfriends buzzing around? All of us do. Maggie still has to and she's been with Kyle for four years now and they have a kid."

Tate nodded. "I know. At first it really sucked, but now I'm just sort of used to it. He never flirts back. He may be friendly but he never looks at them like he looks at me. I figure if I got upset every time I ran across someone he'd had naughty play-dates with I'd be permanently pissed off."

Liv snorted. "Very true. And that's a great attitude to have. Because, and I've seen this happen three, no, four times now, when a Chase falls, he falls. There's no in between. They like a woman or they love her. Once they love her, that's it. Matt straying is not something you'll ever have to fear."

Some moments later, Matt came out onto the deck and as Tate's gaze was drawn to him, she noticed the blonde across the deck stared at him too.

"Still, I'm gonna be honest with you, Tate, 'cause I like you and all. I'm gonna look at him. Because he's mighty fine to look at." Liv took a look at Matt and then winked at Tate.

"Remind me to tell you about visual donuts," Tate murmured as she looked her man over. He didn't notice the other woman at all. His gaze scanned the deck until he found her and he moved straight to her. The fear edged away a bit as his eyes held nothing else but her. He sat, giving her a kiss as he circled her shoulders with his arm.

"Hey there, Venus. Man, I needed that." Winking at her, he leaned around Tate to blow a kiss at Liv. "How you feeling, gorgeous?"

"About a thousand months pregnant. Swollen. Sweaty. But I've convinced your lovely girlfriend here to like me. I feel much better."

Matt flicked his worried gaze back to Tate, who'd come to realize Liv Chase just said whatever the hell came to her mind. What wasn't to like about that?

"I told her I already did like her but that it sucked that she was all gorgeous and stuff and I was like a little blonde dumpling and you'd seen us both naked."

Matt paused, trying to figure out what the heck he could say and both Tate and Liv laughed.

Matt cupped her chin and brushed his lips over hers softly. Just enough to make her nipples hard and her pussy sensitize and ready for him. "Tate, I love you. You're beautiful. Liv is my friend but you're my woman. Do you understand the difference?"

She nodded enthusiastically and he grinned.

"Hi, Matt! Fancy seeing you here." The other woman had made her way over and sat, no, bounced her way into a chair across from Matt, her knees touching his.

"Well, Liv's my sister-in-law so I don't think it's that unusual I'd be here. I just came to get cake and steal Tate away. Do you know Tate Murphy?" He moved back a bit so their legs no longer touched.

"Yes, she used to clean our house." The blonde's voice went flat, snotty. "I think she does a better job cutting hair, or I hope she does. I go to Atlanta to do mine."

Matt blinked several times and sick humiliation seeped through Tate, replaced quickly by rage. Who did this woman think she was? But before she could speak, Matt did.

"What is it with people? You owe Tate an apology. You've just been really rude and I don't like it. Tate doesn't deserve that sort of thing and frankly, I'd have thought it was beneath you."

"Don't you care about what people are saying, Matt? *She's* beneath you. Look at her. Have some self-respect."

"Sometimes. And sometimes I'm on top. And you're not. That's what bugs you isn't it?" Tate kept her voice low so Sal had to lean in to hear it. The other woman sat back and gasped but Liv laughed before getting serious again.

"You need to shuffle your ass on out of here right now, Sal. This is my party and Tate is my friend. I won't have her insulted by the likes of you and if you make me get out of this chair I'm gonna be even more upset." Liv sat forward. Seeing that, Marc hurried over and Tate wanted to crawl away. Every damned time she was with them, something dramatic happened. She should have just kept her mouth shut.

"I'm just saying what everyone is thinking, Liv."

"Everyone? I'm not thinking that. Are you, Matt?" Liv asked him and he glared at Sal and shook his head.

"What about you?" Liv looked up into Marc's face before looking back to Sal. "Because see, you might need a dictionary so you can look up *everyone* to see what it means. *You* might be thinking that. Melanie might be thinking that, but I'm not and I'd wager most people don't, especially those of us who actually *know* Tate so *everyone* isn't thinking it, Sal."

"Hey, beautiful, what's going on?" Marc put a hand on Liv's shoulder, caressing it. "Everything all right?"

"Fine. God, it's fine." Tate stood. "Liv, thank you for inviting me. If you ever need a sitter and Polly will let the baby out of her hands for five minutes, give me a call." She bent and kissed Liv's cheek but Liv grabbed one arm and Matt the other and they both hauled her back to sitting.

"You're not going anywhere, Sal is. She's insulted a friend and she's leaving, now." Liv turned her gaze back to Sal but kept her hand on Tate's arm. Tate felt the warmth of friendship in the gesture and relaxed a little bit.

Marc looked to Sal and back to Liv a moment. "Okay, Sal,

you've upset my wife and my brother's girlfriend. I'm going to ask you to go."

Sal hurried out, mumbling under her breath and within three minutes more, her sisters and Polly arrived and the story was told over and over until Tate stood and made the *cut* motion with her hands.

"Enough! If one more person asks me if I'm all right like I'm a hunchback who lives in a cave I'm gonna lose it. It's over. I want it to stay over. Please. Now I really do need to get home. Thank you, Liv. It was a lovely shower and I'm glad we were able to chat."

"I'll drive you home. We can talk." Matt moved to the door with her.

"No. I drove here with my sisters. I'll get them home. Visit with your family. I'll talk to you later."

Nothing made him angrier than when she tried to pull herself away from him like that. As if he were associated with those stupid people, or like he believed it. Well, as he'd done every other time, he simply ignored her attempts as he pulled her to him.

"You go and take your sisters home. I'll see you at the house in an hour. I haven't eaten. Won't you take pity on me and feed me?"

He loved the way she got flustered when he didn't let her win her silly attempts to hold him away. And when she knew he'd be licking her from head to toe when he saw her next.

"Fine."

He laughed, kissing her quickly, and walked her and her sisters to the car, seeing them off.

When he'd come back inside Liv had moved to the couch, her feet in Marc's lap. Maggie looked pissed off and Cassie was in a heated discussion with Polly on the deck.

"What the hell happened here?" Matt sat down across from Liv and Marc.

"It was fine until Sal came over. I can't believe that. I feel so bad." Liv's color had returned to normal but Matt didn't want her getting upset again.

"It's not your fault, honey. Tate doesn't blame you, I know she doesn't. I just can't understand all this stuff. Just a few days ago, Ron Moore cornered me in the hardware store about it. Some bunch of bull about Tate's mom and how I should watch my pockets. I've known this guy since third grade! He's met Tate one time and when I asked him for specifics he said he'd *heard it around.* Apparently Melanie has been saying stuff all over town." Matt exhaled sharply. "I didn't mention it to Tate so I'd appreciate it if none of you did either. Now what's all this about Tate not liking you?"

Cassie and Polly came inside.

"Tate and I had a very long talk, cleared the air. I've been dying that she likes Cassie better than me."

Cassie laughed.

"I still think she does, *hmpf.* But she's been feeling insecure about any comparisons between us and I've been feeling a bit, oh I don't know jealous maybe? Not like that." She looked quickly at Marc who rolled his eyes, apparently unconcerned. "But you know, you look at her in a way you never looked at me or anyone. It's hard at first. But she and I got past it and were visiting and laughing but Sal kept on staring. Lots of people stared. They're curious, Matt. Most of it wasn't hostile. You came in right after she'd asked about Sal."

"And you told her?"

"Look, Matt, it's no damned secret you tasted the nectar of many a flower here in Petal and the tri-state area. Tate's not stupid. But she wasn't upset about it either. She didn't like the attention but she laughed about it and it wasn't her covering up for being uncomfortable. She and I talked about the big issue for all Chase wives."

"Ugh, the constant female attention," Maggie spoke from the chair near the doors.

"Yes. But she's okay. She gets that Matt isn't interested in any flower in the garden but her." Liv shook her head. "But the thing with Sal wasn't just about her jealousy that Matt had settled down with one woman. This whole *oh there's an outsider in town, quick hide the silver!* thing is just weird. I don't know exactly what to do about this. But I do know we have to make a stand."

"Yes, we do." Polly sat down. "Cassie and I have been talking and we thought it would be good to make Homecoming our big exclamation point about Tate being part of our family. That is if Liv hasn't gone into labor by then."

"You'll have to excuse me if I most fervently hope to have given birth by next Tuesday much less two weeks from now."

They all began to plan.

"I can't believe that bitch!" Anne exclaimed as they drove away. "Sal has some nerve."

"Every fucking time I'm with the Chases some kind of drama ensues. It's downright embarrassing. I hate it." The fuck habit was back.

"It's not your fault, Tate. Sal was way, way out of line." Beth turned to her. "Don't let it get to you. That's what she wants. That's what they want."

"I've been thinking on this a lot. Matt was the last single Chase brother, they all wanted him. But you landed him. They can't stand it. In truth, they'd find fault with anyone who snatched the last Chase standing," Anne mused. "So screw them all. They can suck it. Who cares about them, Tate? You're the important one. You're the one he loves. You're better than the Sals of the world."

"Every time I'm with him in larger social settings I feel totally out of my depth. Beautiful ex-girlfriends every three feet. All his friends don't trust me and they talk about stuff I don't know a damned thing about. I'm not one of them and they know it."

They pulled into Anne's driveway. "Tate, Matt loves you."

She shrugged. "He wants to be with you. You love him. I've never seen you so happy. Who cares about them? His family adores you. We adore him. It's all good." She hugged her before getting out. "I'll see you later. Call me if you need me. Love you."

Beth scrambled into the front seat and gave her basically the same speech when they arrived at her apartment complex.

She loved her family and she loved Matt but she hated the anxiety and didn't know what to do about it.

Some half an hour later, Matt walked through her front door, looking very intent. Without taking his eyes from her, he threw the locks and pulled the cord to the front blinds, casting the room into pale light.

"Bend over the couch arm, Tate."

Frozen, she stood and looked at his face, his features sexy, aggressive. Shivers worked over her at his manner, far more dominant than his normal laid-back sexual playfulness.

Eyes still locked on hers, he pulled his belt loose, unbuttoning and unzipping his jeans, freeing his cock. One of his eyebrows slowly rose. "Tate?"

Stifling a nervous giggle, she shrugged and walked around the edge of the couch, bending forward over the arm. She closed her eyes when she heard the condom wrapper and felt the cool air on her bare thighs as he drew her skirt up to her waist and her panties down. She stepped out of them and let him widen her stance.

His fingertips drew a path up her inner thighs, brushing through the folds of her pussy, finding her wet.

"Just what I thought. I've been so damned hard since I saw you sitting there on Shane's deck, your hair gleaming in the sunshine."

The head of his cock found her gate and nudged into her body slowly. He made love to her, his hands stroking over her back and thighs, his body pressing deep and withdrawing. Gently at first until the heat between them built and built to scorching and his speed increased along with the intensity of his thrusts.

One hand reached around and he found her clit, ready and slippery. She pushed herself back against his body, rolled her hips, wanting more and he gave it to her.

The fingers on her clit were slow, teasing and he brought her up, built her orgasm like a masterpiece and when it crashed around her, she had to yell into the couch cushion. The sensation was too much to bear, it drove her mindless, pleasure blind as the hand at her hip tightened and she felt the muscles in his abdomen grow taut and his cock harden impossibly.

"Matt, please. I need you to need me." She didn't know where the words came from but they came and brought a gasp from him followed very quickly by his orgasm.

Still breathing heavy, he kissed the back of her neck and withdrew, returning in moments, his pants still unzipped.

He looked pleasure wild, slightly feral and holy shit, he was hers.

Dazed, she managed to land herself on the couch and he sprawled alongside her, his head in her lap. Immediately, her fingers sought the softness of his hair as they enjoyed the silence for several minutes.

"What brought that on?"

He heard the amusement in her voice and was relieved he hadn't pushed too far.

Lazy, his eyes closed as he enjoyed the way she massaged his scalp, he smiled. "Dunno. I'd planned to waltz you into your bedroom and take you nice and slow but when I walked in the door and saw you, I had to have you right then."

"It was very inspired."

He laughed. "I'm glad you enjoyed it. I was concerned you'd be upset after the shower."

She sighed but didn't tighten up. "It's a cross I have to bear, Matt. She's not the first, she won't be the last."

"To talk to you like that?" He sat up and faced her, his arm along the back of the couch resting on her shoulders.

"Yes. And I did clean her parents' house. I did a good job, even though my own house is messy. I work hard." Her chin jutted out and he kissed it.

"Who cares now? It's what? Fifteen years ago? Venus, some people live in the past. And I wish you'd tell me when people said things to you."

"Why, Matt? What could you possibly do except feel bad?"

"Why? So you're not alone in this. Do you think I like it that people treat you this way?"

"Do you think it makes a difference whether you like it or not?"

"Damn it, Tate. Why are you so hard sometimes?"

"Because people I don't even know stop me on the street to accuse me of trying to steal your money. Because your friend Ron cornered me at the public library to warn me that you'd see past a piece of ass soon enough so not to get comfortable with my newfound position."

Anger, hot and nearly unmanageable, rose in him like bile. "He said what? Ron Moore said that to you?"

"Yes."

"Who else?"

"Doesn't matter. None of this matters. He'll only deny it."

"I don't give a fuck what he says. He's lucky if I don't knock him into next week for talking to you that way. Tate, I'm sorry this is so ridiculous. I'd say it doesn't matter but being treated that way does matter. What doesn't matter is anyone's opinion but yours, mine and our families'."

"I know."

He smiled. "You do?"

"Yes, I do. I know it's not easy, but I love you, Matt. I love being with you. If people don't like that, there's not much I can do about it but I'm not letting what we have go because people who don't know me don't like me."

"Yeah? Because Tate, let's move in together." He'd almost asked her to marry him but he knew it'd be too much for her right then. "I want to be with you every day. I want to wake up with you every morning."

"I don't want to leave this house. I love it here. And I'm not giving up Martini Friday with my sisters."

She was full of surprises, he'd thought they'd have to argue over moving in together. "Like I'm going to complain about a house full of tipsy, beautiful women. Although if we could plan it so you hung out at The Pumphouse first and invited Cassie, Liv and Maggie back here too, I'd like that a lot."

"I hate The Pumphouse, you know. The last time you invited me everyone stared at me. Still, okay. For you. I suppose if we just came and sat with Liv, Cassie and Maggie, people will get used to it eventually." If Petal was meant to be the place they were to be together, she had to work harder to make it more of a positive place in her head. Let go of the past and build a future.

He kissed her. "Thank you. I love knowing you're there as I play pool. It's sort of sucked since we've been going out that you've been here when I was there. Speaking of that, I love it here too. Thing is, it's small for two people although my place is even smaller. But I have a suggestion. This is a huge lot. It wouldn't be hard to add on at all."

"I've been thinking about that for the last year or so. I'd be open to that."

"Who are you, ma'am, and where did you put my girlfriend?" He leaned in to kiss her again and then once more, licking his lips afterward like she tasted good.

"I had this long talk with Liv and then with my sisters. I fucking hate how people react to this relationship and to me. But to give in and let them chase me off isn't who I am. I've been letting it get to me when there's nothing I can do to change it. All I can do is live for me. And for you. You say you want something with me. I want that too." She shrugged.

"Well, to start, this dining room needs to be about three times the size it is now so we can have all the Murphys and Chases over no matter the weather. We need another two or three bedrooms and a den I think." He winked and they planned.

Chapter Eleven

Things began to settle in. That next week, Matt slowly moved his stuff into her house. She hadn't been too surprised to come home from work on Friday and see several sweaty Chase brothers with sledgehammers taking out a side wall to enlarge the kitchen. William and Tim were out there too.

"You aren't mad?" Matt asked as he came into the kitchen, freshly showered.

"We talked about this. You had someone come out here Tuesday to check the load-bearing walls. You got the permits in next to no time, I'll have to thank Liv's connections with the mayor's office for that one I guess. You promised to do something and you're doing it. Far from making me mad, it makes me very happy. How long have you all been at it?"

"I got off at noon. Kyle had a half day and came with me. William showed up after he got off at two. Everyone else came as they got off work. We'll get a solid amount done tomorrow and Sunday too. But for now, it's time to play pool. Marc called to say Liv hasn't been feeling well. She'll probably have the baby any day now. Everyone has their phone on. But I'll stay away until ten since it's no boys allowed. In fact, we're all headed to Nathan's after pool."

She smiled. "Really? That's nice. I like to hear that you're all doing stuff together. And I know about Liv. I stopped by there on my lunch hour today to bring her a few things."

It was his turn to smile. "I like to hear that too. You're a good person, Tate Murphy. Oh and about next week."

She froze. *Homecoming.* A shudder of revulsion rode her spine. Tate dreaded it. Hated it with the heat of ten thousand totally clichéd suns. She'd been trying to talk her way out of going with the Chases for weeks but Matt would not let it go.

"So I ran into my momma earlier. She wants to know what we're bringing to the picnic next Sunday. And don't forget dinner at my parents' house after the game on Friday. I've already talked to Nathan and Anne, they're both coming and bringing dates."

She ground her teeth in frustration. The stress of this damned town event and her father's increased demands for money weighed on her more and more. He'd come back several times and each time he wanted more money. His behavior had deteriorated and he'd begun to threaten showing up at the kids' school in the afternoons, saying they should get to know their grandpa.

The thought of the way Tim and William would react to that little kernel kept her paying him. Her family was finally enjoying normalcy and she wanted it to stay that way. And once he found out Matt had moved in, it would get worse.

She'd had to juggle a few bills the week before to wait for payday, not easy when you own the darned business. But she had some money in savings if she needed it, which it looked like she did. And now the expansion of the house. It was a lot at once.

She knew it would get out of control. She knew that moment wasn't too far away and eventually she'd have to deal with it and tell someone. She couldn't afford to pay him forever.

But right then, she felt cornered by Matt's going around her to her siblings. "You did what? I told you I wasn't going to any of that fucking stuff. You know how I feel about Home-coming."

"Oh, *fucking* is it? What crawled up your craw?" He tried to tease his way into her arms but she slapped his hands away and took a step back. His grin slid off his face.

"What crawled up my craw? You went around me to Nathan and Anne to get them to go to this crap so I'd go too. That's what crawled up my craw. And it's crawled up your ass, not craw." She crossed her arms over her chest and glared at him.

"I did no such thing!"

She widened her eyes before narrowing them to angry slits. "Yes you did. I told you three weeks ago I wasn't going. And you acted like you didn't hear me. I told you two weeks ago, ten days ago, a week ago, three days ago, yesterday. And you thought, *oh, let's be sure Nathan and Anne are there so she can't say no.* Well, I've got a news flash for you, tightass, I'm not going. You all have a good time."

"Why are you being like this? It's a damned picnic and a football game! My family loves to go, we do it every year without fail. You think you're too good for a football game?"

Hurt welled in her stomach. She put her shoes on and grabbed her purse. "If you think *I'm* the one who thinks she's too good for anything you don't know me at all. Go to your fucking snobby game and your fucking snobby picnic and while you're at it, try noticing for the first time in your shiny life just who *isn't* there. And you tell me it's *them* who feel too good."

She pulled at the door but he leaned against it, keeping it closed. "This is something you have to tell me, Tate. How can I understand if you don't tell me?"

"I have told you! I've told you six times I don't want to go. You don't listen. Now let me leave. I don't want to be here right now."

"Too bad because I want you here and I want us to work

this through. This is our house now. Why don't you want to go?" He drew his knuckles down her cheek gently.

"Why do I have to give you an explanation to make it valid for you? Do I ask you for an explanation? When you say you don't want to do something do I make you? Do I demand you explain why? Do I disregard everything you say and try to manipulate you into it?"

He sighed. "No. You're right. I just want you to be with me. I won't go if you don't. It's a family thing, I want you at my side. You're part of that now. I want to show you off, I want to have you part of those memories. Please?"

His voice was so sad she knew she couldn't hold on to her anger any longer. Knew she didn't have it in her to refuse. She leaned her forehead on his chest. "All right. I'll bring baked beans and potato salad. I'm sure your mother is frying eighteen chickens and Maggie is making pies."

He tipped her chin up so he could see her face. "Your pies are better."

"I'm not usurping Maggie's spot. She's the one who makes pies and cakes and stuff and she's really good at it. Stop making trouble. You're very spoiled you know."

"I do. Thank you for agreeing to come. Will you make that pasta salad too? The kind with the feta cheese in it?" He fluttered his lashes and she sighed.

"Pushing your luck."

"I know. But I'll make it worth your while. We've got about twenty minutes until we have to go…"

She growled but allowed him to guide her back toward their bedroom.

Hell had a name and it was the Homecoming game. Well, no, probably the game was purgatory and the picnic would be hell. She could hardly wait to see.

"You look like you sucked on a lemon." Shane seated himself next to Tate and Cassie grinned around him, waving her hello.

"Do I? Because I was only thinking happy thoughts. Do you think I'll be able to fly?" Tate asked in a singsong voice.

Cassie snickered and Shane allowed an upturn of one corner of his mouth.

Matt squeezed her against him. "You know how sexy I find it when you get all snarky, don't you?" he murmured into her ear and she laughed.

"It's hard to take a grown man who still wears his high school colors to a game seriously." She arched a brow at him and the green and white he wore.

Shane laughed aloud at that. He squeezed her from the other side, kissing the top of her head. "It's not that bad, darlin'."

"Hmpf."

But they'd surrounded her, blocking all routes of escape. Chases and Murphys all around her. Well, Tim and William had begged off, the traitors. They had wives and kids so they got to stay home. She'd get even for that. There were two drum sets with her niece and nephew's name on them for Christmas. She prayed Liv would hurry up and go into labor so they could leave.

It wasn't that she didn't like football. She did in fact. She enjoyed the game a lot. It was the atmosphere at the game she hated. Her kind had never been welcome at Homecoming events, that had been spelled out, bolded and underlined as she grew up.

She'd shielded the others the best she could, taking the brunt of the abuse, but her memories of all the tears they'd shed over it still lay inside. Beth had told her it didn't matter now, that she'd made it all right and they'd be there for each other but judging by the hostile looks she was getting just then, it wasn't going to be an easy night.

"Walk with me to get some sodas and stuff?" Matt kissed her nose and winked.

Feeling claustrophobic and hemmed in by the wall of Shane Chase to her left, she agreed. He led her out and down the bleachers toward the concession stands.

Matt loved the way Tate looked that evening. Her hair hung loose, a wide, shiny red band holding it away from her face. Her sweater matched the band and the skirt was long and flowing, just to the ankles of the seriously sexy high-heeled boots she had on.

"Venus, have I told you how sexy you look tonight?" He stood behind her in the line, his arms wrapped around her shoulders, holding her to him.

"It never hurts to hear it again." She tipped her head back and looked up at him.

"Thank you for coming tonight. I know you're not thrilled about it."

"Yes well, I've thought of escaping but you've got my routes blocked. It's my only hope that Liv goes into labor tonight."

He laughed. "So charming. If I didn't know better I'd think you were avoiding my company."

"Order your stuff, goober." She indicated the window and he held her, one arm around her waist while he procured enough sugar, hot chocolate and food to keep the group happy.

They took the stuff back, arms full of food, and passed it down the row before sitting down. Matt realized he needed to hit the men's room and excused himself. Kyle came along.

"Don't try and run for it, Venus," he called out, laughing as she gave him a subtle scratch to her nose with her middle finger.

Kyle laughed all the way to the head. "Your woman fits in just fine."

"She does and I think she's finally seeing that too."

"Matt!"

Matt turned to see Ron Moore approach with a few of their other friends. He narrowed his eyes and Kyle tensed too.

"Just the man I was looking for." Ron had the audacity to smile at him.

"Yeah? Why's that? So you could talk shit to me instead of harassing my barely five-foot-tall girlfriend in a public library like a pussy?"

"I see she ran right to you. I figured she would. Make herself look better. She's working you, Matt. What the hell is wrong with you?"

"Whoa!" Justin Fields, another friend, stepped up and put a hand on Ron's shoulder. "Hey, what's wrong with *you*? What is Matt talking about?"

"This chick is working him for cash like a two-dollar wh—"

That's all he got out of his mouth before Matt's fist landed square in his mouth.

Kyle waited until the punch landed before stepping in and pulling Matt back. "Okay, it's done. Let it go," he murmured in Matt's ear.

"Don't you ever, *ever* talk about Tate like that. You don't know what you're talking about. You've been my friend since third grade and you harass a woman you haven't bothered to get to know. Does it make you feel like a big man to terrorize women?" Matt stood over Ron as Justin helped him up.

"Tate's good people, Ron. What are you talking about? You're harassing her?" Justin turned to their friend.

"Melanie told me she was working you for money."

"Melanie is a jealous, bitter, angry psycho. I live with Tate, she won't let me pay half the mortgage. She's never asked me for money although she's made dinner for my entire family on dozens of occasions. She usually makes me go dutch on dates. Melanie has issues, Ron. She's taking them out on Tate."

"You don't know what she gets up to, Matt."

"Ron, you don't know her at all. What do you think she gets up to? She owns a small house, an old car and works sixty hours a week in her own business. When does she have time to work out-of-town businessmen for their wallets? Why don't you share with us just what you think Tate gets up to?"

"She's a gold digger. She's reeling you in for your money."

"You've said that and I've told you she hasn't asked for a cent in all the time we've been together."

"You're the fatted calf, which sort of makes sense since she's a cow. Shit!"

Matt hit him again.

"You said to tell you!" Ron yelled from the ground. Justin didn't bother trying to help him up and a crowd had gathered.

"I told you to explain your accusations, not insult my woman."

"Holy fuck."

"Tate! Get back here," Shane ground out and Matt closed his eyes for a brief moment as he heard Tate approach.

"Just what the hell is going on here?" Tate demanded as she shoved her way into the group knotted around them. She looked at Matt and then Ron's face. "Did you hit this asshole?"

Matt couldn't help it, he started to laugh. "Why yes I did, Venus. Twice in fact."

She took his hand and kissed the knuckles. "He's not worth a hurt hand." Shaking her head she looked up at him. "What? Did you think I'd be mad because you punched him?"

Still laughing, he hugged her. "Of course not, Venus."

"Tate," Justin said, "I want you to know I don't think the same way Ron does. I think you're good people and I've never seen Matt so happy."

Matt lifted his chin at his friend in thanks.

"You've ended a friendship by believing someone who isn't trustworthy, Ron. If you so much as look in Tate's direction without an apology on your lips there's more where those two came from."

Shane finally pushed his way through the crowd. "What's going on here?"

People mumbled and began to wander off.

"Anyone see anything? Matt, you want to tell me why Ron is covered in dust and has a bloody nose?" Shane asked, stifling a smile.

"I think he fell," a passerby said.

"Yeah," someone else echoed.

"I fell." Ron brushed himself off. "Not a problem. Don't come crying on my shoulder, Matt."

"I'd get a rabies shot if you're planning to hang out with Melanie much more." Tate turned her back on Ron and Matt kissed the top of her head.

Matt caught the speculative looks from other people as they walked back to their seats. Some curious, some approving and some angry. His glimpses into some of the ignorance Tate had to deal with were maddening.

Admittedly, it was a relief that he also saw friendly faces too. Friends who saw them and waved, people who were nice to Tate, genuinely accepting of her. He felt the steel of her spine relax a bit as they neared the row where their seats were.

The rest of the game passed relatively without incident but on the way to the parking lot, he noticed Tate protectively watch over her siblings and felt like a heel for manipulating her into coming. Fierce protectiveness burst through him as he watched her say good night to her brother and sisters. She was his and damn it, he'd make sure no one harmed her or made her feel wanting.

"I tried to hold her back but she caught sight of something going on and shoved past me. She's really fast, like one of those little dogs." Shane laughed as he kept his eye on Cassie and Maggie with Tate and her siblings. "I would have had to arrest you for assault you know, if Ron hadn't denied you hit him."

"Would have been worth it. Asshole. Called her a whore and a cow. He's lucky I only hit him twice."

"He said what? I'd have hit him too. Hell, I want to go find him and hit him right now. Why is everyone so hostile to her? She's so damned nice. Sweet even with that sharp sense of humor she's got. She goes to the damned old folks' home and cuts their hair for criminy's sake." Shane sighed.

"Some people get nervous and defensive when everything they know gets threatened. It's easy not to think about class stuff when you come up where we do. Most of us, most of the people in this town don't care but there are people like Melanie who are only happy when they feel better than others. The stuff about her parents is a symptom. Essentially here's this outsider who came in and stole the last Chase brother. That's how they see it." Kyle joined them.

Matt shook his head. "It's like some stupid movie from the fifties or something. Honestly, it's totally unreal. She's been trying to tell me and I've been thinking she was oversensitive because of how she grew up." He paused. "She's trying to act like it didn't bother her but I know her. She's very sensitive, no matter how tough she tries to act."

"We'll make sure the picnic goes smoother. There's gonna be a lot of us. Put her near Momma. No one will mess with her then. Oh and Maggie too. We'll be on the outside. No one's gonna hurt her, Matt. We'll keep her safe. One thing we all need to keep doing is let this town and the people like Melanie know Tate is one of ours and we believe in her."

Matt didn't know what else to say. Family did what family needed to do. Still felt good though.

He caught up with Tate. "You still up to dinner at my parents' house?"

She sighed. "There's no choice. She's bound to have gotten at least five calls by now and she'll just hunt us down at home if we don't go over there and tell her the story firsthand. And speaking of hands, yours looks like hell. I want to clean it up better and I'm quite sure your mother has first aid supplies."

He grinned. "Come on then." He waved at everyone else. "See y'all in a few."

Polly met them at the front door, anxious. But instead of cooing over Matt's hand, she pulled Tate into a hug and it made her want to cry. She towed Tate down the hall and into Edward's study, closing the door behind her and leaving Matt in the foyer.

"Let it go now, honey. Give the tears up to me and be done with them," Polly crooned as she rubbed Tate's back.

As soon as Polly gave her permission, it was like her body just let it go and a sob so deep wrenched from her body that it buckled her knees. But Polly just went to her knees with her and continued to rock her and rub her back while she wept.

"It was wrong, Tate. What he said was wrong. What they've done to you is wrong. They're wrong. You're a good person. You love my son and he loves you. You're worthy of this wonderful gift you and Matt have. Don't you let them take the certainty of who you are from you. You're strong. You survived worse than those idiots in town who can't stand to see anyone else happy. You hear me? You give me those tears you've been holding back for so long and let them go. You're safe here."

So Tate let it go. Cried and cried and cried until there was nothing left and long minutes later, totally spent, she let Polly help her to the couch.

"I'm sorry. I didn't mean to fall apart like that. I don't even know where it all came from." She accepted a box of tissues and a glass of water from Polly who sat across from her and clucked. Her voice was rusty and every few seconds she hiccupped.

"It came from inside you. Where you've pent it up to be strong for everyone else. Tate, I know you, girl. You take everyone else's burdens for them. But you can only take on so much before it breaks your back. Sometimes you need to let it out. Tonight must have been very ugly."

"He called me a whore. A whore." Tate shook her head, still shocked. "I didn't hear it firsthand. That was the first time Matt punched him apparently. But I heard Matt telling Shane everything Ron said. Men. They must think we can't hear them at three feet away."

"They don't know we multi-task as well as we do." Polly nodded. "You're not a whore. He's wrong. You know that."

"I do. But it hurts anyway. He accused me of being a gold digger. Polly, I'd never use Matt for his money. Not ever. I've worked hard for everything I've achieved in my life. I love Matt, I'd never hurt him like that. Ever."

"I expect it does hurt, being misunderstood and misused. It's shocking to be faced with so much hatred. I know you love Matt. Matt knows you love Matt. Hell, honey, anyone with eyes in their head can see you love my son. They are bad people. Wrong. The people in the world who count know the truth and that's all that matters. As for the rest of them? Don't let them see you hurt, Tate. They aren't worth it and you're better than they are. You hold your head up because you have every right to."

Tate nodded, blowing her nose.

"There's a bathroom right through there, sweetie. Wash your face and come out when you're ready. I expect Edward is holding Matthew back out there. Can I let him in? I know he wants to help."

Tate needed that, needed to see Matt, to be held by him. "Yes. Let me get cleaned up and I'll be out in a minute."

She went into the bathroom and looked at the ruin of her face. Her eyes were red and swollen as was her nose. Every last trace of eye makeup was gone or dripping down her cheeks. She looked like she had the starring role in a B-horror movie.

Still, after a few minutes of cold water compresses she began to look and feel better and she knew it was time to face the music.

The first gut-wrenching sob broke Matt's heart. His father had simply put his arms around him and held him as they'd listened. Edward had urged him to let her cry it out, to let Polly mother her because she needed it desperately.

Matt wanted to rush in and take over, wanted Tate to open

up to him that way but he understood Tate never would have let him bear the pain she held inside. Thank goodness his mother had been there and known just what Tate needed.

For long minutes she'd cried and cried and Matt had wanted to climb the walls. Her siblings arrived and they'd all stood in the hall and listened to her grief leave her body. Maggie held tight to Kyle, Shane to Cassie. The Murphys clutched each other and they'd all held vigil.

Twenty minutes later, his mother had come out and told them all very quietly that Tate needed a few minutes to clean up and to go on and get in the dining room. She sent Matt in to her, knowing they both needed it. Before he closed the door, Anne approached him quietly and said, "Melanie Deeds has a bill coming due." He couldn't have agreed more.

The door to the bathroom finally opened and her bottom lip trembled as she stepped into his embrace.

"Oh, Venus, I love you so much. I wish I could protect you from all this."

She didn't answer, instead just pushed herself closer to him.

After several minutes he kissed her gently. "You okay? Do you need more time or do you want to go and eat dinner?"

"I can't face anyone. You all must have heard."

"Heard what, Tate? Heard you being human? Heard you being mothered instead of doing all the mothering for a change? We love you. I'm glad my mother could help and I'm sorry you had to see all that tonight. Come on, everyone is waiting and they want to love you. Let them comfort you for a change."

"They've all got enough to deal with."

"Tate, don't be selfish right now. They need to help. *I* need to know you'll lean on me from time to time. You take so much on, give us all the gift of being the strong ones every once in a while."

"You're going to make me cry again." The way she clutched

his shirt made him want to keep her indoors and shield her forever.

"It's okay to cry you know. It's not a weakness."

She made her little *hmpf* sound and he knew then she was on her way back to being all right.

They walked out into the dining room and her siblings came to her, pulling her into an embrace. Matt put his arm around his mother and they watched until Liv burst in, pregnant and pissed as hell.

"Where is that Melanie and who's gonna hold my earrings?"

Marc came in after her, grinning. "Liv's a little excitable after we got a call about what happened tonight. She wanted me to drive her around looking for Melanie but I talked her into coming here instead."

Cassie laughed and Maggie joined her as the three of them hugged each other and then Tate.

"If you'd just gone into labor early this afternoon none of this would have happened. Truly, Liv, I blame you." Tate blinked up at Liv, who laughed and hugged her again.

"I'm trying, sweet thang. Orgasms, spicy food, cod liver oil and this baby is blowing me off. Gets it from her father. Oops, did I say her?"

Marc burst out laughing as everyone excitedly discussed Liv's slip and the gender of the next grandchild.

Matt pushed Tate into a chair and made her a plate. "Eat it."

She shrugged, obeying him as she began to eat. Others noticed and began to fill plates and eat. His momma beamed at them all, doting over everyone, making Liv sit and get her feet up.

The dinner was a nice way to exorcise the demons of the evening. Being with family washed that all away.

Back at home they'd just gotten out of Matt's truck when she saw her father lurking near the garage.

"I'll be in in a moment, I just need to get something from my car."

"I'll get it for you, Venus. What is it?"

"I need to be alone for a few minutes, okay? Please?"

"Honey…"

"I'll be fine. I just need to let this all go."

"You have three minutes and I'm coming back outside if you don't come in."

"I've lived here alone for the last several years. I can handle the driveway, thank you."

He smiled at her acerbic tone and headed inside.

She waited until he was gone before she charged over to the other side of the garage where her father stood.

"What? What are you doing here?"

"A fine way to greet your father." He stank of liquor and she fingered the pepper spray in her hand.

"Get the hell out of here. I have no money. I gave you all my cash. I told you, go away."

"Now that your boyfriend is living here, you should have more money coming in."

"I'm not letting him pay rent! What do you think I am? Her?"

"Don't you talk about your mother that way, girl," he slurred and moved forward but her anger over that evening spurred her on.

"Stop confusing her sins with mine. I have no more money to give you. If you push me too far and go through with your threats there'll be no more cash so shut up and go away until after payday."

She spun and stomped back into the house, triumph warring with fear.

She locked up and turned to see Matt leaning against the kitchen counter, looking at her speculatively.

"Who were you talking to?"

"Myself."

She bustled past him and took another look at his knuckles.

"You really hit him hard. You're going to be sore tomorrow, it's bruising already."

"It was worth it. I don't scrap as much as I once did. When I was younger, my knuckles were nice and hard from duking it out with my brothers all the time. God, we used to be such a mess! Marc rarely got into the physical stuff but he used to work us all, set us up. He's a wily one."

Tate laughed. "Mindfucking. He and Liv really are perfect for each other. I used to think he was softer, more laid-back, but he's a lot more intense than he appears to be."

Matt nodded. "You're very observant. I don't think he understood that himself until he and Liv got together."

"Like you didn't realize how hard you worked until you got together with me? Or that you rode yourself too hard and thought you were shallow because a lot of things came easy?"

He started a moment and took a deep breath. She'd hit home with that one. *Good.* He needed some introspection too.

"Let's go to bed. Taking her hand, he drew her to their room and slowly undressed her before they settled into bed. She lay quietly, waiting as he stroked fingertips up and down her back while he thought about what she'd said.

"Most things have come easy for me. Do come easy I should say. Then I get bored and lose interest. I usually only stick with stuff that challenges me. Firefighting is one of them. It's a physical challenge every day and a mental one too. You have to be on your toes when you're at a fire or you'll get hurt. Hell, even if you're on your toes you can get hurt. But it's exhilarating, that work I have to put into it."

She stayed quiet as he processed. He liked that about her. She let him work through stuff without interrupting even though she had all that energy.

"And women? Well, okay, that's been easy too. And so I suppose people have looked at me and thought I was a happy bachelor. I have been at times but really what I wanted was a woman who engaged me, challenged me, made me dig and work and be a better person and I never found that. Until that day I walked into the salon and you choked when you saw me."

He chuckled as he felt the heat of her blush against his skin. "I walked in there and there was this laughter. Feminine laughter, drew me right to you and your sisters. Pretty women, all of you. But I couldn't take my eyes from you. You were like this golden, shiny thing in the midst of my gray life. And you choked and got all embarrassed and then you teased me. When I teased you back you blushed. You are *real*, Tate.

"And I couldn't stop thinking about you and we started our lunches and I had to work to get to know you, to get past your defenses and every day I work because you make it worth my effort. Working to make a relationship is meaningful with the right person. It's not just something I do because I'm not quite bored enough to find something else. I wake up each day excited to work with you, looking forward to whatever new experiences we'll have, wondering what memories we'll create. I love you."

She snuggled close and kissed his chest. "I love you too. I was afraid at first. We're different. But you're everything a man should be and I'm so damned happy. You make me feel safe with you. That's not something I've felt a lot in my life. Excited, thrilled, desired, cherished, loved and safe."

He needed to hear that. It touched him deeply, soothed him. "You looked at me and saw past all the stuff most people see. That's… I don't even know if I have the words to express how much that means. I watched my brothers find the women of their hearts and I saw how that made them into better men, *whole* men, but I didn't quite understand the process until it happened to me. You complete me because you love me. You *know* me, Tate. I'd do anything for you."

"Good, you can make me come."

He laughed, rolling her on top of him. "If people only knew the sex goddess who lurked behind those innocent-looking blue eyes of yours. Well, I'd have to beat them off with a stick."

"Mmm hmm. Put your money where your dick is then, bub."
And so he did.

Tate was finally a part of something bigger than just her small universe with her siblings. When Liv went into labor some days after Homecoming and baby Lise came into the world, Tate was a part of it. Lise wasn't just the baby of someone she knew, Lise was a member of her extended family and she had to admit, seeing Matt hold the tiny baby made her heart sing.

Petal lost some of its unfriendly feel as Tate realized she had more there than she'd given credit for. She had friends other than her sisters for the first time. She had lunch with Maggie and Cassie, she visited at Liv's, checking in on her and the baby. She went on shopping excursions with Polly. The past was letting go or maybe, it was the other way around and Tate was letting go.

In any case, the only real dark spot was her father. His unrelenting presence in her life and the increasing weight of the secret she kept.

Halloween came and Matt began to suspect something was wrong. Tate was tightly strung, more than usual and she'd even let him pay for half the mortgage that month.

He'd confronted her about it but she denied there was a problem. She'd come home late a few times in the last few weeks, clearly upset and he had a feeling it had something to do with the things people had said around town.

It had died down a bit as they'd been seen more regularly and the Chases had so obviously taken Tate and her siblings into their family, making it clear they believed in her.

Fury rode him when he thought about her being talked to badly by people who didn't know what a remarkable person she was. If people couldn't look at Tate and see how much she cared about him, about her siblings, they didn't have eyes and they sure didn't if they couldn't see the way Matt looked at her right back.

They'd added on another bathroom adjoining the master bedroom, and another bedroom was being built to the other side of the kitchen. He found he loved coming home from work and making the place theirs. He also loved walking across the street from the station on the days he got off when she did, to come home with her.

Waking up with Tate nestled against him was the best feeling he'd ever had.

The weekend before Thanksgiving was the Harvest Dance at the Grange. A community fundraiser for the local food pantry and it happened to be one event Tate looked forward to.

Matt came home with a big white box and several smaller boxes, tossing them on the bed. "Just a little something, Venus."

She grinned. Still uncomfortable taking presents from him, it got a little easier each time and it made him happy to do for her and her happy because who didn't like presents?

He hopped on the bed and watched as she tore into the box and gasped, pulling out a beautiful deep blue dress.

"Matt, this is gorgeous."

"I thought it would look dead sexy on you. Will you wear it tonight? There are shoes and a purse in the other boxes. Anne helped me with them to be sure they matched and all."

"Yes. I was just trying to figure out what to wear and now I have the perfect thing."

How she loved watching him there, on the bed. On *their* bed, eyes lazily taking her in but she knew he paid attention to everything she did. It made her feel wildly sexy, the way he devoured her with his gaze.

They'd begun to make a life together in her little house. It was theirs now, getting bigger every day. The chaos of the constant construction was worth it to see the space grow into a home for them.

Having him there made her happier than she'd ever been, than she'd ever hoped to be. At first, she expected him to grow disillusioned or impatient with her family and other commitments but he didn't. He made room in his life for what was important to her and she found herself eager to do so for him.

Those times when they babysat for her nieces and nephew or Nicholas and baby Lise, she allowed herself to see their future as parents together. She wanted that with him very much.

Her father was a menace in her life, yes, but she'd do anything to protect this precious thing from his poison, from his evil, nasty darkness. She'd protect Matt because he meant everything to her and his family was too good to be sullied by the stain of her father. And she'd protect her own family too. At least he didn't physically scare her anymore although despite not wanting to care, she wished he'd get help. His drinking continued and in the periods right after her mother ran off again, he got worse. She wanted him to get better, wanted a chance to mend things but she knew it would never happen. So she held what was truly precious close and would protect it with her dying breath.

Matt watched her as she got ready. Hard didn't begin to describe the state of his cock by the time she'd blotted her lips and turned.

"Man, you're the most beautiful thing I've ever seen," he murmured, putting his hands at her waist. So perfect. She was soft and sweet, curvy, feminine. Her breasts were showcased quite nicely at the neck of the dress and the skirt was full, coming to her knees. The shoes were sinfully high and whatever she'd done with her hair and makeup made her look glamorously pretty.

She blushed and he grinned. "Thank you. You do too. I love it when you dress up. I can't complain about you in jeans but in a suit? I'm not so sure I even want to leave just now."

"We could stay here. We could play senior prom. This could

be the hotel room and we only have a few hours until you have to be home."

She burst out laughing and hugged him. "I love you."

"That means we have to go to the Grange doesn't it?" He pouted and she nodded.

"But only for a few hours. Lise is with Susan and William along with Nicholas. I'm absolutely sure Maggie and Liv won't want to stay too long. We'll make our exit when they do."

"Oh, good plan." He kissed her neck and twirled her. "Perfect. The dress is perfect for dancing."

"It's a swing dress, it's made for dancing. Good choice, Matt. Thank you for thinking of me."

Once at the Grange, they checked in at the table but quickly headed out to the dance floor. He loved dancing with her. She was so good at it, people often stopped to watch her. And with her heels she fit him nicely, soft against the hard wall of his chest. Perfect.

"Look at them. Goodness sakes, there's love for you." Polly squeezed Edward's hand.

"She looks lovely tonight. In love too. I think moving in was a good choice. I know you want them married and having babies already but she's had a rough road to get to this point. She can see every day how much he loves her. How she fits into his life and his family. And people round town are starting to notice too."

"Mr. and Mrs. Chase, how are you tonight?" Melanie appeared at their table and Polly turned a narrow eyed gaze on her.

"Better once you move yourself away from my sight."

Edward smiled. "Now, lamb, I'm sure Miss Deeds here is only going to tell us she's been powerfully wrong about our Tate and how she's sorry she's been spreading such lies about her all over town."

"No, Mr. Chase, can't you see? She's a bad, bad person! She's had Matt move in to pay for her house. She's making it bigger on his dime. She's just using him. I loved him, I hate seeing you all taken in by her this way. She's a gold digger plain and simple."

Polly snorted and Maggie tossed a crouton at Melanie's head. "Hit the road, Melanie. You're an idiot plain and simple. Suck it up, Matt chose Tate. He broke up with you long before he found Tate. If you don't shut your mouth now, you're looking at a tableful of trouble. I promised to hold Liv's earrings when you got out of line again and she's still wild with pregnancy hormones."

Liv laughed and Marc patted her hand.

Cassie looked Melanie up and down. "What's your deal anyway? You're the nastiest piece of work I've seen in a long time. We don't like you. We think you're a hateful twit and Tate is one of ours. Matt didn't want you. There are other men in Petal, not our men, they're all taken and we don't share. And we don't take kindly to our own being attacked by the likes of you."

"You girls scare me. I'm glad you're on my side." Shane winked at Cassie.

"Well, you've said what you needed to say and you're wrong of course. But you know that and that only makes you even more pathetic. As I told your mother last week. And as you've continued this nasty campaign against our Tate, it's been hard but I've had to shift my business to another florist cross town. Now, if you had any actual skills and say, a job or a business, I'd threaten that but you just live off your folks. Which sort of makes the whole idea that anyone *with* a job and a business is the gold digger instead of you very ironic and ridiculous too. But I suspect you'd need a dictionary to know you were just insulted. So scamper along now before a drink gets spilled on you." Polly waved her away and Melanie stomped off with a wounded squeal.

The men at the table clapped and each woman gave a bow.

* * *

"Matt, I think you should take the river road." Tate looked out the window at the clear night sky, the stars twinkling bright above them.

"Okay, anything for you, Venus."

She rustled around and held out her panties. "Good."

"Jeez, Tate, you're going to give me a heart attack!" He tried not to speed as he headed down the rural road that edged the river leading to the lake.

"Park, Matt. I can't wait much longer."

And she couldn't. Tate needed him desperately and she wasn't quite sure why but he had to be inside her and as quickly as possible.

He pulled off, parking under an old willow tree and she turned, moving the dress out from beneath her as she crawled toward him.

Scooting toward her, he met her halfway and she hopped on his lap, grinding herself against him as he kissed her. His hand cupped the back of her head, holding her to him as he ate at her mouth, devouring her sighs and moans.

The other hand found its way under her dress and between her thighs. "Holy shit, you're scalding hot," he whispered into her mouth and she squirmed against his hand.

"Please, put your cock inside me. Please."

"You undo me when you need me so much."

She lifted up and yanked his pants open, freeing him. She slid the head of his cock through her wetness before guiding him to her gate and sinking down on him.

"What brought this on? Not that I'm complaining." He thrust up into her and she arched her back.

"I've needed you all day and we were rushed but dancing with you, your eyes on me all night, you're so fucking handsome and sexy. I just…yes oh like that…needed you so bad."

"Take your breasts out for me, Tate. Hold them so I can kiss and lick your pretty nipples."

She gasped softly and undid the side zipper enough to reach into the bodice and free her breasts.

Holding them out as he made love to her, his mouth torturing her nipples, cock deep inside her body, she felt like another person, a sexy person, and she realized she was. He made her feel that way and she'd accepted it.

"Since your hands are busy, let me ease you some." Matt reached down and captured her clit between his fingers and squeezed gently over and over as she sped up on him.

"You're a sex goddess, Tate. So damned sexy I can barely hold on. I need to come so you have to too." He bit her nipple gently and then a bit harder and thrust deep, fingers still plumping her clit.

Tipping her head back, her back bowed as she came, the cab of the truck echoing with the sound of her voice and his whispered replies.

Chapter Twelve

Matt walked into a full house two days after Thanksgiving and caught part of a strained conversation between Tate and her baby sister, Jill. After they'd finished the renovation of the dining room, his parents had given them a nice, big table that filled the space.

Several Murphys and Cassie wandered around, gabbing and laughing. He loved that their house was a hub of activity. He caught sight of Liv sitting in the rocker in the living room, baby Lise a pink bundle against her chest, a shock of black hair peeking out from beneath a hat. She waved in his direction and he blew her a kiss and waved at Marc.

Tate stood in the kitchen, she hadn't noticed him just yet. Usually the moment he entered a room she alerted to his presence, their gazes meeting until they could make physical contact. He'd noticed her stress level had ramped up in the last two months but it didn't seem to have anything to do with their relationship. Still it made him nervous that something was clearly going on and she wouldn't share it.

Stress marked her face as she listened to her sister.

"They're books I need for this stupid final paper. I won't get the second part of my student loan money until January. I know five hundred dollars is a lot of money but I'll get it right back to you when I get the check."

"You'll have to give me a day or two. I don't have it right now. I have to move some money around."

Matt stilled. She hadn't said a damned thing to him about money trouble. They'd just paid off part of the renovation that they couldn't do themselves, several thousand dollars' worth. He'd wanted to pay it all himself but she wouldn't hear of it. So he'd told her it was much less than it truly was and taken on a far larger share without her knowing it. The last thing he wanted her to deal with was money trouble.

"Oh, I'm sorry. Tate, let me talk to Tim. I didn't know and I haven't even asked him yet. I just came to you and that's silly of me. You shouldn't be expected to do it all, all the time," Jill said.

And Matt agreed with that wholeheartedly although he'd never voice that to her. He knew what it meant to take care of family and so he never second-guessed how she dealt with hers.

"Can it not wait a day?" Tate sounded testy and it took him aback. She never spoke to her siblings like that unless they were fighting or nagging her about something.

"Sure. Tate, I'm sorry. I don't mean to make you upset." Jill wrung her hands and Tate saw it, pulling her sister into a hug.

"No, I'm the one who's sorry. I snapped at you and I've always told you and Jacob to come to me if you needed stuff for school. If you need it today, I'll give you my credit card number and you can charge the books that way. If it can wait until tomorrow, I'll get you cash."

Damn it. There was something wrong and she wasn't telling him. He turned before she saw him, catching Nathan's and Tim's eyes, motioning them outside.

"What's up?" Tim said as they walked out onto the front porch.

Matt told them what he'd heard.

Nathan ran a hand through his hair. "She takes on too much. I can swing the books no problem. I'll talk to Jill and Jacob, tell them to speak to Tim, me or William before going straight to Tate."

"It's more than that."

Both men looked to Tim.

"What do you mean?"

"Two weeks ago I saw her walking downtown, my father was headed in the opposite direction. Then I stopped in to get a haircut and I'd forgotten my lunch at home. Tate told me she'd loan me a ten to grab lunch but she had no cash in her purse. She got all weird about it. And with the first installment of the tuition this semester, she had to juggle for an extra few days. She wasn't late, but she's usually early and this time it was exactly on the day it was due."

"What the hell is happening and how is this connected to your...are you telling me he's working her for money?" Matt's anger simmered.

"It wouldn't be the first time. You know she paid him to let us take the kids when we first moved out. And over the years she's given him money. We all have I suppose but about five years ago he and I got into it and he won't come around anymore. He threatened Susan. Of course now apparently he's focused on Tate."

"And my guess is that Tate is taking this all and keeping it quiet to protect the rest of us." Nathan began to pace.

"I'll talk to Tate."

Nathan and Tim looked at him, pity in their faces.

"What?"

"Matt, you're hers now as much as we are. She'll protect you just like she's doing us. She's not going to tell you anything."

"I'm not playing this game." He leaned in and called to her. Surprised, she looked up and came toward him, the stress on her face smoothing as she got closer.

"Hi, whatcha all doing out here?" She joined them on the porch.

"Talking."

Her back straightened and one brow rose. "Want to enlighten me or is this a guessing game?"

"What's going on with your money situation, Tate?"

She took a step back and looked to her brothers who tried to keep stoic and tough but it didn't last long.

"My money situation? What do you mean exactly?"

"You know, I go out of my way to be honest with you, Tate. I know you're having money problems and so do Nathan and Tim. Tell us what's happening so we can help."

"Oh, you mean like how you told me Melanie came onto you at The Sands before the Grange dance when you were having lunch with Justin and some guys from work? Or about how you nearly got into a fight two weeks ago at the post office when you got lip from someone about me? Honest like that?"

Hell. How did she do that? Did Tim just chuckle? He glanced over and saw nothing but he suspected the line of Tim's lips might have curved up ever so slightly.

"That's different." He folded his arms over his chest.

"Is it now? How so?"

"Oh for fuck's sake! Knock it off. You're trying to muddy the waters, Tate. Give him a break. What is going on?" Nathan interrupted.

Damn, she had been. She was good, almost as good as Polly Chase. He'd let her push the argument away from the subject.

"Traitor. My money problems are no one's business. I just had a lot of stuff come down at once and I got a little overextended. It's not a big deal. In a few weeks everything will be fine."

"What's Dad's role in this?"

Matt had almost believed her story about a temporary problem until he saw her reaction. Her eyes darted away from Tim quickly and he saw her fists clench for a moment and then she smoothed them down the front of her pants.

"I don't know what you mean."

"Bullshit. Don't lie to me on this, Tate. He's working you for money, isn't he?" Nathan stood closer to her, grabbing her shoulders, and Matt wanted to intercede but he saw it was necessary, saw Tate would protect them all unless she was made to reveal the whole story.

"It's none of your business!"

Her raised voice brought Anne out onto the porch and when she saw the scene she intervened. "Nate! Get your hands off her."

"Dad is working her for money. Has been for a while. Long enough that she's having trouble paying her bills on time." Nathan said it without taking his eyes from Tate's and Matt's simmering rage began to bubble.

Anne closed the door behind her and approached Tate, moving Nathan aside. "Honey, is that true?"

Tate's bottom lip trembled a bit but she didn't say anything.

"This is stupid." Matt grabbed her hand and spun her, putting her up on the porch rail so they'd be eye to eye. "You're going to share this with me, Tate Murphy, because I love you and we cannot have this between us. That's what he wants. I won't let anyone hurt you, you have to know that."

"None of us is going to let you off this porch until you tell us what's going on," Anne added from behind them.

A tear broke loose from her eye and rolled down her cheek and he hated making her so upset. "It's nothing," she whispered.

"It's everything, Tate. Tell me. Share your burden with us. We love you."

She took a deep breath and told them. Told them everything from the first night until the last demand for payment of a thousand dollars.

"I couldn't have him harming you or the kids. Everyone

was finally living normal, happy lives and I wasn't going to let him upset that. I'm not sorry!" Her chin jutted out and he shook his head, kissing it.

"You've had this weighing on you for five months now. Oh, Venus, honey, no one should have to bear that alone. I've asked you if something was wrong and you told me no. Didn't you trust me?"

"It's not about that."

But in a way it was. She hadn't trusted him not to run off when faced with her father and that hurt.

He helped her down and kissed her. "I thought we'd worked through that. I thought you'd trust me to stand by you, to protect you."

"I do trust you, Matt. I just...the thought of him showing up at one of your mother's Sunday dinners, of what he is touching that just... I didn't want that to ruin what we have."

Her voice was quiet, but hurt that she didn't come to him still seeped into his gut. She'd been terrorized by this jerk and she hadn't thought enough of him to seek his help. Hadn't trusted their love and his commitment to her that he'd protect her.

"I have to go for a while. I'm hurt, Tate. I'm hurt you didn't trust me to stand by you."

"You're leaving?" Her voice sounded small.

"Not forever. I need to think. I'll be back." He went to his truck and as he pulled from the driveway he tried not to be affected by her face as she stood there, watching him drive away.

Matt sat at a table in The Pumphouse when Nathan stalked in. He picked up the beer and tossed it in Matt's face.

Shocked, Matt stood. "What the hell?"

"You asshole. You begged her to open up to you and when she did, you threw it in her face. You proved her right. You dumped my sister for sharing with you. Bravo. She's never, ever opened up that way to anyone before. I actually encouraged her to do it. I'm a fucking fool and you're an asshole. Your shit will be out on the street by nine tonight so don't bother my sister to come inside to get anything." Nathan spun to leave but Matt grabbed him.

"Wait! I didn't dump her. I just needed some time away from home. I'm not moving out!"

"Yes you are. Leave her alone, Matt. You blew it."

"That's my fucking house! You can't tell me what to do. Tate is my woman. I get that you're her brother and all but this isn't your business."

"It's my business when I have to listen to her cry. It's my business when she blames me for making her tell you something she didn't want to tell you to begin with because she wanted to protect you and the rest of us. You promised her you wouldn't let anyone hurt her and you did it yourself."

Matt reached out to grab his arm when Nate turned to leave again and Nathan shoved him back. "Don't touch me, asshole. I thought you'd be good for her. But you're just like the rest of them."

Shane came in and quickly moved to them. "What the hell is going on? Cassie called me and said Tate is holed up in her bedroom and her family is packing up your stuff. You broke up with her? Are you out of your mind?"

"Packing my stuff? I didn't break up with her! Why won't anyone believe me? Jesus! She holds on to this fucking horrible shit with her father for *five* months! She thinks I'd just walk away from her if her father showed up at my doorstep? How much trust does that show? Am I never allowed to feel anything? Only Tate gets to feel pain now? She didn't trust me to stand by her."

"No one ever has!" Nathan yelled it so loud and his words were so filled with emotion that everyone who hadn't already been watching the scene unfold stopped and turned.

"Yes, she should have told you. She should have told all of us but you can't know what it cost her to keep it to herself.

Have you thought of that? How alone she must have felt as he terrorized her?"

Nathan took a step back and sneered at him. "Damn you, Matt Chase. This isn't about you, not in the way you think. I got more out of her, she's paid him seven thousand dollars. Why? Because she adores you. She loves you and she wanted to protect you and your family from the sickness we've had to endure our whole lives. From the *shame* of what we come from. Probably part of it was she was worried that when you were confronted with the reality of Bill Murphy you'd walk away. And until you've spent ten minutes with him, you can't possibly understand what a powerful motivator that is. He's..." Nathan shuddered in disgust "...he's a horrible man. He's poisonous. She wanted to shield you from him. And not just you, he used everyone she wanted to protect, our nieces and nephew too because William and Tim are the ones other than her hurt the worst by my father. This isn't about her not trusting you, it's about her protecting you. That's what Tate does in case you hadn't bothered to notice."

Matt's head spun. He didn't know what to think. There was no question he loved Tate. He hadn't broken up with her, he just needed some damned time away to nurse some hurt feelings.

"She sold a bracelet I gave her two years ago to send Jill spending money. She dipped into savings to pay for the renovation but didn't want to take more because it's where she keeps the money for their tuition and any other emergencies. So feel your pain, Matt. You go ahead. She told you she was broken at the very beginning and she is. But you're wrong to turn this and make it about you."

Nathan moved to leave but it was Shane who stopped him this time, looking back at Matt, who had to grab a chair as he took in the words.

"I'm not moving out. You can bet on that, Nathan. When I get back, Tate and I will work this out. This is not about you."

"Fuck you, Chase. For the better part of my life Tate took

responsibility for me. Paid my father hush money so my siblings and I could live safely and be fed. That's why we're always at her house. She feeds us emotionally and physically. There's never a bare pantry at Tate's house, not in her heart or in her kitchen. This is about me because Tate is about me. Tate is more of a mother to me than the woman who gave me birth. I owe Tate everything I am and I won't stand by and let *anyone* hurt her. Not my father and certainly not you. Get out of my way, Sheriff Chase, unless you plan to arrest me."

Shane sighed and moved to the side. "Nathan, don't do this. Tate needs Matt, she loves him and he loves her. You know that. I know you're upset but you have to let them work things out."

Nathan said nothing more but left The Pumphouse.

"Whatcha gonna do?" Shane looked down at Matt.

"I'm going to go home and kick people out. Tate and I need to fix this without an audience."

"I'll go with you. I don't think it's going to be as easy as you think." Shane rode over with Matt.

"I just needed some damned time to nurse some hurt feelings. I didn't tell her I was breaking things off. I told her I'd be back," Matt explained to his brother after he'd told him about the payoffs.

"I understand why you'd be hurt, Matt. And I think Tate does too. But you're going to have trouble getting past her siblings who're all going to gang up to protect her from any perceived threat, you included. We'd do it in their place. I see their perspective very well. Cassie told me Tate walked past her and into her bedroom after you left, like there was nothing left to her."

"Damn it. Okay, okay. I shouldn't have left but…"

"But you felt like a failure for not protecting her. So you gathered up all your righteous indignation that she hadn't told you so you didn't have to feel like you'd failed the person who matters most."

Matt licked his lips as he turned down their street. "Yes. Shane, she's so small, she's mine to protect and cherish and I didn't. And she didn't trust me to."

"Do you really think that? Do you really think this was about her not trusting you to protect her? I'm not saying you don't have the right to be mad that she kept it to herself, I see why you are. But it's who she is. She's going to choose to take on burdens to protect people she loves. You knew that going in, Matt. If you can't handle that or this messed-up family situation get out now. It's unfair to keep going with this relationship if something like this is enough to break you up.

"Worse things will happen. Loving someone means they can get to you in ways no one else can. There are going to be times you're so pissed off at her you want to rip your hair out, where you have to leave before you say something that'll hurt her. But you do leave, or you do take a deep breath and go get a soda because you'd rather hold back than harm her. That's what love is. And until I was with Cassie, no one meant that much to me other than my family."

"I don't want to leave her. I love her. I love being with her. I don't know what to think or feel or do. I've never felt so fucking scared in my life other than when I first got to the hospital in July when that bastard put her there. I wanted to be the one she turned to, the strong one. And when she did turn to me I ran. Fuck."

Shane snorted softly. "You'll both get over it. You'll work it out and the next fight y'all have you won't turn tail, although you'll make new mistakes because that's the way of it. It's not earth shattering. You had a fight. It happens. Now go in there and fix it because makeup sex is the best."

Laughing, Matt pulled into the driveway and saw boxes of stuff stood on the porch and Tim sat out there with Beth.

"You need to grab your shit and go. We'll pay you back for the renovation when we can." Tim blocked the door.

"This is my house. I'm going in, Tim."

"No you're not. You've done enough damage." Beth shook her head at him.

"You're just making things worse. Come on, you know I love Tate. This is a huge overreaction."

"Overreaction? And you'd know this because you saw the damage you did firsthand? Oh, no you couldn't have because you were off at your little bar drinking and looking at chicks." Beth's eyes narrowed.

"I wasn't looking at anyone. I'd never do that to Tate, and I'm not interested in looking at other women. Don't mistake me for your father either. I had *a* beer, most of it I didn't drink because Nathan tossed it in my face."

"You're right, the running off when things got hard thing is more like my mother. Hit the road." Matt hated it that Tim was so mad. He'd always considered Tim his greatest ally with Tate.

"Actually, this is his place of residence so he has a right to go inside, Tim." Shane, thank God Shane was there.

"I see, you're going to use the sheriff in your pocket to hurt my sister now?"

"Oh stuff it!" Cassie pushed her way past. "This has gone on long enough. Tate is worked into a frenzy in there and none of you are helping!"

"Of course you'd take his side."

"This isn't about sides! All of you get the hell out of here." Tate thundered out onto the porch, anger sparking in her eyes. She looked at her siblings and then Matt. "*All* of you. I want to be alone and I don't need or want anyone speaking for me, thinking for me or taking responsibility for me. How dare you all pack Matt's things and make that choice for him and for me."

Matt nodded. "They're just trying to help, Venus. They love you."

"And you! You don't know a damned thing about it." She pushed Anne gently but firmly out and slammed the door, locking it. "None of you has the right!" she yelled from the other side of the closed door and turned out the porch light.

They all began to argue until Shane's cell phone rang. He answered, listened and started laughing as he snapped the phone shut.

"That was Tate Murphy, she's called the sheriff to file a noise complaint about a public nuisance in her front yard."

Matt scrubbed hands over his face. This had all spun out of control so fast. He didn't want to be arguing on her, *their* lawn, he wanted to be inside, holding his woman.

"Y'all go on home. I mean it. I'm going in there to work this out with Tate. If you love her like you say you do, you'll know she loves me and I love her too. We're gonna have arguments and she's going to be hurt and I'm going to be hurt. That's natural and normal and truly, no one deserves normal more than Tate. So go. Please. I'm sorry I've upset you all and we can all work this out later but Tate is in there alone right now." Matt sighed as he looked at the front of the house.

"Please," Cassie added. "Please, guys. You know they're good for each other. I know you're hurting for her but you're the ones who started packing all this up. It wasn't her idea. She'd have done it herself if she'd wanted to. It's just a fight. God, if you all only knew how many fights Shane and I had our first year together. Okay—" she grinned at Shane and he laughed, "—still have. Tate is a strong woman and Matt's easy-going but they will have disagreements. If you gang up on him every time it happens, they'll never make anything work. Let them make up. If they don't, you know where Matt works. If you can get to him before Polly does, you can kick his ass."

Matt heaved a sigh of relief—ignoring the comment about his mother—his moving out hadn't been Tate's idea.

Her siblings moved and Matt nodded at them, reaching out and squeezing Cassie's hand when he passed. He unlocked the door and opened it slowly. When nothing took his head off, he went inside and found her scrubbing the tile in the bathroom.

"Hey, Venus. Whatcha doing?"

"Scrubbing the tile around the toilet."

He leaned around. "Tate, is that my toothbrush?"

"Hmpf."

Ouch. "Oookay. Well, luckily there's a spare in the medicine cabinet then. Will you talk to me?"

"I already did."

"Tate, not that I don't like the view and all, your ass looks particularly lovely and I can see your breasts coming out the top of that shirt reflected in the shower door, but can we move this to the living room? Our bedroom? Someplace we can be face-to-face?"

"Matt, what are you doing here?" She turned and tossed the toothbrush, *yep his*, into the trash and took off the yellow rubber gloves, laying them under the sink.

"I live here. I told you I'd be back." He held a hand out to help her up but she ignored it and stood, brushing her hands off on the front of her pants and left the bathroom.

He followed her into the living room where she took the chair so he sat on the table, leaning in and taking her hands in his.

"I'm sorry you had to deal with this insanity with your father alone for all these months. I can't imagine how scared you must have been to keep it secret."

"Fine."

"Fine? That's it? Your fucking family moves my shit out onto the porch and you scrub the toilet with my toothbrush after you hide something important from me for *five* months and all you give me is an okay?"

"Who's got the fuck habit now, buster? Anyway, my family did that, I didn't. And what's more if you'd been here, they couldn't have done it now, could they? And don't you call them my *fucking* family, only I get to do that. I'm beginning to wish I'd fucking gotten in my car and headed to Atlanta for a few weeks like Liv did."

"And Marc went insane with worry!"

"Yes, because it's always about you people!"

"Back with that 'you people' thing? Liv is from my side of town too!"

"Oh shut up! I mean you people with penises, not you rich people. God. Look, you *asked* me to tell you. I did. And then you ran off. You can't expect me to just be all, *hi, honey, nice to see you, want a beer?* when you come back. You're the one who's always all, *I hate it when you try to run off* and then you did."

"You're right. I was hurt and I needed to be away from here for an hour or so. God knows why I imagined hell wouldn't break loose if I left."

"You left, Matt. When things got bad you left. I may have been wrong for not telling you, and I'm sorry I hurt you, I am. But I've been trying really hard to make a go of this. Even with all the insanity, even knowing you don't tell me everything to protect me, I stay and I try and today I trusted you enough to tell you and you threw it in my face and walked away."

"I felt like a failure out there on our porch this afternoon. You hid this from me when you should have been able to come to me and let me protect you. It shouldn't be the other way around."

Her anger softened and her eyes searched his face. "You're not a failure, Matt. My family is just too messed up. I'm messed up. You deserve more than that. Better."

"I want you to stop that talk right now. There's no breaking up here so quit it. I told you I'd be back. Okay, so I handled it wrong. I should have stayed and we could have talked it through without all the packing and yelling. But we're together, Tate. We'll work it out."

She listened to him and took a deep breath. The tentative smile fell away and her eyes narrowed. "Why do you stink of booze? It's hard to concentrate right now with you smelling like that. Bad memories I suppose but I'd really rather you not go out and tie one on when you're pissed. I don't mind drinking, I do mind coming back so bad off you smell like a brewery."

He laughed and then tried to get serious again. "Sorry." He put his hands up. "I'm not drunk. I had three sips of one pint of beer. Nathan threw the rest on me. Why don't I go shower and change and we can continue this?"

The corner of her mouth slid up a bit. "Nathan threw a beer on you?"

"Yeah. I thought he was going to pop me one and I'd have had to pop him back and you'd have been really mad at me for giving your baby brother a black eye. Luckily, Shane interceded so no blows were thrown."

"*Hmpf.* Go on."

He wanted to go to her and give her a kiss but his clothes stuck to him and now that she'd pointed out the smell it began to make him feel slightly nauseated.

"I'm saving the snuggles and sugar for after I'm cleaned up. But I've been running a tab."

When he finished showering he found she'd moved many of the boxes back into the house and was in their bedroom putting his clothes into drawers.

He approached her from behind wearing only a towel and put his arms around her.

"I could have done that." He kissed the top of her head.

"It gave me something to do. Anyway, my family made the problem, I'll undo it. They really didn't get most of your clothes. I was in here so they didn't touch what was in the closet and dresser. I think they took stuff out of the laundry. I'd done a load earlier today."

He turned her and his chest constricted a moment as he looked at her face, the features he loved so much. He could have lost her over something silly. That was untenable.

"First things first. Tate, we're going to fight sometimes you know. But unlike what Beth might think, I'm not your mother.

I'm not going to abandon you. I shouldn't have left. I'm sorry. My feelings were hurt and I was upset with myself too, I needed a bit of space but I should have handled it differently."

He'd moved her back toward the bed and with a flex of his hips, bumped her onto the mattress.

"If I thought you were like my mother I'd have done more with your toothbrush than scrub the tile with it. I love you, Matt, but I'm not a doormat. Even if I gave in to my father, I'm not someone you can walk all over. I won't allow it." She put her fingers over his lips as he loomed over her. "But that's not what you did so calm down. I'm just saying that's not what you did and that's not who I am."

Frustrated at being unable to pull her T-shirt off, he grabbed hold of the neck and ripped it down the middle. "That's much better." He kissed the exposed mound of each breast and her skin broke into gooseflesh.

"I'm sorry I hurt you with this whole thing about my father. I would never want to make you feel like a failure. You're not. You're my hero in so many ways. You do make me feel safe." Her voice shook and got breathy as he traced along the edge of her bra cup with his tongue.

He kissed her, nipping her bottom lip quickly. He sighed, rolling off her long enough to rid himself of the towel and start yanking on her jeans.

"Venus, I love you. We're together and we'll learn more about each other as we go. You *will* stop giving that bastard money, do you hear me? I *will* pay the next month's mortgage on this house. I've been here three months and you haven't let me pay my share. We'll work it out with your brothers and the school and with Shane to make sure the kids are safe."

"It's hard to concentrate when you're naked and ordering me around." She may have complained but she lifted her ass so he could pull her pants and panties off. She sat up, removed her bra and tossed the ripped T-shirt aside before pulling the blankets back.

"Tough. Now you're naked too."

"I noticed. Why are you over there?"

"I like looking at you laying there naked, your chest heaving because you want me so much even when your eyes are sparking at me because you're mad."

"You really should write all this stuff down. You could turn it into one of those books that teaches guys how to get a woman into bed. You'd make a million dollars. Oh and you're not paying my bills. That's not going to happen. Half the people in town already think I'm only with you for that. Although I question whether or not they've actually seen you because anyone with a brain knows I'm with you for the sex 'cause you look so good."

He laughed. His Tate was back. Their rhythm was back. Relief crashed through him as he knelt between her spread legs and skated his palms up her thighs.

"I'm paying *our* bills and I'm not arguing. I may be good in bed but I don't want to be a kept man." He winked at her.

"Well, that's good since I've got three dollars to my name and you're worth way more than that."

He frowned. "Tell me you're going to let me pay next month's mortgage or there'll be no sex. I'll withhold it and everyone knows you're only with me for my cock."

"I don't want you to think I'm after you for money." She writhed beneath him though, grabbing the body part in question and squeezing lightly. He didn't hide his smile.

"Tate, that's not what I think. I live here. This is my house too, right? Don't you want me to feel at home? How can I if you won't let me pay my share? And hello, in case you haven't noticed, I'm a firefighter. It's not the kind of salary my father makes. Between the two of us, we do fine. But the whole after-my-money argument is based on what my parents have, not what I have. We can talk more about how we'll split the bills after the sex. You've avoided the conversation so far but this situation wouldn't have been as bad if we'd talked more openly about finances before."

He wet a fingertip and drew it over the hardened point of her nipple, making her arch into his touch. Pinching it enough to make her moan, he bent to kiss the hollow of her throat and across her collarbone as her free hand slid down his back.

Tate needed him so much right then she felt like she'd die from want. Needed to feel that reconnection with him, making them two as one again.

She knew he hadn't broken off with her but it hurt that he'd beg her to reveal something and then leave. Still, hearing that he'd felt like a failure, knowing she'd hurt him when she'd only meant to protect him made her realize just how important it was that they communicate with each other.

He kissed down her neck to first one nipple and then the other. She grew wetter, felt her pussy ready for him. The bristles of his beard abraded over the sensitive flesh of her breasts and what started out gentle took on an edge as they both realized the intensity of their need.

"Matt, please, please," she murmured and he kissed down her belly and settled between her thighs.

"Glad to oblige, Venus." He pulled her open with his thumbs and looked at her for long moments. It should have weirded her out, the way he gazed at such an intimate part of her body, but instead, it made her feel beautiful.

Even more when his thumbs slid inside her and his mouth finally brushed across her, tongue flicking quickly over her clit until she panted. He backed away, licking slowly, avoiding her clit until she arched her hips into his face like a floozy.

He rolled her over and pulled her hips up. He'd never taken her quite like that before and it thrilled her. She pushed back against him and he laughed. "All in due time. I haven't finished what I started."

With that, he spread her thighs wide and bent, his mouth finding her again, making her groan into the pillow. With his hands on her upper thighs, he held her wide and steady as he devoured her. All she could do was hold on and be glad she walked as much as she did so her legs were strong enough to hold her up despite her trembling muscles.

Edging into her, sharp and bright, the pleasure of her climax burst over her emotions as the depth of her love for Matt Chase rushed through her.

She wasn't sure exactly what she said but whatever it was, the neighbors probably heard it, she said it so loud.

She didn't have much time to wonder though because within moments, Matt's cock began to press into her pussy, her body parting for him, accommodating him as it always did because she was made for him.

"So beautiful. Do you have any idea how beautiful you are right now, Tate? The curve of your back, creamy and pale, your hair like moonlight against your shoulders? Spread out before me like a banquet and I didn't get nearly enough to eat."

She squeaked at the rough eroticism of his words but there was no denying he turned her on.

"You're mine, Tate. From the first moment I saw your face you worked your way into me. Mine. No one else's. Even when I'm an ass, you're mine. Even when you hide things you should tell me and your brother throws beer in my face. Even when you scrub the toilet with my toothbrush, minx. You're mine as I'm yours and we're getting married. You got me?"

Surprised but still realizing there was no way she'd say no, she nodded enthusiastically into the pillow.

"You realize I just asked you to marry me, right?"

"Yes," she managed to gasp out and he reached around and toyed with her clit, idly, as he fucked into her body.

"You're not going to argue with me?" Amusement laced his voice and she tightened herself around him, bringing a grunt from him.

"Do you want me to? What, it's just idle sex talk?" She smiled, pushing back against his thrusts.

"Seeing as how I've wanted to ask you for months, it's not idle at all. Holy...damn, Tate...that was...shit!"

Laughing, she tightened again and swiveled.

"Oh it's gonna be that way, is it?" He leaned over her body and bit the flesh where shoulder met neck as his fingers on her clit sped. In that position he totally controlled everything, her movement, his depth and speed. It was beautiful and erotic. He was nearly a foot taller than she was, muscled and very strong, but she knew he'd never hurt her.

And today had only underlined what she'd already come to learn—even emotional hurts would be something they could get past because, as improbable as it seemed, he was the one.

Unbelievably, another climax hit just as he pressed hard, fingers digging into her hip, the others still playing against her clit, teeth digging into her shoulder. A long groan came from him and she realized then he wasn't wearing a condom. The third time in a few weeks. Moments later she realized she never wanted him to again either.

He fell back against the bed and pulled her against him. "I love you, Tate. With everything I am. Will you marry me?"

"I love you, Matt, with everything I am. So yeah."

"You make me very happy. I'm sorry we didn't make each other happier earlier today."

"It's gonna happen. I'll try to keep my family from moving you out next time. I know my family, or my parents, are a mess. I'd understand if you were wary of that."

"Tate Murphy, I love you and your crazy brothers and sisters. My family loves you all. Your father, after Shane speaks with him and you get yourself a protection order in place, won't be an issue. My father would be happy to guide you through the process and Cassie too. She's done the protection order thing before."

"And it protected her really well."

"Hey." Reaching back, he turned on the lamp and looked at her closely. "That was a very different situation. In the first place, I know how much of a priority Petal's law enforcement puts on protection orders and family violence prevention. Shane, even before Cassie, cared and now the department is even more committed. I'm here too. And my dad is the best attorney around and the judge who hears protection orders is really good. First thing you need to do is tell him he's not getting a dime from you again. And then we'll take the next steps."

Chapter Thirteen

Christmas Day and the Chases' home was filled to the absolute rafters and Polly was in her element. Tate bustled around the kitchen along with Maggie, Matt's aunt and both his grandmothers.

The backyard held a makeshift touch football game with players from one to ninety-five. Fourteen Murphys plus Royal, Anne's boyfriend, twenty various Chases and Cassie's brother visiting from California wandered around laughing, talking, snacking and laying out plates and preparation for breakfast.

Tate had made a turkey and a ham at their house, Maggie also made a roast beef and another turkey and Liv brought a ham as well. Add to that the three turkeys and two hams Polly had baking and the side dishes nestled in Tate's, Maggie's, Liv's and Cassie's kitchens and they were good to go for dinner. But for the moment, they needed to finish up breakfast so they could get the presents as the kids were begging every three minutes.

After dishing up the scrambled eggs and putting a lid on the large bowl, Tate grabbed Lise from Liv, who laughed at Polly's snort.

"Y'all never let me hold those babies. Stingy, every last one."

Tate snickered. She'd had to race to get to Lise first because Polly hogged every baby and child in sight. Her own nieces and nephews included. She glanced at Liv over the baby's head. "I think she looks more like you every day. Her hair is so dark but she does have green eyes like her daddy."

Liv grinned. "She's so amazing. I never imagined it would be like this, you know? Marc's so good with her too. Gets up with her in the middle of the night, rocks her."

Tate nodded. "You're very fortunate to have such wonderful parents and grandparents, Lise," she crooned to Lise before kissing her forehead.

"And such wonderful aunties too." Maggie picked up Nicholas who'd run in with Kyle on his heels.

Everyone else filed in and sat at the long tables. Edward at the very head, Polly on his right. Matt put an arm around the back of Tate's chair, his nearness bringing the reality of the moment home. How fortunate was she? Despite the blight of her parentage, she had amazing brothers and sisters and a new extended family with the Chases. Her life was very good.

Edward rose. "Welcome and Merry Christmas one and all. I'm not one to talk a whole lot. Because Polly doesn't let me get a word in edgewise." Everyone laughed, including Polly. "But today I have to tell you all how truly thankful I am. My goodness look at you all. My boys grown into men. It was just yesterday wasn't it, that I had to yell at you to get your cleats off the front porch? You wanted to borrow the car for a date? You lost your first tooth?" He had to pause a moment, pressing a hand to his stomach.

"And today you're here, two of you with children of your own and finer babies I've yet to see. Polly and I have been gifted with four new ready-made grandchildren in Belle, Sally, Shaye and Danny. I admit to my share of worries at first with the bird-brained women you used to squire around but you never brought anyone home who wasn't perfect. Maggie, girl, I just adore you. You came into our lives and you brighten them every day. Your fire and caring, the way you mother my grandson, I'm proud to have you in this family."

Maggie gave him a wobbly smile and blew him a kiss.

"And you, Cassie. When Shane brought you here that first time I was simply bowled over by your beauty. Truly, there are few women walking this earth who are as physically stunning as you are. And yet, what sticks with me every day when I think of you is how strong you are. How much you give to Shane, how much courage and tenacity you have. You're every inch a match for my oldest."

Cassie leaned into Shane and blinked back tears.

"Livvie. Oh, girl, you knocked my Marc out, you know that? I remember him coming over here and telling me about his feelings for you. Smart. Blunt. I love that. You say what you feel and you decided what you wanted and went for it. That's the kind of girl my boy needed. You're a good woman, Olivia. A beautiful mother and a fine wife and you keep Marc out of trouble. You two were made for each other. Happy first anniversary."

"Thank you, Edward. If it weren't for Marc and Polly, I'd have snapped you up already."

He winked at her and chuckled before his eyes settled on Tate.

"And Tate. Well, your path here, like my other daughters, hasn't been an easy one. When I watched you stand up in court and tell the judge about your father, I realized something about you. You're small but your heart, your courage is large. Even with extortion threats, you cared about the man who'd harmed you. And you let Matt in, and you let him help and you let him love you. Each time I wondered if you'd run away from the ugliness some in this town have hurled your way, you stood up and you stuck it out.

"Matt is a good man but you don't let him coast. You appreciate the outside of my boy, but you love the inside. Polly told me about how you told her why you loved Matt earlier this year. And then you and I had lunch. I came over to your house on a Sunday and you made me a very lovely meal and we sat and talked. Your eyes, when you talked about Matt, your eyes practically glowed. No one has known my boy as well as you. Thank you, beautiful girl, for loving my son. Welcome to our family."

Tate put her hands over her face. These people were so wonderful and they were real. They meant it.

Edward came over and hugged her. "Hey, sweetness, I didn't mean to make you cry," he said softly.

She hugged him back. "Thank you for making Matt."

Polly shook her head. "Y'all are too good to be true. I'm a lucky mother-in-law."

Matt looked around the table as his father went to sit back down but before he could speak, there was a pounding on the front door.

Tim stood and put a hand out. "Tate, you sit your butt down." He craned his neck. "If you will all excuse me a moment. It's for me."

William perked up and moved to follow.

"It's my father," Beth whispered.

"Everyone, please sit." Shane stood and put his napkin down.

Matt got up. "Don't move," he admonished before he and the rest of the men at the table got up and left.

"Oh for goodness' sake!" Tate stood. "This is ridiculous."

"Tate, let them handle this," Polly spoke. "Let Matt do this. He needs to. You exorcised that demon with the protection order. Let him feel like he's protecting you. It seems silly but that's what men like to do."

"I've ruined yet another gathering with my drama."

"You sit your butt down, Tate Murphy! I will not have you making this about you. It's not. It's about your father, who is a bad man. You all deserve better. Now you let those boys kick some tail and we'll crack the windows here to hear what's happening." Polly raised an eyebrow, daring her to disobey, and moved to open the windows.

Matt felt nothing but the ice of resolve to end this bullshit once and for all. The oily fucker had come to the firehouse to try and work him for money a few weeks before and he'd sent him packing.

Tim was standing on the porch, menacing Bill Murphy when Matt came out. Shane stood in the doorway, letting Matt handle things.

"I don't know what you're doing here but as Tate is inside, you're violating the protection order even being this close." Matt stood next to Tim with William on one side and Nathan on the other.

"I been hearing around town how my girl is using you for money. I figure if you want me to keep quiet about it, you need to provide incentive."

"You're aware that this kind of thing is illegal. It's called extortion, might be considered blackmail but I'd go with extortion. You'll do more jail time that way," Edward spoke lazily from his place on the porch but Matt heard the steel in it.

"You've been warned to remove your carcass from this property and that you're in violation of the protection order. Get your sorry ass away from here. I'm not going to let you hurt Tate ever again, you got me? This has gone on long enough with your pathetic abuse of your daughter." Matt stepped forward, pleased to see Bill step back, his bravado failing.

"Why doesn't Tate tell me herself?"

"*We're* all telling you. You've threatened my children, you've threatened my wife, you've hurt my brothers and sisters and it's not happening ever again. I beat your ass fifteen years ago, you want another helping?" Tim asked.

"You're a weak, pathetic excuse for a human being. If the only thing that makes you feel like a man is abusing a woman a foot smaller than you who's never done a damned thing to hurt you, no wonder your wife doesn't stay at home."

Tim gave him a sideways glance that held a cringe. Matt knew he pushed hard but damn it, his woman had been terrorized for most of her life by this piece of shit, he was done trying to reason with him.

Bill lunged at him but Matt was ready and his fist was cocked back to deliver a very satisfying punch to the nose. The other man howled in pain and stumbled back. "You hit me! I'm going to sue you for assault!"

"You're on my property, you've been advised to leave and you attacked him. It was self-defense and there are plenty of witnesses to say so." Edward chuckled. "Now get your drunken ass off my lawn. If you so much as look at my daughter-in-law-to-be again, or any of these children you were gifted with but threw away, I'll come up with ways to sue you until the end of time."

"I don't have anything for you to take, Chase!" Bill moved back to the sidewalk.

"Certainly not pride. But it'd amuse me to mess with you for a good long time. My grandchildren are in the house, we're having Christmas breakfast. You get on out of here."

"Go on now, Bill. You're in violation of the order and if Tate wishes it, I'll arrest you right now." Shane moved his hands to his waist.

"No, I'm just fine, Shane, thank you." Tate came onto the porch and leaned into Matt, who put an arm around her. "If he leaves now. If not, arrest him." She looked at her brothers, the Chase men and finally Matt and smiled. "Thank you. Now, food is getting cold and there are some children who want to open presents, oh and me too, so let's eat."

"I love you," Matt murmured as they walked into the house after watching Bill stalk away.

"Me too. Matt?"

He stopped and looked down into her face. "Yes, Venus?"

"You're really going to get some tonight. You're very sexy when you're tough."

He laughed, leaning down to kiss her quickly. "Thank you for letting me handle that."

"Come on already!" Liv called out from the doorway and Matt sighed, dragging Tate into the dining room.

As they ate breakfast, Polly watched the children, her grand-babies as well as her new, ready-made ones, play and laugh. Children should grow up safe and knowing they were loved.

She looked at Tate who held three-year-old Shaye, kissing the top of her hair as she buttered a pancake one-handed. Polly realized the sins of the parents hadn't damaged those children. They'd pulled together and held tight against all odds. Tate Murphy was extraordinary. Polly couldn't remember the last time Matt actually got worked up enough to get into a fist fight with anyone. Even with his brothers it was more of a wrestling thing and they'd get tired and do something else.

Shane had his share of fights, even Kyle. But Matthew had been her lazy boy, nothing got him passionate enough. Until Tate. She knew she should be frowning on two fights in a few months but in truth, it made her happy to know he'd found something worth fighting for.

"I vote we leave the dishes until after presents and then the men can clean up," Polly announced to a cheer.

Everyone adjourned into the large formal living room where the tree took up most of the front windows.

Pop, Edward's father, put on his Santa hat and began to hand out presents. The process, which in the past had taken multiple hours, lengthened as more members had been added to the family and Gramps, Polly's father, stepped in and they double-teamed the effort.

At the end, nearly four hours later, after several pots of cof-fee and snacks throughout, Matt stood, helping Tate to her feet. "We've got a few things to tell everyone."

Polly beamed at them and Matt slid a ring on Tate's finger. "Finally! When's the date?" Cassie asked.

"Yesterday as a matter of fact. Tate and I got married yesterday at the justice of the peace in Riverton. Obviously if we'd gotten married here at city hall, you'd have all heard about it in two minutes."

"You did not! You eloped? Why? Matthew Sebastian Chase, you should have let us plan a big wedding for you. What's Tate going to think when we threw weddings for the other girls and not for her?"

"Aren't you happy for us, Polly?" Tate asked.

Polly jumped up and hugged them both tight, followed by forty others. So many Tate was dizzy with all the love they showed her.

"We wanted to keep it simple and quiet and it was sort of a surprise. We'd planned to announce the engagement officially today and get married in March.

"But I'll be showing by then and I'm already embarrassed enough."

Polly blinked rapidly and burst into tears, hugging Tate as she hopped up and down excitedly.

"So you're happy then? You're not mad that I, um, got her pregnant before I married her?" Matt laughed.

"Mad? Oh, Matthew, Tate, you've both made this day even better! A new daughter-in-law, a new grandbaby, it's all fabulous. When are you due?"

Tate took a deep breath. "August thirteenth they think. I'm afraid to even announce it this early, we just found out for sure three days ago." She winked at him and he kissed her hard and fast. "An accident but not so much." She shrugged. "More like throwing caution to the wind one too many times. And this isn't something I want to go into more detail over with all these grandparents and children in the room.

"So you can't throw us a wedding but you can throw me a shower if you like." Tate hugged Polly and her sisters all hopped around squealing with delight.

"Well, you can throw a double shower." Shane stood and

pulled Cassie up with him. "We're expecting in late July, right around Nicky's birthday."

Polly had to grab Edward, who laughed delightedly.

"Always have to beat me don't you?" Matt asked Shane, grinning. "We just signed a contract to have a second story built onto the house and a back sun porch put on too. We'll live in an apartment for a few months. They should be done by May."

"An apartment? No, you'll live with us!" three different people exclaimed.

Tate looked around the room. "My heart is so full. You have no idea what you all mean to me. I used to wake up in a panic when Matt and I first started dating because I was terrified it would all disappear. And then I worried my father would ruin it. But through it all, he's been there. And you've all been there. All my brothers and sisters, my new family in you all. Thank you for believing in me and for believing in me and Matt. This baby couldn't ask for more."

Cassie hugged her and they started talking about baby stuff.

Polly stood back with Edward and looked over the room. Paper everywhere, children pushing trains and trucks, dancing around with dolls. So much love and she was so lucky to see it all, to have it all in her life.

"Each year, lamb, each year things just get better. First it was just me and you in that tiny apartment on Oak, you remember? And we had our own announcement at Christmas with Shane. And each time we brought a new baby home, our lives got bigger and better. And they grew and moved out and then Kyle brought home Maggie and so on." He kissed Polly because he couldn't do anything else. Smart, small, sexy and all his, Polly Chase had been the center of his world since he clapped eyes on her when he was just nineteen years old.

"I love you something fierce, Edward Chase."

"Ditto, lamb. We're gonna be grandparents again. I can't wait to keep on getting older and better with you."

"I can't wait until everyone leaves so we can get better when we're naked."

Edward laughed, heart racing and thoughts wandering, just what she'd intended.

* * * * *

Subscribe and fall in love with a Mills & Boon series today!

You'll be among the first to read stories delivered to your door monthly and enjoy great savings.

WE SIMPLY LOVE ROMANCE